Fight for Love

A Novel

Sarah Michelle Lynch

Copyright © Sarah Michelle Lynch 2023

The moral right of Sarah Michelle Lynch to be identified as author of this Work has been asserted by her in accordance with the Copyright, Designs and Patents Act of 1988.

All rights reserved.

No part of this publication may be reproduced, stored in a retrieval system, or transmitted in any form or by any means, electronic, mechanical, photocopying, recording or otherwise, without the prior permission of the copyright owner. You must not circulate this book without the authority to do so.

All characters in this book are fictitious, and any resemblance to actual persons living or dead is purely coincidental.

For more info: sarahmichellelynch.co.uk

Prologue

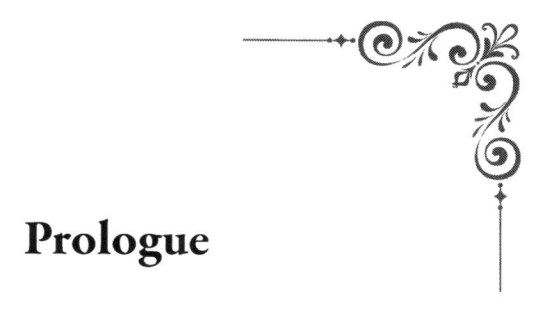

IT WAS LATE AT NIGHT, and Blake Rathbone stood beneath a large sycamore tree, observing as the new father arrived home tired and yet beaming. Caelan parked the car and walked to the front door of their renovated house, fiddling with the keys for a second before he noticed a wrapped gift on the doorstep.

Caelan immediately looked around, scanning the area. Flora had only just given birth. They hadn't told anyone yet. Caelan was only home to catch a bit of sleep before he went back to the hospital.

Well, a grandfather knows more sometimes than he might ever let on.

Blake, in one of his favoured tracksuits, which were all the rage in Florida, remained hidden. Black clothes, black hat. Thankfully it was the darkest month of the year.

Caelan picked up the wrapped gift, then walked inside.

Smiling, Rathbone turned and walked away. He got halfway to the nearest taxi rank, when a shadow popped out from nowhere and pointed a gun right at his head.

"*You*," said Caelan, lowering his weapon.

"Me, what?" asked Blake, amused.

"You're breathing."

"I am." A pause, to consider. "Did you think I'd tell anyone I was cured? Did you think I'd not use Sherry's murder attempt to take my second chance? And get away from that viper. Become the man Flora always wanted me to be."

Caelan's chest heaved. "You've a grandson."

"I know."

"Flora should ken you're alive," he insisted.

"She can never know."

"Why?" demanded Caelan.

"I was never going to leave this world until I'd seen my daughter safe and happy. Knowing how stubborn she is, she'd probably try to have me in her life. But then she'd not be safe, nor happy."

Caelan nodded in agreement. "How'd ye ken I wouldna hurt her?"

He chuckled, eyes beaming. "Just did."

"I see." Caelan's eyes glinted.

"My daughter and you... you're the same, you know?"

"I'd no go so far. I'd say she's a much better person."

"Agreed, man. But..." Blake rubbed his bottom lip. "I had people check in on her for me over the years, and one thing changed after you came into her life."

"What was that?" asked Caelan.

"She started walking in that way she once used to, kind of with a spring in her step, maybe even a skip. She was like a girl again." Caelan smiled with surprise. "You both kept love at arm's length, until in each other, you found a fellow big kid. Someone who, deep down, had retained their goodness. The type of goodness, raw curiosity even, that nobody, not even people like me, your mother, father, Jimmy could eradicate."

"Dinna flatter me, Rathbone or I'll shoot ye for causing me to like ye an ounce."

Rathbone started to back away, grinning. "Tell her the gift is from you."

"You're just leaving?" asked Caelan, aghast.

FIGHT FOR LOVE

"I already left, lad. Besides, I know my daughter like I know my own name. If you put a foot wrong, she'll come down on you like a tonne of bricks."

"Aye."

He turned back just before he went around the corner. "And Caelan?"

"Yeah?"

"You never cashed the cheque but I always honour my bargains. As you shall discover."

Caelan cocked his head. "Okay..."

"Oh, and Caelan?" He turned around one, last time.

"Aye?"

"It was a stroke of genius, how you dealt with Sherry."

Caelan feigned ignorance. "You've lost me."

Rathbone raised one eyebrow. "Like that, is it?"

"A pal o' mine might've owed me," Caelan conceded.

Sherry now languished in prison. Meanwhile, the younger Rathbone girls had been taken in by a friend of the family...

"If that's what you're going with, fine. But those were some nice adventures you had, son. Especially liked the hostage situation you negotiated for the Royals."

Caelan scratched his head. "I've nae clue what you're blethering about."

"Not one word to Flora then," Blake asked. "Like me, I know you can keep secrets."

"Aye."

"Good."

Rathbone had a bit of a spring in his step, nearly vaulting his way to a taxi.

WHEN CAELAN ARRIVED home, he picked up the gift from the hallway table and unwrapped it without much precision, then took the lid off a small box. Inside, there was a silver rattle, but also a picture of a beautiful Scandinavian-style log cabin, the Cairngorms in the background, an address typed in bold font at the bottom. There was also a small note: *It's ready for you and will be cosier than the castle, better for the bairn. Only what I owe you, plus interest, of course. My own rates. Let the past stay in the past. B.R.*

"Arsehole," said Caelan, chuckling.

He found a single key too and smiled, knowing just where he'd take Flora and the new baby for Christmas this year.

He'd take them home.

Chapter One

April 2023

I STOOD BEFORE MY MASSIVE worktable, rifling through piles of photos that pictured the late Queen's many, many outfits on mannequins. Taking a deep breath, suddenly the task I was faced with dawned. This would require more members of staff than we had and many more years than some of them had left. Apparently, I was the youngest person to ever head the Royal Collection's wardrobe department—but since I'd done so much for the Duchess, now Queen-in-Waiting, including introducing her to my friend Wendy over lunch (an incredibly body-positive black woman who the Duchess hit it off with straight away)—I had gained myself a shoe in.

The new Prince of Wales was right when he said they couldn't pay me what I was really worth as merely his wife's dresser. However, the Royal Collection could, so there I was at Buckingham Palace this time, having just returned to work from maternity leave, starting this new and exciting adventure—collating collections to be put on display one day, when the time was right.

My knowledge of fabric and its restoration, not to mention preservation, would be put to its best use. Collections would be showcased in the palaces, castles and country boltholes where Her Majesty's clothes had been worn: her tweed, tartan and wax jackets up in Balmoral; the gowns, dresses, jackets and suits she wore for state occasions, garden parties and other major events at Buckingham Palace; then the casual wear she'd donned at Sandringham or Windsor. Indeed, the late Queen's clothes didn't only speak of her life, but of Britain's identity—through fashion. For me personally, the fabrics and their evolution told a story all on their own, but the meaning behind each colour choice, each brooch or hat or pair of shoes... these would be museum pieces for all time and I needed to get them ready to become more than just clothes. They would tell stories forever. This is what I dearly loved about dressing; it was about so much more than creating an appearance. It was about attitude, politics and projecting power. It was about personality. I adored my new job already, even if it were a gargantuan task that lay ahead.

It was decided a few months ago, just before I went off on maternity leave, that long-term, our Queen-in-Waiting would need someone with more stylistic experience to take her to the next level. Cue me introducing her to Wendy, who wouldn't just bring the clothes, but would boost the confidence of someone destined to be Queen. I was all professional manners and logic, whereas Wendy boasted a creative, endearing touch. Not to mention people in the Royal Household would dare not say a word wrong to her. Wendy adored that she had them all on tenterhooks whenever she spoke to them, lest they say the wrong thing. Not only did she grow up in a poor New York neighbourhood, but she was an orphan and a self-starter. It's hard to make small talk around that. She was beyond most people's comprehension, but especially theirs.

My phone beeped with a familiar tone and I knew it was him. Pulling it out of the back of my jeans pocket, I found an image of our son Logan pictured alongside the dog, Jet. Both of them lay in a sunbeam near the French doors, Jet with one eye winking open because he knew he wasn't supposed to be sharing the baby's playmat. How-

FIGHT FOR LOVE

ever, shelties are incredibly protective creatures and so we knew he would never hurt the baby, he only wanted to protect him.

They did look gorgeous lying there together and I grinned so much, I nearly didn't notice someone else walk into the room—until he cleared his throat. Replying with a heart, I pocketed my phone and looked up to see the King's private secretary had just walked in and was hovering near the doorway of my workroom. He had nothing to do with our business, but he sometimes liked to show his face. He didn't interfere, he just wandered, occasionally.

"How are we today, Flora?" he said, in that stiff suit of his, bushy eyebrows raised.

"Very well, thank you, Marcus." I shuffled papers around, attempting to look too busy to chat.

"The King requests to see you, Mrs Cameron."

I gazed sharply at him, then. Not only had he just gone formal on me, but he'd mentioned the King.

"What could he have to discuss with me?" I chuckled nervously.

"I don't know, Flora." He wore a vague but slightly worried expression.

"Now?" I said, aghast.

"Yes, he just arrived and you were the first request he made."

"Jesus," I said under my breath.

I stacked the photographs in neat piles, then followed Marcus out, grabbing my blazer on the way. I wasn't dressed to meet the King, that was for sure.

I was taken through the labyrinth of the backstairs of Buckingham Palace, then along eye-wateringly long corridors, until eventually arriving at the Green Room. Marcus jerked his head after the equerry opened the door for me. The equerry likely knew my husband. Like everyone else here—even the King himself. I opened my mouth to speak, to protest that there must have been some mistake...

but from the look on Marcus's face, it was quite clear there was no way out of this.

"Mrs Flora Cameron," came the announcement, then I walked indoors.

He stood by the window playing with his cuffs, apparently a nervous tick of his. I'd sort of met him once before up at Balmoral. Caelan, the bairn, Jet and myself spent the Christmas just gone up in Scotland. The baby at that point had been but a month old but my better half had just bought me a push present in the form of a brand-new log cabin. And while in the area, we'd been invited to a Hogmanay party up at Balmoral Castle. The King never really partook (so I'd been assured), only showing up to make sure his staff were having a good time before shooting off back to Birkhall. So, it'd been a case of Caelan introducing me, "Your Majesty, this is my wife..." and that was that.

I moved gingerly into the Green Room and the King turned, smiled politely and then extended a hand. I did the curtsey before we shook hands, wondering if I'd got it wrong and should've curtsied before ever waltzing over. Anyway...

"Good morning, your Majesty," I said evenly.

"Please," he motioned, beckoning me to sit on one of the gilt chairs upholstered in green Chinese silk. "Do be seated."

Yes, he really did speak in that warm, plummy way of his, even in private.

"How can I be of use today?" I asked the King of England, Northern Ireland, Scotland and Wales.

Jeepers.

He looked down at his lap. "Well, you see..." Holding his hands together, his mouth pulled tight at the corners and he bared his teeth, tension showing.

I read that expression instantly. He felt awkward.

"It's about Caelan." I guessed.

FIGHT FOR LOVE

He looked up at the ceiling, ashamed, and waved his hand around in that royal way.

"It is," he said, seeming to labour over two very small words.

"He's home right now," I said, shaking slightly. "Here. He just sent me this."

I grabbed the phone from my pocket, showing him my baby and the dog.

"Totally gorgeous," said the King, catching me off guard with his raw sensibility.

My eyes grew hot. "He won't do it, sir. Whatever it is, he won't do it."

The King took a big, deep breath. "He has already refused, yeesss. I hate intervening, but of course, I know the serious nature of what it is... that is to say, the..."

He lost his bottle, or perhaps, he wasn't allowed to say very much. Strictures extended even to him, it seemed.

"You mean only Caelan is capable of solving whatever problem it is you have," I stropped, yes, in front of him. "I mean, I never thought I'd be sat here saying no to you, sir of all people. But Caelan promised me he wouldn't do it anymore. He promised. That's a husband's promise. You'd be shattering a husband's promise!"

He got up and came and sat in the chair beside mine. I was shaking and nearly crying. I couldn't look at him. He placed his hand on the arm of my chair and said, "It is very rare indeed for a monarch to be asked to intervene and yet... it has been done before. I don't mean to liken this situation to the War, but that's the level of crises we're unfortunately facing here. It falls on me to plead with you to ask him to reconsider just this one situation. Just this, and then, all shall be righted."

I shook my head, over and over. "Please, find someone else."

"We both know that another of him does not exist."

I inhaled sharply. "What about Eric Holmes?"

"Captured, along with his team. They were carrying out a special operation."

I turned and shot him a grave look, gasping. "That's the mission you want him to carry out? Retrieve them?"

He winced and stared down at his lap.

"And Caelan knows about all of this?" I persisted.

"Commander Cameron is a man of his word. So, if he made a promise to you, then he intends to keep his promise. Eric and his boys know the job and its risks. They all do. But the asset they were meant to retrieve... Let me put it like this, there is more at stake here than just their lives."

I left my chair to stare out of the window. The gardeners were busy, it being springtime. Then there were vehicles moving about, people in livery marching around, a hive of activity.

"He's turned it down because if Eric couldn't manage it, he thinks maybe he couldn't, either."

"I think partly that, Flora," he said.

I turned and looked at the ageing man who looked more like a father, grandfather and husband in that moment than I'd ever seen him look. He appeared entirely empathetic.

I turned back to the window. "If Eric and the guys are dead losses, and Caelan would only be going in to rescue the asset... I'm thinking that's why he won't do it."

"I think that's about the size of it," he said briskly.

"I don't believe I'm standing in his way, sir. If he judged he could make it happen, he would."

"No, quite. However—"

That a King would condescend to speak to me, and ask me... of all people! The daughter of a gangster and a murderer. This had to be bad!

"I'm his wife, sir. But I can't tell you his mind any better than anyone else who knows and loves him. And some of them have known him for much longer than I." I caught my breath, feeling like I was having an out-of-body experience. "What I do know however is that Caelan can judge situations like nobody else. If he's saying no... it's for a reason."

"Yeesss, but Mrs Cameron, I would still put it to you, that just a little gentle persuading... from *you* in particular, might make all the difference," said the King, wincing, because he hated himself for having said it—knowing the sheer danger my husband might face—and also the chaos that might ensue if Caelan didn't get involved.

The King pressed a buzzer and the doors opened. I understood it was time for me to leave.

"I wish I could tell you more, to convince you of the need for action, but Caelan knows all," he said, like he had no hope left—but me.

I pursed my lips and stared at him. "I wish I could say it's been a pleasure, but it appears even monarchs have to do some dirty work, now and then."

I gave him a mocking bow, then walked backwards three steps before charging out of there. I didn't wait for Marcus to show me the way, in fact I growled at him to stay out of my space, then charged for the staff car park. I wasn't going to put up with this.

ON THE DRIVE HOME, sitting in traffic gave me chance to think and calm down a bit. I went from mentally drafting my resignation email to going over the whole conversation again and again. The poor man. He probably had no idea what sort of stock I came from. Not really. I'd not be cowed, not even by a king.

My department called my mobile just as I was pulling up on our street in Notting Hill. It was Sandra, my assistant.

"I've had to take some personal time," I said, before she could ask any questions.

"Yes, Marcus said something along those lines. He said you would take as much time as you need. Does that mean I can...?"

"You can take off early today, Sandra. I'll see you tomorrow, love."

I heard a muffled curse down the line, then she said, "No problem!" and hung up.

I waited in the car for a moment, then got the distinct impression I was being watched. Turning my head slowly, I saw him standing in the open doorway with the baby in his arms. Daddy Caelan was just about the most erotic thing on the planet. White t-shirt, denim jeans, bare feet, messy hair, tired eyes and a big grin, not to mention those ridiculous forearms.

I took a deep breath and left the car, switching to mummy and wife mode, plastering a smile on my face. He kissed me on the doorstep and I rubbed my nose to his, staring up into his concerned eyes.

"It was quiet and that picture you sent made me yearn for home."

Caelan steered me indoors and there was Jet, waiting patiently in the middle of the hallway, tongue hanging loose, panting. He'd been told by his master to wait, and he would wait. Shelties were clever enough to know that a human like Caelan must be obeyed.

"Come, Jet. Come!"

At that, he came bounding to me, nearly jumping right over me.

I caught him against my chest and found two very bright brown eyes gazing up into my own, his hot breath in my face, his front paws on my shoulders, his tail wagging between the arms that held him to me. He was shedding terribly now the weather was heating up, but it was impossible to be annoyed at anything he did, his glorious tan and black coat silken and thick, so beautiful. He was a supermodel dog.

"Beauty," I giggled, and for that compliment, I got a lick in response and started spluttering with laughter.

FIGHT FOR LOVE

Logan was fast asleep in Caelan's arms as my husband gestured for the kitchen. Caelan must've only just got him to sleep and was afraid to put him down. Meanwhile Jet snuggled on his bed in the corner, well trained. Caelan held the baby as he put the kettle on.

"I canna believe they got to ye," he said, because he knew me well enough now to know when something was wrong.

I sat down and shook my head. "You won't believe the conversation I had today."

Chapter Two

CAELAN PUT LOGAN DOWN in the living-room crib, having just heard from me what went down at work today. I'd paced a lot while explaining the King's command, and now found myself much in need of the sofa cushions to fall into. Caelan stood at the back of the room before the French doors that led to the patio out back, eyes fixed on all the green out there—perhaps a calming view. Jet had moved stealthily to lay by Master's bare feet.

"Are you shocked they've taken it to the very top?"

"Aye, a little," he admitted.

"But not entirely shocked."

"Nae, no when I ken what it is that's gone doun."

He always seemed to don his true accent whenever he found himself at home in Scotland, or in this case, in a pickle. Since we'd been mostly in London this past year, with the Notting Hill house renovations having kept him busy, he'd pretty much slipped into that in-between tongue (only slightly Scottish) whenever he had a gang of cockneys to placate—or intimidate. He seemed to be one of those people, a chameleon, who could easily assimilate.

"I take it you're not allowed to tell me what exactly has gone down?"

He shook his head, that dark look in his eyes.

"And what about what's stopping you?" I said, watching him like a hawk.

He dipped his head and looked across the room—at our son. That had changed the game for him, entirely.

He wouldn't leave our son. I could protect Logan, but not nearly in the same way Caelan could.

"What about if Logan and I head to Scotland, to the lodge?"

He shuddered at my words. Perhaps it was the thought of getting stuck in again; it made him shake with excitement. Or else, it was my willingness to let him go.

"I only want you to do what you think is right, Caelan. I don't want you to regret it... if something happens to Eric and the others."

He agreed with me, nodding, then turned his back to me. I watched him stare out into the back garden, which was my domain. When I'd been heavily pregnant and could only get around comfortably on my hands and knees, I'd taken to scrabbling around. We'd had it landscaped already by that point! I really didn't realise I'd inherited it off her, not until I had my own garden. Then I realised, there was such joy to be found in a garden. I was green-fingered, after all.

"You'd go to the lodge?" he asked, still with his back to me.

"If you needed me to be safe... away from here."

"What about work?"

"I think we both know they'll cater to whatever, just so long as you say yes."

I absolutely hated the thought, more than I hated the past and all our enemies—hated it even more than the fact I grew up motherless—but if he had to go, he had to go. It was who he was.

I'd watched him quietly yearn for a challenge these past months. Even renovating a heap of old bricks, then helping me through thirty-six hours of labour still hadn't really fazed him.

The house renovations should've taken years but he'd got it done in eight months once he knew we had a baby on the way. Some rooms still needed prettying up, but we'd moved in. It was a marvel, everyone said so. We'd transformed a shack into a £15million mansion. Or rather, he had. I'd only given him the fancy ideas.

"Do you want me to go?" he asked, a tremor in his voice.

"I want that less than I want a cactus up the arse, baby. I want it less than I want to put Logan back inside me and go through it all again."

He swivelled and appeared dejected but relieved, too.

He shrugged and I walked to him, held my hands at his elbows and gazed up into his eyes. "I knew what I married, Callie. I love you more than ever, but I knew what I married."

He moved in and kissed me, the world fading away.

LATER, AFTER DINNER, he went quietly into the study downstairs. Having just loaded the dishwasher, I picked up junior from his living-room cot and walked out into the hallway.

Our glorious hallway, with polished flooring covered in extravagant green wool rugs. The staircase wallpaper above the newly added wood panelling was bold with bright red flowers. The wall lights and even the overhanging lights were shaped like little lanterns; there was a grand teak mirror before the cloak area and all the doorframes, skirting and railings had been revarnished. He'd given this place the feel of a "wee Scottish castle" and it was unusually warm, cosy and gaudy for a London townhouse. I loved it. Before climbing the stairs and sinking my feet into the green stair runner, I caught sight of my husband through the open door, sat at his desk pensively studying whatever was on his laptop. Jet lay near Caelan's feet with a grumpy expression, as if sensing something was going on. I winced because I knew if Jet was given even half a chance to accompany his master, he would probably dive right into hell alongside him.

Deep down I'd prayed for him to say he wouldn't go. Not a chance, I'd hoped he would say.

FIGHT FOR LOVE

It wasn't even like I'd feel better knowing what the situation was. Even if I was given an ironclad guarantee Caelan could handle it, and would get home safe, just the thought of him going away and not being beside me was sickening.

He didn't notice me looking at him, or if he did, he decided not to return my stare, lest he give himself away. I took Logan upstairs and the boy started to wake from his evening dreams. I changed him and he cried blue murder, then we settled in my rocking chair in the corner of our bedroom and I began feeding him. He had nothing to cry about then.

After feeding, he went down and I changed into a nightshirt, wandering kind of aimlessly around the house.

It was a beautiful house and was Caelan all over. The way he'd carefully sanded, varnished, painted, added new covings, mouldings, all sorts. It was crisp but warm. Stunning. I did wonder if we'd ever get some rooms finished, there were so many, and we really only lived on the ground and first floor.

For example, as I was wandering the attic, which was now mostly a store room for my odd artwork that we hadn't found a place for downstairs yet, the walls were finished finely with just white paint and all the holes had been filled in. We'd laid a plain grey carpet and it was bland but ready to be used. Some of the rooms on the second floor were the same. Fine, but empty, aside from the guest bedroom which I'd done out like a Royal boudoir with purple everything.

I knew I could've pushed Caelan to fully finish everything else, even done most of it myself, but some part of me felt like this wouldn't be forever. We'd made the living areas our own, but these extra spaces... spoke of a life yet to be lived. A life not yet fully settled.

He found me sitting on the attic floor looking through some of the old boxes my father had kept. I'd thrown out most of my childhood odds and sods, but some remained... and I was holding the leaflet my friends had knocked up to sell my virginity.

Dad had even kept that.

Looking over my shoulder, Caelan snickered. "Who was the highest bidder?"

I tucked the piece of paper back within a packet of other bits and bobs. "It was a joke to wind my father up. Of course, it was my artist boyfriend who eventually won me."

Caelan knelt beside me, his breath whispering through my loose waves. "I dinna wish to go, Flora. Tell me not to."

"Don't go," I said quickly, no thought.

He dipped his head and kissed my shoulder over the nightshirt. It was a foregone conclusion. If it hadn't been me forcing the situation, it would've been someone else. Caelan would regret it forever if he didn't do something.

Sighing, I said, "You can't tell me anything about the operation?"

"I canna and we ran through this before."

I'd tried to understand his life, exploits... the way he worked. He wasn't able to tell me anything. Most of his life would forever remain a mystery to me because of that bloody Secrets Act.

"The artist." He paused, and I saw him out of my peripheral vision rubbing his lip. "Did ye love him, Flora?"

"No."

"What was it like, yer first time?"

I swallowed past the tension in my throat. Now? He'd ask me now?

"We'd been dating for a year already. He'd been very patient. Sometimes we shared a bed and he didn't even try to sneak a hand into my pants, or dry hump me. But when he booked a hotel for my twentieth birthday, you know... some country place... I decided I couldn't hold out any longer. So we did it."

Caelan stroked both calloused hands along my upper arms, my gooseflesh meeting his gentle but unmistakable touch. "What was he like?"

FIGHT FOR LOVE

I closed my eyes trying to remember. "That first time? Or in general?"

I looked over my shoulder and he shrugged. "That first time."

Staring ahead, I said, "I don't remember."

"Ye dinna remember?" he exploded.

"I was so scared, I... don't remember." My teeth chattered slightly which was odd. The large slanting windows in the attic made it warm most of the time, especially if the sun had been high in the sky, which that day it had. Caelan took my hand and rubbed his thumb over the back of it. "It was just something I wanted over and done with. Afterwards, I wasn't hurt and was surprised. I even let him try again. But I didn't love him, or really want him, Caelan."

"So... why?"

I nearly choked on shock. "We've been married nearly a year and a half and you wanna know now?"

"Sometimes I wish we'd found out more about one another before we began, Flora." He gnashed his teeth. "Other times I realise you wouldna huv married me otherwise."

I had to chuckle at that. "True."

Something shifted in the air between us and he said softly, "We huvna made love since the bairn."

We'd cuddled, I'd felt him hard against me, but I hadn't felt horny yet. I loved to have him hold me, kiss me, but it wasn't easy. I thought I owed him some titbit, anyway.

"My artist lover had a bad time of it with me. I wasn't ready. I thought I was. I wasn't. Maybe he wasn't so bad, but he had a time of getting me to reciprocate. I guess it ended toxically. He probably thought it was him. It wasn't. It was what'd happened in the past."

Caelan moved up right behind me on the floor, wrapped his arms tight around my waist, then buried his face in my hair, his legs outside of mine.

"I love ye so fucking much, Flora."

His words thrilled me, reminding me just why we married, how we ended up pregnant. I stroked my fingertips through the golden silk of his forearm hair, and said, "I love you wildly, Caelan."

"Then be with me. Let's... try. It's me. Ye ken me. I'm yer husband. I yearn for ye so deeply, lass. Yearn for ye like ma heart might burst if I canna love ye."

I nodded and stood up, then offered my hand to help him up. His gaze held promise and quiet joy, but also restraint. I led him out of the room and down two flights to our room on the first floor. The baby was sound asleep and I unclipped the monitor from the pocket of my nightshirt, switching it off and placing it on the nightstand.

Caelan trembled with longing as he got undressed. I lay on the covers unsure of myself.

"Turn out the lights," I said.

"I see my loving wife," he said shakily. "My gorgeous, sexy wife."

I stared hard and he eventually switched off the light.

We got beneath the covers and he was already hard, his naked body pressed to my clothed one. His breathing was hoarse and he grasped my hip, my bottom, his eyes shining in the darkness.

"You don't know how to be gentle, Caelan."

"I ken how to win. And if ye tell me to win ye by being gentle, that's what I'll be."

Sniggering, I said, "Be gentle to win me, then."

"Okay."

He held himself up over me and for some reason I thought of our first time, writhing and reckless on the rug in front of the fire, the way his body was sweaty from his run around the loch, the tang of the outdoors in his hair. How he'd loved me like nobody else ever had. I hadn't thought twice then... when I didn't know what it really meant. Before I knew how deeply he'd love me, and how deeply I would love him.

FIGHT FOR LOVE

"Caelan, wait," I said, and reached for my shirt, yanking it off. He gasped as our chests met and I could feel his heart thwacking against mine. "Use a condom."

"I already put six under the pillows. Just in case."

I threw my head back laughing. Then I looked at him, so powerful and crazily handsome, at my mercy. I still sometimes didn't believe it. He leaned in and kissed me so tenderly, softly, smothering but also loving.

I'd forgotten this.

THIS.

Him.

How could I have forgotten it?

My belly was soon a pool of molten lust, and I wrapped my arms and legs around him, letting him kiss my mouth, face, throat... then my breasts. He was slick with sweat by the time he had my nipple in his mouth, softly agitating until he could taste a bit of our baby's milk. Growling, he cursed, "Fuck!"

He yanked my knickers down between us and rolled on a condom. I pushed my breasts up towards his chest and groaned as he slid through my folds, teasing his head against my clit.

He waited until I spread my legs wider, until my nails were in his buttocks, my mouth open and my eyes wide, and he plunged home, causing me to moan and him to bite his lip trying to restrain himself.

Then a second later, we seemed to see one another again, properly, for the first time since I'd told him I was pregnant. It was us again. Just us.

"Kiss me, Caelan. God, I love you."

"I'll no stop until ye tell me to."

He didn't, either. We got swept up for most of that night.

It was the closeness, the love, the longing and the cuddles that were the best.

Neither of us wrestled with the sheets that night; we slept so soundly in each other's arms.

Chapter Three

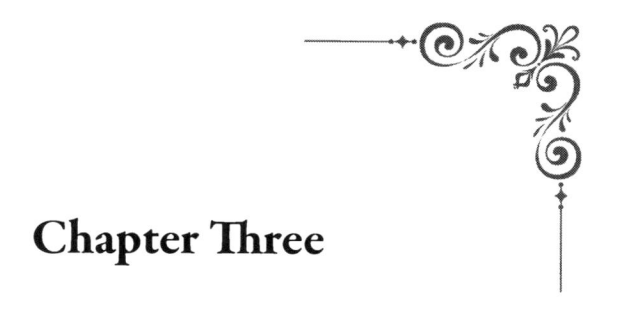

WAKING UP NAKED TOGETHER was gorgeous, but also soul-destroying. He was already awake and had been studying me. The love in his eyes was unmistakable; then the memory of his impending departure hit. I was humming from our lovemaking, deliciously sore and feeling more myself again. Then I heard the baby kicking around in his crib and cooing, my heart racing for a moment before I looked over and saw he was fine.

"I fed him some from the freezer," said Caelan. "To let ye sleep. It's only 7.30."

"I should get ready to go to work." I'd normally leave before eight.

"Nae, lass." He wrapped his arms tight around me and kissed my shoulder, then tucked my face into his chest. The warmth, solidity and smell of him almost carolled me back to sleep.

"Tell me one thing, Caelan."

"Aye?"

"When it's done, will it be truly done?"

His chest rose and fell sharply and I felt the tremble in his touch. "I swear it. I swear on Logan's life. I'm done wi' it, Flora. I have been since we met. I swear it."

I pulled my head out of his chest and looked up into his face. "Then why have I felt for a while now that our life isn't enough for you?"

"Because it isna, Flora."

Shocked, I could barely meet his eye—and we'd made love that was so intoxicating last night, I'd come multiple times, his worship of me that intense. Seeing my obviously emotional response, he elaborated, "Flora, ma heart is in Scotland. I realised it when it dawned on me we'd be a ma and pa. I realised where I'd like to bring him up. I'm sorry."

He was a man of contradiction. Once upon a time, he'd told me he couldn't hack Scotland—it was too quiet and didn't offer enough to keep him occupied.

"But I thought—"

"I miss home," he said in a sad, soft voice.

I bit my lip and rubbed my eyes. "Yes, I miss home, too."

"I miss the castle, I miss the land, I miss Harold and Morag. I miss everything. Miss letting the dog out to hunt and roam free."

I smiled and sighed at the same time. "We can't raise a baby in that castle."

"I ken that," he spoke softly, stroking my hair behind my ears. "Now we have the lodge, maybe I could start renovations on the castle."

I searched his eyes, seeking the truth. "That's what you want?"

"We could gi' it a go, make a business out of it. How about it?"

"You've worked so hard on this house, Caelan."

"Maybe I caught the bug and want to keep renovating."

I rolled my eyes. "You're good at everything. You could do anything."

He nodded, seeming to imply he knew how out of left field this was. "Things change, Flora. My love for you though, nae. Now I've been honest, I'm no gonna say it'll be easy, but we'll figure things out."

Swallowing hard, I said, "I really thought it was that you were missing the job."

FIGHT FOR LOVE

He took a deep breath and grimaced. "I left that job a long time ago. The freelance gig was just... killing time. I was lost before I met you."

Leaning forward, he kissed my nose. My cheek. Curled his fingers into my hair, then kissed me softly on the mouth, stirring my desire... despite him having serviced me plenty last night (our first time together since the birth).

"Caelan, if you could tell me about this mission, would you?"

He stared down his nose. "I wouldna."

"Why?"

"Well, I'm gonna huv to do some crazy shit to get it done."

I saw his dark sense of humour in those big hazel eyes of his and felt slightly reassured.

"When will you go?"

"When I've assembled my team."

"Don't they have one ready and waiting for you?"

He shook his head side to side, slowly. "I need a team who'll care nought for rules, Flora. If they want someone to get this done, then they will damn well let me do it... my way."

"I don't like it, Caelan. Not one bit."

"A week," he said. "I'll need a week to prepare."

He forcefully rolled me so I was tucked into him and we were spooning. His arms were tight around me, the baby was quiet, then his deep breathing seemed to intimate I should go back to sleep. Just like that.

So I did.

A WEEK PASSED TOO QUICKLY because it was a beautiful week. When he wasn't on his laptop, and I wasn't taking calls from the office to advise them, we'd play with the baby. Watch him sleep. Take it in turns to change him, burp him, the usual. Since I'd gone back to work, Caelan had been a stay-home father and he loved it. I saw that now. He wasn't itching to kill again, if he had ever itched for it at all. He only had a hidden desire to settle down where he belonged, and it turned out, he didn't belong here. The truth was, I wasn't sure where I belonged. I'd been a Londoner my whole adult life. I'd never not lived in the south. Heading for life in Scotland would be a whole new ballgame. Sure, it wouldn't be like those terrible holidays at my grandmother's in Perth, but it would be an enormous shift... and I liked my job. I really did. Loved it, in fact.

The night before Caelan was due to set off for who knew where, I sat staring at Logan with wonder as he drank his supper. Blond like his father, blue eyes like mine, though there was still time for all that to change. Whether he'd end up like me, a wildcat, or a lethal tiger like his father, who knew. Maybe he'd be none of that. Perhaps he'd be nothing like any of us, especially not Blake Rathbone, little Logan's deceased grandfather. My dad.

Caelan strode into the bedroom, the one room in the house I'd designed, decorated and furnished all by myself. The thick pile carpet was champagne in colour, matching the silk drapes. A wall of sliding wardrobes, white, with lots of mirrors, existed opposite the bed. There were matching dressers on the adjacent side, then our large divan bed with a silk-upholstered headboard in line with the other décor. All complemented by crystal chandeliers, corresponding table lamps, pillows filled with feathers, layered bedding and a super comfy mattress. It was feminine, warm, with a splash of colour in the Vettriano hanging above the bed. The dancing couple.

He had packed already, I knew. I'd seen his duffel earlier in his dressing room down the hall (he had a lot of jackets and shoes, not to mention suits). Hence my clothes stayed in here, Junior's in the nursery, and Caelan's in his own special room. Originally, we were going to turn the en suite off this room into extra storage space, but just as Caelan was about to create a huge walk-in, I'd decided I didn't want that. I'd keep the en suite. That's what happens when you decide to have a child and know at any minute, you might need quick access to that bathroom. For myriad reasons!

He sat on the edge of the bed near us and rubbed his hand up and down my leg.

"I'll be back before ye can blink," he said.

"Don't make promises, Caelan."

A wave of anxiety came over me now and again at the thought of where he might be going. With whom. And what for...

"I've always wondered something, Callie." He looked away, mentally anticipating my next snippy comment. "How many times did you save my life before we ever spoke?"

I watched his throat shift dramatically as he swallowed. He kept his eyes on the floor, avoiding looking at me. "Maybe if ye'd prefer to sleep at night, I shouldna say."

"I suppose so."

He rubbed my ankle and murmured, "Harold will pick you up from Aberdeen tomorrow."

"I know."

As he was going his way, I was going mine.

I knew he wasn't going to tell me anything, but I still said, "Where are you going?"

"Within Europe," he said, but that still didn't give me comfort—not if my husband had been requested to do this on behalf of the King.

The King!

Dangerous people still existed in Europe. Just because it wasn't the Middle East...

Then, I realised.

We looked at one another at the same time. "Ukraine."

"Aye."

Shit. An actual full-blown war zone.

The look he shot me was one of utter determination. "I'll get it done."

"I know you will, even if it takes your life."

He sighed and moved closer, stroking the baby's head.

Once Logan was fed, I got up and went into the en suite to shower. While the water heated up, I heard Caelan tending our son, burping and then singing to him.

I was halfway through my shower when Caelan walked into the space behind me and wrapped his arms around my waist and breasts. Arching into his touch, I groaned and shuddered the moment his mouth touched my throat.

"I saved ye from her clutches at least ten times," he growled.

"I know."

I turned in his arms and kissed him, lashing my tongue at his. He backed me to the wall out of the way of the water spray and I jumped into his arms.

There was utterly no thought whatsoever as he fucked me deep, hard and religiously. He came inside me so violently, I sobbed after. In the moment, it didn't enter my head about contraception. I think he needed it, maybe so did I.

It was already too painful this parting, and it hadn't even happened yet.

Whatever was to come, whatever state he came back in, it would be too much.

I just knew it. This was going to end badly.

But there was no other way.

He withdrew carefully, then kissed my nose and drew me back towards the water again to keep warm. Even with the spray buffeting the pair of us, I thought I saw tears in his eyes.

"When I return home, we'll make plans, I swear it," he said. "We'll figure it all out. Everything will be fine."

FIGHT FOR LOVE

I let him wash my hair, kiss me under the spray and hold me. I wanted so much to believe that everything was going to be all right. I knew it wouldn't be.

Chapter Four

WE ALMOST DIDN'T LAND in Aberdeen, it was so misty. We were circling for a while until finally, an act of God or something must have made it possible. I thought of the dog in cargo, the poor thing. Still, he was better off where he was. The baby screamed blue murder as we descended. No doubt his ears were popping.

After waiting forever to collect the dog, I found Harold in the car park huddled beside Caelan's modern Range Rover, which we now kept up here.

We said nothing to one another, he merely nodded and I gave a small smile.

He put our things in the boot with no complaint and I leapt onto the back seat with the kid, feeding him as Harold drove us away. Thank goodness for tinted windows. Needs must, when you've just been on a packed plane with a load of leering golfers tutting and scoffing. Meanwhile Jet panted in the front seat beside his grandpa, Harold occasionally reaching out to stroke the beautiful beast's head.

The lodge was situated on the other side of Towie, right on the edge of the Cairngorms National Park. Our first home, Castle Cagair, lay a few miles north, a little west of Kildrummy, in a small valley that almost nobody knew of. I'd got to know the landscape a lot better since those crazy early days.

Morag was waiting on the porch with a look of worry and sadness. She didn't even make a song and dance about the baby. She saw my face and took Logan from me quietly, not even making a sound when he threw up a little bit on her plaid shirt.

I heard some whispered words between the pair, then Harold made himself scarce around the back of the lodge, no doubt throwing a ball for Jet.

For a moment, I sat in one of Caelan's high-back chairs by the wood burner, watching the birds and squirrels racing around outside the window opposite. Then, I fell apart. Morag passed me the baby back and I held him tight to me as tears slid down my cheeks. He was alert and sucking his thumb, but probably oblivious.

"Aye, a good cry, lass. And I'll make ye some tea."

I caught my breath. "Have you made scones?"

"Aye, course I have," she chuckled.

"All right, then."

ONCE I'D HAD MY TEA and scone, I felt much better. The baby had a nap in Morag's arms on the couch and eventually, she said, "Where's himself, then?"

I gave a wry smile. "Oh, has Harold not said anything?"

"Wouldna say a thing."

She sat there in her thick plaid shirt, her grey wiry hair sticking out in all directions, her jeans splotched with muck here and there. Well, she'd married Harold, so...

"You wouldn't believe me if I told you!" I began.

She squeezed her eyes tight shut. "Try me."

"The King himself asked him to help with a diplomatic situation."

Her jaw dropped. "Nae, lass! Nae. What a thing."

I looked into her eyes, eyebrows raised. "A bad thing, yes."

"It'd have to be dangerous for them to be asking yer bawbag, Caelan." I loved the way she said his name. Thickly, barely pronouncing it, she sounded it out *K'lun* instead of *Kay-lun*.

Chuckling, I admitted, "Yes."

"Och, weeel... seems there's nought to do but wait for ye big idiot to arrive home. And we can have fun in the meantime, right? Young master?" She cradled him tightly, looking down into his sleeping face. "While I'm babysitting, why no take yourself to Balmoral and such." She gave me a determined look. "Mark my words, that lad'll be back. Tough as auld boots and them some. The thick-eared wee bastard. He'll be back."

I truly, truly hoped so. Or, I didn't know what I was going to do.

Chapter Five

Caelan

THE PLANE THEY'D CAUGHT a ride on was carrying humanitarian aid to Ukrainian refugees who'd crossed the border into Poland. His team had dressed in the bibs of one of the charities coordinating this aid but at some point, Caelan and his men would quietly break off from the unloading party. After they crossed into Ukraine, they would be outlaws, or as good as. This was a mission of the utmost secrecy. No trail, no evidence, no record of their trip whatsoever. It was a diplomatic mission of the tallest order.

Thankfully they were able to slip away from the refugee encampment they'd been "helping" at without notice, the aid workers they'd flown in with all having been sworn to secrecy.

After trekking through wilderness from late evening and into the night, Caelan and his men found a spot to take a few winks of sleep, huddling in their fur-lined, all-weather jackets beneath a dying willow tree, the stars up above out in full force.

"Wants me some filth," complained Cain, his voice full of grit.

Caelan sat next to the pockmarked East Ender whose reputation for ruthlessness preceded him. He was two stones heavier than Caelan, but much less clever.

"Take five winks, ye wee piece o' shite," Caelan growled, and Cain grumbled, responding to the order.

Even he wouldn't cross the boss. Caelan didn't just have a rep; he was a legend.

They had a long day ahead of them tomorrow. A day of reconnoitring and sussing the landscape. Five winks… or maybe two for Caelan, would have to be enough.

AT DAWN THEY RELIED on their army rations to get them moving, chomping and drinking as they went. It wasn't difficult to find an abandoned vehicle, and once they were on the road, Caelan instructed their driver Cliff where to go. No main roads.

Cliff, an army driver with fifteen years' experience, had retired a couple of years ago. The man had got himself involved in some shady stuff since finding civvy street a tough adjustment, so Caelan had had to get him out of jail for this—because, Cliff could really drive. He could take anything across rugged terrain, much to the chagrin of Cain, Chuckles and Richards in the back, grunting every time the crappy SUV they'd piled into nearly lost suspension due to a pothole or an unavoidable boulder.

It was hours before they made it to Lviv.

Everyone sat supremely still then and watched out for any kind of threat. They were wearing generic army wear and had the yellow and blue patches of Ukraine displayed on their jackets. People in the streets gawped at five huge men packed into a relatively small car, but they also nodded and waved them on.

The city was one of the least affected by the war, but still, the cultural heart of Western Ukraine was damaged here and there.

"We stand out too much, boss," Cain grumbled.

"There's nae time to lose. Beggars canna be choosers," said Caelan, ever the optimist—or maybe he just enjoyed hurling himself into danger.

"Here," said Caelan eventually. "Stop here."

They came to an abrupt halt on a long, tired street dominated on both sides by towering apartment buildings, all in the Soviet-era style.

Trash lay in the streets, debris and God knew what, plus an air of something hung about the place. Perhaps the people they were here to see had been tipped off by spies at the refugee camp.

Caelan turned to Cain and nodded. There was understanding and a plan they'd made earlier. Richards and Chuckles would go their own way, and they, theirs.

"If things go wrong, dump this and we meet at the rendezvous," Caelan reminded Cliff, though he didn't need a reminder. They'd all taken note when Caelan had warned them back in London: *"This could see ye all deid, but ken the Treasury will see ye families right if it do. And it'd be a hero's death at that."*

Indeed, Richards and Chuckles were mercenaries the British government had been looking for forever. It had taken Caelan two days to find the inseparable friends lurking in a cave in deepest Wales. He'd contacted them through their radio. Even the most cloistered of people have need of some connection to the outside world.

"Aye, boss," said Cliff, a fellow Scot Caelan met years ago in Afghan.

Cliff, despite his foibles, had saved a dozen lives that tour with his driving skills.

People don't remember that though, do they?

Just the bad.

"With me," Caelan said, and he and Cain left the vehicle.

Cliff skidded away with the other two who'd make themselves comfortable on the roof of another apartment building nearby. Backup. British spies in the city had stashed weapons on that roof, ready and waiting for their use. Richards and Chuckles were the best sharp shooters in the Northern Hemisphere. It didn't take a genius to figure out they'd been seduced by the wrong kind. Hence evading the authorities in a cave. Because Caelan knew they sure as shit weren't lovers, so it wasn't to shack up or anything.

Meanwhile Caelan and Cain strode across the street, heading for the place where at least Eric was meant to be being kept. It was no doubt why the entire street and neighbourhood was eerily quiet, why there were no children on the streets, not even a beggar or two out to filch some copper from their wallets.

"Ain't right," muttered Cain.

"Be ready," said Caelan.

Cain had been brought along for one reason and one alone.

Size and therefore, the appearance of might.

He even intimidated Caelan (not that Caelan would ever admit it).

Cain was the only other who'd been SAS. Before retirement Cain had been controllable, but now out of the forces, he was a loose cannon taking part in illegal boxing matches and bodyguarding some of the slipperiest bastards around. Caelan's thoughts turned dark as he realised he wouldn't be so sad to lose Cain; it'd mean some of the foulest gangsters and pimps around wouldn't keep getting away with the stuff they were.

Though he'd assembled this party of renegades, on the whole ex-serviceman and women were good people. It was the aftermath that wasn't good to them... hence why some went rogue and earnt themselves prison, homelessness or even worse situations.

The door to the apartment building was open, swinging on its hinges. They walked right in, clambered over the trash lying around the hallway and headed for the stairwell. They climbed three flights of stairs before they reached the corridor leading to their destination.

Again, deathly quiet. Not a sound. True, they were acting on British intelligence, but even that on occasion was wrong.

FIGHT FOR LOVE

And they had nothing. No weapons. No equipment. Just themselves. Oh, and two rogue assassins across the way, potentially having been intercepted as they made their way into the building opposite.

"Nowt for it, boss," growled Cain.

They reached a door which had a bunch of scratches and boot prints all over it. The lock had been broken, repaired, broken, repaired...

Caelan took a deep breath. He'd been in worse situations. Not to say this would be a breeze, but it wouldn't be as bad as some of the other hellish encounters he'd dealt with and escaped... somehow. A few times barely by the skin of his teeth.

Caelan knocked on the door and then there was noise. So, they weren't expected.

Boots shuffled in the room and hushed voices spouted commands.

"I don't think they knew," said Cain.

"Quiet," Caelan commanded.

Bolts and other locks (no doubt makeshift ones) were released.

The first thing that poked out of the crack between the door and frame was a shotgun. The chain was on but a quick kick of the door had it open and the soldier fell flat on his back on the floor.

Caelan stepped over the felled man and strode into the revolting space in which twenty men had obviously been contained together for quite some time. A poky living area not more than twenty-metres square. Someone flushed and came out of some cupboard of a bathroom just as Caelan moved into the centre of the room, Cain hot on his heels. Most men stared, dumbfounded.

So, they knew who he was then.

Eric was tied to a chair alongside another man, the asset. Both were bloodied and pale.

The rest were Ukrainians.

Caelan made it his business to always learn some of the language wherever he went, and he'd been to Ukraine plenty before on exercises, so he said in their tongue, "I'm not armed. I'm here for negotiations." His pronunciation was awful. Some of them snickered, but it got the message across. "Check, if you like."

The guy he'd just sent flying checked Cain first, patting him down, perhaps because he looked like more of a threat. Then it was Caelan's turn. Again, they discovered no weapons.

One of the Ukrainians stood and nodded to Caelan, then said in heavily accented English, "You're here to negotiate?"

"Aye, I'm here to negotiate," said Caelan.

Men around the room then turned to one another, eyes wide—Caelan's accent seeming to confirm for them who he was.

"You *are* Scot?" asked the man who seemed like their leader.

"He's the fucking Scot, all right, you bunch o' wankers!" growled Cain, throwing his neck back and forth like a pigeon pecking at the ground.

Some of the Ukrainians stood straighter, fingers resting on triggers, so Caelan urged Cain back and to stand out of the way—which he did.

For a brief moment, Caelan and Eric locked eyes.

A lot passed between them in that moment, but there wasn't time to dwell.

Then Caelan caught a look at the asset. He was more bloodied up than Eric and weaker, by the looks of him. His head rolled around on his shoulders and he was in and out of consciousness.

"I need to take both of these men," said Caelan, two fingers gesturing at the men in question.

None of the Ukrainians moved a muscle or made a single facial expression. In his experience, the Ukraine people were some of the toughest on the planet. As evidenced in that here they were, not moving in the face of one of the toughest soldiers on the planet. They stared at him blankly, psyching *him* out.

"What's it gonna take?" he asked.

"Much more than you can offer," said the Ukraine spokesperson.

Caelan swallowed hard. It was a tricky situation.

He would ask to speak to Eric alone but Caelan wasn't sure he wanted to hear what might come out of Eric's mouth. That in itself could jeopardise the mission. Caelan stood with his arms folded weighing it up, and eventually, his stare provoked the leader to speak again.

"We are not letting Russian scum out of our sight, nor the man who saved his life."

The Russian scum was the asset. A spy for the West. He'd been buried deep, deep in the heart of the Kremlin, but in recent months, had come under suspicion. He'd been sent to Ukraine as part of a secretive diplomatic force, with a mission to broker some kind of peace, but he'd scarpered before the meeting between Ukrainian and Russian officials could go ahead. He'd lost his head, terrified he'd come undone—fleeing Kiev, the site of the meeting, like a thief in the night.

In fact, he was right to scarper.

The Kremlin bombed the meeting place, having sent only suspected traitors to bargain on its behalf. They'd killed all the Ukrainian diplomats, too. Respected, revered men in this country.

Caelan could understand that these men wanted blood, retribution and vengeance more than they wanted answers. In their eyes there were wounds, let alone on their bodies; there were traumas, animal instincts in charge, survival at the forefront; they were quietly terrified, hungry and cold, longing for homes that no longer existed. He had to do this right.

Caelan gestured for everyone to sit and calm down, hands out in front of him, patting the air. Taking a deep breath, he crouched on the floor and looked around the room at all of them, nodding he understood.

"This man, I can vouch, is no like those other Russians. You'll just have to take ma word for it."

The shaking of heads was their response. Tetchy was an understatement. They were emotionally wrought and wouldn't give up either man easily.

From what Caelan had gathered, Eric and the team had chased the asset across country as he tried to evade capture. When they did eventually apprehend the Russian double agent, at an abandoned warehouse outside Lviv, a bomb hit killing everyone but Eric and the asset.

Eric had secured the asset in a shelter but everyone else bought it.

Too bad as the debris flew, this group of Ukrainian civilian fighters had come to check nobody was injured, then they'd recognised the asset—Russian official, Ogarkov—and now here they all were. Stalemate. It was Caelan's understanding that Ukraine simply did not have the resources to send anyone official out to deal with Ogarkov—and these men were feeling reckless enough to want to wait it out, so they might intercept any rescuers and die for glory and revenge rather than see Ogarkov go free. It was obvious Russia had given up trying to kill Ogarkov, the cat with nine lives. Or maybe they knew enough about the man who'd rescued him... to know to steer well clear of the white-haired SAS commander, the most revered pupil of the infamous Scot.

For sure, Caelan didn't know everything, but he would interrogate Eric later. Including on how he'd survived alongside the asset, while the rest of the team met their end. Including Caelan's oldest army buddy, Hamish. He didn't have time to think about that. Not yet.

FIGHT FOR LOVE

"Britain is a friend to Ukraine, yes?" Caelan asked, and nobody disagreed. "I am a friend to Ukraine. I am asking for this man to be freed so that we can process him properly."

He wasn't sure if Ukraine knew Ogarkov had been feeding intelligence to the West or not. He couldn't risk telling these men too much. Russian spies with flimsy allegiance were everywhere. Suspicion was high. Spies from the West... everywhere. Churchill always knew future wars would be fought through intelligence, information hoarding and psychology. He was right.

Caelan had seen enough during his almost-forty years of life to know that nothing was ever black and white and the blurred lines between good and evil meant life always teetered on the edge of catastrophe.

"We *cannot* let either man go," said the Ukraine.

It was clear they were acting on their own initiative, and for them, this was how things had to be. Any Russian on their soil, in these times, could not go free. Nor could the person who'd apparently rescued such a criminal—especially since everyone else in that warehouse had died.

True, a spy could be a double or triple agent. With no true allegiance to anyone. Yet Caelan had read enough about Ogarkov to know he'd helped the West immeasurably. At the same time, he wasn't about to start listing all the pieces of intelligence Ogarkov had gotten the West about what was happening inside the Kremlin.

What was *actually* happening.

The West couldn't reveal what they knew.

Or this asset, and every other asset, would be compromised.

Churchill... he had it right.

Ukraine's friends needed information so they might anticipate if things were to become really hot in Moscow. Like volcanically hot.

"Listen, gentleman," said Caelan. "I'm gonna give ye ma final offer, and then, we're all gonna leave this cesspit of a place."

Some moved uncomfortably in their seats when Caelan stood and paced the room; Cain in his peripheral vision folding those boulders he called arms. Indeed, the tang of the last bloke to use the shitter had filtered through the place and wasn't lifting.

Caelan had to get Eric and the asset out of here. One, because Eric never fucked up, but he'd fucked up with this, so there had to be some plausible reason why—and this would not be discovered if he died here, in Ukraine. Two, the asset needed to be secured over in the UK, interrogated, information gathered and then, decisions would be made as to his future. Because dead he was worthless. Alive, he could perhaps tell Ukraine's allies what Russia might do next. He knew how they worked over there, could interpret their manoeuvres.

"My friend Cain here is gonna take Eric and Ogarkov and get them over the border to Poland." Cain nodded arrogantly that it was going to happen, whether they liked it or not. "And I will stay here as guarantee."

Eric fought with his bonds, mumbling through the gag in his mouth. This wasn't what he had intended, but this was what was going to happen.

Some of the Ukrainians laughed at Eric, others hushed when Caelan shot them a feral look.

"Chuckles, shave the hair off Ogarkov's head for me," said Caelan into his concealed mike.

At this instruction, people gawped and began to stand, but then the window made a small *pop* noise, and indeed, a bullet shaved just a small amount of hair off the Russian's thick mop before blasting a hole through the concrete wall opposite.

Ogarkov, who was still pretty much unconscious and whose head lolled around, never knew anything about it, including that Chuckles had been forced to calculate the rate at which the head lolling might affect his shot. Caelan saw this wasn't lost on the Ukrainians.

FIGHT FOR LOVE

"I've two talented sharp shooters on your soil, and you're gonna turn down the chance to not only utilise their skills, but also, learn something from me, too?" Caelan hooked his fingers into the belt loops of his khakis and stood akimbo, smirking at the lot of them. Some of the Ukraine's looked out of the window, even touched the Russian's hair and gulped. "Dinna make me do something I will regret. If ye ken anything about the Scot, it's that I get it done."

Which is what he thought he'd taught Eric, but...

Ogarkov had been a hot asset, but something had gone terribly wrong, Caelan could feel it. Eric was tormented, conflicted, it was obvious.

The whole team. Dead. Including Hamish.

Caelan couldn't even process that yet.

It was unthinkable.

He was glad Eric had survived, but it seemed to have come at a cost.

The Ukraine leader looked around the room, and they all did that thing with their lips, sort of grimacing in agreement.

"It's a deal," said their representative.

Caelan nodded at Cain to help free the two prisoners. As soon as Eric was on his feet, he began trying to speak, but Caelan pinned his furious eyes on his former student.

"Sshhht," he insisted, and Eric said nothing.

The Russian needed help standing and moving, so Cain gave him the support he required.

"I'll be there in two minutes," said Cliff through the comms system they'd all set up beforehand.

"Crazy bastard signing us up," said Chuckles, and Richards was laughing, too.

Their voices became echoey as they left the roof and went back indoors where the reception was obviously lousier.

He'd known they would relish the chance to take out some Russian scum.

But nobody could know.

They weren't active soldiers, just independents, but, they were going to be paid by the British government for coming at Caelan's behest. And they were all ex-forces. Trained in the UK.

As Cain shouldered the Russian out, Eric approached Caelan and tried to speak, but again, Caelan wouldn't allow a word from him. Eric kept shooting warning signals, until at last, Caelan could hold in his fury no longer. He pinned his eyes to Eric and whispered, "I will find out everything. Everything."

Eric appeared shocked more than guilty. Maybe it was Caelan's coldness, but probably, it was his very presence here. Perhaps Eric had been close to escape and now, Caelan had ruined everything. Caelan doubted Eric had been at all close to resolving this. He knew something festered in that man's heart. Had done for years.

Caelan looked over his shoulder and Cain nodded that he had this. He'd see it done.

Minutes ticked by, then Richards and Chuckles entered the room; the screech of tyres in the street down below told them that Cliff had his cargo safely on its way.

"Now, then, where do we start?" asked Caelan, a wolfish smile accompanying his new tone of voice. Amused, but deadly.

Even as Richards and Chuckles appeared at first glance to be the most brutish of the three British men standing in the room, anyone really looking into Caelan's eyes would've seen the killer hiding inside that cold, calculating stare.

A killer who'd get no pleasure from killing with a gun or machete. Not even a knife. Only with his bare hands would he ever truly enjoy it. And only after he'd psychologically reduced his enemy to near rubble before that last, vicious swipe came.

FIGHT FOR LOVE

"Well, my friend," said the Ukraine man, squaring his shoulders in the face of potential doom. "Shall we have a drink, then maybe we can have some fun?"

"The Ukraine sense of humour is undimmed, I am happy to discover," snickered Caelan. "It will serve you well, believe me."

A ripple of nervous laughter rang out in the room, and in those short moments, it was immediately established who now held all the cards.

Part of Caelan had only agreed to this because he'd missed it, badly—and he could see these people needed him.

They needed hope.

They needed fighters.

And Caelan?

He needed the truth... and knew he would only find it here.

Chapter Six

THE ODD COUPLE LEFT Caelan's side the next day. By "absconding", the cave dwellers wouldn't be getting paid as such, and if they were here just for some fun, Caelan figured that was okay and not a potential threat to international diplomacy—if they were independents merely getting paid in food and drink. Caelan had known they'd slip off eventually—and it might as well be to hunt Russians. They were headed east to the more contentious zones with some of the Ukrainian men who were in awe of their skills. Something about the deadness in Richards' eyes as he'd left told Caelan that he was on the hunt for rapists, especially.

Meanwhile Caelan followed the leader of the gang who'd kidnapped Eric and soon found himself in Kiev speaking with military leaders who needed his advice. He listened to everything they said, a translator explaining all strategy in great detail. It seemed to him they were already doing everything they possibly could and there was nothing else they could do within the limits of international law. Nor could Caelan be seen to lead missions or execute even one person. Someone like him launching into battle would be an absolute declaration of war. The most renowned SAS man of his time. He could do nothing.

At best he could go home and plead Ukraine's case, but...

The UK was already doing so much for the country.

An island nation in enough hot water as it was!

FIGHT FOR LOVE

In the end, Caelan told the president's military advisors that their best bet was someone like Ogarkov, who would be questioned thoroughly on his return to Britain and would hopefully yield something of importance. Maybe something even he himself hadn't yet realised to be significant. Caelan didn't tell them Ogarkov was probably one of dozens. To these Ukraine's a Russian was a Russian as far as they were concerned.

Lviv being so close to the border, as soon as the asset was in Poland, that would be it. Russia had no jurisdiction. No powers, unless, they wanted to start WWIII over one traitorous spy. Caelan hadn't got word Cain and Cliff had successfully escaped Ukraine with their two assets in tow, but since nobody had heard anything at all, it seemed safe to assume they'd made it.

To appease the Ukraine's for having stolen vengeance from out of their grasp, Caelan offered all he had to give, telling an assembled room of military men and women, "I will visit your fighters," he told them, "and I will tell them I admire them, and I will inspire them to keep going, never accept defeat. I will show them how to fight. I will show them how to win."

Cheers erupted in the room and Caelan felt a thrill he hadn't felt in so long.

It was purpose.

He'd had purpose with Flora and Logan, but this was different. This was where he belonged, on the very outer reaches of what was possible. He would help these men achieve something never before seen. An underdog coming from behind to prove its quality.

He hoped she would forgive him, understand, and be patient.

More than anything, he hoped she would see through Eric when he inevitably showed up on her doorstep.

Chapter Seven

Flora

HE'D BEEN GONE NEARLY two weeks when there was a knock on the door I hadn't been expecting. My heart immediately lurched for the worst-case scenario, of course.

After I was brave enough to peer through the entrance hall, and look beyond the glazed glass that gave a slightly blurry view of whoever was outside, I saw Eric's outline. He was unmistakable. Not much taller than me, but a barrel of a man around the shoulders and chest. Plus with that light hair...

I swallowed all my anguish and answered the door. His light-blue, almost silver eyes studied me carefully. His platinum hair was tied back. For a man meant to be in the military, he seemed to get away with a louche sort of short bob which was shaved underneath.

A commander like Caelan once was, Eric could get away with a few things, I supposed.

"He stayed behind," said Eric, unemotional about it.

I caught sight of the cuts on his face which were scabbed up, then the slight bruising around his neck. When I didn't react, that seemed to unnerve him.

His eyes even widened when he saw I could mirror him, if I wanted to. I gave no reaction because I knew this man couldn't be trusted. Or he wouldn't have come here like this. He'd have called ahead if he were anything like a decent human being.

I hadn't for one second thought Caelan dead. No. If he were, I'd not be looking at a man upright, but a shadow. He seemed haggard but together.

"Come in," I said, and he gingerly stepped over the threshold, since it was still quite chilly in Scotland.

A green bomber jacket, tight grey t-shirt beneath, comfy jeans and black boots. Despite the inconspicuous dressing, his arrogant swagger, cold eyes and the way he dressed his hair told people immediately he wasn't ordinary.

"I've got rather a lot on my plate, but I can offer you some tea if you would like."

I stood in the entrance hall with my arms folded, mentally prepared to defend myself against whatever passive aggressive comments he was about to make.

"You're not worried about Caelan?" he asked, staring around the room, utterly nonchalant.

He was no doubt seeking ways into our world, little tells of what our private life together was like.

"My husband will be back. He's just doing whatever it is he's got to do. I know him. He'll be back." While I knew all that was true, beneath I was a quaking bag of nerves, not sleeping at night, not showering without crying... every single day.

I comforted myself whenever my despair got too much, thinking of his return home and how sweet that would be. It would be forever this time, too; no more missions, no more nastiness.

No more Eric.

"I'll take some tea," he said.

He followed me to the kitchen and stood by the sliding doors which looked out onto the garden and the forest beyond that. Somewhere in the wilderness Harold was walking the dog. I was expecting them back any minute.

The log store from winter was still full owing to the fact we'd spent much of our time lately down in London, what with the new baby and all. It was one of those things Harold loved to do whenever he came over—he'd potter around chopping wood for us, check the water butts weren't overflowing, the drains etc. Anything he could do to make himself feel useful, since the land he used to tend had been sold off and he'd officially retired soon after. Having shared with the new caretakers all the knowledge he possessed, Morag had been able to persuade him to finally rest at seventy-seven years old.

"Milk, sugar?" I asked.

"Just milk thanks, Flora." He leaned against the frame of the sliding doors with one hand on the top bar, his other hand in his pocket.

"I really thought you'd be more mad he stayed behind," said Eric, eventually.

I placed his tea on one of the coasters lying on top of the circular breakfast table. He heard me stamp it down and turned, plastering a fake smile on his face as he picked it up. I held my tea close to my face, blowing the steam off the top, my back propped against a sideboard. Logan slept upstairs and would soon wake needing to be fed. I hoped Eric would be gone by that time. Later on, I had a video call with some staff of mine and wouldn't want him around for that, either.

"Why would I be mad? Caelan is the master of his own destiny." Sad, yes. A little mad? Maybe. But not in the way he was insinuating. I wasn't some simpering, needy little woman.

His gaze nearly turned feral as he angrily slurped tea that was still too hot to be guzzled.

"You took him away from us," he accused.

I shook my head slowly. "Don't be such a princess, Eric."

FIGHT FOR LOVE

He ground his teeth together and that jaw of his which could probably cut diamond suddenly appeared even more angular, the tendons in his neck jumping to attention, too.

I smirked while preparing to cut him down. "I don't know what this dance between you of all these years has entailed, but you need to move on, Eric. That's all I know. I am not some siren who stole your best mate. He left that life willingly. Ages ago. Before I even came along. So us marrying merely drew a firm line underneath what was already done with."

Eric had some scrapes of a few days' old on his hands which I studied as he lifted the cup to his lips once more. It occurred to me that Eric might have intentionally placed himself in a tricky situation in the hope that Caelan would come and rescue him.

Eric chuckled, shook his head, then pinched the bridge of his nose. "You don't even know who he is."

"No," I said, vehement. "I do. I know who he *is* and I don't care who he *was*. I know who he *is* now."

He inhaled deeply. "Well, fuck knows when he'll be back. They're all over the place out there. He'll see that things need to be done and he won't be able to stop himself. To him all that chaos is like a big sweet shop and he won't be able to resist the shiny wrappers of all that needs doing out there."

"Maybe he's what they need," I retorted.

Realising I was no safer here than in London, a plan began to form. I'd head back home and get on with my life. Maybe Logan could come to work with me and I would stop at intervals to feed him. I wasn't going to stop living my life because of these idiots.

"Caelan will never stop being who he is," warned Eric. "It's ingrained. He's not meant for domestic bliss."

My face turned red with fury and I had to hold my tongue despite the rapid-fire expletives threatening to break free.

The first strains of Logan waking filled the house and Eric ground his teeth again.

"That's my cue to leave, is it?" He pushed his tongue into his cheek, the arrogant prick.

"I'd thank you kindly to never darken my door again."

He pulled his bottom lip inside his mouth, then bit it to stop himself saying whatever it was he had on his mind.

"I shall show myself out."

I said nothing, but when he'd gone, I bolted that door.

Bastard.

MORAG COOKED DINNER for me in our kitchen that night while I dealt with Logan's nightly routine. Meanwhile Harold sat in Caelan's wingback downstairs, petting and telling the dog off.

Harold had seen Eric's Jeep leave the property earlier but when he'd asked what he was doing here, I said it was to tell me that Caelan had got caught up with something but he would be home soon. The look on Harold's face told me he knew there was more to it. Then when Morag had shown up to cook dinner, silently getting on with it, I was fairly convinced that neither believed me to be all right about everything going on.

When the baby was finally abed and we all sat around the table for haggis, tatties and neeps, plus the most delicious red onion gravy known to man, that's when I saw in their faces they were preparing to make their feelings known.

"Can he no tell ye himself?" said Morag out of nowhere, in a sharp tone.

I was angry with him, too. I'd known beforehand he wouldn't be allowed to take a phone with him into a country he wasn't supposed to be in, but surely, they were still allowed to make some calls out of Ukraine? Unless your name was Caelan Cameron, of course and your very existence in such a place might trigger all-out war.

"I'm going to have to get on with my life, aren't I?" I said in a forthright manner. "Because he's getting on with his."

It'd only been two weeks, but that was a long time without one word. I had to continually push down those horrid thoughts, such as, "He doesn't care, he's forgotten me," or, "He cares about them more than me."

I had to remind myself he was there to *help* people and that was important to him, and to me. His work certainly didn't lessen his love for me and the baby at all.

"I dinna think ye should return to London, lass," said Harold. "He would want us to look after you and the wee 'un."

"I know that, but..." I couldn't bring myself to say I was eager to get back to my job so I could have a distraction from all of this—and not have to look at their concerned faces as I appeared to get on with things.

"He's right, lass," Morag added. "Caelan would want ye here, wi' us."

"But what about what I want?" I said, my temper rising.

Morag reached for my hand. "What do you want, lass?"

"My husband!" I cried, and covered my face with a hand when my composure cracked.

Morag's arms were around my shoulders immediately. I knew they both understood, but what I didn't know, was when he was coming back and that utterly killed me.

"That fucking bastard, Eric!" I exploded. "He did this, I know it! He did this."

The silence coming from Harold and Morag was deafening. Eventually Morag merely whispered, "Aye."

Then Harold said, "T'would seem the lad has never been able to move on."

"Aye, the way he would linger at the castle after all the others had gone home." Morag sat in her own chair again while I dabbed my eyes with a napkin. I eagerly awaited more. "Like a leech, wouldna let go. Something about him, something cold. He'd get this look in his eye, lass. If yer man didna give him the attention he so craved, aye, he'd wear something like frozen rage inside those wolverine eyes."

I swallowed and looked to Harold. He nodded and said quietly, "He's nae good, Flora."

I ate some more of my dinner, then decided, "I've got to get rid of him. Or he'll never leave us in peace. He found me here, he can find me anywhere."

If the man thought that it was better for Caelan to be trapped in a war-torn country than at home safe with his wife and infant child, what did that say about him? It said he had a warped sense of what love was, that's what.

"Aye, perhaps it's time," said Morag, one bushy eyebrow raised.

Harold raised two bushy eyebrows and smiled crookedly.

"Time for what?" I felt like there was some mystery here to be solved, the way they were giving each other a knowing look.

"For someone to take him doun," she said.

"And you think that person is me?" I looked between them, seeking answers.

Harold sniffed. "Who else?"

I TOSSED AND TURNED that night. Part of it was the fear of him coming back to slaughter us during the night. Another part of me was absorbing all I'd learnt and what it meant.

Eric would never leave us be. He'd helped us get rid of Sherry, for sure, but part of that was for his own sake. So he could keep Caelan safe from the woman.

FIGHT FOR LOVE

For an hour or so I stood by Logan's cot watching him sleep. We'd named him so because it was a strong name for a braw lad, but also because, Caelan's mentor in the beginning had shared this same name. Logan McCarrick. He'd raised Caelan from a wee scrote, as my husband would say, to the machine he'd become. Then Logan tragically died while skiing in Canada—instantly promoting Caelan. An honour he'd reluctantly accepted.

My husband was out in the world, at that very moment, perhaps in a bunker beneath ground, or sleeping beneath the stars in a trench, maybe even some slightly more homely barracks.

I couldn't stand knowing nothing about where he was, with whom and for what purpose, exactly. All I knew was that I had to have faith. He was no ordinary soldier and he could help those people in ways even I couldn't comprehend—and I was married to him.

Why now, I thought? Why now? When I'd only just gone back to work and everything was fine. Why had this happened now? Or had Eric been waiting for the perfect opportunity? When Caelan and I were least expecting it.

Scary scenario: Eric never orchestrated this and all he'd said earlier was true.

Caelan would never be able to truly leave behind soldiering. It was in his blood, marrow, in the very fibre of his soul.

Whatever the truth was, I would find out.

I would go back to London and the snake would slither its way back into my life... eventually. Morag and Harold would have to accept they couldn't help. This was my task and mine alone.

Chapter Eight

London

IT WAS HATEFUL, BUT with no word from Caelan, no family nearby and no trusting many people, I had to put my trust in someone. So I put it in Arabella, my posh friend, who told me about the nanny she'd just let go—her kids were all in school now and a friend of hers would act as a childminder if and when her husband had a project on the go. What wasn't in there was how much the price of everything had crept up and how, potentially, Arabella had found a more cost-effective mode of childcare. Pride and all that. Anyway, the nanny hadn't taken a new position yet, so I swept in and she leapt at my offer.

Amy was lovely actually, very calm and centred. I wanted to say it but didn't—how I thought only someone like Amy might be able to ply and please someone like Arabella.

For a couple of days, I worked from home and oversaw Amy's technique, checking she had everything she needed, that she and Logan might get on, which they did. Finally on the third day I felt confident enough to go into the office for a morning's work.

Just the morning.

Then I'd be back.

Amy had her instructions not to answer the door to anyone. Under any circumstances whatsoever. Let the canvassers and delivery

FIGHT FOR LOVE

men come and go. Only when I got back would we walk out together, and, with pepper spray hidden in my bag.

Nobody at work dared speak to me about anything but work. What could they say? How's the baby? *Practically fatherless.* How are you? *In a perpetual cycle of nervous energy.* When's he coming back? *How long's a piece of string?*

I got some more ideas together for various collections and scheduled in what would need tidying up, preparing for storage or sending to other places. It often struck me how much money could be made for charity by auctioning off even just one item of clothing, but that wouldn't be happening anytime soon, I knew. Some of the pieces were utterly priceless. Monetarily and to the family. Moreover, of historical and future significance.

It wouldn't be until I got to the ballgowns for state dinners and foreign tours that the real work would begin. Right then, I was still on the day dresses, suits and travel clothes.

Just as I was about to leave my office and head to the break room for a cup of tea in the late morning, I got handed a note in the corridor. Some nameless boy in livery serving some page or whomever. The note simply said in scrawl: *Green Room*

I took a deep breath and abandoned my break time, heading through the labyrinth of corridors and tunnels. Nobody batted an eyelid even though I was unaccompanied. It was only when I reached the very door of the location itself that I was noticed—one of the pages grinning with a little bit of a crush, I thought. A feat I'd made it, really since I'd only made the same walk once before and the place was a veritable maze!

I wasn't announced and the King wasn't even in attendance.

It was his son, the heir.

The door was closed behind me and I realised formality had been dispensed with for the humbler and more modern prince.

"You're looking well," he said, clearing his throat. "Despite circumstances."

In a blur, well, on my part anyway, we shook hands and I was gestured to sit.

I began to imagine I was going to be told he was dead. It was inevitable the prince had some experience of this, once having served himself.

"I'll cut to the chase. I'm not meant to know a thing but a friend of a friend of a friend heard Caelan is in Ukraine and alive. Well. And busy."

I'd expected air to rush out of me, but truly, all I felt was flat.

"Eric Holmes came to see me. So I'm not entirely unapprised. Hence my lack of reaction, sir."

The prince's eyes narrowed at that. Even darkened. I could see he was thinking very carefully about whether to say anything.

Hell, if my father could see me now—bowing and scraping.

He'd laugh his socks off at me, deferring to anyone.

Feeling like I had to explain myself to anyone! What had happened to me?

That's not what my father had taught me to be.

I wasn't a servant. Yet here I'd ended up, somehow:

Accepting my purpose was to serve other people who went about living their lives while I put mine on hold. One could argue I'd done that in my former job, too...

"Is the child safe?" the prince asked.

"Yes, he is. Caelan installed the security system. The nanny worked for my friend. She's utterly flawless. Crime wise, I mean. Looks wise... well, my friend's husband did have a wandering eye."

The prince looked vaguely amused, perhaps at my oversharing. Or indeed, his own reputation as a bit of a flirt was warranted.

"Best not to trust Eric Holmes, Flora. I'll let it slide this once, but he shouldn't have left the London area, not even to visit yourself."

FIGHT FOR LOVE

So, the prince knew I'd been up in Scotland and that a visit from Eric had no doubt brought me back down. What else did he know, then?

"Why's he been told to stay put, sir, may I ask?"

His Highness took a deep breath. "You don't seem to be aware that the whole team was killed." I lifted a hand slowly and covered my mouth, shaking my head. He nodded. "Except for Eric, of course, and the asset whom we now have in our possession thanks to Caelan."

"It was a bargain then, a swap?"

"Indeed, though until Caelan actually got into the country, I don't think he knew what he'd be facing. He didn't go with the intention to stay, if that's what Eric has tried to convince you...?"

That was a leading question.

"Eric couldn't convince me of anything; he only paid a visit to stir the pot." The prince looked assuaged as I looked him firmly in the eye. "So, if I understand this right, Eric is under investigation and grounded until further notice?"

"Precisely."

"And I'm here because...?" I certainly couldn't help them where Eric was concerned; he was as oily as they come.

The prince crossed his legs and rubbed his index finger under his bottom lip. I made him nervous. Or the topic of conversation did.

"The Russians suspect Caelan to be in Ukraine. They've sent a kill squad to find him."

I nodded my head. "Good."

He frowned deeply. We didn't know one another well, so he didn't know if I were joking, being serious, or if I was in denial.

A little of all three.

"If they do catch up to him, he'll kill them first," I clarified.

He cocked his head and tried to press home with a serious gaze how desperate the situation might become. "If they find and capture him, Flora... do you know what it might mean?"

"No, elucidate, please," I said abruptly.

He let me have that and said quickly, "It could mean a great deal of trouble for diplomacy."

I had a slew of vile retorts on the tip of my tongue, but I was bigger and better than that. I sat there and mirrored him, crossing my legs and pursing my lips, eyes fixed on him.

Eventually, he broke the silence. "You were a friend to my wife, so I am trying to be a friend to you, Flora. You should find somewhere safe."

I inhaled deeply. "Safe? Safe? If you're as knowledgeable as you claim, then you have to know I've never been *safe*."

He rubbed his nose in response. "Hmm."

So, he had looked up who my father had been and what he'd done for money.

"Sir, if you think for one second Caelan did not meet his match in me, you are very gravely mistaken. You'd have been better employing me as your wife's bodyguard than her dresser. I don't appreciate being treated with kid gloves, like I'm some pathetic little woman. I'm the wife of a man who has done all kinds of things for this country. I know and see more than you could possibly imagine. I'm the—"

...only one who really knows Caelan, I wanted to say.

But I stopped, breathless. He nearly got up, but I scowled so hard it made him blush with embarrassment.

"I insist on you taking a leave of absence, Flora. No qualms, please. My father agrees. Whilst this is in play, you need to be with your son. It's what Caelan would want. And the job is going nowhere. We're none of us in any rush to see Grandmama's things on display like doll's clothes."

FIGHT FOR LOVE

Indeed, she had been like a doll. A seemingly weak and feeble little woman, though no doubt she'd put all of these peacocks in their place.

"What you're really trying to tell me is that you don't want to have to look at the woman whose world might be ripped apart."

"Flora, what I'm trying to press home is that, yes, Eric Holmes is potentially a very dangerous man and as a father myself with a wife ferociously protective of her cubs, I know without doubt who the best person in the world to protect a child is."

I'd hurt him by insinuating he didn't care; he'd hurt me by not being straight from the start.

I already had known Eric was bad news, right from the very moment I first set eyes on the bastard.

This was an impossible situation.

"You're doing other people's dirty work, and I'm sorry," I said, struggling to prevent my lip from wobbling.

"I am sorry, Flora," he said as gently as he could.

"Let me have my work. Trust me, Logan will be fine." If Amy had survived Arabella...

He took a deep breath. "Your unease makes others here uneasy."

"I can't help that. But if you expect me to carry this alone, fine, toss me out into the cold."

I lifted my head and gazed sharply at him. Here I was, a nobody, bartering with the future monarch like he was nothing but a dodgy market trader and I was down to my last copper.

"My work keeps me sane. So put surveillance on me, on my house. Do what you will. I will do better at pretending everything is okay. You can do this for me, for Caelan. You never know, being frustrated might force Eric to make a misstep and you could have him."

"I wouldn't risk Caelan's wrath for anything, not even your sanity," he chuckled.

I wished I could have laughed along with him, but my chest was a basic cavity capable of nothing more than shifting up and down in that moment.

"Please," I said again, a hand over my mouth, a tear balancing on my lashes as I stared out into the lush gardens.

"It'll be done," he said.

Without a word, I got up and left.

Back in my wing, I closed my office door... and screamed into a cushion.

Chapter Nine

I KNEW THERE WAS SOMETHING wrong a few days later, when I was driving with the baby in the back of the car through Brighton, and I saw the same blue Range Rover in my rear-view mirror I'd seen all the way from London. Four men packed into the vehicle, four. The government wouldn't send four. They'd send one and maybe a drone. At a push two men, one of which would be a trainee. No. It felt different to the lazy junk-eaters who sat at the end of my street in baseball caps doing their crosswords. Basically, near-retired cops who would report in, nothing more. Those men in that blue vehicle were no babysitters. They were beasts.

I'd driven out with the intention of giving myself some breathing space, but had I fucked up?

Maybe the prince was right. I should've never left Morag and Harold's side.

I drove around as if I were trying to find the perfect parking spot, perchance a mother and baby space right near the beachfront (yeah, right). I actually did end up parking in such a space, but in a supermarket car park nowhere near the front. I'd gone round and round in circles, in some kind of heightened state by that point, a frenzy if you like. I buckled Logan into his buggy while scoping the borough. The other vehicle had disappeared... or was nearby.

The prince wouldn't send out his own personal protection squad of beefcakes to follow little, inconsequential old me to the seaside... would he?

Doubtful.

I purchased donuts inside the supermarket and bottled water, pretending everything was normal. They'd hidden themselves well, because when I decided to vacate the supermarket car park altogether and head to the beach, again, nobody I passed screamed berserker.

Convinced it'd been nothing, I lapped up the scene of too many people in too few clothes for the time of year. Couples and gangs of friends, families and loners, everything was here. Nobody looked scared. I even began munching on one of my donuts as I walked.

When Logan let out a little yelp and a cry, I knew it was time to find a place. So we went to a café and I fed him, drank tea and told myself everything was going to be all right, even though it felt pretty similar to the time I'd known Caelan was stalking me—and I'd ignored it.

We went out and about again after the café and Logan was fast asleep once more. As Amy had quickly learned, Logan was a pretty good baby.

I ended up on a packed street of dancers and revellers, some kind of festival going on, when my head started spinning as I got pushed and shoved. The buggy nearly got away from me and I was dizzy, only just managing to keep a grasp of the handles.

That was when the noise suddenly died as I realised, I'd been herded somehow into a quieter little side street away from the main action—the four men from the Range Rover encircling me.

Colour and noise, people and smells, heat and light, basically all that I'd just been engulfed by—enough to overwhelm my senses—evaporated at the sight of them. Their cold faces. Dead eyes. Shadows were their companions and the world became black and devoid at the sensation of them trapping me, here.

FIGHT FOR LOVE

Silence. Dark, deadly. Silence.

Before I knew what was happening, four shots rang out, like whispers on the wind. As dead as their eyes had been before, they really did look dead as they fell one by one to the ground.

My eyes darted around until landing on the source of those shots.

Eric, with his unmistakable physique, hair and slick movements, crept across a girder above my head where he'd been hiding or had just positioned himself for the purpose of...

After walking the length of the girder, he leapt off an extension roof.

I started to go into shock when he wrapped one arm securely around me, tucked his gun with the silencer still on into his jacket, then turned around the buggy with that one free hand as he directed me and the baby back out into the chaos.

"Do what I say or you'll both die," he said, every word bitten out.

I knew I had no choice.

Chapter Ten

IN A DAZE I FOLLOWED his lead. Back to the supermarket, into the car—him driving. The baby was mercifully asleep, didn't know a thing about all the crap going on around him.

The journey back towards London happened in a blur. I was under no illusion that even if he was just as much of a protector as Caelan, I was unsafe. I didn't know if I could trust a single atom of him, let alone who my true enemy really was.

No words were spoken. I felt like if someone touched just a hair on my head I might explode and I didn't want to kill anyone—ever again.

Once was enough.

He'd just killed four men in seconds like it was nothing.

The car suddenly stopped and I realised we'd ended up in a rough part of town.

Perhaps I was in survival mode, trying to stay quiet and small and the opposite of obnoxious, because I blindly followed as he grabbed the car seat and clicked his fingers for me to move faster and follow him towards a terrace property.

When he walked straight indoors, I was all at odds. He hustled me in and shut the rickety wooden door behind me, locking it, then popping on the chain. The place smelt grimy and when we passed a kitchen as we walked along the hallway, everything was Formica, lino and stains.

FIGHT FOR LOVE

There was an unkempt woman in a corner watching the horse racing on ITV. She didn't look up at either of us, or the baby who'd started to make a little bit of noise in his seat. He stirred.

"Ma, it's me," he said gruffly.

She waved her hand around as if his voice was a far-off annoyance.

"Has anyone been here?" he growled.

"Only you pissing me off," she grouched.

Scanning the room quickly, I saw old photos of a white-haired gangly boy. Siblings, too.

A distant memory hit and I remembered he grew up in Bromley. That was where we'd ended up, then.

Eric did a quick scan of the downstairs rooms, checked in the back yard, then returned. He handed me his gun just as I was about to pick Logan up. The baby stirred and yet...

"I need to pack. Hold the fort. You can use a gun?" He gestured at the gun he'd just shoved into my hands.

I swallowed hard. "Use a gun?"

"Yes?"

I nodded I could.

Yes, I could use one if the need arose.

He chased upstairs and through the thin floors, we heard him throwing open drawers, cupboards, crashing and smashing about.

She kept watching TV like nothing was amiss, those dead eyes never losing that glassiness, though every time the house shook as he thrashed around up there, I noticed her flinch slightly. If she wasn't licking the corner of her mouth, she was furiously biting her bottom lip. She never once glanced my way, never acknowledged the baby.

So he'd been raised by monsters, then.

Telling.

I rocked the car seat with my foot and the baby dropped to sleep again. He wasn't due a feed, he'd just been disturbed by the change in temperature from the car to indoors. Her house was dank and dark; light only hit the front of the property in the late-afternoon sun, not the back where she sat. Whereas the car had been warm during the drive over... and perpetually in motion.

Eric arrived back downstairs with a large case, holdall and a cardboard box full of computer equipment and other paraphernalia.

"I've gotta go, Ma. Don't know when I'll be back."

"Sooner you piss off, the better," she said.

I lifted the car seat off the ground and followed him out as he made 40kg of stuff look like a couple of bags of feathers.

As he filled the boot and I buckled the baby back in, he said, "Your place isn't safe."

"Were they Sherry's cronies?"

"I think so."

"I've got stuff at the place in Scotland for Logan."

He gave a sharp nod. "Then we'll go there."

I knew it might all still be a trap of some sort, but I also knew those men weren't friends of Eric's—or anyone else I knew, for that matter. Those sorts of men could only be associated with my evil stepmother, no doubt controlling things even as she languished in prison.

He started driving and eventually once we were on the M25, speeding along, I said, "How did you know to follow us?"

"He really doesn't tell you anything, does he?" he snorted.

I couldn't find it in me to say anything. Clearly, the danger Sherry posed by still existing in the world had been kept from me. A lot had been kept from me.

Prison or no, I would never be safe so long as she lived.

"It'll be fine," he said, as we chased for the M1 North. "We'll get there... it'll be fine. You've got me. He taught me everything he knows."

That was what worried me most.

Chapter Eleven

THE NIGHT WAS WELL on its way to dawn by the time we made it to the cabin. A few pitstops to feed the baby and ourselves, use the toilet, refuel, etc, and it was around 3am before we got there.

So I was surprised while feeding at 6am to discover Eric was out there already, scouring the land. Out of the windows which were the width of our bedroom, I could see him checking the traps Caelan had laid. Testing them. Checking them again.

He went all around the perimeter doing this as I fed the boy, winded the boy, changed the boy, then put him down again.

I was using the toilet and about to head back to bed when I heard a kerfuffle downstairs. I arrived, knotting my robe, just in time to catch Harold pointing a shotgun at Eric's face.

"Harold, stand down," I ordered.

The old man grimaced, chewed his lip, and grimaced again. He could barely contain his rage.

"Trust me," I reiterated. "Trust *me*, Harold."

He shrugged his shoulders. "Coulda told us ye were back, lass."

"I was going to. We've only been back a couple of hours."

Harold's eyes flicked from me to Eric and back again. "Trouble?"

"Nothing we cannot handle," said Eric.

"He's right," I agreed. "I'll speak to you and Morag later. Dinner, maybe?"

Harold gave a sharp nod. "Aye, we'll be back for dinner, lass."

He took his leave.

We watched Harold walk back down the lane, gun resting on his forearm, his steps faltering slightly as he went around a carefully concealed trap.

Alone again with Eric, I watched him begin to make coffee. He had no intention of going back to bed, then. I was nearly dead on my feet.

"The Prince of Wales himself warned me about you, you know."

He showed barely any shock, just one slightly raised eyebrow, and made an artform of his drink as he did that thing baristas do to create a feathering on top.

"You having one?" he asked, holding it out to me.

I shook my head. "Heading back to bed."

"He warned you and yet, here you are, comfortable enough to fall asleep in my presence."

I kept my face expressionless. "You're disavowed while they investigate you, I take it?"

He chuckled, back resting against the kitchen counter as he sipped his drink. "You watch too many films, and read too many books. I'm just on leave following a period of intense action. I've filed my reports. They're watertight."

"On leave?" I scoffed. "That's not what I heard."

"The Prince of Wales dislikes me because I'm much cleverer than him. End of."

I picked at my nails. "But he likes Caelan?"

"Ha! A master of disguise, your man is. I told you, Flora. He doesn't tell you anything." He put his coffee on the side, shoved his hands in his pockets and looked up the ceiling, jerking his head at this or that, as though the cabin was a bit of an extravagance or novelty. "Checked the paperwork for this place, have you?"

I didn't like his insinuation—and I didn't want to know.

FIGHT FOR LOVE

"Someone on leave doesn't go back to the hovel they grew up in." I intended to pry, to hurt, to upset. "Not unless they're in dire straits."

He only looked at me blankly. "Question my sanity, sure. But question my ability? Now, that would be your downfall."

"Your ability is directly linked to your sanity, especially if Caelan's involved."

"This isn't about Caelan. And it's not about you." He thrust his hand out to press home the point, a red, angry vein popping in his temple. "It's about people who want information and will do anything to get it."

That stopped me in my tracks and made me feel hopeless. Astonished this wasn't over yet, I said barely above a whisper, "This is about my father. Some other secret he kept?"

More money hidden away? More ... something.

Eric said nothing and intended to keep his mouth shut, I could tell, turning his back and taking up his coffee again.

I was almost at the staircase and ready to go back to bed, when I turned around and headed for him, my finger raised in his face. "You were raised by animals and I know what you are. I know what you come from. I know they were monsters. And that you could be a monster, too."

He pinned those silver eyes on me. "Unlike your husband, I'm a man of many words. So you'd better watch your mouth around me because it takes a monster to know one. And if you keep coming at me, I'll give you both barrels back and then some." He leaned in closer and snapped his teeth, smiled darkly, then whispered, *"Monster."*

My nostrils twitched and venom threatened to rise within me. I clucked my tongue and spun out of his space. Monster, indeed. Fucking fucker.

OVER THE NEXT SEVERAL days, not much happened. Morag and Harold dropped off food every now and again but largely left us to it. It might have had something to do with that first night of trying to be civilised across a table and Morag (not Harold, surprisingly) dramatically failing at civility, at least where Eric was concerned.

I could tell Eric was getting bored. First, he stocked up the wood shed with kindling. He polished all of our knives and some of his own. He cleaned the gutters, washed all the windows, cut the grass, dug the borders, cleaned the drains and scrubbed nearly every surface, floor, appliance and crevice in the house.

He would also go out running, of course. And use the baby as weight training all while Logan laughed his socks off. It was those times I caught myself accidentally smiling.

We didn't talk except to say things like, "Pass the salt." Or, "Does he need changing?" Sometimes, "Is it his bedtime?" Other times, it'd be me: "Caelan can't even manage one thirty-second phone call?" Eric would inhale sharply when I tried briefly to probe on that. If people were out for Caelan, calling home was certainly out of the question.

Work had been gracious, even relieved, when I had called to say I was going to take that extended leave of absence, after all. I'd spoken over the phone through gritted teeth. Hadn't said anything about when I'd be back—if I'd be back. Even I had to admit the likelihood of any return was low.

It was around a week since our arrival when I caught him scrubbing one of the pans from dinner. It was already mirror-shine worthy but he was still going at it with a scouring pad and I had to say, "Eric, what's wrong?"

He looked at what he was doing, then at me, cursing under his breath. He rinsed off the pan, emptied the bowl, wiped around, dried his hands—then tried to barge past me upstairs.

FIGHT FOR LOVE

I implemented one of my defensive moves and got my arms locked around his shoulders, his back against my body, held firmly in place. "Don't walk away from me when I am talking to you."

"I'm not going to hurt a woman, but don't tempt me," he groaned.

He smelt of the outdoors, from the trees to the streams to the grass, to the cold winds over the nearby hills. He was outdoors a lot but never far away.

He tried to get away but he wouldn't have been able to without hurting me, snapping back at me or something, and he knew it.

"Tell me what's wrong. Tell me what you know. Tell me everything," I demanded.

"I'm not telling you anything because there's nothing to tell. I'm just bored and angry. Most men are. It's not a new thing, I promise."

I squeezed my arms tighter and he nearly succumbed to elbowing me to get himself free. I kept him still, however.

"I can't abide a man who doesn't say what he really thinks."

He laughed at that. "Says the woman who married Caelan."

My arms loosened and he wrenched himself free, turning around to shake his head at me.

When he tried to grapple me, I kneed him in the stomach, gave him a throat jab, then grabbed his balls and shoved him up against the nearest wall.

"I never had to use physical violence..." He grunted and I hissed. "...*much* physical violence with Caelan."

"I could kill you with one blow to the head, Flora. Have at me. I can take it if it makes you feel better."

Always baiting me with that coldness.

I twisted his balls and his eyes watered. *"Stop."*

I did as he said and stood back, ashamed of myself and annoyed at the situation. It wasn't anything to do with him, not really. He was just our babysitter until Caelan got back.

With every day he was absent, it felt like he got further and further away.

Maybe that was what ate away at Eric, too.

His light eyes narrowed and he dipped his head, those bones of his seeming ever sharper. "You've proved you can take care of yourself, Flora. But some men aren't just strong. They're psychologically damaged and will do things to you I can't even utter in the presence of a lady."

I tipped my head back and huffed. "Lady? Ha."

Amusement lit his eyes too and I had a thought.

I went into the liquor cabinet and gestured we take the Ikea rocking chairs positioned by the floor-to-ceiling windows. The solar lights outside would soon come on and I always liked to sit here at dusk, watch the owls come out, the stars start to twinkle, the foxes in the distance begin their nightly scavenger hunt.

"Tell about your mother," I said in a German accent.

Eric couldn't help a little laugh and it made me happy to see him actually smile for once.

Handing him a few fingers of neat whisky from Caelan's top shelf collection, I watched as he drank a nip, then threw back the rest. We hadn't drunk since we got here. We'd both been on high alert.

I would pump before bed and hope by morning my milk was ABV-free again.

I poured him some more and stuck to my two fingers, sipping slowly to savour the small dram I was allowing myself.

"You saw her," he said, swirling his remaining liquor around the edge of the glass. "She's a shell. She exists, that's it."

"And your siblings?" I asked.

He avoided my eye. "Caton lives in America. We don't speak."

"Why not?"

"He left us."

"Ah, he's the elder."

Eric shrugged.

"There was a sister, in the pics?"

He stared daggers at the floor at any mention of her. "She died of an overdose."

Rather than say, "I'm sorry, that must be hard for you," or, "How do you cope with that?" I went to the window, pressed my nose against the glass and tried to push out memories that flashed before my eyes. No amount of squeezing my eyes shut worked.

White powder.

Dazed, naked men.

Schoolfriends on hospital beds.

Then me trying not to succumb, too.

"Caton was the strong one. If he'd just stayed..."

"Your father must be dead, I take it?"

"I don't know. I could find out, but I don't want to."

I heard the raw pain in his voice. He'd wanted love, a relationship, but they hadn't ever had one. I got the impression there was no chance of it now, so his father may as well have been dead already.

"That's why she's like she is, then? Your sister?"

He looked up, blinked, then stared into his glass. For the briefest second, he'd looked like he was thankful I could read the situation myself without him having to say much.

"She is a monster, she turned a blind eye to the abuse we all suffered, but *yes*. She was a victim, too. She shut down after Betsy died. There's nothing left in her but shadows and lies. Lies she tells herself to survive."

He was well-spoken for a South London boy. "Did you get a scholarship or something?"

He put an elbow on the arm of his chair and held his chin in his hand, a sign he was starting to relax. Maybe the whisky.

"No, I'm just very good at pretending," he said with a smirk.

"An actor, like Caelan, then?" I said, making his eyes snap to mine.

"I'm not even close to his level. You have heard him talk in different accents, no?"

I shook my head. "No, but, I can imagine." Sherry had insinuated Caelan could play anyone he liked. Had to come in handy in his line of work.

I stared into my glass. "Were you in his life when he was with that other lass?"

"Dani?" His voice held no emotion. I nodded once. "I knew Dani, yeah."

"What was she like?"

"Tough." He paused, considering his next words. "She was kind of sweet, cute, one of the lads. She wasn't glamourous, or beautiful, like you. I'd only just started working with them and they'd already been together a while. Everyone knew they were shagging. Everyone knew she wanted more. We kept it from the top brass for the sake of the team."

Our eyes locked and I saw he was telling the truth. There was a clearness there, no spite or darkness. Just a guy telling it how it was.

"Did he hurt her?"

I held his gaze and he didn't look away, but he wasn't giving me any inkling, either.

"Did he?" I persisted.

"Yes," he said. "But I don't think he meant to."

"How did he react when she died?"

Eric inhaled so deeply, his already broad chest seemed to take on a Hulk-like quality, expanding massively. "He shagged anything that moved after that."

I bit my lip. "What about you?"

Gulping, his eyes widened. "What do you mean?"

"How many women, how many men?"

FIGHT FOR LOVE

He chuckled and seemed shy about it. "I've been with a lot more women actually. This was when I was his wingman and he didn't know about the guys."

"So you have a preference for women, or... just...?"

Pursing his lips, he said, "Caelan sort of crept up on me. I'd known I liked men too, but he was... so unavailable and it just sort of..."

"He did what he does with everyone. Makes you need him, love him, adore him. Charms his way into your heart like a deadly serpent."

He threw one hand up. "Pretty much."

Eric took time to consider, then he said, "There have been a couple of guys, but all it was, really, a BJ in a pub toilet kind of thing. I would probably do the full thing if I ever met and loved a man, but the only man I ever loved would never wanna fuck me, so..."

We both had a giggle about that. I might've poured myself a bit more whisky, and him, a lot more whisky. I liked relaxed Eric. He was funny and straightforward.

"I guess I've always had too much respect for women, hence my father's dislike of me, his hatred even. Maybe he thought my friendships with guys were weird, that I should've been shagging girls from the age of sixteen and using and abusing like he did." Eric looked at me darkly then. "Sometimes I like that a guy is a bit rough. And I can be rough back. Guilt-free. Ish."

"You're frightened of becoming like him?" I paused for dramatic effect. "Your father."

He didn't deny it, staring straight ahead. "I'm frightened of being someone who closes themselves off. I see people's personalities and that's what attracts me. You could say I'm sapiosexual and see beyond gender, so if that person has a big brain I wanna shag, well..."

"Ohhhh... ohhhh!"

We both had a laugh about it. Actually, I was the same. I'd been in far too many dalliances with men I knew I could never love, because they weren't on my intellectual level. I'd used them for sex, the same as they'd used me. I wasn't a victim or a damsel in distress. I'd been getting what I wanted without any strings. Had it furthered my career? Perhaps. But mostly, I'd done that through hard work and grit. The sex was a bit of a bonus on the side. An exchange. Nothing more.

"But were you ever like Caelan?" I said quickly to catch him off guard and hopefully get a truthful answer. "Did you ever just fuck for the sake of it?"

"No," he replied instantly. "It always... there had to be something I found irresistible. Like it'd be a mole on their cheek, the shape of their breasts, or their eyes, a tight butt, their laugh, maybe they had really good hair, or we got on... something... that got me off. For Caelan, he buried himself in nothingness. In vague attractions. Fuelled by alcohol. Lots of alcohol."

I'd been afraid of that—of the darkness that lurked beneath. That responsibility weighed on me a great deal sometimes—because without me, I knew he'd go right back there again. I didn't even need Eric to confirm all this. I'd felt it, all this time, that I was the one thing preventing him going back to that lifestyle. That darkness.

"Did Caelan tell you I killed his uncle?"

Eric's jaw dropped. A man his size and with his brutality looked shocked.

Part of me revelled in being able to shock someone like him. Another part of me was terrified he'd judge me forever... see me differently. Treat me differently. No longer like a lady he would allow to bruise him while he did nothing in return.

"We're trauma bonded, you see, we two. Me and him. I've not been able to talk about this with anyone else for fear of judgement, shame, mostly judgement."

"I would never judge you, Flora," he said softly. "There must have been a reason."

"Yes." I gulped and rubbed at my chest, staring into space. "Jimmy was working for my father, got high and drunk one night, tried to rape me... and I killed the bastard with a tool one of the stable lads had left lying around. Dug it into the femoral artery... maybe in more than one place."

I didn't look up, but I could sense Eric taking it all in. "So, he was looking for the killer... and found you."

Nodding, I met his eye, finding only acceptance and sympathy there. "This is true, Eric. He might not have stopped his pillage through life... if Sherry hadn't put him onto me, as a way of exacting revenge on my father." I had to take a breath. "The thing about that woman is she's conniving and clever, but so mean. Oh, so mean. She saves information for when she knows it'll hurt the most; when it has the potential to destroy rather than just break." Another deep breath. And Eric had sat forward, still shocked and astounded by the whole thing. "I truly think she would use Caelan for her own ends, if she could. That she's always planned to break her son so thoroughly as to make him her weapon. I think she knows, even from her current position, Caelan is breakable."

"He often spoke of Jimmy like he was a hero." Grave words from Eric.

I'd been afraid of that. "He won't speak of it at all. We don't talk about it. I made that decision, to draw a line, to forget, because I know— I know—if we do have *the talk*, then we can't go on. So if he's angry he never says, or if he's sad, but I know... he did love his uncle. More than most kids love an uncle."

"Not just his hero, then... but, like a—"

"Father?"

"Yeah. I sometimes felt jealous." Eric considered, rubbing his index finger and thumb across his bottom lip. "But also, something told me Caelan was... hero worshipping because he'd died, maybe... making it seem more than it really was. Like, I'd ask when he last saw him, did they spend every weekend together, what was the last thing his uncle said to him... and it'd be different answers every time."

None of that surprised me, and, it only made me sad, not angry. Sad.

We'd both shared a lot of information in a short amount of time and in that moment, as it all sank in, an awkwardness descended. We'd got pretty familiar really quickly. A week of passing each other on the way to the bathroom or politely queueing for the coffee machine...

Yet it was only that night we actually spoke, finally meeting properly for the first time.

"You should never be sorry for protecting yourself, Flora."

I swallowed hard, smiled sadly and said, "I think that's it, I'm not."

"What's happened, why he's out there, it has nothing to do with you, okay? He's just... stuff happened. It's a war zone." He sat even further forward on the edge of his seat, gesticulating he was sure of this being the case. "He's not happy if there isn't a problem to be solved. That's who he is."

I wasn't sure if he was lulling me into a false sense of security, or, if I really did like Eric, after all. Going with my gut, I decided, I could trust him and I did like him.

"I know exactly what it's like you know, Eric."

His jaw twitched at my serious tone. "What do you mean?"

"Trying to be good when everyone else around you is bad. I know what that's like. What it takes. What reserve of hidden power that requires. What tiny morsels we cling to in order to preserve our true selves."

He said nothing but I could tell, this time, I'd really shocked him.

FIGHT FOR LOVE

"What barriers we put up, the front we put on, the personas... the masks."

He threw back the last of his drink and suddenly stood up. "I'll say goodnight."

There was a tight smile, then he bounded for the stairs.

I'd said too much.

Chapter Twelve

WE AVOIDED ONE ANOTHER for days after that. He went on extra-long runs. I used Caelan's punching bag in the downstairs mini-gym and focused on taking care of Logan—often inviting Morag over for tea and cake once Eric was out running off steam.

It was during one of our tea and cake sessions that something new came up in conversation.

"Has it crossed ye mind what ye'll do if he dinna come back?"

I shook my head, revolted by the notion, giving her a flat, "No."

"What about the bairn? He'll need a father."

I stared at her blankly, wondering where she was going with this.

"I mean, what about yon Eric? He loves the bairn, clearly. Reminds him of his chieftain, no doubt."

How'd she come to this conclusion? A few days ago, she couldn't stand the fella. Now...

Unless, they'd been spying on us through the windows and she was fishing. They had seen that whenever I had a shower, Eric made sure he kept an eye on the baby, or...

"What are you trying to say, Morag?"

"Weeeel, himself surely should be home bi'now."

"Yeah, true. But that doesn't mean he's coming back dead."

She grimaced and smiled, or maybe both, at the same time.

"You're not cheating on the lord with the laddie then?"

FIGHT FOR LOVE

I threw my head back laughing. "What the hell gave you that idea?"

She shrugged. "Man acts like he's running off the world's biggest erection."

"True," I deadpanned, and she nearly fell off her chair wheezing with laughter. "Which means I haven't let him anywhere near me obviously." She raised one shrewd eyebrow. "He's just... Eric. He's bored and would prefer to be back out there, but he's on leave."

I hadn't told her or Harold about the episode in Brighton. I hadn't wanted to worry them. I'd only told them that work had forced me to take time off and that they'd suggested Eric as a temporary bodyguard. They didn't know the half of it.

She pursed her lips and wasn't convinced, I could tell. "Something is afoot. How could he nae be attracted to a woman such as yeself?"

"He really isn't."

"I've barely been down here, lassie but it's obvious ye could cut the air with a knife."

That was true, but I kept telling myself, that was just because of the stuff I'd figured out about him. He was feeling exposed, I'd decided—vulnerable.

"Caelan will be home. You know Caelan. He goes off and has an adventure, then he comes home. Nobody will replace him as Logan's dad. End of."

"Aye, expect you're right lassie, as always."

"Yes, you'll see. He'll be home."

I wished I believed that as deeply as it sounded like I did.

IT WAS A STORM ONE night that forced us to start talking again. One that swept in late evening, battered the cabin and the nearby forest, shrieks of noise sounding like one thing, when they were actually another.

He'd just come in from having secured the corrugated roof on the wood shed, when I made it downstairs to see why the power had gone out.

"Let me check the fuse box," he said, after having had to shove the door shut, then lock it tight because of the wind.

"Power's out," he shouted from the cupboard under the stairs.

"Thought so."

I grabbed matches and candles.

Logan was dead to the world but I wouldn't sleep until the storm had quietened down a bit. The constant thrashing of wind against the roof was enough to wake the dead.

I opened a bottle of red wine while he set the coffee machine going. We both felt like it'd be a long night, and while I needed medicine to get through it, clearly, he was of a more practical mindset.

The winds could get up to 80mph around those parts and it was scary at times. There were no power lines near us, but even a newish roof wouldn't withstand mother nature if she was fixing to batter us silly.

I sat in one of the rocking chairs sipping wine, watching the odd bit of trash, tree or a bucket roll around the fields outside. Gusts hit the house and seemed to want to crack open the windows, but the place stayed intact.

Eric remained where he was in the kitchen sipping his coffee in the shadows. Yet the air crackled with that tension between us. Perhaps I'd hurt him, I wasn't sure. If I knew what I'd done, then maybe I could put it right.

I was about to tell myself I had nothing to apologise for, I hadn't done anything wrong; this was my own home and the mess we were in wasn't my fault, or his particularly—we ought to be grown-ups about being thrown together, though sworn enemies we still were.

"Caelan wants us to live in Scotland full-time," I blurted out of nowhere.

"What?" he gasped, and my words brought him over to join me.

"I know. I can't abide it!" Pointing at the stormy world outside, which was proof enough, I added, "I don't know what it is with him."

"When did he say this?"

I cursed under my breath, shaking my head. "Just before he left. He wants us to talk about it when he gets back."

"But... didn't he just do up that place in Notting Hill?"

I tipped my head back and snorted. "Yep."

"What's the dude's problem?"

"I have no idea."

A pause while we both considered.

"What do *you* want?" he asked.

I didn't have to think very hard. "My work. My friends. My lovely big mansion. London, basically. London." I shot him a look, only a brief one, to gesture I couldn't live up here full-time.

"You don't have to convince me." He held his hands up, one side of his mouth raised in a smirk. "I'm London through and through, too."

"I can handle the odd trip here. I adore Morag and Harold. I adore the place to an extent, but a full-time existence here? This remote lifestyle?" I shook my head, lips pressed together. "Maybe I could run the castle or something as a business while he farms or hunts or runs his little bootcamps or whatever. But my work is important stuff. The preservation work, particularly. It's my skillset. It's where I'm needed."

Eric clapped his hands together, and hunched over, staring at the floor. "He's not settled, then?"

"Nope."

"You're gonna hate me for saying this but despite what you may think of me, why am I not surprised? Why are you not surprised?" I had to concede, I wasn't surprised either. "He's just... not happy unless he's trekking about."

"Aren't you the same?"

Eric sniggered. "My work is my work. One day I'll leave it there."

I was incredulous. "You'd just... quit. And do what?"

"Teach," he said with immediacy, "in some capacity. Yeah, I'd teach. What? I don't know. But I've been told I'm a really good teacher."

"That's... nice."

Nicer than being a gun for hire, muscle for hire, advisor to thugs... etcetera.

We listened to the wind trying to wrench the chrome chimney outside off its hinges, the flue of the wood burner indoors rattling enormously with the force coming in from the outdoors.

Something struck me; a hint he'd made before. "You don't know what I think of you, Eric. You only imagine."

His silver eyes were lined with long dark lashes and in that moment, as he smirked in that rakish way of his, I thought he looked simply gorgeous. I almost forgot we were meant to be having a conversation.

"You think I'm completely besotted by him, that I think the sun shines out of his arse," he chuckled lightly. "Well, you'd be wrong. I know his faults, warts, and all."

I was surprised that's what he thought I was thinking. It wasn't at all. What I was thinking was that Eric had been messed up in childhood and still hadn't dealt with that, not properly. I pitied him more than anything.

"I love him like any man loves a best friend, but am I sceptical as to why he married you? Yeah! More that than some simple jealousy. I accepted who he is and what we are to one another a long time ago." Who was he trying to convince? "Yeah, I wonder... and I'm intrigued... but Harold and Morag and even Caelan have me all wrong.

I'm not some blind fool. Sometimes I'm just playing Devil's Advocate because I can see what a bunch of others can't."

I hated to admit it, but one of the attractions of Caelan was that he was such a mystery.

In general, people couldn't help but gravitate towards him—if only to figure out what'd shaped him that way. His stature, charisma, supernatural strength and intelligence...

"You can see a person's faults but still love them entirely, Eric. Like I love him."

He let out a long exhale and smacked his lips together in annoyance. Putting his head in his hands, he gave a sigh that was more one of amusement this time. "But you do not fully know him, so how can you know it's love, and not this... what did you call it?"

I reluctantly whispered, "Trauma bond."

He raised one eyebrow and clucked, "Yep."

Eric made me feel uncomfortable and ill at ease, he always had. He wasn't just a beautiful man, he had a stillness in those silver eyes of his, and it was more than his training that'd made him such a cool customer. I thought he'd always been like it.

Then there was that hair. White-grey like silk, shaved underneath, with the long parts (which probably reached his chin if I had to guess) always tied back, only the occasional stray piece coming loose. He had to have some idea how gorgeous he was, how cruel he could come off, and this coupled with his beauty was incredibly disarming.

"Can't you for one minute not be analysing everyone all the fucking time?"

He gave me an upside-down smile. "I wouldn't be any good at my job otherwise. He's like this, too. He just doesn't say what he sees sometimes."

My cheeks started to heat. "Can't you just be kind to the woman you're bodyguarding, after everything I've been through? Can't you just shut the fuck up and be fucking nice?"

I had a small baby. An errant husband. A past full of ghosts, shadows and dangers.

A future that looked uncertain. A storm that was nearly driving me insane.

In fact, just as I had that thought, some noise outside made Eric shoot to his feet, gun out from wherever he'd been hiding it.

He looked around and wandered to the hallway, checking the front door. The wind was so strong, it'd sounded like someone had been trying to break in.

"Just a patio chair. Thought I'd secured them all," he muttered, "wait right here."

The howling wind swept through the house and made me shudder as he opened and closed the door. It was nearly May, but up here, as weather fronts fought for supremacy in the battle between the last of winter and the beginning of summer, it could still feel the loneliest, most brutal of places.

Wondering if to get myself to bed before he came back, I realised there was no saving face as he fought his way back in, shutting the door again.

"Fucking hell," he shouted. "Mayhem out there!"

It was no small amount of undiluted joy I got upon seeing his perfect hair all out of place. However, as he retook his seat, undid the tie and let it all fall around his face, something tightened in my stomach and that's when I knew it.

He unnerved me not just because he'd once had a thing for Caelan, but because, he was another god like my husband. And yet, this god—this particular one—made me feel as though I could say anything at all because he'd rather any truth or dark revelation over any bit of fake boasting any day. That's what scared me: Eric was someone who hunted out truths, wanted to know a person deep, deep down and would stop at nothing to get there.

He was real.

I wasn't as cold and as calculating as Caelan could be which made me fear I might accidentally tell Eric everything about myself and then he'd get bored of me. Was it the mystery of Caelan that kept him intrigued? And would he use my truth against me? Or would he thank me for my honesty, and we'd become the best of friends?

"Tell me something true, and then I'll tell you something true," I offered, trying not to grin.

His eyebrows rose to the middle of his forehead. "Too easy."

"We'll see."

"Well," he said. "I can see what a wonderful mother you must've had, because of how you are with Logan."

Way to slice me open. It felt as though I'd been winded.

Wetness appeared on my cheeks in no time.

Of course, Caelan had told me what a wonderful mother I was, but he'd never said it must be because of my own. We didn't talk about our parents. Any of them.

I used the heel of my hand and Eric frowned deeply, unsure if he should come over or what he should do.

I raised my hand to show it was fine. "I needed to hear that."

"Oh... good." The relief then in his features was quite endearing. To know he could be affected, too.

"My turn," I said, quickly wiping my nose on my sleeve.

"Oh, god," he groaned.

I smiled gently, then I said, "It wasn't your fault."

His hand shook as he lifted it to his lips. He managed a small smile behind his spread fingers, then he murmured, "I know."

I threw back the last of my wine and he took that as a cue to escort me upstairs. All the while I heard his every breath, felt his every step behind me and smelt the outdoors in his hair, clothes, then the coffee he'd drunk, the particular fabric softener he liked that we'd had to go out and get.

In bed, I dangled my hand over the edge and into the cot so Logan could clutch my finger. He occasionally squeezed as he dreamed, meanwhile, Eric sat in the corner in Caelan's big tub chair.

We snagged eyes and he said, "Not that anyone would try to make it here in this hideous weather, but I'll stay awake while you sleep."

The wind seemed to be dying down anyway, but I didn't argue, just closed my eyes.

Chapter Thirteen

BEFORE I MOVED OR DID anything in the stark morning light, I watched as Eric slept. He snored a little with the angle of his neck; perhaps he'd fought sleep and not been able to last a second longer. The man barely ever let himself off the hook and it was nice to watch him like that, completely dead to the world. Aside from workout clothes, he never wore anything but those jeans he favoured, never downgrading to sweats like Caelan often did. Eric was still in his brown suede jacket and a white t-shirt beneath which stretched across his chest. I had to admit he probably was one of the most good-looking men I'd ever known. All a matter of taste, of course. Personal opinion. But even though Eric was my age and had lived, he still had that ethereal quality of a young Orlando Bloom playing Legolas in *Lord of the Rings*. His bones were immaculate. Those strangely long black lashes fluttered on razor-sharp cheekbones every now and then.

Surely, surely, if my husband had any sense, he'd come home already! I lifted my head slightly and saw the baby was busy sucking his thumb, head tossed to the side as he continued to snooze. It was still only around six o'clock but the kid definitely took after me, being able to sleep the way he did. My dad used to say I'd been a good sleeper and it was the one saving grace as my mother battled post-natal depression.

I thought about going back to sleep for just a moment, but then my eye snagged on something outside. It looked like a trampoline from a nearby farm or perhaps, even, a faraway farm had blown all the way out here. It'd smashed into a tree and caused some damage to it, though the most damage had been to the trampoline itself, if the mangled metal poles that'd once kept it upright were anything to go by. Luckily it hadn't blown right into my car which was nearby. Absentmindedly, I got up to look out of the window and to inspect if there was any more damage, this movement snapping Eric from sleep, his hand reaching for the gun again. I made a mental note—he kept it in his inside pocket.

A few seconds passed and he took in the scene, realised all was fine, and relaxed.

The first thing he did was get up and look at the baby in his crib. Logan had begun to stretch and mewl, nothing more.

Eric sat where I had just been sleeping and let Logan squeeze his finger tight.

"Just a weird trampoline, like it blew in on a Mary Poppins breeze," I said.

"That's good, if that's all there is."

"Do you want a hot drink? Some tea, perhaps? Instead of that tar you drink all the time." The South American blend that was Strength 5 or whatever.

"Yes, if you're offering."

Just as I started to walk away, the baby kicked out a powerful yell.

"Want me to change his nappy?" he asked as I kept on walking.

"Please! Back in a tick!"

I made quick work of the tea and by the time I was back in the bedroom, Eric was jiggling the baby in his arms to keep him quiet, though Logan kept turning his face as if to say, "Where's my boob?"

Putting his tea on the windowsill, I popped mine down on the bedside table and hopped up onto the bed, taking the baby from Eric. Without even half a thought, I unbuttoned my pyjama jacket and Eric's face was a picture as he witnessed Logan eagerly latch on to my engorged tit, the glands having filled overnight. Sod it, I'd forgotten to siphon some off after the wine. Well...

Logan was eagerly going for it, the noises kind of embarrassing. It got to the point where Eric didn't know where to put himself so kept looking out of the window, though gradually we both seemed to realise we'd come this far...

He sat in the chair and didn't stare, but, he wasn't avoiding my eye either. He'd seen my breast now. So what? It was a feeding unit for Logan.

(The blush in Eric's cheeks and the glint in his eye told me it was not just a feeding utensil.)

"Did you sleep well?" he asked.

"Full eight hours, I suppose."

"Good."

"What about you?"

"Probably fell asleep around two when the house had finally gone silent."

"Figured as much."

Another silence. That time he was watching me as I fed. I could feel his gaze on me as I stroked the baby's hair and let Logan grab my other boob beneath my shirt, as if to say, "That's next."

It was a routine well practised by that point, but Eric seemed fascinated as I took Logan off, gave him some burping time, then passed him to my right breast instead. All the while I kept my modesty as intact as possible.

When the baby had taken his fill, I held him against my naked chest as I walked him around the room, my pyjama jacket still loose around the sides. Logan was so warm and smelt so good, I felt nothing but bliss as I waited for his burps to come up, which they did.

Stroking his back and kissing him, he eventually dropped back to sleep and I lowered him back into the cot.

Before I got back into bed, I quickly did up my shirt and threw down my cup of tea, sinking back beneath the sheets.

We looked across at one another.

"What?" he said.

"What?" I said.

We chuckled.

"You're so beautiful, Flora. You really are. I can see perfectly well now why he might change."

I smiled graciously. "Might being the operative word."

He grinned and left the room, shaking his head as he moved out of my maternal space. I closed my eyes and dreamed of those fields I used to run through with Mum, the gardens she planted, the wildflower meadows and the baking I'd come home to after school. Yes, she left her mark on me. Yes, that love never left. It kept me strong.

The men in my life—Caelan, Eric, my own father—never seemed to have had a protective mother in their lives.

How sad.

REELING FROM THE STORM, and needing some time away from the cabin, later that day I drove us away to the castle to check out the potential damage. Harold was already there tugging his hair at the ends. Morag wouldn't be far.

The tower was fine, but the other side... worse. The roof had caved in a little more and tiles had been tossed off. Inside, no doubt, more water had got in.

We would have to decide what to do with it—and soon—or else the decision most likely would be taken out of our hands.

"What do you need help with?" Eric asked Harold.

"Weeeel, now you're askin.'"

FIGHT FOR LOVE

I left them to it and went indoors with the car seat. Morag was crying in the kitchen and it really scared me seeing her like that; she'd only ever been stoically together up until that point.

"Och, lass. I wasna expecting ye." Quickly wiping her face, she tried to plaster on a smile but failed to banish her despair completely. I shoved her into a chair and popped the car seat on the table in front of her. She cooed over Logan, a distraction.

"Let me play mother," I insisted.

I made the tea and went in the cupboard where she kept the really good shortbread for emergencies such as this. You know, the elderflower flavoured stuff.

After a certain amount of patience, that is, me waiting and munching, she said, "He winna settle. He canna settle. He's lost wi'out his gillie'ing."

Ah, the marital tiff. It was more than the storm and any damage out there.

It was on the tip of my tongue to tell her about Caelan's desire to come back, renovate the castle properly, perhaps take some land again—a smaller amount, this time.

I said nothing.

Everything was up in the air.

"It's bound to be a period of adjustment."

"It wasna just a job," she said, sniffing into her sleeve.

"No, it wasn't. I can imagine." But it had been a year or more now.

"Most men his age huv been retired fifteen years already."

"Yes."

She looked so disconsolately into her teacup, as though answers might arrive... in the tea leaves at the bottom.

They wouldn't.

"Caelan had to sell that land, Morag. It was not just that it was getting difficult for Harold to cope with alone, Caelan needed a fresh start. To cut ties with the past. Free himself."

"Aye, aye, ah ken. Ah ken."

"No, I don't think you do."

She looked at me sharply, and slowly, I began to tell her about the attack on my chastity—my life. All those years ago.

Uncle Jimmy.

She nearly fell about hysterical at the thought. The reality... slowly sank in.

"I think Caelan, in his way, sold it all to make a break from the past."

At least, that's what I'd told myself in the months since. Not that Caelan had sold because he'd been afraid of Sherry... and had wanted insurance. A reserve in case of... all eventualities.

Whatever may come.

"As sorry as I am aboot ye pain, as wretched as that was, as much as I ken it true what ye say, lass... my husband is no gonna be able to move on with his life. He canna. The land is in his soul. He needs a job."

Another casualty of Caelan, huh? Seemed to be becoming a theme.

"Where's Jet?" I asked, the thought suddenly occurring. I'd left him with them the last time I was up in Scotland, owing to me going back to work and it not seeming fair to lump a dog on the nanny, too. I'd half-expected him to be here today and was dying to see him, but I also knew it would confuse him—like Eric's presence would, hence why I hadn't had him come over to be with us again, not just yet.

"Running riot nae doubt on his pup date. With his wee brothers and sisters. He's doing just fine, the canny lad."

"That's nice," I said.

"Aye."

FIGHT FOR LOVE

It did seem Jet belonged up here rather than down there.

"God, we're all at sixes and sevens, aren't we?" I groaned.

She wiped her eyes again and took a deep breath. "He's gonna drive me to murder, lass. I swear to gawd!"

You had to laugh, so we did.

ON THE DRIVE BACK, he asked, "Is the old woman okay?"

"What do you mean?"

"Heard some bawling, or something."

"Oh," I giggled, "yeah, she'll be all right. What did you make of Harold's mood?"

Eric shrugged in the passenger seat. "He'd have died on those hills, Flora. If he'd had his way."

"Aye lad, aye," I said, adopting the local accent. "Aye, he most certainly would."

"Wow, you got it down."

"My grandma was Scottish," I said, not dropping the accent.

"She was?" He thought back. "Yes, he said you had Scots in you."

"I'm a quarter."

Another silence. We tended to have those now while he thought carefully about his words rather than brashly passing comment.

Tapping my fingers on the wheel, I said, "Harold isn't doing well. I think he takes it out on Morag."

"I got that feeling. He was trying to give me orders until I firmly said he could have my help, but he could bloody well ask nicely!"

I laughed loudly. God, it was so nice to have someone to talk to who wasn't so dour all the time, so... moody and withdrawn, on occasion. So fucking Scottish.

"Why can't he just get a fishing boat and have done?" Eric snorted.

"Oh, he has one," I barked, "but he is not happy unless he's got several hundred hectares to manage and not enough time in the day to do it all."

Eric grunted and shook his head.

"What is it?" I asked.

"In my not-so-expert opinion, the oblong part needs tearing down. The fissures are too big, and, the longer they leave it, the more the structural integrity of the tower and what's still habitable will be affected."

"But a real sort of, like, enthusiast for it… they might restore it, right?"

"You mean Caelan?" He blinked several times.

"I do, lad." I went into accent again.

"I'd say he's capable of anything, Flora. Whatever he puts his mind to… yeah. A slim possibility, but one he'd run with, nonetheless, if he really wanted it done."

I knew he didn't just mean the castle.

Chapter Fourteen

ONE THING THAT STRUCK me the next day as we ate breakfast together, was that since his return to the UK from Ukraine, Eric hadn't spent much time mourning his fallen blades. It occurred to me maybe this wasn't the first time he'd lost people. Wouldn't be the last. Still...

Perhaps they'd merely been soldiers he'd inherited from Caelan's squadron—numbers, workers, means to ends. Maybe they weren't really dead. Hamish, the oldest friend of my husband's, gone? Seemed hard to believe a man wider, taller and even more brusque than Caelan might succumb. Yet perished he had, allegedly.

Or had he?

I didn't know if he would react well to what I was really thinking. Maybe I didn't want answers; I guessed he wouldn't give me them anyway; or even, scary thought, I was enjoying the friendship we were beginning to build.

"You're chewing your lip," he said, tutting, "must be thinking about something."

He was scooping scrambled egg up into his mouth like a man with no time to waste. Four eggs. Every day. Ugh.

"Don't you mourn them, when they're gone?" I said, feeling adventurous.

"The dead?" he said so flatly.

I was aghast at the way he spoke, but I kept a straight face. "Yes."

"None of them were my friends, they hated me."

Shocked by where this was going, I pretended to be concerned about Logan, stroking his face as he lay in the mobile cot right next to me.

"Why did they hate you?" I stared at my sleeping son.

"Because I was their boss, not their mate. It's very rare for a boss to be liked in the way Caelan is."

I looked up and felt my feminine intuition trying to tell me something. His silver eyes danced at my confusion... intrigue.

"Like Caelan is...?"

"Respected, admired... and loved."

"So you were just respected and admired, I take it?" I deadpanned.

He snorted and finished his plate, standing up to wash it at the nearby sink.

"I never really wanted to do this job," he said, washing an already clean plate, his eyes studying the world beyond the window rather than the bowl. "It was... my father. He wanted me to go into the military... and... I guess..."

"Then Caelan. He saw potential when nobody else did. He changed your life?"

"In a nutshell." He finally put the plate on the drainer.

Then it was the egg pan, getting the scrubbing of its life.

I pushed the last of my soggy muesli around a bowl.

"We'd have those group get togethers, you know? Our weekends at the castle. But I'd endure them only because it'd mean time with Caelan and away from London."

So, he didn't entirely *love* London.

"No love lost between you, Hamish and the others?"

"None. They only hated me more when I was promoted and put in charge. Caelan's decision to leave, but I still got blamed, for no logical reason other than I wouldn't be carrying them all like he did. I made them work. And they didn't like it."

Men! How did they survive all these millennia? No wonder women lived longer and happier.

I pursed my lips because a lot didn't add up, and he was still scrubbing that pan, avoiding my eye and staring out the window.

"The only reason Caelan agreed to go was because he knew if you hadn't been able to get it done, then literally the only other person who could would be him."

Eric jolted and then turned swiftly to look at me, like he'd just been hit by a thunderbolt.

"He said that?"

I nodded. "If you'd... he knew it had to be bad."

He turned back to the window, still scrubbing that gleaming pan, the suds in that bowl nearly overflowing with the motion.

"In certain types of warfare, especially one in which you're untested, things can happen. Paranoia is rife in that country. Spies everywhere, both sides... our intelligence was bad. Something... someone... but not *me*, Flora. *Not me*," he insisted. "Hate them I did, but not enough for all that. They were my team. Now they're gone. I can't change that."

Finally, the pan went on the drainer, then he emptied the bowl even though I had my dishes yet to wash up. I nearly snickered when foam blew past the window, thrown up by the wind from the drain outside. He seemed upset, I thought and wouldn't appreciate me laughing. Even though he claimed not to care, it was clear, he cared a lot. I kept a straight face.

"Caelan will sort it all out," I said. "That's why he went."

"I hope so," he said, "because I did nothing wrong, Flora. I swear it."

He leaned forward against the sink unit and seemed to stare disconsolately at the hills in the distance, like he'd run for them if he had to.

THE NEXT MORNING, I knew something was wrong the moment I woke. Not only was I groggy, the fog of sleep with its claws still in me—meaning I'd been woken unnaturally—but there was a scent. Metallic. Not like steel, but like the outdoors. The moment I looked up from my pillow, I saw a figure clad all in black.

Dark eyes peered at me from out of the slits in his ski mask, and he said, "Come and we will not harm the child."

An accent, like he was Middle Eastern. Indeed, his eyes were deepest midnight.

I nearly shot off the bed, but, he held a hunting knife in his hand and it was pointed at where my son lay in his crib next to the bed.

Slowly, I rolled over and sat up, staring at him. Willing myself to give nothing away.

Abominable things flashed before my eyes. Flesh tearing. Bones breaking. Blood welling from his wounds. Bloodlust hit me so suddenly, so forcefully, it was almost like an orgasm waiting to be released.

It was still there, buried inside me. Deep down. The real me.

The killer.

Hunger for violence had me. Entirely. A hunger I'd always closeted. Guarded. Though in the quiet, I'd nurtured her, taken care of her... melded her within myself.

Fury itself.

"What do you want with me?" I said in a flat tone.

"Information."

I shook my head. "I have no information you could possibly want."

FIGHT FOR LOVE

"We'll see about that."

"Is this about Cae—"

He held the knife closer to the child and I saw red, and black, and blue.

He would not live.

I rose slowly from the bed and walked around it. His eyes were on me the entire time, wary. They knew whose wife I was. As I got closer to the window, I saw their vehicle at the end of our little lane, my eyes briefly flicking to it. A small, nondescript saloon. Odd. Not the same guys as last week, then? No 4x4 for the terrain around these parts. No more than four bodies his size could fit in a car like that.

A knife rather than a gun. The guys the week before had had guns bulking out their jackets.

What the fuck was going on?

"May I put on my slippers to go?" I asked, gesturing at the footwear which sat beside my son's crib—my calm tone of voice telling him I'd agreed, I was coming, I just wanted my slippers and to have one last look at my son.

He jerked his head to say it was okay, but warned with his eyes I should not make sudden moves. I inched past the man who smelt like rain and earth, making my way to my leather slippers. Slipping my feet in, I used the seconds to decide how.

Once I'd turned around, I knew when.

Once I'd sidled up to him, I knew his weakness.

A pretty lady.

I blinked my lashes and for a brief moment—just long enough—he was drawn under. Realising he'd been lured into a false sense of security, he was about to raise the knife, when I lurched forward, covered his mouth with a hand, my other hand on his shoulder, my knee swiftly buried in his balls—his cry of pain masked by my hand over his gob.

The right pressure on his neck made him pass out, then I laid him gently on the bed, silent as a mouse. I would've slashed him to bits for threatening my son, but there was little time. I nicked his throat at the artery and blood started spurting out. He'd die painlessly. Too good for a bastard like him.

Giving myself a moment to try to calm my pounding heart, I took some deep breaths, flicked the droplet of his blood off the knife, then tiptoed for the floorboard where Caelan kept a handgun beneath.

It popped open easy and I heard Eric's voice muffled by a gag down the hall. There'd be three more. Probably one downstairs. Two trying to hold Eric.

Soundlessly, I moved along the corridor. Steady breathing, though blood rushed through my ears. Hopefully Logan would never know anything about this.

I reached the room, peering around the door.

"Where is that stupid fucker with that bitch?" one of them said—same accent as the other.

As my face came into view, Eric's eyes widened, then they saw something had caught his attention behind them. I quickly whipped back, out of sight.

"What was that, dickhead?" one of them said.

"Leave it," said the other, "probably a trick of his."

Yet the first one was too stupid to abate his curiosity and came towards the doorway. I pressed myself as flat as possible to the wooden wall and wrapped my fingers tighter around the knife.

The moment he was outside the door, I swung my arm and dug the knife in his guts.

A nine-inch blade sharpened like a butcher's knife. His guts dripped to the floor as I dragged the knife across, towards me, then yanked it out. Barely a sound.

Until his body hit the floor.

FIGHT FOR LOVE

I climbed over him, going for his friend next. Two pops in the brain. Easy.

Eric and I caught eyes. He gestured there was one more and to beware of him coming up the stairs.

I hid again, behind the door this time. Dangerous, I knew. My son lay unguarded and I'd just killed three of the fourth man's friends.

He climbed over the bodies looking for me, cursing in his mother tongue. He was about to raise a knife to Eric, as if he'd had a hand in it, still trussed up as he was—because, of course, a woman would never be capable—when I appeared out of the shadows, using the mattress on Eric's bed to fling myself up and around the man's neck and shoulders.

We fell back on the bed. I had my legs holding his arms still, then one arm locked around his neck, held in place by my other arm.

"Tell me who you're working for," I demanded.

He struggled against me, but those were legs that'd kicked in the heads of instructors, martial arts champions—even Caelan Cameron, Lord of Men.

"I will break you bit by bit. You know who I am. *Tell me*," I demanded.

My victim grunted, refusing to say anything. He wheezed and I let loose only slightly, giving him a chance to speak.

"One name and you'll get a quick death."

"Go to hell—"

"My pleasure."

I squeezed hard and waited, gasping as he tried to thrash, but he didn't manage it. Every ounce of me had to hold him to keep him steady as he fought and fought.

When he finally gave up, I sagged with relief and threw him off me.

Standing up, I spat on his corpse and shook my head.

Eric mumbled and I moved to him, removing the tape from his mouth and the cable ties from around his wrists.

One could argue cable ties wouldn't curtail such a man, I thought, but brushed it aside.

Eric got up gingerly and surveyed the carnage. After he'd seen the hallway, he went and threw up in the bathroom.

I looked down at myself and shook with the aftermath of adrenalin and fear. It wasn't so much the blood on me, but the energy leaving my body. Quickly, I walked to the bedroom. Logan was safe, still asleep. It was but 5.30 in the morning.

We had to act quickly if we were to survive, so I ran downstairs and checked the doors. They'd used some sort of high-tech cutting tool to get in through the front door. We were no longer safe here. The security system at the Lodge wasn't exactly basic, but they'd somehow disabled that too, because I always set the alarm every night to let us know if someone had broken in.

I looked out of all the windows around the house. There was only that one car and no others in sight. An ambush, yes! Why would they expect to not achieve their goal of taking me?

Idiots! They weren't as professional as the others. Maybe the bounty was bringing all sorts out of the woodwork, from the professional to the amateur.

Eric came downstairs in his t-shirt and long underwear. Both grey. His face wan, he looked like he'd been drained of all life.

He dove straight for the rucksack he'd been keeping his laptop in. In one of the inner pockets, there was his gun with the silencer on. He checked for bullets and nodded.

"You truly are his wife," he said, trembling.

He was afraid. Petrified even, though our opponents lay dead.

I'd gone calm suddenly, blank, like ice.

Frigid, deep, ice.

"You didn't believe it?" I said, stock-still, not meeting his eye.

FIGHT FOR LOVE

A part of me was waiting for more. A corner of me had yet to relax.

"You enjoyed it," he said.

"I did."

"What was that?" he asked.

"What was what?"

"Inside you?"

I took a deep breath. "It was a mother protecting her cub. A mother with blood already on her hands. What could a few more ounces of the stuff do?"

My groin was already pounding before he came over to me. Vicious, stabbing pangs of desire had me gasping for breath. Then he put a finger under my chin and drew my eyes to his. He was still pale but there was an admiring look in his eye. Every inch of me stung with lust.

"You're a monster inside there, Flora."

I blinked once. "I am."

He moved in, nipped my lip and groaned. I nipped back at him, my core throbbing with need—to get rid of this thing inside me. This raging, violent tempest.

It had been a nightgown that night and he reached under the layers, dragging my knickers down my legs and discarding them. All I felt was lust. A violent need of closeness to another human being. He seemed to know this, studying, searching my eyes, seeing I was this roaring dragon beneath the veneer. A creature of depravity that'd survived all those years of London, alone. I'd avoided love, anything real, because my true self was wicked, violent and a beast. I'd had to hide her. He knew that. Knew it and didn't shy away. I'd even hidden parts of myself from Caelan, the Lord of Men. A gentleman. Perhaps because he would baulk, even him. Yet this man before me, I knew—scared though he was, felt drawn towards my darkness.

He backed me up against a tall cupboard door in the kitchen. I was untying his drawstring while he cupped my breast over my dress and then squeezed my nipple. Our eyes were nearly level and he looked into mine as I looked into his, without shame or guilt or hate.

It was so quick. I saw a flash of his gleaming abs which were hairless, then his pubic hair shaved close. His cock risen. Thick thighs, rock-solid, twitching with anticipation. His skin was milk-white and flawless. My walls were already clutching before he entered me, and it was fast, hard and ruthless as he squeezed my bare buttocks beneath the nightdress and drove into me, again and again, my legs around his waist, arms clinging to his broad shoulders. I didn't even know my own name. Just that I was getting the fucking I desperately needed.

"Eric," I moaned, as a shiver ripped through me.

I came from my scalp to the tip of my big toe, a whole-body orgasm laying waste to anything I was before. In that moment, for the very first time in my life, someone saw me for exactly who I was—and loved me.

He came outside of my body on my thigh and I continued to twitch around nothing, empty inside. Diabolically empty.

He knew I wasn't satisfied. Knew it completely.

I was laid on the kitchen island and I removed my nightgown myself, tossing it somewhere. He feasted on my breasts, ridding himself of his own t-shirt and bottoms while he licked, teased and sucked. He thrust fingers inside me and made me come again, spurting over the tiled surface. Then he was between my thighs, drinking all of the arousal he'd made, making love to me with his tongue and lips, occasionally his teeth. He was so different, sort of kissing me, completely worshipful and so tender. It took my breath away as I arched off the counter, hands clutched around my breasts, coming on his lips.

FIGHT FOR LOVE

Eric dragged me closer and fucked me hard as he stood and I lay there, getting railed by his thick, lovely cock. His wildly sensual arms, which I'd dreamt of a couple of times now, sort of Hulk arms, both of them heavily tattooed with full sleeves, were wrapped around my thighs as he pounded ruthlessly through all of my orgasms, sucking my big toe as he tried to keep my flailing limbs in check.

"I want it," I said, nodding at the olive oil nestled in the kitchen caddy nearby.

"But you haven't before...?"

I shook my head.

"It's not the right time," he said, pleading.

"I'll tell you when's the right time. *Now*."

He took some of it and lubed up his already slick cock.

We didn't speak of it—how he knew I couldn't have done it with Caelan, not with his size. Not just that, I'd never... been so unhinged before.

Eric put both of my heels on his shoulders and said, "Open."

So I bore down, and slowly he nudged in... and I relaxed, letting him. The juices from my pussy slid down as I watched him gurn and curse, his immaculate body a thing to behold.

That frozen, ruthless beauty... mine. For now, at least. For those moments. He was weak for me. Vulnerable.

Eventually he got all the way in, and I took a breath, groaned... and he let loose.

He came roaring my name and filled me, filled me so full I yelled his name back.

Afterwards, he dragged me closer, touched his brow to mine and wrapped his arms around me. Those silver eyes were trapped behind flickering lids, his breath coming out ragged. Then he moved in and gave me a tender kiss. So soft and gentle. Maybe since he threw his guts up only a little while ago, that's why he hadn't properly kissed me yet.

I saw beneath it all, he was a gentle, caring, loving boy. A sweetheart.

I encouraged him to rest on my chest, face between my breasts, as he panted away his exertions.

"He'd kill me for this," he murmured.

"He'd kill me first."

He lifted his face and stroked my brow. "You're so beautiful, it hurts, Flora."

"I could say the same, but I won't."

That made him smirk, then even, smile quite a bit. He lifted away and pulled me to sitting. Looking me in the eye, he held my cheek as he spoke.

"I can lie to you no more," he said, swallowing.

"Tell me everything," I begged, holding his hand.

"Your father is alive." I slapped both hands over my mouth to keep the surge inside. He looked sad, continuing, "This house is the gift he gave you both for making him a grandfather. Caelan received a visit, you see, when you were in hospital, newly a mother. Caelan left you for Ukraine even though he knows Sherry's been trying to find Blake so she can hang everything around his neck. That's what this is about. She thinks maybe you know something about where he might be. But Caelan is the best at keeping secrets. And don't we both know it."

"I can't—I can't—"

"We have to go. We'll talk later."

So I let him pack my bags for me, put me in clothes, and I fed Logan on the back seat of the car as we drove off—the cabin aflame behind us as we chased away.

As far as I was concerned, this all started with Blake, and it would end with him, too.

The sooner Caelan got back, the sooner we'd be able to tell Sherry where Blake was—and it'd be done. Finally.

Chapter Fifteen

Ukraine

IT WAS HIS LAST NIGHT in Kiev but he'd been all over—Dnipro, even Mariupol and Kharkiv. His presence had been much-needed. Weapons training, tactical systems, even the basics like homemade bombs as ordinary people engaged in guerrilla warfare. He'd taught a lot of people from generals to boots on the ground to people on the street who were starving and needed money to buy food... a few pence to start growing it themselves. He'd worked solidly, sixteen-hour days, in all the time he'd been here. His body knew it. He was tired. He had become more machine than man again; all the protein rations he'd slugged down his throat; all the drills he'd led and demonstrated. All the runs he'd broken men in on, the hiking up and down mountains, along riverbanks, sometimes even training them beneath ground in sewer networks if the bombing outside made the threat too great (training in sewers was actually valuable to spatial awareness and overcoming fear of the dark). He'd fought to be able to go back home and now a Jeep waited downstairs outside of the president's palace.

Nearly every night he'd been offered women, drugs and cheap alcohol. He'd abstained from all. He'd needed a clear head. That was him all over: professional to the last. Around him men smoked like chimneys, drank their sorrows away, had their dicks sucked for a few pennies... anything to combat the reality of having their lives, families—sometimes even their souls—torn apart.

However, he had to admit he'd been tempted once. Though the contraband Russian vodka was very risky indeed, he missed whisky and he missed home. The strong vodka had offered him that oblivion he craved, yet, abstained he still had.

Women were nothing. Nobody but Flora meant anything to him. He yearned to get back to her.

Yearned to tell her everything, even though... some of it would destroy her.

The president himself met Caelan before the secret exit. They clasped forearms and Caelan looked the man in the eye as an equal. (Though Caelan did indeed stand a foot taller at least.)

"You will be back?" said the president in raspy English.

"Aye, I'll come back. In better times."

"To a hero's welcome, a feast," insistent the president.

"Nae bother wi' that," chuckled Caelan.

"We do not forget," said the president. "Those who raised us when we were on our knees."

Caelan nodded his head, a vein under his right eye twitching. "Maybe some things would be better to forget... in time."

The rape, abuse... the suffering. The broken bodies, the uncertainty, the obliteration of a once-glorious culture.

"We are strong, we will prevail."

"Aye," said Caelan. "Ye shall. Braw people, ye are. Braw indeed. Seen that spirit myself, I have. In your smiles, your jokes, your banter. And there will be another side of this. I've given yer people everything they need."

The president agreed with a sharp nod. "Goodbye, warrior."

Caelan grinned from ear to ear, winking. "Later, Chief."

The president offered a chuckle.

FIGHT FOR LOVE

Caelan's getaway car whizzed through the streets as though it was the president himself being spirited away. Outriders flanked them, traffic was scarce and his drivers were both armed. In the back seat, Caelan studied his fingernails, so broken and dirty, bloodied and in need of care.

The only way he'd been able to secure his safe departure was with a bargain. He would make sure the truth came out about Eric Holmes and the Russian asset he'd saved. The British authorities would probably try to dumb it down so they didn't look bad, but he would use what the Ukraine people had told him to get to the bottom of what had really happened here. It was entirely possible Eric had sacrificed his entire team so that he could achieve this goal of sneaking a double agent into Britain—for money. Caelan wondered if Ogarkov hadn't been sent to Ukraine to bargain as a diplomat; perhaps his entire raison d'être was to stir up trouble wherever he went—his ultimate goal to get into the UK. Masquerading as a spy for the West but really, working as a double agent. Knowing Eric, if he had been paid to keep Ogarkov alive, the money trail would be non-existent, but Caelan had other ways of getting the truth out of people.

Caelan had always known Eric had the potential to be corrupt, but this? After the sickening stuff he'd seen in this country, he'd never imagined his protégé could possibly stoop so low as to betray a worthy cause.

Then again, hadn't Eric only ever been in it for the money? He'd never really cared.

A private plane awaited at the nearest airport and Caelan was flanked by six burly soldiers as he crossed the tarmac before jumping up the steps to the plane. Once he was on board, the doors were locked behind him, his guard of soldiers rushing away across the tarmac.

Caelan wandered into the cabin and was met by the Deputy Prime Minister, the Defence Secretary and the Prince of Wales.

"Tell us everything," said the prince, and so Caelan started talking.

They had the flight to be open and honest about everything, because when he got back to Britain, he would be debriefed and tell the other bods only what they needed to know.

He was going to deal with Eric himself—and that would mean keeping a very tight circle indeed.

Chapter Sixteen

Scotland

AFTER THE EVENT, WE headed to the castle. It being as remote as it was, the front door having such solid locks and the windows all being too small for a human body to pass through, it seemed like the safest bet around.

Harold was running towards the car as we approached, his shotgun waving, his face as red as I'd ever seen it. He must have heard or seen something because he collapsed in front of the vehicle as we got near, out of puff. I raced to his side with Logan asleep in my arms and helped him up. Eric remained in the car. I wasn't sure why.

"We're okay, Harold."

"Smoke... smoke," he repeated, gasping.

He must have been out on the hills when he'd seen smoke coming from the direction of our cabin. I'd had Eric set it on fire because it was full of dead bodies—and it'd been bought with blood money. It would burn quickly and there were no trees close enough to get damaged. I didn't think any of the neighbours knew who owned it, they were all too far away, and the deeds were probably still in Dad's name... or whatever.

In that moment, I didn't give a rat's arse about anything.

"We'll need more guns," said Eric after winding down the window. "Lots more. Hope you've brought reserves, Harold."

The old man looked from Eric to me and seemed shocked. "What, in, the, hell, lass?"

"My father's alive," I said, "and his wife is out for revenge. I'm unsafe."

He rolled his eyes and limped away, then walked back again. "That wee shite Blake Rathbone?"

"You know of him?" I sounded surprised. I was.

"The lad told me all about *him*," said Harold.

"Yes," I sighed, "I can hardly believe it. Then again, why wouldn't he do something like this? Pretend to be dead so he could escape his bitch wife and begin anew. He stashed money everywhere, why not stash some abroad somewhere, too?"

That had to be where he was, and quite possibly, Caelan knew precisely where.

I stomped towards the castle on foot while Eric said to Harold, "Get in mate, you need a sit down, pal."

They crawled along behind me until eventually we pulled up into the grounds where Eric could park the car. I was in survival mode and went into the castle to find Morag in floods of tears, but all I could say was, "Listen, we're fine. Now, please let me just have a moment."

She gawked at me as I climbed the spiral steps with the boy.

Once I got into the suite on the top floor, I placed Logan between some pillows and let him rest. Then I started running the bath, and in it, I shivered even in the hot water.

What the fuck had I done?

―――― ⚜ ――――

ERIC BROUGHT ME DINNER late evening, something no doubt Morag had put together. I ate it in front of the fire, sat on the floor in nothing but my robe. I'd been here in the suite all day, staring into space.

FIGHT FOR LOVE

"Morag and Harold won't leave. They're both armed to the teeth, vowing to protect you."

I ignored him. He was part of this... this mess.

I'd let him...

I'd killed three men. No, four. Four.

Plus, Jimmy.

Jimmy, the man my husband had idolised, worshipped. Loved.

I was no better than this faker before me, this charlatan, this fraud.

Deep down I knew it, but my despair, my fear... my self-loathing... was in charge.

I knew why I'd done it, why I was going to do it again.

"You don't have to feel guilty about anything," he said, having squatted near the rug I sat on. The food gave the baby food, I told myself. To me, it tasted like ash and shards of glass, but it was for the baby. My baby, with Caelan, my husband. The man I really loved. That man was the true man. This man...

A day spent staring into space, thinking on my sins, had made me see. Finally, see.

Too much didn't add up.

Truth? What even was that anymore? I didn't know. Couldn't feel. Couldn't see straight. Not without Caelan. Bereft, unsure, broken, I truly was a shell without him.

That had to be why I'd done it, not because I was falling for Eric, the potential liar, the fake.

I couldn't be *in* love with him, could I?

Yet I'd come...

I couldn't bear it.

The thought.

He caught me grimacing and got on his knees, crawling towards me. He took the empty plate from me, put it on the hardwood floor nearby, and then lay me down on the rug beneath him.

I couldn't help the way my heart pounded as he removed his t-shirt, untied his hair and looked down into my eyes. I ran my hands over his scarred body, tattooed arms, the familiar bumps of the SAS inking on his back—like Caelan's—even almost comforting. Perhaps Caelan would see past it and forgive me. This was just while he was gone, to stave off the insanity.

Deep down, I knew he would never forgive me. Maybe get past it, but…

Sliding my hands into Eric's silky hair, I inhaled sharply when he nudged his cock between my legs.

"My cap," I said. "In the bedside drawer."

He went over and fetched it. He even helped me with it. Then I loosened the belt on my robe and he stripped himself naked.

What we did next wasn't filthy or depraved. He kissed my mouth so lushly, making the pangs in my belly pulse so hard, I thought I'd die. I shook inside his arms as he pushed inside me, rocked with me tightly, never ceasing his worship, his kiss.

"I love you, Flora," he groaned, right before he came.

Maybe that I could believe. His silver eyes seemed to shimmer, confirming it. He moaned as he drained himself inside me, like he truly was in pain for the wanting of me.

We moved it to the bed, huddling together for comfort, warmth, sleep. The baby noticed nothing. As I buried my nose in Eric's trunk of a neck, then wrapped my leg around his middle, my arms around his shoulders, I might even have felt like I loved him a bit, too.

Chapter Seventeen

Caelan

A FEW DAYS AFTER LANDING back in the UK, he arrived home in Scotland to discover the log cabin had gone up in smoke. It'd burnt itself out, but when he looked closely, there were human remains.

Four adult males, if he had to guess.

His guts churned.

No baby. No woman.

Who'd done this?

He couldn't figure it out.

The first thing he did was call Harold.

He picked up at the cottage they'd bought themselves with their severance package.

"Is that really you, lad?"

"Aye."

He groaned down the line. "I'm afraid it's as we feared."

"Aye. I'm at the cabin."

"Aye. They're at the castle."

Caelan's fury built inside him. A throb inside his skull. His knuckles clenched, the skin stretching around his bones uncomfortably.

No, he told himself, Eric would pay. The right way. At the right time.

Hamish would have his vengeance, so would the other lads.

"How was it?" Harold said after a time.

"Like the bowels of Hell itself."

"Like old times then, eh?"

"Aye, Harold."

The old man sighed deeply. "He's a canny one."

"Nae cannier than me."

"Verra true."

"Do something for me?" Caelan asked.

"Anything."

"Take Morag abroad. I've got a friend who owns a place. I'll set it up."

Caelan could nearly hear Harold nodding. "Might do us some good. Nae been the best, I admit."

"Soon we'll be back home altogether. Start something new. I swear it."

"Aye, but..."

"She will see the truth. I ken her better than she kens herself."

"While that may be true, the lengths he might go to..."

"Aye, we've been here before."

Eric had done this before, more than once. He would pretend Caelan's girlfriends were in danger and make them feel safer with him. Most of the time the lass would figure out who it was Eric was really in love with. Few fell for his act. The funny thing was Caelan was never serious about any of those girls, but the slightest whiff of one of them falling for Caelan, and Eric would swoop in and shit all over it. Caelan used to laugh it off. Not this time.

He never thought in a million years Flora would be the one to fall for it, but perhaps that was on him. Caelan had left her alone with the baby... and she was still hurting about Jimmy, Sherry... so much.

"I'll speak to ye when I speak to ye," said Caelan.

"Aye, stay sharp, lad."

"Dinna fash, Harold."

He hung up.

Caelan surveyed the scene, shaking his head. He'd seen things these past few weeks... but now he faced this. After everything he'd given in life, over and over, and always, he seemed to get treated like shit.

He saw the car nearby, took the number plate and fed it into a database on his phone he wasn't meant to have access to. Within seconds, a result came back.

Hire car. An overdue hire car.

He got the details of who'd last hired it and hunted for more information about this person.

A Syrian national. Former asylum seeker. Someone desperate enough. Someone who'd only been able to hire this piece of shit car due to their dodgy credentials.

So Eric had hired a bunch of dickheads to scare the fuck out of Flora?

What the hell was going on?

Gutting Eric would be too easy.

"Nae, wouldna like to make it easy on him," Caelan said to the ghosts.

He would fight for his and Flora's love. He would purge them of this annoyance, once and for all. This time Eric had gone too far. His blind obsession had to stop.

No more Mr Nice Guy.

Caelan would punish them both.

And he would win the girl.

Because winning was what he knew.

And losing?
He didn't know what that was.

Chapter Eighteen

Flora

THREE DAYS SINCE THE event, I woke knowing something else—someone else—was in the room alongside us. I'd know that smell anywhere. His saltwater and pepper scent, that fresh shampoo and sandalwood soap.

Lifting my head from Eric's chest, I saw I wasn't wrong.

His head was turned to the side and he wore fatigues. I'd never seen him look so cold and aloof. He couldn't even look at me.

"Caelan," I whispered.

He didn't turn or flinch. He'd heard me, knew I was stirring, which was why he'd turned away.

Eric bolted upright in bed and saw what I saw. Fear had him in its grip. Blind panic, then dread.

"I swear this isn't what it looks like," said Eric.

Caelan rubbed his fingers along his jaw, his wedding ring glinting in the light.

"Forgive me if I have ma own ideas about what the fuck this looks like."

Cold, icy even, empty. He sounded... as if he'd checked out.

I made a grab for my robe. Caelan kept looking away.

It was as if he couldn't... wouldn't... see this scene.

This treachery.

Before I got to him, he held up one hand in the air, beckoning me not to move closer.

"Keep yer distance, whore. Lest yer wicked lies get someone else kilt."

His vicious tone told me that his private name for me would never be spoken in a loving tone ever again. He still didn't look at me.

"Blame me, it's my fault," said Eric. "Blame me."

I heard Eric shuffle into his long underwear behind me. The baby had already had his milk in bed earlier and was sleeping off his draught.

Caelan swallowed so hard, his Adam's apple bobbed several times. Whatever bait Eric was trying to dangle, Caelan wasn't falling for it.

Yes, I'd known all along Eric couldn't be trusted, but I'd still got myself involved. There was no going back. He'd made me come harder than Caelan ever had, and that was saying something.

"The four men," said Caelan, his voice rough, "who killed them?"

My legs were unbearably heavy and I shuffled backwards, calves hitting the end of the bed, my bottom plopping onto the mattress. Out of my peripheral vision, I saw Eric's shadow lurking near the window.

"I did."

My husband chose that moment to finally turn his head, and with a fury in his eyes I thought nobody could contain for long, he spat, *"You?"*

"One held a knife near our child. I tricked him, knocked him out, then pierced his throat. The next one, I sliced open his belly using his friend's hunting knife. The third one I shot with your gun from beneath the floor. Then the fourth one was going to hurt Eric, who was tied up, so I jumped him from behind, then strangled him on the bed."

FIGHT FOR LOVE

Caelan got up from his seat and paced the room with a hand over his mouth, his expression as unreadable as ever. I wasn't sure he believed me, but perhaps it was that he admired me and didn't want to show it, or else he was ashamed he'd left me here in danger. Probably the latter.

"There was a thing in Brighton, too. Four men followed me in a Range Rover. Eric took them out. That's how we ended up here. It's a long story, but..."

Caelan couldn't believe what he was hearing, kept shaking his head, pacing the floor as if he'd wear out the wood if he weren't careful... leave scorch marks everywhere.

Caelan's head whipped around and he pinned his eyes on Eric's, growling in his direction like the revolted commander he was—snarling at an underling upstart, a puny little interloper. I watched as Eric moved back against the window, realising he had nowhere to run, his fear palpable.

Which told me Eric knew what Caelan was truly capable of, or he was very good at playing the part of someone who got scared easy. That didn't seem to add up.

"This is what he wants, Flora. For me to play the big, bad wolf. Punish him. He's a sick wee shite."

I looked across the room and Eric did indeed have a massive erection. I was disgusted. Eric's cheeks were rosy. He couldn't take his eyes off the aggressive, dominant alpha in the room.

The true alpha.

How did anyone get beneath Caelan Cameron without getting a lashing? I was yet to find out.

"You've seen only what you've wanted to see of me," I blurted, trying to bring my husband's attention back to me. "You forget what I grew up with. You forget. If this has happened, blame the fact that Eric doesn't shy away from what I really am."

"Dinna talk to me of who you really are," Caelan growled, so loudly, so viciously, the baby awoke.

Eric took one step towards the new crib I'd recently bought—and that was it—Caelan saw red. He moved so fast across the room, he had Eric's body lifted off the floor by his neck before anyone could do anything. It was like fifteen stones meant nothing to my husband, as if some powerful force of nature bade him overcome the laws of physics.

I held my breath, covering my face. If he did it, I wouldn't blame him.

Although...

"Please, Caelan," I begged, voice barely above a squeak.

Eric's face turned blue and he had no way of getting free. Caelan eventually dropped him on his arse like a sack of potatoes and Eric went on his hands and knees trying to catch his breath, winded and choking, all at the same time.

"Touch my son, ever, and you die," Caelan warned, in a hollow, ghostlike tone of voice. "Touch that whore all you like, but not my son."

The fact he wasn't in tongue, enunciating perfectly, told us both how anguished Caelan was.

Caelan picked up Logan and held him to his chest, the boy quieting instantly. A boy knows his father. When he passed me as he went out of the room, he spat on the floor between my feet and hissed. I deserved that... and more.

Eric and I looked at one another. He was horrified. Defeated.

Whatever game he was playing, it had backfired, big time.

I LEFT ERIC STEWING in the suite as I went downstairs having had a quick wash in the sink. I'd dressed and brushed my hair, which now was tied back in a sleek ponytail. I looked less fucked, if that would earn me anything, I didn't know. Caelan was cuddling the boy before the hallway window, staring at the world outside. He'd gone completely into himself, his face now a perfect blank mask.

"Are you going to explain the truth about my father?" I demanded.

"Whatever way he's tried to paint it, I was protecting ye. That's all I ever try to do."

Back to Normal Caelan, then. Maybe that beast upstairs was for Eric's benefit.

"Oh god," I said, nearly dropping to the floor as everything hit me, all at once. I had to reach for the sideboard to keep myself upright. Caelan only glanced briefly before he continued his staring contest with the outdoors.

"Aye," he said, a muscle in his jaw feathering. "It's true."

"I didn't quite believe it until now."

"The Brighton thing, maybe, I could believe. If ye were stupid enough to leave Scotland and go back to London cos ye were bored."

I didn't deny it.

He kept his voice down. "I looked up those Syrians you killed. I canna prove it yet but I would be surprised if Eric hadn't paid them good money to scare ye. It had to be a setup, y'see. Blake covered his tracks impeccably. I checked for ma self. Nobody would've been able to find the cabin wi'out help."

I looked down at the floor, ashamed, embarrassed, revolted, empty. Of course, Caelan had already found out everything—and Syrians made sense. They were much less professional than the ones in Brighton. Amateurs, no doubt.

"What do we do?"

"Ye do everything I say. To the letter, okay?" Caelan whispered.

I nodded and wiped my eyes. "I'm sorry, Caelan. I'm so sorry."

"Come here."

I ran to him, crying into his chest, his heart... his answering shiver reassuring me. He kept one eye on the staircase and kissed my head. Then he backed away, scorn and revulsion in those amber eyes again.

"Get away from me, whore," he hissed, and when I looked up, I saw where his eyes were focused.

Eric had appeared at the foot of the stairs, Caelan's supernatural instincts serving him well.

"I only want to—" I played along.

"Shhhtt," said Caelan, holding up a hand. "Tell it to someone who gives a damn about ye filthy hide."

Caelan walked away into the kitchen and slammed the door.

Chapter Nineteen

HE WAS INSUFFERABLE for the rest of that day, either because he felt like punishing me, or, he was keeping up some sort of act for the purpose of making Eric believe our marriage was already done for. Caelan wouldn't let me have Logan unless to feed him, and even then, he wouldn't let me burp the kid, change him or much cuddle him, either. He had that look in his eye, as if to say, *I've been away, so, I'm owed time with our kid*, sort of thing.

Eric was scowled at constantly even as he came into the kitchen for food and drink to survive. Where was there to go?

None of us could go anywhere else, not yet.

It wasn't safe.

I had a feeling Caelan had spoken with Harold before he got here, that's how he was able to enter this castle and not break something—yet. He'd been prewarned.

My carelessness was catching up to me, I knew it.

I should've been more sick with myself, but I wasn't.

Stained.

I'd always been stained.

Ever since that filthy prick had tried to mouth rape me.

Ever since I'd fought for my life.

And I'd done stuff throughout my twenties. Two men at once. Not as a threesome, but, stringing them along, playing with their emotions. This wasn't entirely a new thing for me.

I'd played it back then for as long and as well as I could, until inevitably, a sloppy little text or something would unravel the whole thing. Guy No.1 would arrive at a bar to witness me with Guy No.2 and the stupidity ended... until I took up with new men, or a new man, stringing them along.

One time a man had actually tried to hurt himself because of me. That's why, after that, I took to doing it abroad with colleagues. People I told myself I needed to keep sweet.

I'd always had a problem with letting someone in.

Scuppering it was better. Easier.

Love wasn't my thing.

Pain was.

Even now.

Caelan thought he knew who I was. Not really. He'd barely scratched the surface.

When nightfall came, Caelan emerged from the suite carrying Logan down the stairs. I was trying to sort through my thoughts in the living room when I caught his silhouette against the moonlight. He'd got changed.

I immediately leapt from my seat and soon Eric was there, too. He'd crept in from the kitchen where he'd been pouring himself cup after cup of coffee, like that might calm him down.

"I'm coming with you," said Eric, apparently with prior knowledge as to why my husband might be dressed in black combat clothes.

"Look after them," he said, his voice fractured.

"What's happening?" I panicked as Caelan handed me the baby but didn't really look at me.

He said with a fierceness that raised the hairs on the back of my neck. "It's time to hunt. They'll be here. Somewhere."

Sherry's men, this time. I thought that's what he meant. Of course, she'd no doubt have heard by now he was back. The castle would be one of the first places she'd have searched for any sign of him.

In front of the hallway mirror, Caelan plastered on some black face paint around his eyes. He had a knife hanging from his belt. There was also a holster wrapped around his arms and he had a pistol.

"Don't you need more weapons?" I trembled with fear... real fear.

"I've seen Caelan at work. He needs only his bare hands," said Eric, and Caelan hissed in his direction.

Caelan pulled on a black balaclava to complete the ensemble and as I stared at him, I saw he'd gotten thicker these past few weeks. More lethal, if that were at all possible. He'd been wrecking himself out there, then. Working for them. Fighting alongside them, as any good soldier would when faced with a barbaric enemy. An injustice.

That's how I knew if Eric truly had done bad things, he wouldn't get let off. Oh, no. Caelan would work on him until he squawked and revealed everything.

And I'd be left to deal with the fallout, whatever that ended up being, because that's what I deserved.

"Bring the truck at dawn," said Caelan to Eric. "We'll take them into the woods and you can bury them."

So sure of himself. So much the commander. It made me petrified for the future. What awaited us now that a man of Caelan's breeding, intelligence and fury knew his wife and one of his last surviving friends had betrayed him? Who knew.

WHEN CAELAN HAD GONE out into the night and I'd put the baby down to sleep, I slid into bed and shook not with cold or fear. With sadness.

Old routines and tricks. Wickedness and lies.

Eric tried to comfort me in bed but eventually gave up as all I was doing was facing the fire, unresponsive to words, touch or his warmth.

He moved back downstairs and I heard the jangle of metal as he no doubt prepared some things—just in case.

For who knew what the night might contain.

I fell deep into a pit of warped dreams: ghoulish monsters, contorted, nearly invisible enemies, and every time I broke out in a sweat, I saw my mother's face. Her look of shame, revulsion and the shaking of her head—nearly stopped my heart, every time.

I knew it, then.

I was more like him than I was ever like her.

But a fragment of her remained.

I was a Rathbone, through and through.

Which meant by the natural order of things, I would always be the enemy of a Cameron, the man I'd married being the last one standing.

Chapter Twenty

Caelan

FLORA WASN'T THE ONLY one who could have some fun. Caelan had provoked this on purpose. Drawn them here to make a point. He needed to kill. It was like a vile serpent under his skin, and until he killed, he wouldn't get it out. This raging demon inside him, this violent requirement to purge and vacate.

His blood hadn't just boiled at the sight of them in bed together, it had evaporated right out of his pores and nearly blinded him with the rage of a thousand men all at once.

They'd looked like ridiculous teenagers lying in one of their parent's beds, trying to get caught just so they could be treated like children instead of the adults they were nightly pretending to be.

Eric didn't know the first thing about loving a woman like Flora. He had no clue about the things Flora had done in the past. Caelan did, all right. He'd hacked the gossipy, bitchy one who was jealous of Flora—Arabella. She still had emails from years ago where she wrote to a gossip columnist about a woman she knew who was playing paramours off against one another... left, right and centre.

He knew the reason behind everything she'd ever done as an adult—it was the thing that'd happened with Jimmy. Even though he could reason it out, all of it still cut him to the quick. He saw through the situation, her brokenness and her battered heart—and he could, in some way, understand—yet his shredded soul hurt, too. Hurt for her, for himself...

...but not for that bastard Eric.

Eric he would kill slowly, painfully. Just as he deserved.

Having dropped some intelligence in the lap of one of Sherry's last-remaining contacts, Caelan was all-too aware Sherry would consider this a trap. He would too if he were her, and because they were so alike, he knew there'd be some... kind of sting in the tail.

But now he knew Flora would absolutely kill for the bairn, and, Eric would probably kill for her—since she was his only route to Caelan—he felt slightly more at ease, knowing they could handle any assault on the castle.

He'd calculated that the men would come in from the east after flying into Aberdeen. They'd find somewhere to leave their vehicle, probably the low-lying hills nearby so Caelan wouldn't see their vehicle lights, hear them or have a good view of them before they snuck around a corner.

Pity they wouldn't know there were a bunch of bogs standing in their way first. Not many people knew about the bogs and their dangers.

The men would have to go around and they'd be brought out into the open valley where on a good, bright night, Caelan would've just taken them out cleanly with his rifle from a few hundred yards out.

Nah, that wasn't going to happen.

This was his arena. He'd make the rules.

He'd have the fun, while all they would receive, was death.

IT WAS 3AM BEFORE ANYBODY crept into the valley. By this point, Caelan had buried himself in long grass and wildflowers near the edge of the valley floor. Lying on his belly, his night-vision binoculars told him they were wary. They half knew it was a trap, but potentially, the bounty was high enough they'd risk it. Risk him.

Large men, ex-military, maybe American seals or some such people. They carried automatic weapons of the "don't fuck with me" variety.

They knew who they hunted, but couldn't resist the temptation—the promise of a share of a million quid or more.

They'd sent six this time. How could she afford it? She'd lost four in Brighton. That would've cost her. No hired gun died without someone paying, somewhere. Who was so desperate to have her freed? Which monster held Sherry's leash and who benefited most from her being let loose into the world once more?

He could only think Rathbone's stupid fucking visit the weekend of Logan's birth had caught someone's attention, somewhere, and it had got back to Sherry somehow. Rathbone, that wily old fox. How could he hate him? He'd sired the greatest woman alive. He could never kill the man, it'd break Flora's heart. But his pride at a grandchild was costing them now, and the worst thing? While sunning himself with his two younger daughters in Florida, he was probably clueless to the shitstorm he and Flora now faced back here!

Caelan wished he knew what was going on at the castle. Eric favoured the silencer and from half a mile away, he'd never hear a thing.

He'd been glad of the five-star hotel in London while he'd been debriefed. It'd given him chance to recharge his batteries. Who knew when he'd truly sleep again, knowing what he now knew.

The six spread out when what Caelan really needed was for them to cluster. They moved carefully across the land, assessing, seeking. None of them came close to the edge where he was, but they clearly expected him to be here somewhere.

He would have to do this by stealth.

Pick them off, one by one.

Each tree would be used, each rock something to hide behind.

Caelan remained in the shadows as they passed by, heading towards the lit-up castle in the distance. It was him they wanted, him who had the information on Blake's whereabouts. They would only use their weapons to intimidate. They had their orders to wound but not kill.

There were a few things he considered as he held his nerve and bided his time:

If the aim were to get back at Blake, surely there were other ways, such as old contacts of his who might squeal. People less dangerous than himself. And why now? If Blake had snuck into the country in December, why now? Nearly six months later. Anyway, there was no time to consider any more of this nonsense. They were starting to get away from him and he had far too much fun planned for these men.

Caelan rolled onto his front and wormed along on his belly, diagonally sweeping more into the middle of the valley, the grass getting rather thin as he got closer to the open expanse. It was the trees around the edges that fed the grasses at the perimeter and made those longer.

An owl hooted and they all looked around, so Caelan kept his head down, moved his limbs inwards and waited. In the dark, they didn't see him, and kept going. Damn owl.

Not helping me, ye damn wee feather sack.

One of them was lagging behind the others slightly.

First one to pick off.

Caelan reached for his weapon and aimed for the man's thigh, his intent to skim it. He'd fall down and he'd hurt, but he'd live. He needed at least one of them to live.

He fired the shot and it reverberated around the valley, a treacherous place to try leading a hunt, when every sound bounced off every tree, small hill and rock, forever ricocheting around and about.

FIGHT FOR LOVE

The man went down and howled, clutching his leg. Caelan lay flat to the floor, the shadows of rocks, trees and phantom night creatures masking his whereabouts... for now.

Caelan didn't dare raise his head. They would be on high alert now, their weapons raised, and even though they had their orders—they knew very well what it was they hunted, its reputation for ruthlessness, its cunning. They were human at the end of the day. With a desire to live.

They began to cluster after the shot, exactly as he'd expected, like that would give them an advantage. It made them weaker. But they were scared of what lurked in the dark, unlike those Ukrainians he'd just been training in the sewers beneath Kiev, whose senses were now so attuned to the dark, they could hear how many rats and what size, just from listening carefully.

Like Caelan was listening now, keeping his wits about him.

One of the soldiers applied a tourniquet to the injured man and then he was dragged by some of the others towards the edge of the field upon which they'd all decided to die on. Propped against a tree trunk, the gun-shot man wept with pain.

Big baby.

A few minutes went by as they congregated and decided what to do next. Perhaps their target wasn't in a killing mood. It was a warning shot?

Their hushed voices carried on the wind but not loudly enough.

Still, their little mother's meeting gave Caelan chance enough to move back into the thicker grasses, quickly elbowing his way through the dirt. God, he'd missed this.

He'd got himself upright behind a tree, when someone seemed to say, "What was that?"

It was obvious to him by this point that these men weren't soldiers at all, or elite killers. They were cheap meat. She was desperate, then. Unless it meant... the real soldiers were at that moment up at the castle readying to kidnap his child, thus forcing him to give whatever she asked for in exchange for Logan's safe return.

No, he told himself.

Flora and Eric would protect the bairn. No doubt about it.

The question was, could Caelan kill all these men? When they didn't really know what they'd got themselves involved in?

Eyes were on the area where he hid, he could tell. Someone had seen enough of his shadow to warrant their suspicion he was somewhere over this way.

Caelan dashed between the trees, running with all the might his long legs possessed, heading for the thicket where he'd stashed some homemade weapons. Some of the men fired shots that didn't even come close. Instead, they smashed trees to bits and in the chaos, gave him ample time to make it to safety.

After that, they came running into the treeline at the edge of a clearing. Caelan squatted low, and when one came within a few feet, he threw a javelin with a razor-sharp point he'd just honed tonight with his blade as he'd waited for them.

Two down.

Four to go.

He crawled, scurried, leapt and used the landscape he knew so well to encircle them, snare, then strike. The dark was his bosom buddy and like best friends, they worked together in harmony, the fear of the hunter so deep in their hearts, buried so irrevocably, they all fell one by one. Until just one remained.

Caelan crept up on him before the man knew he'd been hunted.

Knife at the man's throat, all the others squirmed on the floor with either bullets in their legs or javelins fashioned from the very trees around them.

"Ye can all live, but, only if ye go now. Will ye go now?" asked Caelan.

FIGHT FOR LOVE

"We can't go back without you," said the man in a strangely hypnotic accent—perhaps South American.

Caelan wasn't sure if this was Sherry... or Sherry's former overlords, looking to bring back Blake so they could use him for their own ends.

"Ye winna gi' up this day, then?" asked Caelan.

"We cannot," said the man, fearfully.

Caelan wasted no time.

He shot the leader, then he went around ripping out the javelins, until one by one, they all bled out. The two who hadn't died yet, the ones holding their bullet-ridden legs, squirming, he broke the necks of.

By the time he'd walked back to the castle, the sun had started to come up. Eric waited with the truck keys, swinging them around his index finger. The boot was already open, two bodies inside.

"Was that it?" Caelan asked, ripping off the balaclava and cleaning his face with it.

"Maybe they stupidly thought they had it in the bag."

"We'll need the trailer. There are six more."

Eric wasn't surprised. "We'll burn them on a hillside nobody ever visits. They don't deserve burial."

On that, they could agree.

Sure, men got desperate a time or two in their lives, but to do this? For evil pricks?

They all knew what sort of line they walked, they had to. It was why Caelan felt no guilt.

"Do you feel better now?" asked Eric.

"Aye, ye dinna ken how much better I feel."

Caelan kept it to himself how furious he still was.

Better that Eric believe himself excusable.

Caelan had his sights set on Eric next—for tonight had been far too easy.

AFTER BURNING THE BODIES, Caelan and Eric went to the shower block near the outskirts of the castle grounds, stripped and put their clothes in an oil drum they set on fire, then washed off in the showers. Caelan could feel that man's eyes on him the entire time. Eric had never been shy about how much he craved, coveted and admired Caelan, all these long years. The amount of times Eric had walked in on Caelan with a woman and he'd pretended to have accidentally stumbled in wasn't even funny. The man had a problem.

Caelan needed Flora to see what this was really all about.

He needed her to see right now.

Fuck the potential fallout.

If only she could see the truth...

They grabbed a couple of towels and dashed inside to the castle nearly naked.

Stumbling on the slippery spiral steps, their limbs nearly frozen, they made it into the warmth of the suite to find Flora still fast asleep. It was barely five o'clock. She'd sleep through anything and it'd only got worse with motherhood and all that it drained from her body.

Caelan threw his towel away and climbed in behind Flora's sweaty body, her nightdress damp from fever dreams. *Good*. She didn't deserve to get off scot-free.

He gave Eric a filthy look and gestured for him to stay away on his side of the big bed—Flora between them.

"Dinna touch her," he warned.

Caelan cuddled his beautiful, clueless wife and felt the exhaustion of the night wash over him. All the while it was obvious Eric lay desperate to touch him, feel him out, know more. But Caelan squeezed his eyes tight shut and let himself breathe her in.

No matter what... he'd love her no matter what, he told himself.

Chapter Twenty-One

FOR A FEW BLISSFUL moments, everything was how it'd been before. Him holding me tight, his arms around me, his scent overpowering. My hulking beast breathed like a slumbering dragon, deep in sleep. When I opened my eyes, I saw Eric was awake on the other side of the bed. Caelan had to have barely any room behind me, perched right on the edge of the mattress. For a second Eric didn't notice I'd woken up, then he saw I'd seen him watching Caelan sleep.

He and I stared at one another for a while. I couldn't read him at all. What was he thinking?

If Eric had paid those Syrians to make it seem like a fake kidnapping or something (as part of some plot of his to gain my trust), make me vulnerable...

It'd backfired, hadn't it?

Perhaps that was why Eric had vomited at the scene, back at the log cabin. He'd not expected my violence, my strength. Yet... we'd fucked after. Maybe because he'd sensed my need. Since violence seemed to arouse me.

It'd also been fear... that dire need to have someone close. Someone to reassure me. Obliterate me.

Yet I couldn't deny, something had been brewing between us before that day. Whether it was this shared frustration at neither of us ever being able to truly get beneath Caelan.

I wasn't sure.

The baby let out a little cry, in that way of his, no drama... just a little noise so we'd know he was waking up.

That roused Caelan immediately and he grunted awake, burying his face in my hair before he did anything. It nearly made my heart break, watching Eric watching us.

Had he meant it when he said he loved me? Or was that just another symptom of his quest to get closer to Caelan? Me being the wife of his greatest love, maybe he was just trying to figure out what Caelan saw in me. That's why he liked/loved me. Because I was a part of Caelan.

He continued to look emotionless and blank. Vacant Eric was worse than anything, when he was a person of so many opinions, thoughts and such expressiveness ordinarily. I didn't want to see that look in his eyes anymore.

I rolled over and into Caelan's chest, breathing in his skin, his heart pounding against my cheek. He wrapped his arms tighter around me and threw his leg over me, too. For a second, none of it had happened. I was back home. Everything was safe, warm, and I was loved.

But the problem was, if I were truly safe, loved and secure, I wouldn't need him right beside me all the time to know that. He'd gone away and I'd strayed because I'd doubted him. I'd been right to doubt him. He'd been keeping the truth about my father from me. Woman's intuition had told me something was wrong.

When Caelan buried his face deeper in my hair and groaned, making a show of it, Eric huffed and got out of bed. I heard him dressing, then his feet were like heavy wet flippers across the room as he angrily moved out.

Caelan surrounded my cheeks with his hands and made me look at him. There was worry in those hazel eyes, the like of which he never usually showed unless it was about us. I knew he was the man I loved, absolutely. He was it. But he kept secrets, he wasn't wholly mine. He had a blackness inside him I couldn't reach. He seemed to think I was a perfect goddess, the antidote to his inertia, but I wasn't, and that was difficult, when I was so scared of losing him and wanted to keep him but also tell him the truth sometimes.

Ever since the day Sherry had bombarded me with all those vile revelations... nothing had truly been the same. We'd merely papered the cracks, for the sake of our son.

"Tell me it was just physical and we'll say nae more about it."

I bit my lip and sucked back a sob. "I wish I could say that, but there's a lot to sort through."

His hand shook as he stroked the hair back from my forehead. "While I was gone, ye were all I thought about. Ye dinna ken how much I love ye, Flora."

"Maybe if you were more effusive, I'd know, Caelan." I swotted away a tear.

When the baby gave a more urgent cry, Caelan carefully stepped out of bed and grabbed the boy, bringing him to me. His bum was whiffy but the feed was more important and I let him latch on. Caelan pulled on his underpants and sat up in bed next to me, stroking his fingers through Logan's hair.

"Ye've been careful?"

"Of course." I was angry he would ask.

"How careful?" he demanded.

I looked at him then, caught his meaning, and gulped.

"Ye canna trust that man," he groaned.

I'd let him...

Yes, I knew I needed to be tested, to be sure. He was right.

"What do ye wanna do?" he said.

"What do you mean?"

"Go back to London?"

I nodded my head.

"I'll arrange it."

"What about him?" I said.

"He's coming wi' us."

Caelan left the bed and got dressed.

It was clear, this was far from over.

BY EVENING WE WERE back in London and at the house. The mansion. Eric and Caelan did security checks while I got myself re-installed.

I made it clear I didn't want either of them near me while I bathed, got changed and ate my dinner—a microwave meal—alone.

And at bedtime, I slept the sleep of a thousand dreams, each more terrible than the last.

I didn't see an end to this, nor a beginning to the next part of my life.

All I saw was my son, his needs, and our cocoon.

The scariest part of it all?

I wanted to call up my father, ask him to come get me, take me somewhere far away from both of these men... save me. Tell me what to do. Where to go. Give me the answers I craved, put it all into perspective for me. Show me the way.

Even worse than wanting to speak to my father, I wanted Eric to sneak in with me between the sheets and slide his cock inside me, make love to me carefully like he had done before Caelan came home. No questions, nothing but comfort and calm.

That's all I'd ever wanted, but that night, it felt like happiness was the furthest away from me it had ever been.

Chapter Twenty-Two

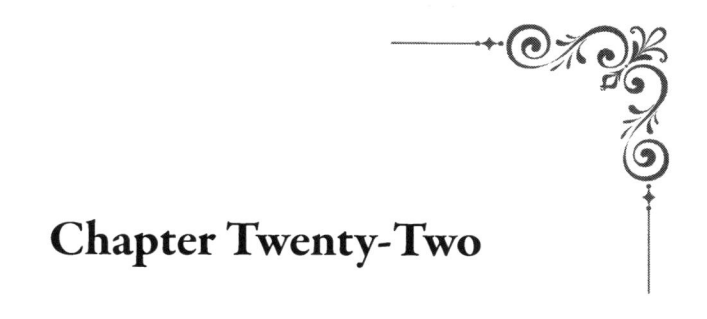

BY DAWN I WAS RESOLVED. Eric had to go. I couldn't see him again. I'd been a fool. This was a mess we could sort out, but just Caelan and I—no third party. Get rid of Eric, then, rebuild: that was my plan.

After feeding Logan and using the bathroom, I crashed into the wall of muscle and man that was my husband, meeting him as he strode down the hallway in his combat clothes.

A thick wave of dread ran through me. What now? What the hell now?

He played with the cuffs on his long-sleeve army shirt. It was obvious he hadn't had much sleep. Had he and Eric stayed up talking? Had he killed Eric yet?

All these thoughts raged and I tried to calm myself down, since there were no scabs or bruises on Caelan's knuckles—and he wouldn't have been so cheap as to shoot a man without a proper fight.

"I huv to go away a couple of days." There was no room for compromise, I could tell. His voice was so sombre, almost hollow. "Eric will remain here to guard you and the bairn."

Avoiding my eye, I knew something had come to light overnight—something he wouldn't trouble me with. Though I'd potentially be able to help if he would only tell me.

"Is this to do with our current situation, or is this more work for the government?"

"Both." He lifted his eyes then and I saw only Machine Caelan, ready for action.

Ready to maim, destroy, overcome—worm his way out of another dodgy predicament.

Even outwit every single enemy until he stood over a battlefield riddled with bodies, yet, ultimately, was able to declare victory.

He wouldn't lose, I knew that.

It wasn't in his nature.

"There's a lot we haven't talked about," I murmured.

"Aye." He wrapped his hands around my wrists and stared into space behind me. "I ken there is."

"What really happened with Sherry? How did she... we've never talked, not properly. How she got you trailing me... what she said. How much you knew. What was your plan? I want to know everything. Including the times you saved me."

Caelan's terrifying beauty hit me then as he pinned me with his eyes. He was hurt, I saw it. Brutally wounded, beneath that stoic masculine façade.

He trailed a finger down my cheek and looked broken when he said, "Have ye ever known me to lie, lass? Ever? Omit, maybe. To protect ye. But I meant it when I said, it was love at first sight. That's all I ken."

He leaned in and kissed my cheek, his body like an impenetrable wall before me, so strange and strong and livid, I couldn't find a way past the barricade in that moment. A ginormous block of marble too intimidating to go round or over.

A force I couldn't comprehend lived inside him. Something beyond, maybe superhuman. A warrior with a heart of steel. He was no ordinary mortal, but for some reason, he loved me. I knew it.

FIGHT FOR LOVE

"I huvna a choice but to do what only I can do," he said. "But I'll be back in two or three days."

He turned to go and I watched him retrieve a bag from the walk-in closet. Small, just the essentials. So many questions bubbled on the tip of my tongue but I couldn't find the strength to utter a single one.

When the front door downstairs banged shut, I remained standing on the landing like a shell-shock victim. And I had one thought, and one alone: *but is love enough?*

I WENT BACK TO SLEEP for a while and when I woke up, I found Eric watching me sleep with Logan on his lap, the pair of them sitting on the other side of the bed. Logan was nearly sitting up alone; Eric had him balanced upright against the inside of his knee, his leg extended across the bed behind the baby. Logan was mesmerised by the tattoos on Eric's arms and kept patting them, scratching his skin and tugging at the fine white hairs silken against all that ink. Eric was wearing jersey shorts and a tight white t-shirt. I could smell the recent application of powder meaning he'd changed the baby's nappy while I'd dozed.

"You were dead to the world," he said. "Logan was just chatting to himself so I came in to keep him company."

Gradually awake, I took a deep breath and sat up in bed. "He's gone again."

"I know." No emotion about it.

"What did you two speak of last night?"

Eric looked empty and shook his head. "We didn't speak. He doesn't trust me anymore. He locked himself in his study and I think he stayed there all night. I never heard him emerge, until..."

"I see."

Logan got bored of Eric and held his arms out to me. I pulled him close, his scent, warmth and squidgy softness utterly electrifying.

I loved him more than life itself. Logan had always been a gentle and tender baby, but when he wanted something, he wasn't ever subtle about it—and he yanked at my shirt to let me know he was ready for a bit more.

While Logan latched on, Eric went downstairs to make tea, returning with a tray and a full pot, milk jug and two cups. It seemed like I'd brought him over to the more mellow side, since he'd started drinking tea instead of coffee that was nearly strong enough to hold a soup spoon upright.

Logan didn't need a full feed, he'd just been wanting to soothe and top up before dozing some more, so when I took him off and Eric gave me that look, that was all it took for me to start unbuttoning my shirt the rest of the way.

He was untying his shorts when I said, "Are you clean?"

He frowned and I frowned back. A standoff ensued before he realised what I meant.

Grabbing his phone, he showed me his NHS records on the app. Modern technology, eh?

"Last tested three weeks ago." I saw it was true, with a negative result for all kinds of things, HIV included. "Done it for years. Even if I haven't been sexually active, which I haven't, in quite some time now. I still get tested anyway, just in case something... appears. Given I'd been in Ukraine, cut several times by my captors, I didn't just get the STD's done, but the full workup."

Shame painted my cheeks crimson and I was mortified I'd allowed...

But didn't I have a right to know?

Yes, I did.

I could tell from the look in Eric's eyes, he knew it was Caelan who'd put that fear in my heart.

FIGHT FOR LOVE

"When was the last time you were with someone?" I asked carefully, still with my shirt mostly unbuttoned, though I remained on the other side of the bed to where he sat.

He pursed his lips and thought for a moment. "A while," he said raggedly, then a frog got caught in his throat. "Since I first saw you, hmm. It's been difficult to look at anyone else."

I wasn't sure why he was looking at me like that and had spoken with that heavy tone, but then...

Something caught at the back of my throat, too and I looked down at myself, it suddenly dawning on me that this was real. He wasn't faking it.

"What? You think Caelan and I being best friends means we couldn't possibly appreciate the same woman?" He grunted and cursed under his breath. "I'm afraid we have a lot more in common than he would ever admit."

"B—but you hated me? At the castle. You spoke..."

I heard him swallow even above my own ragged breath. "I spoke harshly because..."

His softness then made me look up and our eyes met. His eyes were shining with affection and yes, something like love.

"I'm surprised I'm alive, as it happens," he said, worrying his top lip.

I inhaled shakily and closed my eyes, hardly able to believe this was happening.

"Caelan will break you, someday," I whispered, afraid my husband might still hear, even from wherever he'd gone.

Eric sniggered and cupped a hand around his mouth. "Oh, he already did that a long time ago. I just never let him know I'd got past my delusions to see what he really is, beneath."

"Beneath?"

Eric smirked. "He thinks I did what I did in Ukraine to bring him back into the game. I didn't."

"What did you do in Ukraine?" I asked, even though I wasn't sure I wanted to know.

He met my eye without shame and didn't take too long to think about what it was he wanted to say. "It's a war zone, Flora. The people are scared. There's no black and white. Normal rules do not apply." I could buy that, at least. "So, there was a Russian asset I'd evacuated from a bombing. Yes, the team got killed in that bombing, but I had no hand in that, I swear. I nearly got killed myself but it was pure luck I'd been on watch that night and was stationed just outside the blast radius alongside the asset we'd stashed in a bunker." Eric's conviction seemed real. "We unfortunately got picked up by a bunch of Ukraine militia and things got complicated, hence them calling in Caelan to negotiate the situation. However, if they'd just left me to it, I was on the verge of convincing the Ukraine's to let us go free so I could take the asset to the proper authorities... when Caelan turned up and ruined everything."

I narrowed my eyes. "In that swaggering way of his?"

"Yup. But I was playing a long game. I had plans."

"Plans?" I raised my brows.

He nodded and told me defiantly, "I'd convinced the Russian double agent whom I'd rescued that I was bent. I'd given him a bank account to wire money to in exchange for intel from me. I was going to send him back to his handlers with false information which would ultimately destroy the reputation of one of Russia's top military advisors. Because every single man we take out is one less enemy, one more chink in their armour."

I wanted to believe him so badly. After all, wasn't this what SAS men did? Inveigle, unbind enemy lines piece by piece, shatter loyalties, play mind games... then smash. It seemed plausible.

"I could've and maybe should've fought Caelan when he arrived in Ukraine, maybe explained myself more, been forceful instead of a pussy. But he was set on his own plan of attack. Isn't that Caelan all over?" He shrugged and I knew what he was saying. "And maybe I wanted to get rid of him long enough to have a good crack at you, see if you're both really as happy as he always makes out. Well, I got my answer, didn't I?"

My jaw nearly fell open and I had to clench my teeth to keep from gawping. The insinuation was staggering: that Eric had used Caelan's absence as an opportunity to get closer to me. That it wasn't really Caelan who he was obsessed with anymore, but me.

"There's something wrong with him," Eric continued, "something that leaves him without reason. I've never known him be so impulsive and erratic before. God knows what he had to do in order to get himself back home. I wouldn't like to think! He's lucky to have escaped alive." My face fell and he saw. "Me? I'm a single man. But a married man with a kid can't go round doing that anymore, right?"

I felt sick and my palms became sweaty. "I don't know what he was thinking." My thoughts turned dark. "But sometimes, I do wonder, if there are things he purposely avoids. Like real life. He'd rather go to Ukraine than go to the supermarket with me."

A filthy smile painted his face; I'd given him the opportunity to seize upon my doubts. "Last year, I wanted to murder Sherry, to despatch her, eradicate the threat to you entirely. He wouldn't have it, wouldn't let me take her out. Mistake number one in my book." The seriousness of his stare, his tone, told me he was telling the truth. "I knew when I heard on the grapevine Blake Rathbone was rumoured not dead, he'd have heard that, too. And I knew with that rumour Sherry would be on the warpath. But again, my warnings... my plan to have her done away with inside fell on deaf ears."

Violent rage hit me square between the eyes and I wanted to murder something, someone. Smash. Break. Destroy.

Lies, such terrible lies. So many.

"When it comes to that woman, he's blind, Flora. I never imagined in a million years he could possibly have an Achilles heel, but she's it. She's why reason goes out of his head. The thought of her out there still. Doing what she does. I mean, is that what he wants? Me to kill her without him knowing, so he can just wash his hands and be absolved. I don't know..."

I rubbed the tears from my eyes, my hands trembling as I pushed the hair back from my face, the reality of it all setting in. I thought it was more than likely that Caelan had known before heading to Ukraine that everyone but Eric was dead. If he'd have told me that before he left for the war zone, I'd have told him to stay home and not bother.

But he wouldn't have wanted to hear that; because, deep down, he'd been desperate to leave us for the heady heights of all-out warfare once more.

He'd also gone knowing Sherry's goons might eventually catch up to me, but perhaps he'd somehow known Eric would be here to fill the void. It didn't matter which way I looked at it, the fact of the matter was, Sherry was the biggest threat to our happiness and he'd been offered the chance to eradicate her but hadn't.

"Tell me what you've just said is true. Swear on my life. On Logan's. Swear it!"

Eric moved across the bed and sat before me, and I only saw love and desire in that beautiful face of his. He put his hand over mine, a sad smile tugging at those perfect pink lips of his.

"I swear it, Flora. On my life."

His chest was heaving up and down and I saw the heat creeping up his neck. I got on my knees and climbed across his lap, lifting my hands to his shoulders as I sat astride him. He looked in love when he put his hands gently on my waist, waiting for my instruction.

"Eric, I thought he was all for me." My lip trembled and he leaned in to kiss my mouth softly, comforting me.

"He's clueless, Flora. All these years... I've been trying to figure him out. The Jimmy thing makes sense of it all... and his mother." He swallowed and shook his head. "He has nobody to blame but himself for us getting together. He abandoned you. Lied. His uncle tried to assault and possibly kill you. Did he ever say he was sorry you'd had to defend yourself at such a young age?" I shook my head, sad, because that had occurred to me, too. Caelan had been devastated at the revelations, but he'd never told me he was sorry. "He's from a bad lot and I think, some of it might have rubbed off on him."

"What about us, Eric? Did it rub off on us too?"

He peeled the top away from my body and shuddered as he stared at my breasts. The weight of his gaze peaked my nipples and I felt every ounce of my breasts as they tingled, my chest heavy in a way it hadn't been in months. Maybe years. A true kind of nakedness overcame me, to the point where I could brook him being clothed no longer.

Pulling his t-shirt away, he grabbed and yanked it off, then dragged me into his warmth, strength and heat. Nipping my bottom lip, he said, "I'd commit any atrocity, to get one more night with you, Flora. Does that make me bad? If so, I don't care."

I grabbed his head and made him look at me. "Did it rub off on us too, Eric? Tell me seriously."

His eyes sparkled with longing, with amusement and love but also, unmistakably, peace. "Nobody's perfect, Flora. But together, maybe two people can come close to being so." He kissed my jaw and breathed against my chest, making my heart thump harder in response. "Maybe together, people can be better, be dedicated to one another. Nobody else in the mix. Live for one another."

He was describing everything I'd ever wanted, so why did I still feel like I was a pawn in some game between two dastardly, adroit players?

He raised me up enough to drag my pyjama trousers down and I lifted my knees one at a time so he could remove them altogether. All he had to do was shift the shorts he was wearing down a bit and then

I shuffled into place, sinking down onto his shaft. I watched as Eric's eyes darkened as his eyes roved my body, a purely male satisfaction filling his face with wonder.

"Perfect, Flora," he whispered, "utterly perfect."

"Yes," I murmured, my eyes falling shut as he kissed his way down to my nipple, then licked around my areola.

Eric dug his hands into my backside and rocked me back and forth, my wetness sliding along his shaft smoothly, our bodies fully joined. I threw my hands over my head, bucking back and forth, his hands doing the rest to force me up and down the length of him. With my eyes closed, all I felt was sensation: his hardness buried inside my clenching pussy, his mouth hot over my breasts, his cries as I rode him closer and closer getting louder.

And we weren't protected. I'd not had him put on a rubber in all the time we'd been fucking, but I had made Caelan wear one a few times since I'd had Logan.

That time, I wasn't wearing my cap and I wasn't planning on telling him to come on my body again. I wanted that feeling inside me of electricity and unencumbered passion.

His mouth travelled up my throat, hot and wet, hungry. Our mouths met and I leaned into him, wrapping my arms around his head to let him explore my mouth with his tongue.

"Have you ever been truly satisfied?" Eric asked, throwing his hips towards me to bury himself so deep, I nearly shrieked every time. "Have you, Flora?"

"Show me," I said.

He threw me off him and twirled me until I was on all fours, then pulled me back onto his cock until he was slapping his hips against my backside and cursing under his breath at the tightness of it.

"Rub that little clit," he demanded.

FIGHT FOR LOVE

I did as he bade and came in no time, so sure as he dug his nails in my hips and cursed my name that he'd come too, if the satisfied heat inside me wasn't enough evidence.

Eric tossed me onto my back, pushed my knees up to my chest and said from down where his head was, right in front of my very exposed pussy, "I'm going to screw your fucking brains out, slut. My perfect, dirty slut. Who needs shafting as often as possible."

"Yes," I groaned, rubbing my breasts.

He ate me out, his cum and all, slurping away at the mess of our sex. I'd also waited for this all my life, too—a man who would never complain about me needing it, all the time.

Rather a man who would just get on with pleasuring me constantly, no explanation necessary.

It was only after he'd made me come with his tongue, then fingered my pussy, then my arse, then came in my arse again, that we finally lay down in each other's arms.

"Did you never arse fuck anyone before?" I asked.

"Once. Using a condom. She wasn't into it. Not really."

I leaned in and kissed his top lip, then his bottom lip, slipping a bit of tongue in for good measure. He smiled and grabbed my rear, sounds of satisfaction escaping his mouth.

"Do you have some toys?" he asked.

"Why?" I was shocked he'd ask.

"I want to try them out on you."

"Really?"

"Yeah, really."

I rolled out of bed and went into the bottom of my wardrobe, producing a shoebox full of toys. I wasn't sure they still worked; I hadn't had them out in a while. Caelan had never asked if I had toys. Or if he might use them on me.

"Hmm, interesting," said Eric, picking through the box.

He pulled out a wand and pressed the button. Mysteriously, it still held a charge.

When Eric used it to peak my nipples, I arched off the bed and cried out at the sensation of milk leaking free. Eric was there to quickly drink it up, and then as he moved the wand to between my thighs, he didn't stop kissing my breasts.

It went on like that for ages, him alternating between different toys, as one and then another ran out of battery. It was intoxicating but not quite as satisfying as his tongue or cock or fingers.

So when he lapped at my entrance, then dragged his tongue back to my clit, I clawed at my own hair and gasped, "More!"

Eric pounced on me, drilled his rigid cock into my body and groaned into my mouth, "Fucking love you, woman."

He held me in his arms, fucked me violently and cawed in my ear as he came, again, shooting into my depths unencumbered. I came so hard that time I drew blood from his back and thought I would never walk again. I was drained, utterly drained and depleted.

Eric hovered over me, stroking my face and kissing my lips softly as I dozed a little. He rubbed his nose to mine and licked under my top lip. That was a different kind of caress. A loving, tender, playful one.

I rolled him onto his back and kissed his throat, nibbled his earlobe, his nipple, then kissed his face, gently tugging at his hair from the roots. Meanwhile his hands didn't leave my back once, holding me gently as I enjoyed his beauty for once.

We looked into one another's eyes across the pillow and he said, "Will he ever accept me?"

I inhaled sharply, almost at once coming to terms with it. Honestly, my life without Caelan would never make sense. Maybe loving two people was possible? In that moment, I couldn't imagine saying goodbye to either of them.

"I don't know, Eric. I would like to hope so."

FIGHT FOR LOVE

"You think he might?" He almost looked childlike with hope.

"What would you do, if he agreed? Would you try to steal him away from me, like you'd always planned?"

He gazed upon me without maliciousness or jealousy. "Maybe he should count himself lucky. He has two people who love him. And those two people also love one another. It could be harmonious."

Deep down, I doubted Caelan would ever agree to it. However, they were both right about my sexual needs. I only wanted more... and now I was thinking about what it'd be like... having both of them.

Eric read that in my eyes and grabbed the one vibrator that still worked, buzzing my clit until I came screaming into his mouth, the image of him and Caelan worshipping me at the same time having taken me right over the edge.

Chapter Twenty-Three

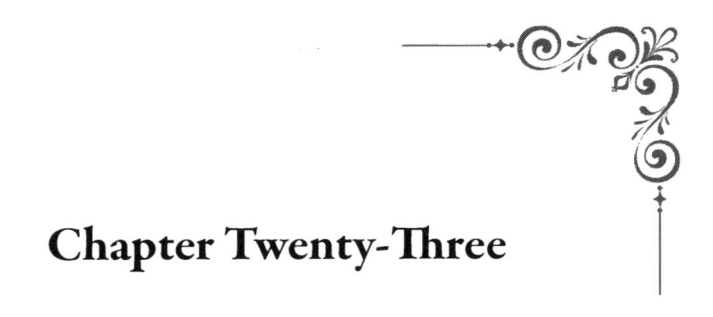

Eric – Past

WHEN HE FIRST SET EYES on Flora, he hated her with a passion. No matter how many times he told himself he was over Caelan, he wasn't. To finally meet this woman—beautiful though she was—who'd so quickly wedded the man he'd loved nearly all his adult life was soul-destroying. He would never truly be able to love another person, not while Caelan still lived. Breathed. Existed.

One night, unable to sleep, he'd bumped into her at some ungodly hour in the castle kitchen during one of their lads' weekends with the other guys. Why the wife had to be present he didn't know. Maybe Caelan had turned over a new leaf after all and needed her close. Maybe it was real. That remained to be seen.

She quickly got the measure of Eric and impressed him with her shrewdness. Then she got down to brass tax about the strange trauma they were undoubtedly bound by—hence such a quick marriage.

Pretending she wasn't scared witless, she said flippantly, "He's worried for my life. He won't tell me the details, but I think, someone wants me dead."

Was she for real this person? He wasn't sure. "What do you need me to do?"

"You need to find out everything you can about my father's widow. And you'll extinguish the threat. Do you hear me? That's how he and I really met. He knows something... he's trying to protect me... from something."

Interesting. Eric had learnt a lot from Caelan over the years, but one thing the Scotsman could never take credit for was Eric's natural intuition. There was a shared history between the star-crossed lovers. Some terrible truth, or something. He'd known it even before that day.

He gave a brief nod, trying not to look pleased to have a way into this sham marriage and its eventual undoing.

"I'll do what needs to be done."

"He can't do it, Eric or he'd have done it already. There's something... I don't know... some way in which he's compromised that I don't know about yet."

"Leave it with me," he said, trying not to laugh at her cloak-and-dagger, almost comical, manner.

"This is not for me, Eric. But for him. You understand?"

Perfect wife? Eric didn't think so. This one had skeletons threatening to pop out here, there, everywhere. He smiled inside. "He will only find peace once I've got rid of this bitch?"

"I'm almost certain."

He played along. "Then, if you keep him happy, I will keep you safe. That's our bargain."

"Thank you."

He got up, moved to her side of the table and hugged her fiercely. *Thank you for giving me a way back in*, he thought secretly.

"You know, Eric... if he was gay, it'd have definitely been you. You're pretty awesome."

He gave a smirk. Gay? He was actually straight. Let people believe it. Let them. He knew the truth. The real truth. The actual truth.

Again, he decided to play along...

"What would you say if I was bi?" he said.

She pinched her lip between her teeth, blushing as Eric stared at her mouth.

Did she not realise she was meant to be married to someone else? He was shocked by the way she brazenly assessed the size and potential of him, probably without even realising she was doing it.

"I'd say that's very interesting indeed."

He kissed her cheek and pushed her in the direction of the doorway, chuckling as she made her way back up to bed—to Caelan.

Back in his bunk with the rest of the guys in the stink-filled barracks-style chamber they had for their stay, he lay there wondering how he would do it.

Well, first he'd find out more about this stepmother of Flora's.

Then he'd figure out how to use it to break apart Flora and Caelan.

It wasn't at all that he was gay though he liked people to think so, and he couldn't lie and say he'd never sucked cock, not when he had, just to find out if it was for him (it wasn't).

He couldn't tell anyone why Caelan. Why him. Why he felt this way about only one person on the planet.

There was something about Caelan that Eric had never been able to get over, and it wasn't even necessarily physical. It was more than that. It was something else... something the submissive in Eric cried out for.

He'd only ever found the cruelty he desperately craved in his former mentor.

Nobody else came close, not when it came to true sadism.

Eric couldn't help himself.

Caelan was the perfect alpha.

Everybody loved him.

No matter who, everyone loved the man.

The King of Men.

The one true leader he'd ever met. The one true gentleman.

FIGHT FOR LOVE

And a total sadist. Through and through.

Chapter Twenty-Four

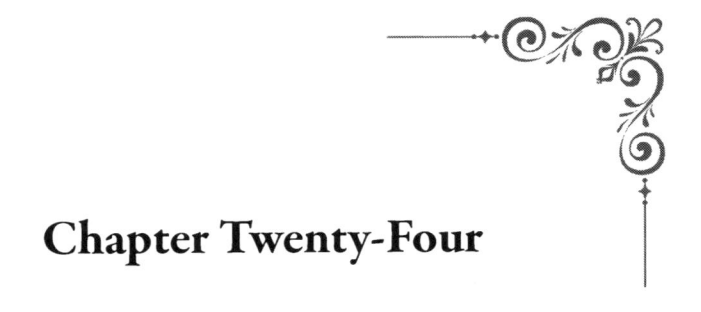

Caelan

HE PROWLED THE INTERROGATION room in his combat clothes to appear like he was still part of the armed forces. Well, with what had happened recently, he'd have a hard time convincing anyone he wasn't still in the forces. Does anyone ever really leave? The life has a way of imprinting so that even when out, you're still in, taking all those lessons learned with you. For Caelan though it felt like he was on a rolling freelance contract, never truly able to clock off.

Ogarkov had been treated very well so far. Three square meals a day. Even Netflix. A comfy bed. A room with a window. A little shelf of books. A notebook. Even an in-room kettle to make himself hot drinks. So far they'd treated him like he wasn't a filthy double crosser. A dirty liar, cheat and a man without any true allegiance. All that Caelan had determined having taken just one look at the fella. Now all he needed was proof.

Ogarkov had passed all the lie detectors. Had told them everything they needed to know. Or so he would have them believe...

Yet one of the interrogation specialists had requested Caelan come on board, see if he couldn't dig up some new information pertaining to Eric Holmes. It was a hunch the woman had—that Ogarkov was hiding something.

FIGHT FOR LOVE

So far, Caelan and he had discussed the weather, the state of things in Ukraine (including the cultural institutions destroyed irrevocably). It was the lack of sadness in the Russian's eyes that told Caelan the man was an evil self-server. Even the most stoic of Russians hated the loss of cultural icons—and the two countries shared such close history, after all.

"So you are here to tell me I am being sent home or something?" the Russian finally asked, since Caelan's prowling about the room had obviously had the desired effect.

"Can I no come here just to check the man whose life I saved is doing okay?"

Caelan shot a glance at Ogarkov and saw that the man was very much suspicious of Caelan's visit. Not at all comforted. Good.

He finally sat down opposite Ogarkov at the interview table positioned in the middle of the dim, spartan room. Ogarkov wasn't cuffed but the man knew he was in a secure building.

"Eric Holmes," said Caelan calmly, letting the name hang in the air.

The Russian's nose twitched. "I don't know this man."

Ogarkov's story so far had been that the rough treatment he'd received from the Ukrainians had kept him pretty much out of it so that he wasn't always aware of his surroundings or what was going on.

He claimed to not know who Eric Holmes was.

"He has verra light hair and the eyes of a wolf," said Caelan, "is a tank of a man with tattoos down his arms, London through and through. He saved your life in Ukraine."

The Russian attempted to appear incredulous he had ever met such a fellow.

"You two made a bargain. Eric himself told me of this bargain."

Caelan let those words sink in, watching as the Russian worked through his choices.

Eric hadn't confessed anything about a bargain; Caelan hadn't even let the man speak to him since he'd found him in bed with his wife.

It was a guess. Caelan's guesses were nearly always spot on.

"What you know of this alleged bargain?" Ogarkov asked, in his drawl, his hand gestures attempting to make him seem indifferent and beyond reproach. "This Englishman lies, whatever he has said. Lies."

Caelan got up and tucked in his chair as slowly and as carefully as possible. He shot the Russian one carefully weighted grin, then turned and began heading for the door.

Those few seconds had to be counted precisely. Enough to give the man space to hang himself, not enough to let him complete—not that day. Let his doubt fester. His survival instinct take over. Caelan had perfected the art of silent intimidation over the years.

"I will talk, but I want immunity," said the Russian.

Caelan looked over his shoulder and snickered. "I don't bargain with Russian scum."

"But—"

He quickly vacated the room leaving the Russian to stew on his options.

Caelan walked to the room next door where a group of people had been watching on security screens. The woman who'd asked for him especially grinned from ear to ear.

"You're not going back in tonight?" she asked, her blonde hair piled on her head in a messy bun. Barely twenty-five, she was one of those prodigies with an IQ through the roof. He'd met a few. They bored him. Nearly always had strange routines they had to keep. Weird proclivities, too.

"Nae, tomorrow he'll be offering everything on a platter. In fact, dinna let him see anyone but the guards before I see him again. Okay?"

She nodded and gave him a playful punch to the shoulder. "Nice work."

Caelan wanted to wash his mouth out with soap as he left the room, then the building, heading for a meeting he'd set up earlier in the day. The person he'd arranged to meet had to have been waiting hours by this point and he wasn't sure he'd still be in the city. He might have chickened out.

Leaving the secure facility behind, he headed in a taxi to the Ritz. On the way, he pulled a leather jacket over his fatigues and left the taxi to head straight for the interior. Nobody looked twice as he strode right for the elevators and pressed the button.

People knew that secret service types met up here all the damn time.

Caelan knocked on the door of a suite on the top floor and the door opened up.

He walked indoors and found himself face to face with Logan's grandfather.

Caelan patrolled the room, seeking gadgets, hidden cameras. Anything.

"You sure nobody followed ye?" asked Caelan.

Blake sat down at the circular breakfast table with a huff, his tracksuit tacky against the surroundings.

"I'm sure," he groaned.

Blake had discarded a wig, hat and glasses on the coffee table over in the sitting area.

"The passport worked, then?" Caelan asked, nervous energy rippling off him.

"I wouldn't be here otherwise. And maybe it's you we should be wary of being followed."

Caelan had made sure he wasn't followed. There was a black spot around the facility he'd been at earlier, anyway. Blake didn't need to know his business—especially not that his daughter was across town, probably screwing a bad man.

"So she's really determined to find me, then?" said Blake.

"Do ye want me to go collect those twelve burnt corpses from Scotland? Or will ye just take ma word for it?" Caelan's jaw clenched and he waited for a retort to his sarcasm.

"Hmm," Blake sighed, resigned to accept the situation, Caelan thought.

"Ma's no gonna stop. And Flora will be the one who'll pay, if we're no careful."

Blake rubbed his bald head in frustration, his fate seemingly already set. Sherry wouldn't stop until someone paid. Until somebody begged.

At least with Eric, Flora remained safe. He wouldn't let harm come to her. No matter how much it killed him, so long as Flora lived, Caelan could deal with anything. Which meant that while they were busy doing whatever it was they were doing, Caelan was free to finally wrap up the shit going on in the outside world.

"What do you need from me?" Blake asked, more than just jetlag in his eyes.

"It's returned, then," Caelan guessed.

Rathbone stared dead ahead. "Yup."

That made him sad for Flora, for his son, for Blake even. All the rigmarole he'd gone through to get one tiny slice of freedom. A tiny slice of freedom... before the inevitable.

"I can't stand to go through it all again," he said, grimacing, "and anyway, we both know I've had more time than I ever deserved. And now my girls have a new and better mother over in the states, they're set. Everything as it should be."

Blake had apparently remarried out there, a shiny new ring on his wedding finger.

"You canna give up, man." Caelan laid his knuckles on the breakfast table, hunched over so he could look into Rathbone's eyes. "No until she's seen ye one, last time."

"I don't think I can." Rathbone didn't just sound tired, but defeated. Ready for the end.

Had he already decided he would give Sherry what she most wanted, just to finish it? Once and for all.

Caelan took a seat and Blake got a good look at him. "You don't look so good yourself."

He tipped his head back and sighed. "I've been caught up in a diplomatic situation."

Rathbone grimaced. "Rather you than me."

"Aye, I'd have to agree there," he groaned.

Rathbone rubbed hands around his face again, as if his skin were crawling. Perhaps whatever had befallen him this time had already progressed.

"What is it she wants?" asked Caelan.

"I don't know if she knows that herself."

It was Caelan's turn to rub his tired eyes. "Should I have her done away with?"

"Could you?" Blake looked hopeful for a second.

"Aye, but..."

"She's your own mother," he answered.

"Aye." Caelan raised his eyebrows. "And I think, there's more to this. Something she's searching for. Money, maybe. Doubt it, though. More likely information, something only you'd know."

Blake thought it through. "She just wants me to suffer because I outwitted her."

"Aye."

"But..."

Caelan sat forward, hands clasped. "What, man?"

"I think at this point she knows she will never go free. The evidence your pal got hold of was far too damning for her to ever get off, no matter if I surface or not." Caelan couldn't disagree. "She's not doing this to get free or get money."

"So, she just wants to hurt us," said Caelan.

"And she won't stop until she does."

Caelan frowned and sat back, arms folded. "So what shall we do?"

"I'll think about it."

Caelan stood up and grunted. "I'll be back tomorrow. I'll borrow an armed guard and we'll take you to Flora."

Blake gulped. "If you think it wise."

"Nae, I think it necessary."

IN THE DIM CORNER OF an ultra-exclusive private members' club, Caelan found the prince with his back to the room, the wood-panelled, leather-accented, high-ceilinged space having been cleared out for his particular use.

Caelan took the leather chair opposite and didn't say no to a rather ancient Scotch, nor a thick Cuban cigar. Such places still existed, and, what a marvel.

The prince had already smoked half a cigar and was now just watching the world go by outside the plate-glass windows, the busy road below full of people.

Caelan had taken a few puffs on his cigar before the prince turned and looked at him.

"How can you stand it?" he asked.

Caelan took a deep breath. "It doesna matter what she says, does, fucks... what mistakes she makes... at the end of the day, she'll still be my wife. My life. The same person she's always been. Just a little more screwed up. But if you truly love something, sometimes, you have to let it go."

The prince's jaw ticked and he disagreed, Caelan could tell.

Sure, every inch of his heart was clawing at the inside of his chest cavity, willing him to throw his sack of shit bones into a taxi, storm into their mansion and kill that fucking usurper.

"You think she'll break him?" asked the prince.

"As sure as I ken ma own name. Because she broke me, your Highness."

The prince still didn't seem particularly convinced. The man had a personal stake in all of this. Among the team killed in Ukraine was a friend of the prince, going back to childhood. A close, personal friend. Someone he needed to see avenged.

"And Ogarkov?" The prince's sharp stare seared.

"He's ready to squeak. Primed, in fact."

The prince took a deep breath. "I want you knighted after this, and, fully retired. No question."

Caelan raised one eyebrow. "I couldna give a shite about a knighthood, sir. Give it to someone who really needs it. Maybe a footballer."

The prince pursed his lips. "That's why you're getting it."

He stood and left the room, two shadowy bodyguards peeling away from other hidden dark corners to follow in hot pursuit of the man's quick steps.

Caelan remained behind and took another offer of whisky, plus a few more drags of the sickeningly heavy cigar, which he ordinarily wouldn't partake of—but needed that night.

Tomorrow would be a big day, but first...

He had something else to take care of.

Chapter Twenty-Five

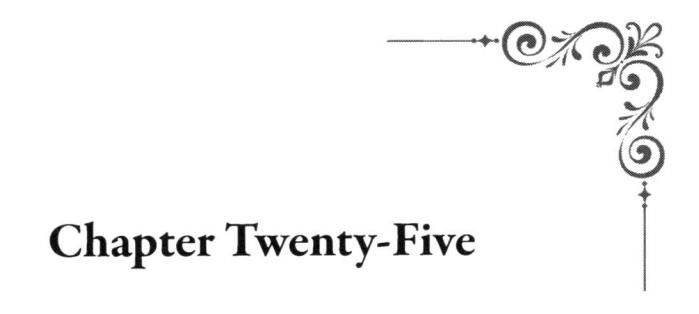

Flora

CAELAN'S RETURN TO the house came two and a half days after he'd left it. He emerged in the hallway stinking of cigars and whisky, his fatigues looking as tired as he did, given that he'd obviously not got out of them in a few days.

"Where's the cunt?" he asked, and I could tell he was a little drunk.

I had a tea towel over my shoulder, dinner in the oven, and the baby asleep in his cradle in the dining room.

"He's upstairs pottering around."

We'd got sick of fucking one another. Well, for five minutes at least.

Caelan beckoned me to follow him into the kitchen and he turned up the fan on the oven hood to its loudest possible setting. We stood beside the oven and he asked, "Do you trust me?"

"Yes." There was no doubt in my mind.

"Then follow my lead. Okay?"

I swallowed hard. "I trust you, Callie."

He looked as if his heart would shatter, as if he was barely holding it together by a thread. Eric chose that moment to enter and Caelan's hand moved so fast, I didn't see it as he turned the oven hood fan right down.

FIGHT FOR LOVE

"He's back," I said brightly, and Caelan plastered on a smile.

"For now," said Caelan.

I watched Eric move into the space like he'd stumbled into another man's house only to find the woman he thought was his wife was actually someone else's.

"Are you hungry?" I looked up into my husband's face.

"Nae, I ate. Let me take a shower, okay?"

Caelan had never needed my permission to do anything. "Whatever you need."

He left the room without another word, Eric trying to keep his expression neutral as Caelan walked right past him without a glance.

A weighted silence descended as Eric poured himself a glass of water and I dished up enchiladas. We were just about to tuck in, when he finally spoke. "Is he okay?"

"I don't know."

"He doesn't seem okay," said Eric.

"I agree. He's obviously had a lot on his plate."

God only knew what he'd been up to these past couple of days.

"Don't you think we should tell him?" said Eric.

Dread pooled in my stomach. "Tell him what?"

"Well, about us."

I swallowed whatever it was I was feeling. Regret. Fear. Disgust. A multitude of things I'd yet to come to terms with.

"When the time is right," I said, avoiding the insinuation.

I was fine playing the role, living out the fantasy of the long-suffering wife with a new, more exciting lover to keep her entertained while her husband was away at war. So long as Caelan wasn't in the house at the same time.

With him seemingly home again, it felt weird, and I thought Eric acted differently whenever Caelan was around. Sort of... unhinged.

Eric said nothing more and got on with eating.

In my heart of hearts, I was sure who I belonged to, and it really wasn't this interloper opposite. I'd known all along this was a sick, sad, twisted little thing that only felt good in the moment. The rest of the time, it just felt bad.

Eric kept saying he loved me and that it was only natural for us to love one another when we were both bound so tight to the same man. I'd never reciprocated those words, never actually told him I loved him, too.

Because I didn't.

Did I?

He was just... something on the side.

A way of vacating myself to someplace else. With someone I didn't care for so much.

LOGAN WAS NOW OLD ENOUGH to be left in his nursery to sleep alone and once the lights were out and the baby monitor set up, I left him to head for the en suite. Running the bath, I added everything I had in the cabinet and then some. I was soaking when Caelan came into the room, shut the door and knelt beside the tub. We'd found him showered and dressed in his grey sweats after dinner, already beavering away in his office. I thought that's where he must have just come from, right before dropping to the floor in here to tell me something.

"What's going on, Caelan?"

"If you say it's still me you love, I swear, I can get through anything. I swear it, Flora."

He was desperate. He didn't just sound it, but in his eyes, there was real fear.

"It's still you," I whispered, my eyes darting to the door. "It's still you."

FIGHT FOR LOVE

I ran my fingers through his thick hair and yearned to bury my face in his freshly washed mane, then have him crawl between my arms and cuddle me all night long.

He sighed with relief and wiped his eyes. There was something terrible afoot and I suddenly realised he'd been carrying it alone and it probably felt like the weight of the world was on his shoulders.

I looked to the door again, my eyes darting quickly between his face and there, just in case Eric were to enter.

"He told me about the Russian, the double agent," I said quickly. "Something about you scuppering the long game he was trying to set up." Caelan bit his lip, angrily shaking his head. "I asked him in the beginning why he wasn't mourning the team. It's as if he felt nothing, Caelan. I don't believe all he says."

My husband nearly popped a blood vessel at the thought of Eric having orchestrated it all.

"He maintains his innocence, but..." I hastily added.

"Nae, lass. The opposite." Caelan continued to worry his lip. "If you trust me, then play along tonight. Let me show you who he really is."

"What is it he's done, Callie?"

Before he could respond, Eric entered the room and narrowed his eyes at the sight of us conspiring. Caelan quickly covered for me, winking and stroking my arm.

"She says you've taken really good care of her while I've been gone."

"He has," I said grinning.

"She's been telling me about her fantasies of two men," said Eric, cutting to the chase.

I saw Caelan had anticipated this; it's what the whole thing had been leading up to.

"Aye, my whore, she is," said Caelan, his gaze fixed on me as he said it. "I always suspected she was a dark horse. With dark desires."

"She's had me doing all sorts to her," said Eric, and the acting it took for Caelan to remain impenetrable wasn't lost on me as I stared into those hazel depths of his, any fury he might have felt buried deep down. "I'm not too big to do her behind."

I kept his gaze and he didn't twitch or grimace, but kept still, perhaps imagining what he was hearing was not really true.

"Aye, I'm no small man," said Caelan, searching my eyes. I tried to tell him with my stare that it was sex, just sex. I'd realised it since Eric's comment the other day about this being about the three of us. Not me and Eric. Not Callie and me. Not Callie and Eric. But the three of us. This was always how he'd planned to get to Caelan; the only way in fact.

"I like it but as we all know, Callie is too big for my dark territory."

"It shocked me when she first told me that you let her call you that," said Eric, who was now circling the tub in the centre of the room, the proverbial vulture.

"How so?" asked Caelan, his restraint showing no bounds.

"We've never had pet names," said Eric, and as I kept my husband's gaze, I saw then a slight fracture in that wall of steel. "We all had nicknames in the squadron, but he would never be called anything but Boss."

"Caelan and I are partners, he's not my commander," I stated, and I looked up, eyeing Eric closely. I saw my words had driven home my point. He looked shaken. "Caelan was reinforcing boundaries as your leader while allowing his team to bond. It was nothing personal Callie, right?"

"Nothing personal," he repeated, still having to work to keep his anger battened down.

"She likes it hard up the bum," said Eric, obviously baiting Caelan, "but gentle in her pussy. I came in there a few times these past few days. But she says it's unlikely to result in pregnancy. Her periods haven't come back yet."

I'd been planning to start weaning Logan off, but I feared that would mean another baby if I did. Contraception didn't seem to be my strong point.

Caelan saw me gazing at him and seemed to come to some realisation. "She's a whore and needs us both, it seems."

"She came one time at the thought of us both touching her. Simultaneously."

Instead of looking horrified that time, Caelan looked pleasantly surprised as Eric remained stood behind him. Therefore, Eric didn't see that gleeful look in my husband's eyes that said he was well on the way to catching his latest prey.

This was music to his ears; that Eric now believed he'd won the prize he'd set out to pinch.

How to break a man, truly...

I thought Caelan had decided how he was going to do just that, in those moments during which Eric was blissfully unaware of the trap he'd been drawn into.

Not the other way around.

Chapter Twenty-Six

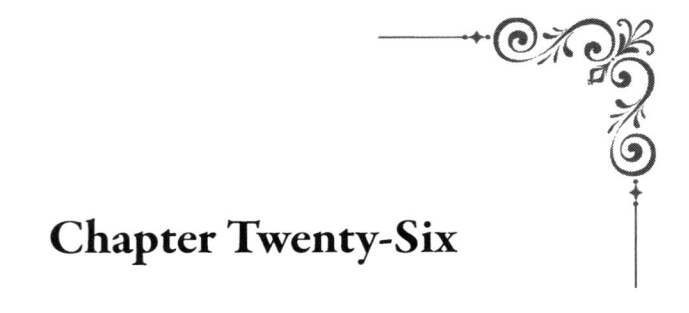

WE WERE ALL NAKED BUT I couldn't tell if they were hard yet as they knelt on the floor before the foot of the bed. I lay with my legs wide open near the edge of the mattress, my feet spread as far apart as they would go. Their heads were between my thighs. They'd covered me in shaving cream and had taken it in turns to make me bald. Each of them had commented on my anatomy down there, like they were purveyors of pussy or something. They'd really taken their time in shaving me completely bald.

"She's tighter since the bairn," said Caelan.

"How's that possible?" laughed Eric.

"Dinna ken, except maybe we didna fuck awhile and she closed back up, or maybe, she does exercises that've made her snap back."

"I do exercises," I confirmed. "But it's common, I hear. The body goes into overdrive repairing itself and some women's bodies snap into better shape than before."

"She's not wet yet," Eric complained.

"Nae, because we're getting her ready. She's no gonna waste her precious juices, are ye, darlin'?"

I winked and wriggled around a little bit.

As much as I knew this was a ploy to show Eric he couldn't break us up, I also knew this was going to be pretty much a one-time thing that I should probably not think too deeply about—and just enjoy. I think Caelan knew that too and was more relaxed now he'd been able to show off the delights of his wife's genitalia to another man. Something about the anatomical nature of their exploration perhaps reassured Caelan this night was about sex and nothing more.

Eric was given the honour of patting me dry and taking the first few licks of my clean, freshly shaved pussy.

"So good," he chuckled, and I writhed a little as his warm breath skittered across my clit. "She likes it when you do it like it's kissing."

Caelan watched how I responded as Eric licked my clit, occasionally kissing as he'd just described. The expression in Caelan's eyes as he observed told me he knew it wasn't the same; the way I looked when it was him doing that to me was different. This was just a novelty.

"My turn," said Caelan.

Eric moved away and kissed my hip while Caelan shoved his tongue deep inside me and held my hand as he slid through me, punishing me with a much larger tongue than Eric's. At one point while Caelan's tongue was writhing around inside me, Eric rubbed my nubbin lightly and I was shaking with my first orgasm in no time at all. Caelan's eyes were dark as he felt me spasm around his tongue. I'd never done that before. I'd come around his fingers or cock, but his tongue? Such a thing was an indulgence, a rarity to manage to pull off. It was the way Caelan was looking at me, as though Eric didn't even exist in the room. Feral and lusty, yes, but something else. Love.

For me however, the way these two men were obviously vying for my attention was a whole new level of naughty.

"Now make her come with your tongue," Caelan said, setting the tone as the one in charge.

"With pleasure."

Eric wrapped both arms around my thighs and tasted me, eagerly lapping the place where Caelan had just been enjoying himself. He was gentler and took longer to arouse me. Caelan gradually lifted me further up the bed, Eric following so he lay flat on his stomach before me—but not before I'd managed a good look at his erect cock. Meanwhile my husband lay at my side kissing me, fondling my breasts, my stomach, my sides. I reached down to stroke his hard cock and that thought alone—of their two cocks hard because of me—made me even more wet. Eric saw what I tugged on and grinned. It thrilled him, too. Caelan kissed my throat and I shivered with a swift but deep orgasm as Eric's tongue worked my clit again. He laughed as he licked up the juice of my squirt into his delectable mouth.

Caelan was the first to prop my heels on his shoulders and fuck his way into my body.

"Look how she stretches around me," said Caelan. "Dirty whore."

Eric stood by the side of the bed rubbing his erection. "She's gone full slut. Look how wet she is. Squelching."

"Lick my clit at the same time," I begged.

"Only if you suck it," said Eric.

Caelan nodded it was okay; and that seemed to thrill Eric.

While he straddled my head and stuffed his cock in my mouth, our bodies performing a 69, he licked my clit and probably got to take a taste of Caelan's cock at the same time. All I knew was that Eric's pink, smooth cock was delicious and his tongue twisting around my bundle of nerves even more so as Caelan's enormous penis rocked in and out of my body.

It was as my husband was fucking me that I realised why sometimes it wasn't so easy for me to reach orgasm with him. I needed to be wetter. We needed to give one another more time and effort. He was a big boy and for it to be good, we needed more patience. And then when it was good, it was always really good.

"How do we taste?" Caelan asked, right before withdrawing.

I couldn't see what was happening, but when I heard Eric groaning and his tongue no longer licking me, I caught on.

FIGHT FOR LOVE

"I want to watch," I said, feeling like I was missing out.

"Let me get ma cock soaked with your cum and mine first, Flora. Then let's watch him lick it all off."

"Yes," I groaned.

Eric moved off me and lay at my side sucking my breasts as Caelan pounded into my body. Meanwhile my husband held my legs open with his hands on the soles of my feet, my body rocking back and forth dramatically as I got properly fucked. Meanwhile Eric lazily rubbed my clit and I lay there letting all these things be done to me, sensation ripping through me constantly as I got fucked and kissed, then came, over and over, Eric's finger hitting just the right nerves and my husband's huge phallus filling me in all the right ways.

Caelan grunted and cried as he came and I saw in Eric's eyes, the sight of it nearly made him come too, but he held onto his desire somehow, as if afraid his reaction might not be well received by Caelan.

When he withdrew, his huge cock glistened and dripped with his cum and mine. I saw Eric's greedy eyes and watched as he shifted across the bed and lay on his back, his head right beneath Caelan's balls. Caelan guided his cock downwards and let Eric's mouth devour all that length and girth, not to mention the combination of our sexes. Eric had definitely sucked cock before, it was obvious. Caelan kept his eyes closed, probably telling himself it was me his cock was inside, not another man. I reached into my bedside drawer for my wand and stuffed it inside my pussy, frigging myself silly at the sight of them there, that enormous cock swallowed into Eric's thick, glorious throat. There had never been a happier man in the world, than Eric in that moment. The man was lazily rubbing his own cock, it was glorious.

Then Caelan's eyes snapped open to watch me and he looked feral, seeing me orgasming over and over at the sight of them. There was a growing puddle on the bed beneath me and I couldn't control myself, constantly spurting everywhere.

Caelan's eyes gestured I shift forward and half a thought had me straddling Eric and then taking him inside my pussy. Eric groaned and had no say in the matter, though he didn't seem bothered. I kept using the wand to agitate my clit and soon, I was rippling around him, again and again. His girth was much easier to deal with when orgasming than Caelan's was. Eric was a balm sometimes compared to Caelan's enormous intrusion. When I lifted off him, more cum dribbled down my inner thighs.

I'd wisely put my cap in that night.

Caelan extracted himself from Eric and instructed, "Lick yourself out of her."

Eric only looked delighted, a little dazed, as I turned on all fours and lifted my bum in the air. Eric did as he was told before rimming me, then playing with my pucker.

It all happened in a blur after that. Caelan lay down and pulled me on top of him. Rigid inside me, he was wedged deep and I didn't think there'd be room for more, but when Eric moved in and penetrated my backside, I lost all control as they both fucked me simultaneously.

It was like it wasn't happening to me, but it was, and the all-consuming tightness, their grunts, their sweat, musk and greedy hands roving my body, fighting for the chance to touch my breasts, clit, bum or belly was intoxicating. They were animals in those moments, sharing me in the basest of ways, their noises and eager hands telling me all I needed to know.

However, in the brief interludes of ecstasy, it was Caelan whose eyes I sought, Caelan whose lips I kissed, his heart I felt pounding against my own. His reassurance I needed above all else. He never once judged me for how I was enjoying myself, and in fact, it made him harder inside me when he saw it. I squeezed his hand inside mine even more fiercely and doubted Eric bore witness to the connection we were rekindling, not as he stared at the other cock between my legs—distracted by the physical rather than the emotional.

Eric came again but Caelan held on. I was incredibly sensitive by the end of it and knew I could take no more. That's when Eric got on his knees on the floor and offered his mouth to Caelan.

What happened next was equally arousing and disturbing. Caelan's big penis disappeared into Eric's face over and over and Eric just took it. Caelan didn't look at whose face it was he was using, he just used it, and forcefully gripped Eric's head so he couldn't get away.

Eventually the face fucking became so brutal, I had to look away. Eric was beginning to make noises like he was going to throw up.

Caelan gave a roar and came, and that's when I cried a little bit. Because Caelan immediately withdrew, tossed Eric across the room like he was trash, then prowled back to bed and into my arms.

Caelan lay nestled against my chest while I stared over his shoulder at the other man in the room. Eric was violently sick in one of my peddle bins, and for a while, didn't seem to be breathing properly. It took him a while to get back to normal.

After he'd caught his breath and stopped puking, that was when I saw it in his eyes. Pure adoration. For the monster who'd just hurt him on purpose.

"You see now?" asked Caelan, who couldn't even see the sight I could, his head buried in my chest. "He just wants one thing. Violence."

"Eric, is this what you want from Caelan? For him to be brutal?"

"There was never a more brutal man," said Eric, pure delight shining out of those eyes.

"That was the job he was paid to do," I said to Eric. "That's not who he is."

"Isn't it?" asked Eric.

"She's no ready for that side of me yet," Caelan growled. "And I only gave it ye this once so that now you can fuck off and die."

I swallowed hard. So. This was the truth. I'd married a sadist. He was no different to any of the others.

Eric looked devastated. "But I thought—"

Caelan still didn't turn to look at Eric. "Tomorrow, Ogarkov is going to squeal. When he does, you'll be bumped to the top of their most-wanted list. So as a courtesy to an old friend, I'm now giving ye twelve hours to get the fuck someplace else. Or, ye'll find yourself in less pleasant company come tomorrow evening. Do we ken one another at last?"

Eric looked broken, defeated… a husk. Then he lifted his head and looked right at me with those tearful eyes. "I really do love you, Flora. And I don't believe you deserve him. Nobody does. You know what he is now. We both do. But we can't help ourselves." He seemed to stare at me as if to say, "Look at what he just did to me."

I watched, horrified as he gathered his things, got dressed and left the place. The front door banged shut downstairs, and I thought, well, that's that. He was guilty, after all.

Or he wouldn't have left at all.

Chapter Twenty-Seven

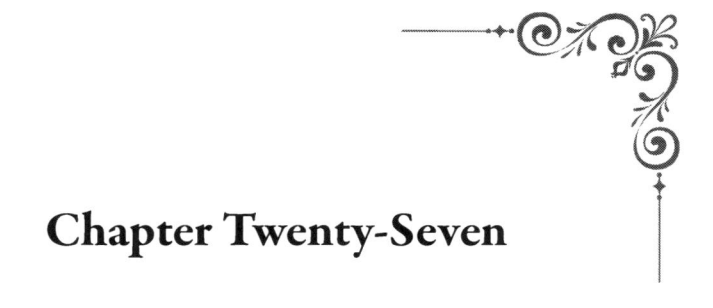

I SLEPT IN THE NEXT day and then spent an hour staring up at the ceiling, reliving the previous night. It was the mouth fucking I thought of mostly and the violent nature of the act. How he'd stayed fully hard throughout. Perhaps he'd really been able to vacate and imagine it was my mouth or another woman's mouth. Or maybe men weren't like that and any mouth at all would do, so long as it was wet, warm and willing. If not those things, then the scent of sex in the air, the things we'd all done together. Maybe they were what had kept him so aroused.

What I was yet to entertain fully was this notion that it had been the violence of the act that'd kept him hard. I didn't want to believe Caelan was like all the other men in his family. I also didn't want to believe he had ever done that to a woman.

There was no doubt in my mind that the pair of them were engaged in a battle of wits and I was caught right in the middle of it. Caelan had wanted to prove that Eric was only doing this to get close to him, while Eric had been hell-bent on showing me Caelan's true nature.

That look in his eyes right before he left last night still haunted me. *Look at what he just did to me.*

I'd watched the whole thing. How Caelan had stuffed himself far deeper into Eric's mouth than seemed possible. Caelan's muscles had tensed and his veins were popping by the time he was coming. Sweat was slick down his body. He'd enjoyed it a lot.

Was that what he really wanted from me?

She's no ready for that side of me yet. Perhaps a side of him only another man could take.

Caelan brought Logan into the bedroom at around 11am and handed me the baby.

"We've had a lovely father-son morning. Lots of cuddles, and he's had a couple of bottles of your frozen stuff… we took a bath. Played on the mat. He's getting so big, Flora."

It was these moments that made me forget about everything else. That light and pure joy in Caelan's eyes ousted all bad vibes. That fatherly pride was pure magic. Whatever else Caelan was, the one thing I could say for sure was that he was an amazing father. This role was the one he'd waited for his whole life.

"I have to go to work today." He stared into the distance. "But it's nearly over, I swear."

"We have a lot to talk about, Caelan."

He turned his head and surveyed me like he'd nearly forgotten I was still in the room. "Aye, lass." And there was gentle, Scottish Caelan again. A different beast.

"Did you push him very hard in training? Is that why he fell for you?"

Caelan looked down at his own hands. "I saw myself in him and decided he could take it."

"You made him like you?"

Caelan sighed and dragged a hand through his unruly hair which had gotten unkempt of late, having not been cut since well before Ukraine. His beard he'd trimmed, but the wild-man look I actually kind of enjoyed.

"I had to choose someone who'd one day take up my place, if the time came, like it did for Logan. But nobody is me Flora, that's the point. Ye ken why they come to me, Flora. Why they always come to me."

There really was only one of Caelan. "And you? Why are you the way you are?" I kept my voice impassive.

"I ask myself that all the time and always come up with the same answer." He gave me a grave look then and grunted. "It wouldna matter where I was born or to whom or how, this is me. With this brain, these hands... and this desire to vanquish."

I inhaled sharply and shuddered. "I agree." I reached out for his hand and he teased his fingers between mine, a loving husband bidding good morning to his loving wife.

Or so it seemed.

"I don't want Logan to be anything like you, Caelan."

His eyes snapped to mine and that feral animal stared back at me.

"He won't be like you. I won't allow it," I repeated.

I remembered how Eric had told me I was a wonderful mother and that part of that was having had a loving mother myself. That had been one of the things that had made me fall in love with him.

Yes, I was in love with Eric, too.

Whether I wanted to be or not.

Lying in that bed for the past hour, all I'd really yearned for was Eric's arms and that tender way he would make love to me. I ached for that ease we'd had. Like being together was akin to breathing.

I didn't really know what the hell I was thinking, but...

"Eric and I talked about being monsters, you know," I whispered softly, gazing down at the sleeping child in my arms. "But he and I only play at it. You are a monster, Caelan."

"Aye," he admitted.

"Would you do it?" His eyes snapped to mine again. "If I asked you to. Would you leave to protect Logan from what you are?"

Caelan's gaze softened as he looked from me to the bairn, his lip trembling. "I think I would."

"That's why I love you," I said, and carrying Logan with me, I moved towards my husband, letting him put his arms around me to hold us both. "I love you so much."

But yes, I also loved Eric.

Chapter Twenty-Eight

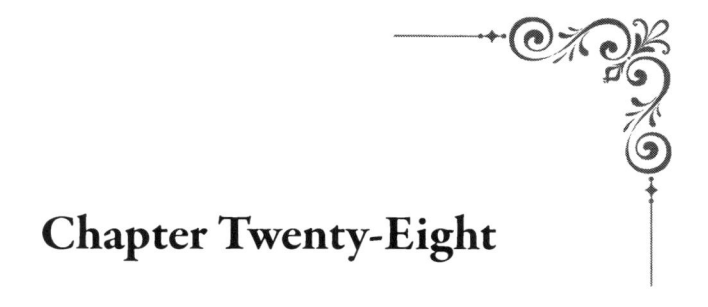

Caelan

"HE'S BEEN DYING TO speak," said Phoebe Thorpe, the blonde who'd been overseeing Ogarkov's time in the interrogation room.

Caelan had just arrived and was watching Ogarkov on the screens. Already sweating, sleep-deprived and shaking with nervous energy, Caelan didn't even know why he was really here.

"It'll be like popping the yoke." Caelan left the room full of psychologists, government bods and intelligence services twats.

When he entered the interrogation room, the smell of Ogarjov's sweat was high on the air and Caelan made a secret gesture for them to crank up the aircon. It wasn't a pleasant smell. Probably the man's diet. Yet the heat in here had served to work up Ogarkov into a state of anxiety high enough that he'd just want this over and done with, once and for all.

"I'm ready to talk."

"I thought you might be," said the Scot, "and your terms?"

"No terms, just truth."

Caelan raised his eyebrows and stood with his arms folded, hip knocking against the wall.

"Go ahead."

"I am proud Russian agent, not agent for the West." His heavy breathing continued even after he'd got it out. "But I plea for immunity at the truth I am about to unveil."

Caelan started to feel nervous. Him. Nervous!

"Eric Holmes tell me to return to my people with intel he offer freely. He gave me bank account I memorise so I could send him money. I recite to you now..." The Russian reeled it off and there was no doubt in Caelan's mind the intelligence services would be on it already. "One of Ukraine filth agree to let us go before you show up. His mother sick, need money, so when it his turn for night watch, he say, he let me and Eric leave. Eric promise the man his diver's watch. Expensive."

This was true. Eric's Seamaster watch was worth at least ten grand. Caelan had a couple himself but usually favoured something more inconspicuous day to day. That made him wonder if Eric had really risked wearing such a watch for such a dangerous mission. Sure, Eric had money too but not money the likes of which Caelan had. Eric wouldn't be able to just go out and buy another like Caelan could. Unless he'd hidden the watch in a pocket somewhere before the Ukrainians got hold of him.

Plus, in a war-torn country, how on earth would someone go about selling such a thing? Having spent time with all those Ukraine men, none of them seemed like they'd be the type to take bribes—especially not from some Russian.

Yet, it was still possible. Caelan listened as Ogarkov continued...

"You know that he speak Russian, yes? That his father was actual Russian. Changed their name. Used to be Herasckow."

Caelan's ears pricked up. He'd never known this. The coffee he drank earlier began to curdle inside his stomach. Maybe that explained Eric's unique looks. Even Flora had fallen for the man and she didn't fall easy.

FIGHT FOR LOVE

"So he tell me that his father, Russian military advisor Lem Herasckow is waiting to hear from him." Caelan had to sit down for this, taking the seat opposite Ogarkov to hear every single word. "I was, what you say? Shock. He tell me Lem should know intel he has and I should get it to him as soon as possible."

Caelan was trying his hardest not to slide towards the edge of his chair but he couldn't help it. Was any of this true? They'd never spoken of Eric's family except for his brother living out in America, the sadness he still carried around at his dead sister, and the junkie mother who still lived in squalor in a cesspit in Bromley. Eric never, ever spoke of his father.

However, this name Herasckow rang a bell. He *was* a Russian military advisor.

"I believe every word he say, damn it," Ogarkov exclaimed. "His Russian was so good, I thought he was one of us for sure."

"And you don't believe him now?" asked Caelan, rubbing a finger around his mouth.

"*Net*, I believe him. Still. Which shock me that I would believe a filthy, worm-ridden Englishman. So what I am about to say, I believe, is true."

Caelan ignored the slight. It didn't matter to him, anyhow. As a Scotsman, he could somewhat agree. "Go on," he patiently encouraged.

"He tell me that we should use you to make example. Find Caelan Cameron, he said, who would enter the country soon to look for us. Then the West would bow and scrape to avoid international disaster and it would all be over. All Russian pride would be assuaged and Ukraine would have to submit... and it would all be arranged before end of month. He said you would enter Kiev at some point and that our spies should be waiting. He would require money to keep his mouth shut, he said. About the danger you'd be in."

Caelan had to swallow hard and looked down at his lap. This was getting too close to the bone. And also, too much like a pantomime.

He gave Ogarkov a tight smile and asked, "Anything I can get you? I think I just need a water. A water, fella?"

"Yesh, a water, would be nice," said Ogarkov.

Caelan left the room and entered the packed room next door. Everyone was silent, some chewing their pen lids, some gawping at the man before them. He ignored them all and began pouring two cups of water from the water cooler near the door.

"What about the bank account?" he asked, and one of the intelligence people showed him their phone.

It was a Swiss account number. A newish one, but Caelan should have known. The SAS used these for emergencies when something terrible had gone down. When one of them got caught in a tricky diplomatic situation and they needed money quick to get themselves out of it. This was a message. Eric wouldn't have given Ogarkov this unless he'd been trying to help the effort, not hinder it. And Ogarkov could not possibly have known about the bank account without Eric having told him about it.

So, had Eric been playing the Russian for a fool? Buying time… or what?

"What about his father?" asked Caelan, feeling like a bloody ignorant pig for never having asked Eric about the man.

"True story," said Phoebe, handing him her tablet.

Jesus, the man was a carbon copy of Eric. This was why Eric looked so different.

Plus this was why Eric was who he was. It had nothing to do with wanting to escape Bromley and get a better life for himself. The military was in his blood, like it was in Caelan's. They were far more similar than Caelan had ever let himself dare understand.

Violent fathers and grandfathers, no doubt. The women they'd loved left broken. Their mothers.

FIGHT FOR LOVE

This passion for the fight, this ... unending need to crush.

Caelan quickly read the brief. Lem moved back to Russia in the early Noughties and rose through the ranks since he'd had no luck finding work in the UK and his marriage had disintegrated.

"This is the short and curlies of it?" asked Caelan.

One of the analysts came forward. "It's in Eric's file. He was questioned about his father a number of times. He hates him. There's no love lost."

"What the fuck does this all mean?" he demanded, and the walking brain that was Phoebe stepped forward.

"At the Polish border, Holmes could've told someone that you'd stepped into the country. As we know Russian spies have died by the dozens since the war began, but there are still plenty around."

"How else did it become rumour that you were in Ukraine?" said one of the intelligence gatherers. "Ukraine itself sure as shit would not have let it out."

Caelan hated this. Warfare. He could deal with the basics, but these politics? Manoeuvres, and such. He'd never enjoyed this aspect at all. These people and their twisted lies and deceit.

For a moment he closed his eyes and he was home, on the plain before the castle, breathing in the pine scent mixed with metallic rain and animal faeces. How he longed for that simple life. To be back there, safe.

"Let's see what else he has to say," said Caelan, storming away from the heady haze of screens, brains and too many questions.

Back in interrogation, Ogarkov eagerly slurped his water. Caelan returned to his seat and merely cupped his hand around his. Ogarkov eyed the other water covetously, but Caelan ignored the man and began again.

"What do you think Holmes meant by stopping the war?"

Ogarkov cocked his head, a small amount of delight glinting in his eyes, as if pleased that some portion of blame might be placed on Eric instead. "They would kidnap you, and given your hero status, they would use you as bargaining chip to achieve attractive terms, thus securing territories and ending the war."

Caelan stared into the distance. "Three kill squads came after me in Ukraine. None survived. Holmes would've known this. You would've known this had you done your homework."

Ogarkov's breathing slowed and he said nothing.

"What did Holmes really tell you to say to his father? How much was he going to pay *you* to get a message to *him*?" It had just occurred to him now that this was more Eric's style. Something more personal was the reason behind why Eric had saved Ogarkov, but not his team, not his career, not even the friendship he was meant to value above all others.

Caelan could still feel the way his cock had bucked into that hungry, desperate mouth, Eric's tongue running wild around him. The fury he'd taken out on him for having fucked his wife and used her like a sex toy had been red hot. It wasn't lust or passion or anything of the sort.

It was hate he now felt for Eric. Nothing but. A hate so strong he'd exploded into his mouth with such violence—his only desire to hurt Eric. Destroy him. Show him just how much of a storm Caelan was inside. A brutal, swirling storm of rage. At the world. The Cameron family. Jimmy. His mother. His existence. His entire life before Flora. He could hardly keep the rage battened down some days, but he managed it, because of her. Their son.

Flora was right. If she had to, she should go. Leave him. Protect Logan. He would let her go. He would return to his hollow work and go on, knowing they'd be better off, but he would die inside at the same time. Die so that they might live in peace. Away from this monstrous thing he was beneath it all.

Ogarkov had been quiet for a while now while Caelan stewed on all he'd been bottling up of late. Then suddenly, he spoke.

FIGHT FOR LOVE

"Eric Holmes told me to tell his father he'd missed him and he was sorry they were sworn enemies now. He also told me to tell him the location of where US and UK military equipment comes in across the Moldova border. That we could easily launch an attack from Crimea..."

"I need details," Caelan demanded, his foot tapping wildly beneath the table.

Ogarkov told him all he'd found out from Eric. Every single tactical detail.

"Have my water," said Caelan, before hopping up from his chair again.

Back with the team, Caelan saw through the monitors that Ogarkov was still licking the inside of the cup he'd just handed him, his thirst raging what with the heat and stress.

"It's nonsense," said Phoebe. "The location is just an empty warehouse and if the Russians had been stupid enough to hit it, all-out war would have been declared over literally a pile of metal and rotting wood."

Everyone in the room groaned.

"If that was all Ogarkov had to take back home with him, he'd have been laughed out of the country by his superiors. If Eric had wanted to make the fella look daft, then... he'd have succeeded."

One of the other analysts said, "Ogarkov has got to be bullshitting, right?"

Phoebe rolled her eyes. "Uh, I'd say the only thing that vaguely adds up is this theory about them capturing Commander Cameron. Although kill squad doesn't exactly scream kidnap or capture. So... back to the drawing board."

Caelan went to the nearest wall and leaned his forehead against it, trying not to lash out at anyone. It was clear to him now why the prince had never really warmed to Eric Holmes. He'd found out about his Russian heritage and deemed him a threat, despite all the extra processes Eric would've been rigorously subjected to in order to remain in the armed forces. More than most people could cope with, probably.

Caelan had been hoping to avoid what came next, but it seemed that was not to be.

"Are you ready to break him?" asked Phoebe.

Caelan turned his lupine eyes on the woman. "No holds barred?"

She looked around the room. None had any qualms about what came next.

Caelan rolled his sleeves up and grinned. "Let's get it out of him, by hook or by crook."

When Caelan entered the room that time, Ogarkov knew all pretence was out of the window.

He sweated even more and snarled, "So they let you loose now. Big man with no tools."

Caelan sniffed. "Tools? What do you call these, then?"

He held up his fists and blasted one right into Ogarkov's nose, breaking it instantly. The man flew back across the room and howled in pain, rolling around on the floor like a wounded animal.

The man began chanting in Russian, then added, "I'll tell you anything you want to know!"

"Aye, ah ken ye will."

Caelan didn't tell the man that whatever was left of him after this, it'd be dropped somewhere near the Russian border and he'd meet his end that way. Ogarkov didn't stand a chance of survival but at this stage, he still needed the man to believe there was a slim chance of it.

Hauling the Russian back into his chair, he handed him a rag for his nose and said sadistically, "Now. We want to know names. Addresses. Ranks. Those your president trusts and doesn't trust. Weapons stores. Codes if you have any. Cities they aren't keeping a

FIGHT FOR LOVE

tight leash on. People whose allegiance you might consider sketchy. Am I clear?"

"Go to hell, Scot," said Ogarkov.

Caelan had the man prostrate on the table before he could find his next breath. Then Caelan's belt was released and he tightened it around the man's balls, scooping the man's most precious possession upwards like it was being hauled for imminent removal.

"All names, or I fetch tools," warned Caelan, tightening the belt with the strength of ten men.

Ogarkov began to talk.

―――― ⸙ ――――

CAELAN'S HANDS WERE bloodied when he walked into the monitor room much later. Most of the staff had left, only a few remained, including Phoebe.

Out in the corridor, a trolley arrived next door to cart what was left of Ogarkov away.

"Weak stomachs," she said, to explain the lack of staff who'd gone the distance. Yet her eyes blazed with excitement.

He ignored her and said, "Did you get it all?"

"Yes... apart from that last bit you had him whisper in your ear."

Caelan smirked. "What bit?"

She gave him a look like he knew perfectly well.

"What did he tell you about Eric, then?" She bit the lid of her pen, desperate to know.

"I got you wee shites a fuck tonne of information. Let me have Eric."

Her eyes narrowed. "Tell me one thing, is he a Russian spy?"

Caelan shook his head, trying not to laugh.

"You know that for sure?" she pressed.

"How can anyone ken anything for sure?" he laughed, grabbing a discarded pile of napkins from someone's lunch order, then cleaning his hands.

"Please, come on. Whisper it to me, if you want," she giggled.

Caelan raised one eyebrow. "He saved Ogarkov's life, hoping to get a message to his father. That's it."

"The message?" she asked, panting with curiosity.

"That Caelan Cameron would make things happen for Ukraine, so he should leave the motherland as soon as things start to go bad."

She didn't believe it might be as simple as that. He didn't care what she believed.

"Come on, it has to be more than that!" she pleaded.

"I've got a family thing so I shall be going, lass. Dinna expect me to answer the call next time! I'm done wi' your lot now."

He left the place with blood still on his hands.

And a nice new titbit about Eric.

Chapter Twenty-Nine

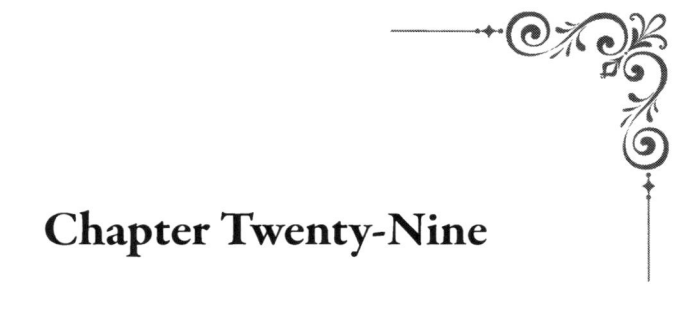

SCOTLAND YARD PROTECTION officers drove Caelan and Blake towards Notting Hill. The whole drive there, Rathbone fidgeted but said nothing. He didn't even ask about the scabs and bruises on Caelan's knuckles. Ogarkov had croaked on lots of things. Pity he couldn't have croaked more quickly, and more easily. The man was now laid up for his troubles in a secure hospital. They'd get him well enough to make the journey home, then dump him somewhere along the Finnish border, not all that far from his hometown of St Petersburg.

"Does she know I'm here?"

"What do you think?" Caelan chuckled, shaking his head.

They reached their street, perfectly leafy and in the full bloom of spring with blossom drifting gently across the pavements and roadways, people out walking their dogs in shorts and t-shirts... windows open, music drifting from a house or two... a couple of artists pitched on the little green nearby.

Blake inhaled deeply, nodding as if this is what he'd imagined for Flora and was glad she had it. As they were crawling up the street in their black state car, Caelan spotted a little spy trying to hide himself in the front seat of a vehicle he'd once owned, an Audi TT. A ridiculous car he bought years ago that he quickly got bored of and sold to his best mate.

The officers in the front seat spoke almost inaudibly into their mikes. When one of them turned and gave Caelan the nod, he knew there'd been checks done and nothing suspicious had been discovered in the vicinity of their house.

Well, except for...

Their black car pulled up outside the gate before the small garden path that led to their front door. Flora was immediately there at the open door holding the baby, obviously having wondered at the strange black car outside. Once she saw her father get out, she burst into tears and Caelan thought he never saw an old dude who was dying scuttle so fast down a path and towards his daughter and grandchild.

Caelan watched them head inside and then gestured for the armed guard all was well. They moved their vehicle so it was still close by but not right outside the door. Caelan used that opportunity with them out of his line of sight to signal to Eric to get his arse inside, too. Their secret signals could only be understood by the two of them. Nobody else. Back in the day, they'd only ever been able to trust one another. Sure, he'd loved his other blades, but sometimes there's just the one who really gets under your skin.

Eric came jogging down the street and stopped at the foot of the steps leading up to the front door, out of puff due to anxiety. "What's wrong?"

Eric's eyes darted to Caelan's hands and he gulped. "Ogarkov?"

"We had a little chat about his comrades today," said Caelan with a wry grin. "And perhaps someone you used to ken, too."

For a moment Eric looked terrified, but then Caelan smoothly transitioned into grabbing the back of Eric's neck like a typical friend might do, steering him indoors. "I canna believe ye never told me about your da."

"You never asked, prick," said Eric, throwing an elbow out towards Caelan and only just missing. "We cool?"

FIGHT FOR LOVE

"Nae, but let's just say I have one more ounce of respect for you today than I did yesterday."

"I can handle that."

Caelan glanced at Eric as they made their way inside. The man clearly thought he was in the clear. Thought nothing could touch him. Perhaps he really believed Ogarkov hadn't croaked that one last titbit. Well, he had... and Caelan was going to carefully hold onto that.

They passed the living-room door and watched as Blake bounced the baby on his knees, Logan squealing with delight in response. Flora turned her head and mouthed, "Thank you."

Eric patted him on the back. "Nice work."

"Let's no get excited, not just yet." Caelan glanced at Eric and sighed. "We should leave them to it."

Eric followed Caelan into the kitchen and they sat around the central island drinking chilled bottles of water. It was a nice warm day out.

"Do you want me to come with you?" asked Eric, reading Caelan's mind.

He shook his head. "No when she kens what you did to get her put away. I huv to do it alone. Before we get rid of her."

How clever he thought he was, this ingrate. Caelan was 99% sure that when he visited his mother, he would find nothing but a woman rotting away in jail. The only reason why Eric would ride along would be to try and twist the narrative in his favour.

Eric was buried so deep in the fiction, even he'd started to believe it.

Caelan felt a sense of purpose now he knew the truth.

"Why didn't you mourn them?" Caelan glared at Eric, the water bottle in his battered hand crunching as his fist tensed. "Hamish, and the others. Flora said as much."

"I never loved them, and, they never loved me," said Eric, steepling his hands in front of him. "I had no hand in their deaths. I couldn't have done anything for them. And we're taught from the beginning, are we not? That this is the reality of our work. And we lost before, remember?" Caelan thought of Dani and those couple of others; they hadn't had time to mourn back then when they were continent hopping. "The Russians likely wanted Ogarkov dead no matter the cost, cos they knew how easily he'd squeal."

Caelan had to agree that made sense and he couldn't deny it. Squeal he had, very loudly.

"Did you visit their families?" asked Caelan.

"Every single one," said Eric, "despite your prince trying to contain me inside London's invisible ringfence."

Caelan snickered at that. "He wants to knight me."

"Eh, why not," Eric chuckled, rubbing his nose. "It'd make Flora a lady, wouldn't it?"

"I ne'er thought of that."

"Getting slow in your old age."

Caelan felt a stabbing in his heart as he looked into Eric's almost pearlescent gaze. "How was Hamish's missus?"

Eric looked away. "She clung to me until she nearly ripped the arm off my leather jacket."

Caelan's hands became heavy in his lap and he bowed his head, shaking it, his heart sinking to hear it. "I'll pop in when we're back in Scotland."

Eric looked pragmatic. "She's a strong woman, she'll get through it. She's got grown-up boys nearly and they'll have families of their own soon. Life goes on."

Caelan used to think of himself as a bit of a sociopath, but whereas he exhibited only slight tendencies, Eric was a full-blown specimen if ever he met one. Knowing what he knew now...

FIGHT FOR LOVE

"We'd moved to London for political asylum, if you were wondering," said Eric in English, before continuing in Russian, a language he knew Caelan had learnt long ago as part of one of his missions. "Eventually when things changed out there, he was offered the chance to be welcomed home with open arms. My mother wouldn't leave her homeland and my brother was determined to provide, so... it was the best thing for everyone, or so it seemed. My father was a brutal, evil pig who made me into what I am, yes. My mother an apathetic junkie who was really no better as a parent. I yearned for a father, someone to look up to. I thought when I joined up, maybe you... maybe I latched on. You reminded me of him a bit. And he would send me letters asking how I was getting on. I would lie and tell him I'd won this and that. Maybe to try and bring him home."

Caelan clapped his hand on Eric's shoulder. "I understand now. All of it." More than Eric could possibly guess at.

Eric reverted back to English. "I understood how evil he truly was when Ogarkov and I got to talking."

Caelan nodded his head. "He spilled his guts to me about your father, too."

"That's when I concocted that plan which would've done very nicely if you hadn't swanned in when you had."

Caelan winced and rolled his eyes, continuing with the pretence. "Weeel, how was I to know?"

"It doesn't matter," said Eric, "someone, somewhere will find a way. Somehow, we always do."

"Aye, verra true," said Caelan.

Flora walked into the room and swung her arms around Caelan from behind, kissing his hair and repeating, "Thank you, thank you, thank you." She hugged him tight and he clasped his hands over hers.

"Dinna get too excited, princess," said Caelan. "We've got a long way to go."

"I know, but let me have this moment with my father. All right?"

"All right," said Caelan, turning to look up at Flora, who launched forward and planted a smacking kiss on her husband.

"He's back, is he?" Flora asked, winking as she moved over to Eric and wrapped her arms around his neck next, her breasts squeezed against his back.

Eric looked pleased as punch to have Flora in his vicinity, let alone with her arms around his neck and her cheek pressed alongside his.

"We cleared up our misunderstanding," said Eric, turning his head and kissing Flora on the cheek. "Does that make you happy?"

"Hmm, exceedingly. This day just gets better!" she yelled, before grabbing two waters for her and Blake.

When she was gone from the room, Caelan observed Eric rubbing at his red cheeks. "You really do love her?"

"She's you, but female," said Eric, smirking.

"She's much more than that."

Eric blushed even more furiously. "She is."

"I'm sorry for last night. It was a lot of pent-up stuff."

Eric swiped his hand out. "Don't mention it. It's done with. You're not gay, I'm not gay. I thought I loved you. I didn't. We had a go. Got it out of our system. My system. But I do love her."

Caelan nearly coughed. "WHAT?"

"I was never gay," said Eric, who looked absolutely serious, "just… searching for something."

"And you think that something is Flora?"

"I know it is," he chuckled.

Caelan growled, "She's mine."

"Keep telling yourself that."

Chapter Thirty

Flora

"HE'S GOING TO BE TALL and strong like his mother and father," said Dad as he saw me approach the doorway while bouncing Logan on his knee. "Not ugly like his dadda, though. Pretty like his mamma."

The babe was enamoured with the roly-poly man holding onto him. I could hardly believe he was here! But he was. I walked into the living room and shut the door.

"Dad, we need to talk."

"I know, I know."

I retook my seat. "No, you don't know. I need help."

He bared his teeth and was immediately on the offensive. "What's that Scotch bastard done?"

I laughed. "Nothing. It's not him. It's the other one. His friend, Eric."

Dad gave a wry smile. "Been sniffing around you, has he?"

Oh, he had no idea. "You could say that."

Dad smirked. "What do you need? A beheading? Four quarters and dumped in the sea? A beheading *and* a burning? Or just a plain old drive-by with a gunshot to the head?"

I laughed and covered my mouth. It wasn't funny because I knew he'd do any of those things for me and not think twice. It was the way he'd said it. Sort of like he'd decided his lot in life had been to deal with the filth of society and his services list was pretty simple, really.

"He thinks he's clever, but he's not as clever as me."

Blake Rathbone, one of the most notorious loan sharks to ever grace Great Britain, eyed me shrewdly. "Go on, love. Tell all."

"Caelan had to go away to save the world, and while he was away, his friend was guarding me against Sherry's goons." My father placed a finger over his lips, sighing. "I've fallen in love with him as well. I love two men, Dad."

He didn't flinch, didn't judge or look at me any differently. "And?"

"He acts weird around me. Like some romantic hero or something, and then when Caelan's here, he's another person entirely. I realised earlier while I was home alone, it feels like Eric... I don't know..."

"Buttered you up?" he growled.

"Nice euphemism, Dad."

He grimaced. "Sorry."

"But yeah," I admitted.

"What do you need, princess?"

"I need you to dig around, send word to every lowlife piece of scum in the city. Eric Holmes. That's his name. What do they know about Eric Holmes?"

My dad's eyes narrowed and he cocked his head. "Eric Holmes, you say?"

"You know him?" My heart was in my throat.

"He's the one who got the dirt that put Sherry away."

"Yes!"

"Why did he do that?" Dad seemed to have got an idea in his head.

"I thought... he'd done it for Caelan... to get the bitch off our backs."

FIGHT FOR LOVE

"Nah." The sceptical look in his dark eyes made me afraid. "Now, there is an Eric Holmes I know of and it's got to be one and the same. His real name is Eric Herasckow. White hair, silver eyes, tats all over his arms. A bit of a street fighter in his youth, so I heard."

"Shit, that's him... that's him!" I bit my nails.

"Well, then. His father Lem was one of the worst types of people you could ever meet. Worse than me. And that's saying something." He looked down his nose and I shrugged. "Back in the Eighties when we were both young, and before we were either of us married, Lem was on the run from the communists, and was working for the much more liberal Russian mafia in London. I got rid of a few motors for them. Well, less got rid of, more redistributed."

"Jesus, it's a small world."

Dad's eyes danced as he made his recollection. "Lem had a reputation for being bloodthirsty and evil all right. I saw his work once. He left a bloke cut into ribbons for having turned up five minutes late for a meeting." The corner of my father's eye twitched. "I wouldn't trust the son of such a man as far as I could throw him. No son of such a man could ever possibly love anyone. Not truly."

I covered my face with my hands and wanted to cry. How had I let such a man into our lives? In truth, I hadn't. Caelan had. Or had he? Had this all been, as Caelan had anticipated from the beginning, just a cunning ploy for Eric to inveigle and break us apart?

"He got the dirt on Sherry for one reason, I believe," said Dad, his eyes alight with a sort of morbid wonder.

"Not sure I want to know."

When Dad went quiet, I looked at him, sat there holding my sleeping baby in the crook of his thick arm, like he'd never known sickness or sadness his whole life. Still as strong as ever, though I knew from the yellowing beginning to form in his eyes that that wasn't true. Not anymore. He looked down at the baby, too and then he said softly, "He did it because that's what people do when they need a way in. They want you to owe them one. That's what every good grifter, conman and lowlife is brought up knowing before anything else. Make them owe you favours here, there and everywhere."

I pursed my lips. "What are we going to do about Sherry?"

"Caelan and I have it under control," he said with an arrogant wink. "Trust us."

When this conversation had taken place—if indeed it had and Dad wasn't just gobbing off to reassure me—I didn't know.

But Caelan had saved me plenty of times before. He'd keep saving me. I just had to have faith.

"Don't let that man anywhere near you. Ever again. Do you hear me?" said Blake Rathbone.

Not my father. Not someone who loved me. But Blake Rathbone was saying that. A former professional criminal was warning me of potential danger. And I'd be dumb not to heed that warning.

"If you say so, Dad."

"I say so."

THREE HOURS WAS NOWHERE near enough. However, we didn't spend any of it going over old ground; but sought to keep to the good stuff. Like Logan, the house renovations. My job. I didn't go into the doubts, unknowns or uncertainties that plagued me. Apart from Eric, of course. Meanwhile he told me a bit about his new wife and how happy the girls were. I tried to ask about his health but he quickly steered the conversation away.

When it was time for him to go, the guys came out of the kitchen and into the hallway to say their goodbyes. I saw there was a black car waiting right outside the gate out front. He would be spirited away back to the Ritz, and in the morning, be taken back to Florida. Caelan had wangled it all.

FIGHT FOR LOVE

My father kissed my cheek, then the top of Logan's head, shooing us back into the living room. "Go in there and let us guys have a chat out here."

I thought about arguing the toss, but then decided not to. I could spy from behind the door.

"Of course, Dad. Safe travels now."

"Bye, princess. Until we meet again."

Who knew when that would be. I tried not to think about it.

I pushed the door nearly closed but left it open just enough.

"I want you gone from this city, this country," said my father, "before morning. Or else I'll call in every favour I'm owed, and pay whoever wants to be paid, to hunt you down like the filthy dog you are."

"She loves me," Eric protested.

"Yeah, she mentioned that." Caelan grunted and so did my father. "But I'm forcing what's called an intervention to save her from the perils of what men like you offer women like my daughter." I heard nothing but snarling for a minute or so. "She doesn't trust you. She won't ever trust you. Not in the way she trusts Caelan. And honestly, even I trust Caelan. So you don't stand a chance pal and I'm here to save her from herself. So, she'll have nothing more to do with you because my feelings are that you are scum and if you don't leave, I will kill you myself with my bare hands. And, I'll enjoy it far too much." Eric had no response to that. "Since you're the reason my daughter is in there now, tormented and churned up because of you, ya stupid cunt... I'd advise you, very strongly, to get the fuck out of this country. Name your price and it'll be done."

"Ten million," said Eric, without any further protest.

"Done. Leave your bank details with Caelan. Then fuck off. I want photographic proof, timestamped, that you're out of the country before I pay ya. And I want Caelan here to have a friend put a trace on your passport so we can make doubly sure you don't fucking come back."

"Fine," huffed Eric.

"If you come back and come anywhere near her, Caelan will have one of my men hunt you down and gut you. Understood?"

"Understood."

"And you swear it?"

"I swear it."

"I mean it, fella. No funny business. I'll have you gone."

"I believe you. As long as I get the money, I don't give a fuck."

There it was. Money. So long as he got his money. Maybe that's what he'd been holding out for. Some kind of bargain.

I smiled because even though I was hurting, I'd known my father would know what to do and how to play this. He'd sorted it out for me and it would be done.

No good could come of Eric hanging around.

I'd loved an idea. Nothing more.

Who he'd pretended to be when he was with me didn't exist.

"Thanks, Blake," said Caelan, his voice uncharacteristically faint.

"Don't say another word. If you leave her again, I'll come for you next. Pray to your god and all the others that you can win her back. Because right now, knowing her as well as I do, she's about ready to run with that bairn and get herself good and lost. You hear me?"

"I hear you," said Caelan, sounding ashamed and solemn.

"Sort it out," said Blake Rathbone, right before banging the front door shut.

I watched out of the window as he chased to the car, got inside, then was driven off into the night.

Out in the hallway, I heard Caelan say, "This is for the best."

"Fuck you, Caelan," growled Eric.

I entered the hallway and found them both glaring at one another.

Eric rushed to me, trying to get me to look into his eyes. I backed away and Caelan snarled, warning Eric not to touch me.

FIGHT FOR LOVE

"Please, Flora. You don't—"

I folded my arms and stared at the floor. "You've got one minute to convince me you're anything but trash, *Eric Herasckow*."

Eric's arms flailed around, then he rushed to say, "Yes, my father is an evil, vindictive, murderous bastard and I was raised by monsters the same as you both were. Yes, I wanted to break you up, ruin your marriage, wreck everything... and had been waiting for the opportunity for a while, I admit. But I didn't create what happened in Ukraine, it just happened, and I wasn't expecting Caelan to fly out and scupper my plans. I never thought in a million years he'd actually leave you. But, anyway... I fell for you, I did. And he knows I love you and hates it." Eric looked over his shoulder at Caelan. "Don't I?"

Caelan only snarled and cursed the man.

Eric pleaded, looking like he was ready to take to his knees, "Give me one more night. One more. And I swear after that, I'll go. You won't see me again. One more night to say goodbye properly and you'll never have to see me again."

I lifted my eyes to look at Caelan, who didn't look happy. Yet he didn't deny me.

"One more night, to finish it, properly. You and me," I said, because deep down, I needed some closure. I needed to know if any of it had been real or if my mind was playing tricks... or worse... he was an evil bastard, just like his father.

"Yes," said Eric, relieved. "Yes."

Caelan nodded his head. "Then he's gone. From our lives. Forever."

"We're agreed?" I asked them.

"Yes," they both said, at the same time.

"Okay."

Chapter Thirty-One

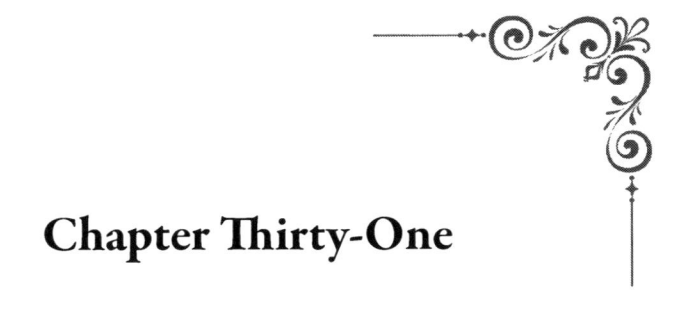

WE ALL ATE DINNER TOGETHER that evening, a strange kind of awkward silence having descended. Then Caelan left the table, took a shower upstairs and came back down as we were finishing dessert. He wore his going-out clothes and had splashed on lots of cologne.

"What are your plans?" I tried not to show my fear. Guilt. Jealousy. I could feel Eric's eyes on me, not on Caelan. On me.

"I'm meeting some guys for beers," he said, "and probably winna be back until dawn."

It wasn't like Caelan to go out for beers, but he wasn't exactly short on friends, either. I understood he wouldn't want to be around for what we were about to do, however.

He grabbed his keys and checked he had his wallet and phone. Before he left he didn't look at me, he just kissed the head of his son who was asleep in my arms.

"The sooner this is over, the better."

Then he was gone.

Eric licked his lips and said softly, "You pop Logan to bed and freshen up. I'll tidy everything down here."

I nodded absently because everything seemed surreal and it felt like I wasn't really doing this—but I was. Logan was nearly asleep having had follow-on milk for dinner. I was slowly weaning him off.

FIGHT FOR LOVE

Upstairs Logan really didn't complain much at all as I winded, changed and put him in bed. I sang to him for a few minutes and watched him after that, his puffy jowls so cute as he slept.

Which of those men would I choose as his father, I wondered. I wasn't sure.

Caelan was Logan's daddy but he had secrets, mysteries and strange foibles that lurked.

Eric wasn't his father but he made me—Logan's mother—feel safe.

Had I ever really felt safe with Caelan?

I'd felt protected, but safe was a different thing.

Safe was peace. And quiet. And calm. Caelan could never sit still. It wasn't in his nature.

I left the room reluctantly and headed for the en suite. I could hear him downstairs still clattering about in the kitchen which meant I had time. So, I made sure my legs, pits and pubis were extra smooth using a close shaver. Once out of the shower, I lathered on cream. Dabbed on perfume.

Brushed out my hair, slipped into lingerie and added a bit of mascara, eyeliner, bronzer and lip tint. The underwear was red with black embroidery. French lace. Balconette bra and matching thong. High leg. I told myself I wasn't going to enjoy this, but in truth, I was already soaking my knickers.

"Are you nearly done?" he called from the bedroom. "I'm waiting."

"Yes, I'm coming."

I went to the door and cracked it open a bit. He was lying on the covers in just his tight white trunks. He saw me peering at him and sat up a bit because I rarely wore make-up so it'd be something new for him.

His gaze was like a tractor beam and I opened the door all the way, then stood there so he could look at me. Eric's eyes drank me in and he smiled with nothing short of pure happiness. I turned around so he could look at my rear and he chuckled, which made me stick out my bum even more and look over my shoulder at him coyly.

I turned back around and leaned against the doorframe, lifting one foot to the wall behind me. He'd filled those shorts in a matter of seconds. I licked my lips slowly. "Are you going to come and get me, or not?"

He jerked his body off that bed and came to me faster than lightning. His hands landed on my waist and he dove straight for my hair to inhale deeply, then slid the tip of his nose along my throat until reaching my collarbone to kiss.

I shook almost violently with desire, my core throbbing so badly, I could feel every pulse of my heart. He pushed me back against the doorframe and tilted my head to him, then licked into my mouth and sealed his lips over mine, kissing me deeply. My hands were on his pectorals as the stabbing in my belly got out of control. He tasted of our Italian dinner and red wine but the taste of him too was unmistakable. Like cucumber and salt. I lifted my arms around his neck and angled myself so he could keep kissing me more and more deeply, our bodies pressed tightly together, his prominent erection digging into my belly.

When he lifted my thigh around his waist, I arched back and gasped. He kissed a path down my throat before sucking at the flesh visible just above my bra cup. He moved me around the doorway and pushed my back against the wall. His boxers were sliding off next.

I could barely see straight by that point. I'd never felt this way before, not my whole life long. I'd always wanted Caelan and I did love him, but this was different. This was a different kind of desire for someone I fit with. Who I really physically, emotionally and mentally fit with.

"I love you," I groaned.

"I know, baby," he murmured against my lips.

FIGHT FOR LOVE

He threw me up into his arms and swiftly yanked my thong to the side, then he was thrusting so hard and fast inside my soaked pussy, I didn't even know my own name. I shattered within about thirty seconds, screaming his name at the top of my lungs. My insides were on fire and I couldn't stop the clenching, it kept coming.

Tears leaked from my eyes and he carried me to the bed, lay me down with his cock still inside me, then reached beneath me for the clasp on my bra and released it. Off with my bra, then a snap of elastic, and he ripped my knickers clean away.

Kissing me, and rocking tenderly into me, he raised my arms above my head and I hooked my legs around his backside. He took the pain away in those moments, not stopping as I cried, shook and could barely believe this was now my life.

He kept on making love to me, holding me close and encouraging my legs tighter around him, his hands wrapped around mine in a lover's reassurance.

"We fit," he said. "We just fit."

I nearly burst out crying and begged, "Don't stop, Eric."

He licked my throat and I lay back, arching off the bed and towards him, wanting him deeper. His lips found my nipple and he sucked hard before heading for my other breast. His tongue slid between my breasts and lower until he slipped out, his tongue then in my navel and swiftly sinking even lower until he pushed it inside my body.

My hands were tugging at my hair, half of my torso was off the bed as he lashed my clit, then sank his tongue back inside me again.

"You taste like new worlds, new horizons and fucking roses, Flora. You taste like heaven. You are heaven."

"I wanna ride your face."

"Do it."

He lay down near the foot of the bed and I crawled over, straddling him so I could see his eyes as I looked down. He held my buttocks in his hands and rocked me back and forth.

"No, let me just ride you as I like. I want to use you."

"Oh, Jesus," he cried.

"Rub your cock a bit while I ride your face."

"If I must."

I rode his fucking face, letting all of that silken skin touch my pussy. His chin and cheeks, his mouth and even his nose, which slid inside me. He devoured me, lashing and sucking, growling and darting and tonguing. I came as I bobbed up and down on his tongue, my vagina clenching around him over and over.

He laughed and rubbed his face in the covers, turning his head to clean himself.

"My turn," he said. "On your knees."

I got on my knees without question and he wanked himself over my face. I held out my tongue and sucked his balls into my mouth whenever he would allow it, which wasn't often, he was so sensitive I could tell. When he came it went everywhere, in my hair, on my forehead, some in my mouth and some dribbling down my chin and between my breasts.

Eric gasped with delight, his chest heaving, his body slick with sweat.

"It's gonna be like this all night," he gritted out.

I was still licking his leaking cock. "I hope so."

I WOKE UP AT FOUR TO him stroking my hair, his mouth resting against my temple, my leg wrapped across his waist and my arms around his shoulders.

"I really love you, Flora," he said, trembling. "And I hate that I do."

FIGHT FOR LOVE

"Why?"

"I've only ever told two people I love them."

I waited for him to speak, but when I realised he needed prompting, I said, "Me, and before that, Caelan?"

"Yeah, and one was a false love, and this real love can never be because of that false love. How ironic."

It seemed he hadn't slept one wink. His voice was hoarse and he was speaking as if he'd been conscious this whole night and all these thoughts were so clear... the situation never more apparent to him.

"Why are you different around Caelan?" I heard myself sound harsh.

"What do you mean?"

"Like... a bloke. Blokeish. Like... carefree. Like... I don't know."

"Hmm. That's what blokes do... act like blokes around other blokes."

"But I thought you loved him?"

"Yeah. Past tense."

He pulled me closer and groaned at the closeness we had, the warmth. It made me shiver. I rubbed my nose against the dusting of soft hair across his chest.

"How could we do this to him? Leave him with nothing? We can't. This is dangerous and you know it is, Eric. It has to stop no matter how much this will hurt. It has to. He'll kill you. I know he will."

"Your father?" He tensed beneath me.

"No, Caelan."

"You're right," he conceded.

"We both know what he used to be. He's always a hair's breadth away from reverting back."

He sighed, teasing his fingers through my hair again. "Tell me you love me. One more time."

I slid on top of him and fed my hands into his hair, getting it good and wrapped around my fingers. I tugged his lips through my teeth and gazed into his eyes, loving how dazed he appeared.

"I love you, my silver fox. My lover. My friend." I leaned in and kissed him lazily, smiling into the kiss, then sinking my mouth into his until we were full-on kissing.

Until we were breathless, we kissed.

Then I went back to being wrapped around him, our bodies absolutely destroyed from a full night of lovemaking. He sighed against my hair.

"This isn't over," he whispered.

"I don't believe it is. But I want you to live, Eric. And this is really hard for me. I need time to sort out my feelings. I need to be a mum."

He kissed my forehead a few times. "Do you want more kids?"

I gulped at the thought. "I don't know."

"Is it because he's Jimmy's nephew?"

"Eric, stop," I begged.

"You've let me come in you, but every time you've been with him, you've used the cap or whatever, haven't you?" I didn't respond, too furious he'd picked up on that.

"I love my son," I said, nearly growling.

"Don't doubt it, but what about the future, Flora? What do you want?"

I sat up and stared at him. "You all make me feel like I asked for this, when I never did. I never asked to have the father I have, nor for the nephew of the man... I..."

Eric lifted his hand and stroked my hair behind my ear. "Baby, don't cry. I'm sorry. Don't worry about me. We'll get back to one another when the time is right. Come here."

He turned me so I was held by his body spooning mine. I was clutched so tight between those big arms of his, I felt a moment of peace. A pure, but fleeting, moment.

"I love you," he whispered. "Just remember that. When you're sad, when you're alone, know that I'll be somewhere thinking of you. Willing the time away until we're entwined again. Like this."

"I love you, I want you, I need you," I said, shattering into a million pieces.

He held me as I cried.

The truth was right there, staring me in the face.

I couldn't get past it.

I couldn't.

I'd ruined Caelan's memory of his uncle and we were broken.

We'd been broken before Eric and I got together.

We'd be broken forever because of Jimmy.

No other reason but that. His uncle. My bane.

I couldn't forget that he was his nephew and had loved such a man, and even if it had only been for a moment or even half a moment, there had been at least a moment where Caelan had considered murdering me for having taken away the only man he had ever loved.

As I settled and stroked my hands over Eric's arms, I realised there were some nasty bumps on the inside of them, just beneath the surface of his skin. He shuddered and drew breath when I touched them, and when I lifted his arm to inspect it, I could see beneath the tattoos there was a litany of scars. Done so that nobody would find them unless they were looking.

"I self-harmed a lot," he murmured. "I found that physical pain was all that took away the emotional pain."

"Of what?" I said softly.

"His hatred of me. Because I was softer. Gentler. That's why I don't act like I do with you around Caelan. I was taught it was shameful to be loving and tender. As a man, I mean. But that's what I am." I rolled back over and stroked the fingers of both hands down his face, his expression crumpling, lip wobbling. "I was confused for a long time, wondering. Not sure. I wanted approval from Caelan. Validation that I wasn't a pussy or a weakling like my dad said. And I liked how he pushed me to be better. It gave me some modicum of pride. He saved me, he did. But love doesn't save people. Love can only comfort, strengthen and bathe a broken heart in peace. Don't you agree?"

I lifted my mouth to his and answered the only way I knew how... with love.

As I was drifting back off to sleep, he whispered in my ear, "Until we meet again, my love. And don't forget, when he reveals the sadist, don't be afraid. If you're not afraid, then he's got nothing to revel in."

I wasn't sure I'd heard right, but I remembered the words when I woke up again anyway. To an empty bed.

And a broken heart.

Chapter Thirty-Two

Caelan

THREE DAYS SINCE HE'D left, and she was still confined to her bed. Caelan didn't know what to do except give her Logan when he cried. At least she responded to him; that was one good thing and gave him hope that she would recover, eventually.

That fucking bastard! If he'd ever cared for or loved Flora, he'd have held his hands up, admitted his sins and left quietly. No. He'd caused her even more pain with his sickness.

Caelan didn't know why she couldn't see it. How much of a liar, pretender and fake Eric was. Why didn't she see it? He'd hoped she would finally see it, but that hadn't happened. She'd only gone further into this fantasy, been taken deeper beneath the warp and weft of his web of deceit.

He needed to visit his ma and if he were to do that, he needed to know Flora and the baby would be safe while he was out of the house. So he had to do something he didn't really approve of, but was necessary.

Caelan packed her bags and made the call. Her friend Sophie's marriage to the banker had broken up and she'd moved back to London with the kids. The husband had stayed behind in France to live out his dream as a landowner. She'd returned to rediscover her dream as a project management consultant. It might have also had something to do with his wandering eye... and past.

Caelan called a taxi, put her and the babe in it and told the cabbie the address.

Flora only asked, "Why?"

"While I finish it," he said.

She gave a brief nod. "Be safe."

"I will."

First thing the next day, he left for the prison. A quick trip down the road and he found himself at HMP Bronzefield. He walked in the place and everyone was wary of him. So they should be. He had the ears of the highest people in the land and one word from him that any of them in there were bent—he'd have them down the Job Centre the next day.

She was brought out into a private room in chains. Her lank hair had turned grey because she could no longer buy bleach. Her clothes were stained, she wore no make-up and she looked every one of her fifty-seven years—and then some. This wasn't a woman who was protected or able to throw her weight around anymore. She'd been broken. No longer was she pulling the strings. So, Caelan's worst fears were confirmed.

Caelan watched as it sank in he'd come to visit her. She was dying slowly and painfully, he could tell. This wasn't her world. It'd been Blake's and all the other disreputable men she'd never known. She'd been along for the ride, but ultimately, she wasn't as tough or as resourceful as any of the men who'd driven her to this.

"Come to gloat?" Her head rocked on her shoulders like she'd been taking some strong medication. "Heard Blake's alive."

"Aye, I saw him a few days ago. Gone back to America, he has. The girls are safe. He has a new wife who cares for them. And his cancer returned. So, there we go."

She gulped. "Small mercies."

FIGHT FOR LOVE

"Canna disagree."

"And Flora? How is she?"

He wore an unreadable expression. "A mother now. We called him Logan."

She looked surprised, then chastened, staring down at her lap. "And you're here...?"

"Wanted to see ye one last time."

"Heard I'm losing the will?" she said, her grimy teeth showing as she gave a half-hearted smile.

"Something like that," he said.

Part of him had always wanted to believe it'd been her pulling the strings all this time, but another part of him had known that not to be the case.

"I'm sorry, if it counts," she said.

His jaw locked and he looked away. "It counts."

"You got a good deal really. The old goats took care of you. You got some dosh, too."

He inhaled sharply. "You should huv told me from the start what'd really happened. With Jimmy."

"I don't know what you mean." She closed in on herself, shoulders hunching to make herself seem smaller.

"You do. He abused you when ye were a wee girl. I figured it out, you see."

She flinched at his words. "So, what?"

"That's why you really wanted me to kill Flora, and why you stayed married to Blake all those years, because you'd loved him. Jimmy. And you were willing to wait to find out who'd murdered him." She squirmed because he'd got it right. "It wasna for money or anything. You were biding your time. And his illness made him vulnerable and gave you an opportunity. To demand he finally tell you."

She shook her head, laughing under her breath. "Do you know? After Blake's death, well, his first death cos it sounds as if the next one is not far off... I found all sorts of papers he'd kept. He'd had all of his men swear themselves to secrecy about Jimmy's killer. Signed away their right to speak about it and everything."

"You hated their love for one another, didn't you? Blake and Flora. Despite the decades and distance." He'd seen that love only recently, undiminished, as strong as ever. He was happy for Flora. He wished with all his heart that Logan and any other children they might have, then their children's children, would only ever know a real love like that. True love.

"Love, hate?" she murmured absently. "I've felt very little for such a very long time. Those are foreign concepts to me now. The truth is, I wanted you to kill Flora because I knew they'd clobber you for motive. You'd go down easy as anything. I didn't think you should've had life as easy as what you have had it. I just wanted to see you suffer even a tenth of my pain."

Oh, how little she understood about pain. His pain was oceanic, so much so, some days it threatened to drown him even as he sat still in the open air. The only person to ever really stand up for him had turned out to be a raping bastard. None of his family had ever loved him. Not really. Nobody had ever truly loved him, not until Flora.

Even though his mother still often spoke like a girl, with a mouth full of stupid lies, he saw her for what she really was. She'd lost her innocence so very long ago, then eventually, her ability to feel, her sanity, and now finally, her freedom. She'd always loved bad men. From the day she was born, sired by a bastard who'd got his student pregnant. Then the half-brother who took her innocence when she was wee and then left her for the spoils of war to cope with her loveless life alone. Making her reckless, aware before her time... worshipping a false idol, much like himself. Abuse comes in many forms. Caelan's had come in the form of a man who said he'd be home, but never was—a man who preferred to play the hero, rather than a father. Caelan recognised that now. Any man who seeks to show himself in a perpetual shining light is not a man. He is a coward hiding behind glory, trinkets and tall stories—for all men are vulnerable, beneath. Even Caelan. And he would allow his own son to see that, to know, it was okay to be a human being—to suffer, love, hate, fail, rise, cry... and suffer some more.

Despite all her hardships and misfortunes, ultimately, his mother had made her own choices.

The same way Caelan had made his.

He watched her as she waited for him to say his final piece, maybe berate her, growl and curse, whatever made him feel better. He'd rehearsed a thousand things he might say but now he was here, all he felt was devastation. For the person she might have been if she'd not had the beginning she'd had. And it didn't matter what she tried to convince him of, because he knew Jimmy had corrupted, poisoned and destroyed his mother—priming her for the next abuser in a long line, the precedent set. It had taken Flora's terrible experience with his uncle for him to realise, finally what it was that drove his own flesh and blood mother to do the hateful, spiteful things she'd done.

"You did one thing right," he said, "leaving me with Harold."

"Did I?" Her grubby face gurned in response.

"I'm the man I am because of him. So as much as you hate ma freedom and everything I've achieved, ye inadvertently caused it, ye daft bitch."

"Maybe so," she said, lifting her nose to sniff the air.

Perhaps that was how she knew what time of day it was, by scenting what meal she was due to be subjected to. In that room, nothing but the floor cleaner could be detected. Oh, and the smell of her. Urine and decay. She looked disappointed it wasn't mealtime yet.

"What does Blake say about being a grandpa?" she said suddenly.

Caelan thought it was a wonder she'd thought to ask. She seemed in her own little world.

"He was fair pleased, Ma," said Caelan.
"Good," she said, "good."
Still, no smile. No light in her eyes.
"Do ye get any other visitors? Any phone calls."
She shook her head.
It was sad.
So sad.
"Nobody from the old days?" he asked.
"Nobody."
"Not even bought a burner off one of the bent screws?"
She shrugged. "I could, but I'm done with it all."
She worried her bottom lip and he stared at her some more. This was no criminal mastermind in disguise. This was a woman who'd been broken beyond repair. A woman for whom the façade had dropped and all that remained was this wizened, shattered shell.

He began to stand up when her head jerked suddenly and she gazed at him fully. "When will I see you again, Caelan?"

"Soon," he said, "very soon."

"I wanted you to kill her to make it better," she said, "but nothing will ever make it better, will it?"

He slowly shook his head. "I'll come back. Soon. I promise."

"Good, I'll have something to look forward to."

Damn him, but he wondered if he might actually return.

As he emerged into the bright daylight of another beautiful summer's day, he wondered at Blake, at Jimmy, at his mother, and at other more recent matters.

They were all of them corrupt in their own ways, but he wasn't. In spite of everything, he'd made a promise to himself a long time ago to never be like them.

Caelan had been incorruptible from the day he became a blade, vowing to always put duty above all else. Duty had been the thing that'd kept him sane when everything else had felt alien.

That duty had made him feel like less of a damned soul.

That duty would get him through this, too.

He put his phone to his ear and a male voice answered. "Is it what we thought?"

"Aye."

"Okay, we proceed to the next stage."

"Aye."

"You okay, son?"

"She's got nothing. No fight left in her." It shocked Caelan that he felt sorry for her, seeing her like that, so obviously reliant on medication these days to get through the day. "Almost seems cruel."

Blake sighed down the line. "You have your mate Eric to thank for that, he did her over all by himself." Caelan grunted. "There's nothing left but twisted hate inside her. Always been the same, nowt new there. The extravagance she'd become accustomed to was the veneer that covered up the ugliness. Now it's on full display, whereas before it was hidden. It's as simple as that."

Caelan grunted down the phone, not wanting to get into it. "It's so fucked up."

"I know."

The man hung up.

Chapter Thirty-Three

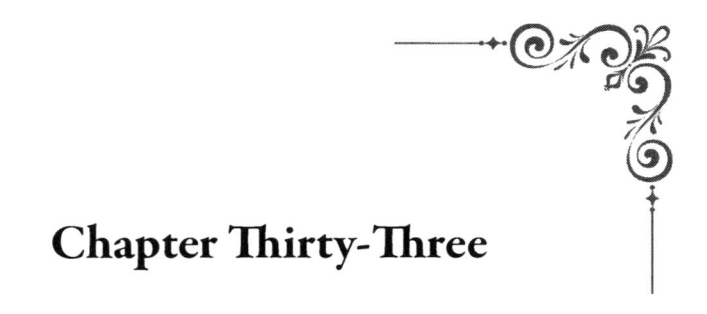

Flora

THREE AM AND FOUR BOTTLES of wine later, we sat at the small cast-iron picnic table in her back garden drunk and wrung out. A couple of empty wine bottles were rolling around the patio with the breeze and the sad strains of Belinda Carlisle rang out from her phone, not loud enough to upset the neighbours, but certainly loud enough for her to look a little pathetic as she mumbled along to the words. Sophie's face was tearstained whereas I was just drunk and angry. Angry and drunk. A mix of the two. She could barely keep herself upright. Mind you, she'd drunk most of the wine. I'd only had about a bottle because Logan wasn't fully off the boob yet.

We'd talked through everything.

Everything.

She'd listened as I'd described the hottest sex of my life, the threesome, then the dead bodies, the chaos. How it was a wonder I hadn't been hauled in for questioning yet. What moves Caelan had likely had to pull in order to cover up certain actions of ours.

"I'm thinking of making a run for it," I said, but she only flapped her hand around, eyes rolling with drink. She'd be of little use to her kids come morning. Maybe she'd needed this blowout and knew I'd take care of them even if she ended up paralytic. "I'm thinking of flying someplace none of them would imagine. Then I'd get in a car and drive and end up somewhere else so he couldn't track me."

I looked across at her. She gave no response. Maybe it had something to do with the fact she'd put her head on the table. I kept talking anyway.

"I love my husband, I do. Much like you once loved yours, babes." She sort of grunted, so maybe she was partially listening. "But do I love him enough? *Do I?* If I did, would I have got into bed with Eric."

"Maybe it was just sex," she mumbled. "Sex is just sex."

"Did you sleep with someone else?"

"God, no. I have three kids. I was amazed *he'd* found the time."

She couldn't call him by his name anymore. Fred had really hurt her, in fucking the local barmaid at the French equivalent of their local. It'd only been the once and he'd told her right after, as if admitting it immediately might absolve him. I could see how for Sophie who'd only ever believed him to be faithful up until that point, she'd had her whole world shaken. Perhaps his admission of guilt was due to knowing that in small places, people talk.

God only knew what he'd been getting away with when they'd been living in London, a ginormous city full of empty faces and strangers.

"I know you want to run away, Flo... but Caelan is a good guy. I know it."

I knew it, too. Deep down, he was.

"He left me alone and afraid."

"Maybe he didn't," she mumbled. "Maybe Eric made you think there was something to be afraid of."

I'd never thought of it like that.

"I should've known the moment Caelan told us that Fred had been accused of rape once."

"Eh, people are accused falsely all the time."

She grunted. "Then why'd he always wanna pretend rape me?"

I gulped. Okay. Maybe for some that worked, but for Soph, knowing her as I did—nope. She wasn't kinky or adventurous or any of that. She'd just wanted to be loved and taken care of.

"Everyone keeps saying it's a chance for me to find my power again, but it sucks like ass!" she moaned, sobbing into her forearm. I leaned across and rubbed her rat's nest of a hairstyle, her long blonde locks in dire need of some salon time. "Three kids, mate! Three! No bloke to help with the heavy lifting. And he's not even moving back here to be close to them. Every time they see their father, which even though it'll be once in a blue moon, I'll be left home alone, wondering what the fuck I did wrong and why I have a broken family!"

She broke down crying for the umpteenth time. Whatever got it out, I supposed.

Once she'd got herself together a bit, she lifted her glassy, drunken eyes to mine and said, "Sometimes I've sat and wondered if it's not men you love, Flora. But the attention."

"Now, hang on a mo—"

"No," she said, holding up a finger. "You listen. You've got at least one good man who worships the fucking ground you walk on. If you throw that away, then you're a stupid bitch and I never knew you at all."

She got up and wobbled on her feet, then stormed off like only a drunken woman could—bashing and crashing into things on the way to bed, but with her face defiant.

After she'd puked up for five minutes straight, I heard her mattress in the room above my head squeak—and then the sound of her snoring.

The trouble was, I hadn't told her about Jimmy. It was too difficult.

The only person I'd ever felt comfortable enough around to really speak about it was Eric—and he was gone.

FIGHT FOR LOVE

THE NEXT DAY AFTER lunch, Caelan showed up. I had fed and clothed all the children. Meanwhile Lady Muck remained sleeping off her hangover.

He found me with Logan on my knee and the two littlest of Sophie's kids doing drawing on the dining table before the French doors. The eldest lad was more withdrawn and had taken to pushing a train around, marvelling at the tracks in left in the thick navy carpet. This was just a rented house while she got on her feet again.

He looked at me like he saw a vision of how it could be between us—with lots of kids at my feet, my hair all askew as it was that morning, not a scrap of make-up on my face, nor a smidgen of sanity as I operated on virtually no sleep. He seemed gutted it might not be our reality.

"I didn't think you'd be back for me so soon."

"Neither did I." Something dark lurked behind those big hazel eyes of his.

"I'm not sure I can come with you, she's in a bit of a state. Had a lot to get off her—"

A bang behind him had us both whirling and standing up all of a sudden. I clutched my chest when I realised it was her, having knocked into the toy box on the floor in her clumsiness. Caelan gave me a look that said, "Shit, I thought..."

I gave him a look right back. "Me too."

"Sorry, I'm a bit... yeah," she said tiredly, before she collapsed on the nearest sofa and dragged the robe she was wearing tight around herself.

"Some coffee?" asked Caelan.

"Tea," we two girls said at the same time. "Lots of it," I added. "I'll sort it."

Caelan came to me and grabbed Logan. When he did, we snagged eyes and there was something weak in his stare, untethered and sad. I made sure the children were okay before I moved into the tiny kitchen next to the living area. Caelan followed me in and we threw our arms around one another, him gasping into my hair and me trying to make sure Logan didn't end up crushed between us—while also trying not to cry, too. Caelan kept the boy high on his chest and I buried my face against the bicep of his one free arm, my hands clutching the material around his waist.

"I love ye so fuckin' much," he said, sounding as untethered as he looked.

"We'll get through it," I assured him. "Somehow, we will."

"Aye, we'll get through it, lass."

I took a deep breath, willing myself to believe it.

"I love you, Caelan."

"Ah ken ye do, lass."

Chapter Thirty-Four

WE WENT HOME AND I saw he'd packed a few bags for us already. I was about to say I really didn't want to go up to Scotland and be stuck in that castle with a baby, especially as the days hotted up, when he said, "D'ye trust me, Flora?"

"Yes. I think so."

"Then let's go away and really blow out the cobwebs. If ye trust me, ye'll no ask where."

I stared down my nose. "Somewhere hot? With a pool?"

He couldn't help but smile wide, his face crinkling up in that extra cute way, and it was so nice to see that handsome man staring back at me I'd always loved but hadn't seen much of lately.

"Aye, perhaps."

"Goodie. I'm in." I stared at the cases. "Plenty of summer clothes?"

"Aye, but we can buy some where we're going anyway."

"Okay. And we'll be safe?" I asked after a few beats.

"With me, ye'll always be safe, my one."

I took a deep breath. "What about him? Where's he gone, do you know?"

"I've an idea. But last we heard, he took the Eurostar... then wasna seen when the train pulled into Paris. So... it's a guess, really."

Pulling my lips inside my mouth, I cringed. "Did he take the money?"

"What d'ye think?"

He'd taken it... and absconded. It wasn't looking good. Still, a tiny part of me believed that he was still, somehow, working to protect me. Perhaps, with a fool's hope to one day get back to me. I saw in Caelan's eyes his distaste.

"Where did you go last night and this morning?" I asked, wondering why he'd packed me off to Sophie's—when apparently, he was going to "finish it". I'd expected to be left nursing my broken friend's heart for at least or week or something. Not that I had my own issues and all...

We'd had to call up Sophie's mum and dad before we returned home; she'd obviously broken open the dam and needed people around her.

"I'll tell ye when I ken more about it all," he said. "For now, let's just go on a wee holiday."

"If you think it wise."

"Aye, ah do."

SIX HOURS LATER, WE touched down in Cyprus. Curious. Lots of ex-military retired to Cyprus, did they not? We'd also flown in one of the jets used by government and Royal family members, right out of RAF Northolt without even any passport checks. Perhaps Caelan had done that beforehand. Security-minded, indeed. To my utter surprise and delight, a rather tanned and happy looking Morag and Harold met us at the gates, Morag with her arms thrown wide open to us.

"What's going on?" I asked, eyebrows crawling off my forehead.

"An auld friend let us have his place here for a few weeks, seemed a tad ungrateful to pass on it," said Harold, with a wink. It was obvious he and Morag had benefited from the sunshine and a different set of four walls.

FIGHT FOR LOVE

Seeing them both in shorts and t-shirts was a new experience indeed. Morag had even used the hair removal cream I gave her over a year ago, for her legs were smooth! I couldn't wait to get out of my jeans and vest top and pull on a dress or jumpsuit. I hoped he'd packed those!

We piled into a large vehicle, one of the security guards we'd travelled with loading our luggage in the back. We were to be chauffeur driven and when I turned to Morag next to me, she shrugged. "They collected us and told us you'd be flying in."

"Did you come to Cyprus because you were invited...?"

"Harold's as mysterious as yer man, lassie. Dinna ask me. I'm just glad it's all free."

I sniggered and kept my suspicions to myself.

THE VILLA NEAR CORAL Bay in Paphos was situated on a hillside overlooking the sea. Typically Greek, with white walls and light furnishings, tiled floors and generous space. Huge kitchen! There was a pool and gardens, it was gated and set within high hedges. It seemed designed for privacy and safety. There were half a dozen bedrooms and as many bathrooms, massive sectional seating in the living areas (including outside) and incredible views if you stood upstairs on one of the balconies, looking out across the bay down below. It seemed like paradise. And strange that so far Morag and Harold seemed to have been staying here alone. Perhaps the plan had always been for us to follow?

Morag went into immediate hostess mode and made us some cold drinks, then had the bodyguard heft our stuff upstairs so she could start to unpack us. They had one of the suites on the one side of the property, and we would have the other on the opposite side. Because our room was so big, they'd already had a net-covered crib put in our bedroom beneath a window. Everything seemed rather pre-planned.

I didn't question it too deeply because I was so tired from my night with Sophie the day before. I'd slept somewhat on the plane, but I really needed a good, proper full night's sleep.

Caelan asked me if I was all right as I slumped on a sun lounger beneath an awning which jutted out from the property to create shade. Logan was indoors having a nap in his car seat in the living room, Harold occasionally rocking him whenever he seemed to complain a little. I'd changed him into little shorts on the plane ride here, but his ears would be ringing for a bit and I'd only been able to settle him earlier on the boob.

He knelt beside me as I blew the loose strands of hair out of my face. Concern was in his eyes.

"I'm just... taking it in," I answered. "I'm too tired to think or do very much right now. Sophie was an absolute mess last night. I thought I had problems but that wazzock of hers..."

"Aye, I'd had a feeling about him," said Caelan.

"You did?"

"Playboy," he grunted.

I stared back at him. "Too true."

I let the sun begin to seep into my weary bones, even in the shade it was delightful. "Have you heard from Dad since the other day?"

"We spoke this morning," he said with a hint of guilt.

"Can I have his number?"

"Nae, mine's secure, lass. So you can use my phone. But sparingly."

I gulped but appreciated I could contact him at all. One day you're bobbing along imagining yourself to be an entire orphan, and the next, your living, breathing father reappears like a phoenix, back from the dead. It was odd but thinking about it, the whole way he "died" had been a little bizarre, hadn't it?

FIGHT FOR LOVE

Caelan rubbed my ankle. "Anything I can fetch you, Flora?"
"Just keep rubbing that like that."
He moved into a better position so he could rub my entire foot. Soon, he was rubbing both. I smiled and closed my eyes behind my sunglasses, groaning. "Keep doing that and I'll be asleep in seconds."
"Go right ahead."
I ended up doing just that.

Chapter Thirty-Five

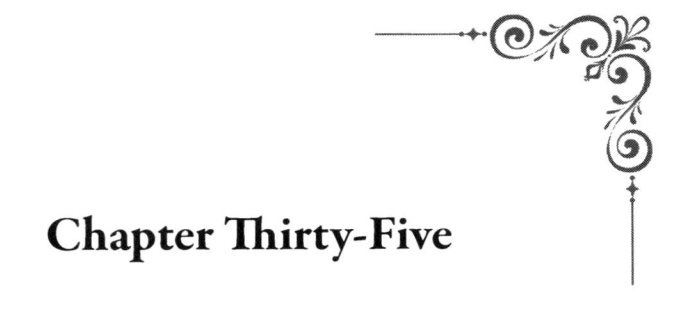

THE INSECTS WERE HUMMING like demons when I awoke a few hours later, having been somehow brought upstairs at some point. It was dark outside but still, a kind of throbbing heat emitted from all the floors and walls. The sheets were stuck to me and I felt sweaty, gross and groggy. I stumbled towards the balcony and peered over the railing to enquire after the al fresco diners down below whose voices had caught my attention. They had some luscious looking salad spread out before them.

"Eh, lass!" cried Morag. "You're awake. I plated something for ye."

"Let me freshen up and come down."

Caelan grinned as he ate with a fork in his right hand, the baby asleep against his left.

I supposed I'd needed the sleep, but I still felt very out of it.

With my hair damp and wearing just a thin playsuit and soft underwear beneath, I arrived to discover the table laden with tuna steaks, Greek salad, carafes containing the most crystal-coloured wine I'd ever seen, plus a bottle of ouzo, of course. Caelan was drinking the latter with water.

I took the baby from his arms and cuddled him close, kissed his head and bounced him to shush him back to sleep. Caelan casually wrapped an arm around my waist as I stood close by and he remained seated at the table. Out of the corner of my eye, I felt Morag studying us closely. So she perhaps knew something, but not everything.

Caelan was clearly merry because he subtly dragged me closer until I was forced to sit across his lap. Then he lay a hand on my thigh and just watched as me and the bairn reconnected. Logan happily sucked his thumb and burrowed into my neck.

"I'll fetch yer dinner, and we'll leave ye in peace," said Morag.

Harold and she stood up at the same time, him bowing his head in goodnight. Morag placed my dinner before us, shifting Caelan's plate out of the way.

"Dinna fash, lass. The bodyguard will clear away after ye done."

I raised one eyebrow and sighed in relief. I couldn't be doing with tidying up the remnants of what looked to have been a lengthy and luxurious dinner. Having passed a clock on the way downstairs, it was ten o'clock at night and there were lots of empty bowls and used plates stacked to one side. Perhaps the bodyguard liked to be especially useful, because my goodness, Morag was not usually happy to leave work for anyone else to do. Hence the elaborate stacking. However, perhaps on holiday, she'd started to get used to "being looked after".

Caelan kissed my cheek, "You eat, lass. I'll take the bairn."

I handed him back and my belly growled the moment I was faced with a plate full of delicious salad, fruits, tuna, dressings, cold potatoes, feta... I was salivating.

Caelan reached over to pour me wine and water and after I downed my water, the wine came next. It tasted as good as it looked. I had half a lettuce hanging out of my mouth when I said to him, "This is all so good."

"Tell me about it. The bodyguard is an ex-marine who also once worked as a five-star chef." I gave him the most confused look possible. He shrugged. "I guess the late nights didn't suit and he came back to work for the Royals at the drop of a hat."

"He's a Royal bodyguard?" I guffawed, and while I was chewing and also simultaneously pouring wine down my neck, I turned my head to see the man sat in the living room playing what looked like Cyberpunk on the ginormous TV in there. "Okay, maybe there are some perks to the job, then."

"The prince loaned him to me."

I turned my head sharply. "That bad, huh?"

Caelan shrugged. "Means I can go down to the bay while we're here and not have to fret about ye while I'm snorkelling."

"Why are Morag and Harold here?" I tried to keep my voice even. "Be honest."

"To keep them safe, too. I brought them out a week ago. A hunch."

I picked a bit of errant salad leaf out from between my incisor and the next one along.

"Do I want to know, Callie?" I stared into my dinner, willing him to say all was well, it was precautionary—nothing going on here.

"Nae, ye dinna fash yourself, lass. Let me handle it. Until I ken the whole situation. Okay?"

"Hmm."

He reached out and touched my thigh. "You look dazzling tonight, princess."

I turned my head and caught him grinning with a set of lusty eyes. "Give me time."

"Aye, I can do that," he said, "so long as I can hold ye tonight."

I agreed that he could and he took a big, deep breath.

"I winna let anything happen to either of you," he reassured me as I kept eating. "You're my life, Flora. I swear it. London, or Scotland. Or wherever. So long as it's you and Logan I'm with, I'm home."

I gulped and avoided his searing gaze. "There's a lot we still need to talk about."

"Aww, no…"

FIGHT FOR LOVE

"I want to know everything, Caelan. About how you protected me while Sherry was at large, what the danger was, really. I want to know it all."

I heard him swallow even as my chewing was noisy and the insects were still going great guns. "Raking over the past doesna do anyone any good."

"Humour me?" I asked, and turned my eyes to his.

He saw how serious I was. "If ye like then, Flora."

"We start tomorrow. Everything. You promise?" He rolled his eyes and reluctantly agreed, nodding. "I want to know about Eric and your past with him, too. Why he would claim you're a sadist."

"I'm no sadist Flora, but when someone provokes me, I can be a bastard when I wanna be."

I didn't doubt it and shot him a look of unsurprise. "If we're to move forward, I need the full picture, Caelan. I mean it. Don't swaddle me any longer. And if you need to know anything from me, too... I'm open to it."

He chewed his lip. "So you're really serious, then?"

"I am more serious than I've ever probably been."

He gulped, as if to say, "Shit."

I LAY ON TOP OF THE sheets in a vest and knickers, some of the sheets bunched between my sweaty thighs. I wanted to put the air-con on in the room but Caelan was afraid the baby would get cold. He was asleep in his crib with the window cracked just slightly so he might benefit from a bit of breeze. All he wore was a nappy and vest, the nets protecting him from mozzies.

The lights from outside cast big shadows around the room because we had left the balcony doors open for air. So I had some faith that we were moderately safe here.

Caelan lay there nearly naked aside from a set of very small holiday pants, as he called them. Y-fronts but even smaller! Ridiculous man with all those long, graceful lines.

"I'm not tired now," I chuckled, just as he moaned a yawn.

"Is that a hint?" he said, one side of his mouth tipping up in a grin.

"No. I think I'm getting my period. I'm retaining water and feel an ache. Here." I pointed at my lower belly and just at the centre of it, there'd begun a dull ache.

He reached out and ran his fingers over my bit of swollen midriff. "Poor baby."

"Is everything going to be all right, Callie?" I reached out and stroked his face which he'd shorn a lot since earlier. Probably the heat. But he wasn't shaved smooth, not like that other man...

Before the image had chance to flash in my vision, his jaw ticked and he spoke softly, "I want to tell you yeah, but I honestly dinna ken."

I rolled onto my back and looked up at the ceiling. "Sophie was angry with me last night."

"Why?"

"Says I don't know what I've got. Etcetera."

"D'ye ken what you've got?"

"Yes, but... I have to be honest, Caelan. The Jimmy thing still haunts me." There, it was out. Finally. I'd got it out.

"It does me, too. It's no easy."

I breathed a sigh of relief. Not that I was jumping for joy at his own unhappiness. Just that I wasn't alone with it made my unease... easier.

"It's difficult for me," he continued, "and that's no anything you've done. I'm still processing what he did. What he was. How ashamed of him I am."

FIGHT FOR LOVE

I heard the dreadful devastation in his tone of voice. He'd not said a thing up to now about how he'd struggled with it. I held my breath waiting for more.

"Harold tries to get me to talk about it. I find myself always changing the subject."

"We're both guilty of that." I sucked in breath, shuddering in spite of the heat.

"I swear he never displayed those... qualities around me." I rolled back onto my side and observed as he lay there staring up at the ceiling, his fingers fidgeting on his chest. "Maybe I remember some stuff through rose-tinted spectacles, but I never—"

"You were a kid," I started to say, because I heard the pain in his voice, couldn't bear it—wanted to smother it, even.

"I was a young fella when he died who still had a child's perception of his uncle as a hero. With the benefit of all my life experience now, I've had to reset how I perceive him, knowing what I know now."

"Again, you were a kid, it's okay—" I couldn't bear to hear him speak this way, would do anything to hear him not sound so broken.

"I dinna wish for ma son to grow up thinking he has to be me, Flora. I wouldna want that for him at all." Caelan took a deep breath and I held in my tears. "I want him to know it's okay to be emotional, because I was ne'er allowed to be and a lot... festered." He swallowed hard and I reached out, stroking his chest. He smiled at that and it warmed me.

"I can understand how it could do that," I said softly.

"Logan doesna have to live up to me," said Caelan forthrightly. "What I am should ne'er be repeated. The things that shaped me would ordinarily kill most other people."

I stroked his hair behind his ear. "I know."

My heart pounded with a need to comfort him, be there for him. I'd longed for him to be this open with me. Pleaded with God to make it happen. I held my breath.

"Carrying things, this is what I do, Flora. What I'll always do." He glanced at me and I saw the full force of his devastation, the look in his eyes nearly reducing me to a wreck. I quickly swiped away a tear after he returned to staring at the ceiling. "For you and the bairn."

"I know," I whispered, swiping at another tear.

"When ma mother wanted you deid, I didna rush to agree with her. My training taught me to research... find out for maself. And I didna believe for one second you were a stone-cold killer, not as I watched ye, found out about yer life. And you're no murderer, sweet Flora. You're still the woman I married." I reached for his hand and squeezed it, taking in deep breaths. "I did want to punish Blake. I believed he was the real culprit. For a time, I might'a let him believe I was trailing ye to have ma wicked way."

"Hmm, that bit sounds true," I chuckled, and Caelan smiled, too.

"I ne'er, not even for a second, ever considered hurting you, Flora. On my life. On Logan's. I swear it." I believed him as he spoke passionately. "But did I want to find out the truth? Aye, more than anything. I wanted to understand if it was my mother wanting you deid for vengeance, or for money—"

"Did you ever find out? Why she did the things she did...?"

He yawned loudly. "Can we talk about this some more later, Flora?"

"Yes, sure."

"Give me your hand."

I reached over and he took my hand, placing it over his heart. "This beats for you and you alone, woman. When I've told you everything, you'll know that for a certainty. Okay?"

FIGHT FOR LOVE

Rubbing my hand over his heart, I thought I did know that already.

That had never been the issue.

It was the difficulty of this shared history.

And the fact I loved Eric now, too.

I looked up at his face and saw he lay peacefully asleep. Yet for a few hours more, I lay staring at my husband, the man who'd made me a mother.

No, he and Jimmy were nothing alike.

It was that I was missing half the story.

Caelan kept so much locked up inside.

I felt like I hardly knew him... yet.

Chapter Thirty-Six

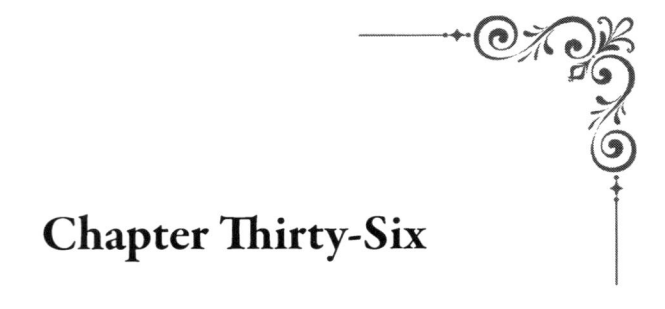

I WOKE ALONE THE NEXT morning, aside from Logan who was cooing in his cradle and wanting out. We spent some precious moments just us, but as I fed him, I realised he was getting less interested in the boob. It felt like it was time.

When I went to the toilet, I had indeed got my period. My hormones were changing and getting back to normal. After I'd sorted myself out, the terrible cramps started and I knew this was going to be several periods in one go. Soph had warned me about this.

"Morag!" I yelled.

She came running and saw me crouched on the floor beside the bed, doubled over.

"Period pain," I murmured.

"Painkillers? Tea? Bed?" she said quickly, helping me back under the covers.

"All of those. And look after Logan for me?"

"Done... and done." She rushed to the cradle. "Aww, braw lad. Had some brekkie already have ye laddie? Beauty."

She left him where he was. "Himself went swimming down in the sea. Will be back in a jiffy with yer medicine."

"Thank you so much, Morag."

After the medicine kicked in, I dozed for a bit. When I next woke, Caelan was on the bed beside me reading a magazine about life in Cyprus.

"Hey, you," he said. "Are you okay?"

"Not especially."

When I got up, I felt really heavy and achy.

"Flo, go steady, honey," he said, and those words left me feeling scared.

He only spoke to me like that when something was wrong.

When I saw where his eyes had gone, I knew…

…and when I got to the bathroom, yes, I'd soaked through.

I sat on the toilet and my thighs wobbled as a really sharp pain tore through me. I hadn't shut the door so Caelan stood there looking concerned.

"Is this…?" He seemed to think it wasn't just a period.

"Six months' worth of periods? Yes."

I sat and winced, and even covered my face as I suffered through more pain, and that's when I passed something that was more than just a bit of blood and my whole body shook. I opened my legs, looked down into the basin and sobbed. Caelan's alarm was palpable and he knelt next to me, took my hand and whispered it was going to be okay. My chin wouldn't stop wobbling and I was pretty sure it was a miscarriage.

"I love you," he said, when all I could do was cry.

He only left my side to start the shower running. I wasn't really conscious as he steered me there and pulled my clothes off before I got inside. I sat in a corner and watched as the pink trail from my body swirled down the plughole.

Then there was a big soft fluffy towel, his arms, and some wadded paper between my legs. Then my knickers filled with pads. An old t-shirt of his which drowned and was the thing that made me want to weep the most.

Morag was just finishing changing the bed when I emerged into the room. She held her arms out to me like she'd heard me crying, knew exactly what it was all about, and didn't need me to say a word. I cried into her heavy bosom as we sat side by side on the bed.

"There, there, lassie, there, there. This wasna the one. This wasna the one." She stroked my hair while Caelan stood behind us, his presence evident but his silence telling.

It was more likely to have been…

"Harold went for a doctor just as a precaution. We'll get ye right again, lass. We'll fix ye up once more, I swear it," she promised, still stroking my hair with a mother's touch.

"Can you get me some more pain relief?" I asked.

"I dinna ken where…" Caelan started to say.

"I'll go."

While she was gone, I turned around and begged, "Please, Caelan."

He came to me instantly and dragged me onto his lap. I bawled into his chest, fisting the material. He shuddered and shook and that's when I knew, even if it had stuck, he'd have loved it anyway. Because it would've been a part of me.

I was eventually soothed, my head buried in his shoulder, when Morag returned with the doctor.

A quick feel of my tummy, and a quick look in the toilet bowl, and he was prescribing antibiotics, hot water bottles and more pain meds.

That's when it sank in: what the fucking hell had I been doing with Eric?

That bastard had wanted this to happen, hadn't he?

Anger brewed silently. At myself. At him.

At the world.

Chapter Thirty-Seven

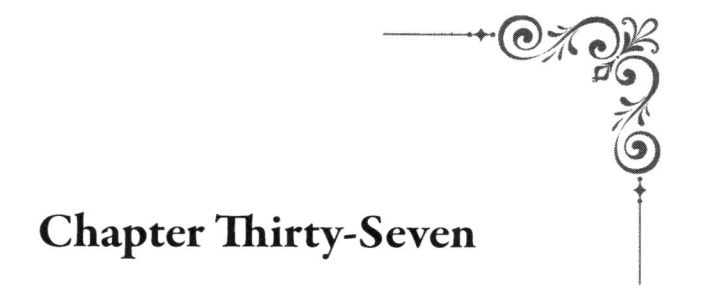

HE NEVER LEFT MY SIDE over the next twenty-four hours, eating his meals beside me, making me chew through bits of fruit and bread, drink water and tea. He read his magazines, even a book, while we stayed in that bed. Logan squawked from downstairs an awful lot and Caelan would play with the boy on his lap whenever Harold or Morag brought him up. A little of the time, he'd lay beside me and we'd stare at one another, Logan reaching out to touch my hand. He would grin and chortle. I would try to smile. He didn't seem to notice how sad I was.

"I think we should take a stroll," said Caelan, just after lunch.

"Why?"

"Fresh air, and maybe, we can talk."

"Am I not getting rid of you, then?"

"Not in a million years."

I heard the seriousness in his tone of voice even as my face was pressed into the pillow. The bedding was fresh yesterday and still smelt lovely even as I'd cried, sweated and spilled my tea in it since the day before.

"Where?"

"Down at the bay. It'll be quiet. People will be at lunch. They like long lunches here."

"Will you dress me?"

"Aye, I can dress ye. Might look like a bag lady, though."

"Bag lady is fine right now."

He rustled through the drawers and after I'd changed my pads again, I stepped into knee-length shorts and a white t-shirt. Perfect.

He drove us there while Harold and Morag stayed behind, the baby joining us. Caelan donned the papoose and after just a few minutes of walking, the babe slept soundly against Daddy's chest. It was like that familiar warmth and smell told him to rest awhile. It was a rare kind of magic, that thing between them.

The smell of the sea was a tiny balm and the sand between my toes felt so good having removed my flip-flops. My big dark glasses hid the shadows.

"There's something ye should ken about me," he said, "and it's a wee bit silly really."

"You're a secret knitter?" I glanced at him, cracking half a smile.

He barked out laughing. "Nae, lass. Although, I can knit. Harold taught me, he did. Scotsman's needs and all, on those hills."

"Bawbag warmers and all that."

He wrapped an arm around my neck and dragged me closer, kissing my hair. "There's ma Flora again."

I put an arm around his waist and leaned into him while he wrapped an arm around my shoulders. "Is it wrong that I should be relieved? That I feel like I'm being cleansed? Relieved of something."

"Nae, I dinna think so. This is a sign whatever it was, it wasna meant to be. The future isna determined. It's yet to be had."

I was in agreement with him, though this feeling of emptiness, hollowness, like being scooped out, continued to rake its nails down my very soul.

"As I was saying, there's a secret ye ought to ken about me," he continued, "and it'd help ye make sense o' this shithead ye married."

"Go on," I lightly giggled.

"I've lived all of my adult life chasing one thing."

FIGHT FOR LOVE

I raised my eyebrows. "That tree thing? The caber, or whatever you call it. Or is it wheels of cheese you lot chase up there?"

He tipped his head back, his nostrils flaring as he resisted laughing.

Then he gave me a wink. "I'm driven by duty. I canna help myself."

"Duty?" I took a deep breath. "You mean, like, doing the right thing?"

I was suddenly afraid of what else he had to say.

He quickly cut off my doubts, adding, "To make amends, for the thing I did when I was wee."

"I see."

"That's why I rush off to save the day; why I am the best of the best. Even now, I canna relax and wanna be off somewhere running, tossing cabers and javelins and whatnot." I guffawed in response. "Because I never feel like I've atoned enough."

I rubbed my forehead. "I never thought."

"Maybe for a wee second I imagined you'd be better off with Eric, or I thought, in some sick, twisted way that letting you go so you could come back to me might be a nice test that'd make me feel better."

I stared at my feet as they sank into the sand, fascinated as my footsteps changed the way it looked. "That's why I never got involved with anyone before you. Not seriously, anyway. I felt unclean."

"I ken that feeling," he said, and reached over to kiss my hair again. "But although it steered me for so many long years, to become something I could never turn ma back on now, my sense of duty wasna what took me to Ukraine or kept me there, okay?"

I turned my head, eyeing him suspiciously. "No?"

"It was that I kent something had gone wrong. And something wasna right. I'd promised to stand at your side, with the bairn, and I'd meant to keep that promise. But all ma experience, all that wisdom, was telling me something was damn well wrong and I was right, Flora. I was on the money."

He wasn't wearing sunnies and in his eyes, as I turned my head slowly to catch what he was getting at, I saw vindication and anger.

"Eric did engineer it?"

"Aye. I'm just waiting for the proof that that sleekit yin meant for all that happened, and all that has taken place since."

The truth shattered through me. "You saw Sherry, didn't you? Visited her. And she had nothing to do with any of it."

"Aye, there can be no doubt, Flora. She's weak. Given up. She's a nobody in there. I got a couple of the screws cornered and forced some truths from them. They confirmed she has no burners, she sees nobody; she eats, sleeps and watches TV, that's it. Besides, I saw it with ma own two eyes. A woman broken. A woman, nae, more like a small girl in an old woman's clothes. She's no got the wherewithal. She doesna care about Blake. She's happy enough he's on his way to the afterlife, too."

I sniffed and tried not to let the image of that woman into my head. "Are you sad she's going to die in prison?"

"No. She hasna been anything to me in so long. I feel sorry for her, though. She really did look wrecked. A shadow of herself. But it's true what Blake said: she needed the money to somehow get through life. Without it, she's now who she really is. A shell. That's it. The victim she is beneath never went away. The life he gave her just made it easier for her somehow to hide her true self."

I sifted through the thoughts in my head. It wasn't easy. So much still unanswered.

"She couldn't be playing a really good game, Caelan? She's not as daft as she seems."

He was vehement. "Trust me. No."

"Then what do we do?" I asked.

"We wait. He'll no let go, Flora."

FIGHT FOR LOVE

I lifted my face to the sun. "We'll be ready this time."

"That's ma girl."

THE REST OF THAT DAY, I felt much more relaxed, and by evening, I was feeling so much better overall. We lay in bed and I was resting on his chest, feeling comforted by his woody scent and that strong rhythm of his heartbeat. Caelan had a really strong heart. It was unmistakable how it clacked against his ribcage, thumping against my ear. Nothing was going to break him, at least not very soon.

His calloused fingertips stroked gently over the back of my neck, then he inched them down until he was soothing my lower back. I was feeling incredibly calm and peaceful when he said, "How about a bedtime story, lass?"

"I'd like that."

"Then, let's go back to the beginning."

Chapter Thirty-Eight

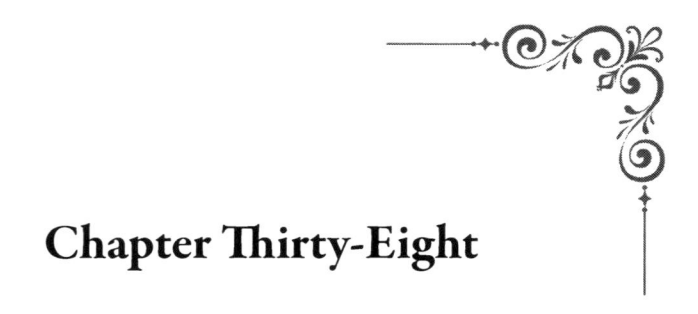

Caelan – Past

THERE SHE WAS. HIS future wife. Beauty incarnate. Nobody else in Venice that day came even close to her splendour, he thought. He'd stalked her online and seen photos, of course but seeing her in the flesh was entirely new. Especially in that Ferrari-red wrap dress. No bra needed for those perky tits. Her skin was flawless, taut; lightly tanned and shimmering against the low autumn sun. Those big blue eyes of hers were breathtaking. Her long, thick dark hair curled at the ends slightly and he had visions of running his hands through it as he stroked her naked back. Ruby-red bow mouth he'd never get tired of kissing. She also happened to have great legs and the most luscious arse. Hers was sensational. He couldn't help the slight push of his cock against the fly of his chino shorts.

Stood on the Rialto Bridge, she had no idea of the danger she was in. She kept taking photos, refusing to budge whenever people tried to elbow past her. Clearly, she was a character.

He'd been spying through binoculars but even through the small scope of those, a spark of light on the opposite side of the canal caught his lens and his attention. In a flash, he'd swapped the binoculars for the rifle he'd already assembled.

Through the rifle's scope, he searched the buildings on the opposite side of the canal. He'd already mentally built a picture of where a shooter on the other side might position themselves and he went right there first. A balcony with a deep wall.

He saw nothing.

If Sherry had forewarned her man that Caelan would be in the city, too and that they would need to do whatever it took to evade him—then where would a man trying to avoid detection hide?

Probably somewhere barely visible.

Caelan's eyes darted right to where his mind told him someone might hide but also find themselves a vantage point.

Not a window. Not a balcony. Not a roof. Right in plain sight where they wouldn't be expected to be. The flash of light from way up above had been a diversion. A red herring.

Caelan searched the area in Flora's immediate vicinity. There were a couple of students who were nearly glued to her right side, lingering close enough that his line of sight to Flora was a little obscured.

They'd expected him to be over here. On this side.

Cool.

So, the real killer would be on the other side.

He was fast, sight sweeping the bridge, the nearby gondolas, the drinks carts, café fronts.

He caught sight of Blake Rathbone trying to look inconspicuous beside a coffee cart.

"Twat," Caelan scoffed, laughing. Good that he'd taken the bait and had come to Venice, though—as planned.

Then, as he surveyed further, he saw the familiar face of Drake Barnett. Notorious gun for hire. He stood in the dark shadows of a closed-down bar with a hand half buried inside his coat. Almost invisible in a dark trench, nothing about him screamed, "Look at me." Which, ironically, had made someone like Caelan look at him.

Caelan fired a warning shot a couple of inches from Drake's head. Convenient that the shots would be absorbed into the thick brickwork behind Drake and unheard by anyone else. That noise would scare him however as it reverberated around the dark, enclosed, echoey space he occupied. Even scum like him could be terrified into submission, the human survival instinct strong in even the toughest of bastards. So, he put another bullet into the slats right between Drake's legs. Drake hopped on his feet, eyes darting around—and when he looked up, Caelan fired another shot that left a nick on the top of his crewcut-head.

Drake flipped him the bird then ran off. It had been a risk and Drake had known it. Whether he'd have actually made the kill with all these people around, who knew? He'd certainly not have managed it with Caelan in the city too, that was for sure.

Caelan swapped back to his binoculars and watched as Flora stepped onto a boat with a bunch of other people. Relief. Pure relief. She'd be safe now. He moved back to where Blake Rathbone hid and found the man scanning the area he was hiding in.

Good, Caelan was ready for Rathbone to follow him instead.

AFTER CAELAN HAD DEALT with Rathbone, both of them having fed one another a pack of lies—Caelan that he was going to take Flora and fuck her up; Blake that he didn't know exactly who'd killed his uncle, Jimmy—Caelan walked out into a typically grey Venice evening and reached the spot he and Hamish had pre-agreed on. A dive bar providing a little bit of privacy in the back.

"What a treat we have here, then," said Hamish, in his slightly more cosmopolitan Scottish accent, as Caelan announced his arrival with the cluck of his tongue.

Caelan grinned wildly at the sight of Drake tied to a steel chair, his wrists and feet bound by rope, tape over his mouth, and Hamish's club of hand holding his forehead so tight, it looked like his neck might snap at any moment.

FIGHT FOR LOVE

"Aye, something told me this wee scrote might be the one she'd send. Dead meat. Since she knew it'd be impossible to get past me."

Caelan had refused Sherry's order to kill the stepdaughter who stood to inherit a big sum of money from Blake—while all she'd get was more debt, more grief and more trouble. The woman was desperate. She'd tried to blackmail her own son, saying she'd go to the police about how he'd killed his own father. Caelan had called her bluff—said if she went and told the cops, she'd also have to admit to having lived the past thirty years of her life under a false name.

She said she would do it, however. If it got to the point where she had nothing left to lose, she would do it, she'd claimed. Caelan had told her to do her worst, while secretly fearing how people would view him if it ever got out.

Caelan sat on another metal chair, sitting on it reverse-ways with his hands resting on the top of the back. He grinned at Drake like he didn't give one shiny shite.

"I thought my friend here, Hamish would enjoy you, hence why I had him trail you earlier."

"Yeah," snapped Hamish at Drake's ear. "You know of me? You must do."

Drake shuddered with fear. From the smell in the room, the man had already wet himself earlier.

Caelan gave an arrogant laugh. "We're gonna take off the tape and you're gonna tell us concisely, no details spared, exactly what instructions Mrs Rathbone gave ye."

Drake nodded.

"Remember, I ken exactly what sort of lowlife piece of shite ye are, pal. The sort who once killed one of our friends. And, someone willing to kill that beautiful woman who doesna deserve death at the hands of Sherry, yeself, or anyone else for that matter."

Drake trembled with more fear and loathing.

Nearly always the case.

Most of them were fucking cowards.

Desperate for a payday.

Weak as they come, beneath.

When Caelan pulled a pair of pliers from his pocket, he said to Drake, "You're gonna tell us the truth, are ye nae?"

Drake nodded slowly, eyes like coals. Caelan nodded for Hamish to remove the tape.

He and Hamish shared a look. No, they weren't going to allow Drake to live after he'd confessed.

Drake seemed to register this because he smiled grimly, stuck his tongue in his cheek, then chewed on something.

"Go to hell, fuckers," he growled, right before white foam appeared.

Then he convulsed. And died.

All Caelan could do was shake his head.

So, the guns for hire all knew what they'd be dealing with in Caelan, then.

And were coming prepared.

He and Hamish growled at the same time.

"Ugh, I was looking forward to cutting off his bits and pieces and feeding him them," said Hamish, seething.

"This isna anywhere close to being over. That bitch is gonna keep coming."

Hamish raised his brow. "Who is this woman?"

"The less ye ken, the better, chief."

His friend's eyes darkened and he kicked the corpse in the room. "This piece o' shite killed too many innocent people to die this easy."

"Then next time we'll search their gob before we string 'em up."

Drake, in his heyday, was a marine with an almost unrivalled kill count of enemy insurgents. Eventually it was discovered that his kill count also included people who threatened his superiority, including someone Hamish and Caelan grew up with—someone who one day stood to surpass Drake.

There was a dark side to the military like any profession, and plenty of grey areas, but Drake's guilt was obvious and yet to save the navy disgrace, he'd been stripped of his medals, given a reduced pension and kicked out into the cold. The type of cold that meant he might easily be lured by the scabs of society into doing their bidding. Like Sherry.

"I love ye, mate. But whatever *this* is, it ain't pretty."

"I agree. But someone, somewhere kens the truth about ma uncle. And whatever it takes, whatever the hell it takes, pal. I'm gonna do it."

Caelan's determination was palpable, so much so, Hamish said, "Good luck to whoever did it, then."

Chapter Thirty-Nine

Flora

IT WAS SO STRANGE TO have heard Caelan's side of the story. About the first time he ever saw me. So strange and sort of romantic, how he'd already decided to try and save the stepdaughter of his wicked mother rather than give into any of her sick demands. Even when he didn't know me yet.

"D'ye no wanna hear more?" he asked, as I scooted closer and wrapped my arms around him.

"No. Later."

I moved in and kissed him. He dragged my body into his and we lost ourselves in the moment. He'd wanted me from the first moment the same as I'd wanted him in Barcelona, which was the first time we ever properly spoke.

Desire and lust had never been the problem.

It was everything else.

He pulled away for a breath and gazed into my eyes. Leaning in again, when he gave me a satin-soft kiss, my belly lurched and I felt it again. That thing we'd lost for a while but had never truly gone away. That love-bond. A real love-bond. That thing which was terrifying and had made me fear him along the way, too. It meant so much more than sex.

He saw in my eyes how affected I was and smirked with male pride. "Aye, you're mine, Flora. I kent it that day in Venice. Thought, there's a bright star for my night sky. A lovely, luscious body to curl into my hard bones. Someone for me to protect and love."

He pulled me closer again and licked into my mouth, groaning as I hauled him over me and let him dominate and devour, his tongue making my belly fizz with joy. I raked my nails down his bare back and lifted my t-shirt off just so I could feel his skin against mine.

We were like teenagers again, hungry and awkward, urgent and at times clumsy in our need. Caelan sighed and shuddered when he came in his pants. I bit my lip and sniggered.

"Now we really are teenagers again!" I cried.

He laughed into my hair and curled around me, spooning up close. He held my breasts in his hands and didn't think to change his shorts. He wasn't bothered and neither was I.

"What did ye think when you first saw me?" he asked.

"Some women were looking at you and I didn't like it."

"Really," he coughed.

"I didn't like it. I still don't like it."

Silence. A few minutes passed.

"I huvna... not even with everything that happened. I huvna been with anyone else. Unless you count Eric's dirty mouth."

I processed that for a while, eventually whispering, "What was that all about?"

"It was me, telling him I hated him. That I was only doing it with the hope he'd get over it and finally leave us alone. That I despise him. Could ne'er want him. Ever." Caelan took a breath. "Only with your scent in the room and the thought of you did I make it. Just to get him to see, he means nought to me."

I swallowed hard. "It was horrible. How he took it. How he didn't seem to mind."

"Aye, I ken how it must've looked. That's the way he wanted it, though. And I wanted him to have it, take it, and be done wi' it, once and for all."

I stroked my fingers through his forearm hair. "He won't ever be done with us, will he?"

"I've a mind to agree."

He kissed my neck and cradled me tight. The wind whooshed through the room and he tossed a sheet over us. It was the last thing I remembered as we sank into sleep.

Chapter Forty

Caelan – Past

IT WAS THEIR FIRST night at the castle together. Earlier that day, she'd tried to drown herself in the loch and he'd nearly had a heart attack. He thought she had a death wish or, in her grief for her father, was trying to make herself feel alive. It had nearly put him in a tailspin—watching her almost drown, barely able to swim to him with those leaden arms of hers—and he was not one for letting situations get to him. He was in love with Flora by then though, hook, line and sinker. Not only beautiful, but she was clever and witty. Broken and in need of protection.

He couldn't help it; he had a fetish for women in need. When he first met Dani, she'd had a violent ex and that's how they got together. Even though he hadn't loved her, it had continued on for some time. Mostly because he was a dick. A little because he didn't like being alone. When Dani died in action, he was more upset than he'd anticipated and became a Grade A wanker, putting it about.

Those were the times when Eric would encourage, "Go on, give her one for me."

He was ashamed of himself for his past. That wasn't really him. He'd never been a shagger, not until Dani died. Eric didn't help, telling him he was free now, he could do what he wanted.

Back to Flora. He had a sense this woman was broken. In ways he couldn't imagine. Deep beneath the hardened shell, she was really very vulnerable—and that night, he was about to find out just how much.

AFTER EATING THEIR pheasant pie, and a pudding Morag had made that might have sunk a ship let alone a human being, Flora and he made small talk. She asked about the land, his age, his horses, such like. He was completely unprepared for the direction the conversation eventually took.

"You've never been married, then?" The food and fire had made her glow and he was busy thinking about her legs in that jumper dress. Throwing her onto the floor and ravishing her...

"Nae."

"Why not?"

"It's not in my nature, I suppose." Too many questions for this early in the day. He didn't really know what he was saying; he was only trying to stop her going deeper.

I'll marry you, one day, though, he thought.

"So, you wouldn't ever marry? What about kids?"

Warning bells! "I'm no sure."

"I see."

"What about you, Flora?" He gazed at her, trying to gauge where she was at with all this.

"What do you mean?" She looked suspicious.

"Have you ever been in love?" *Please say no or I'll have to murder the dunderheid.*

She slowly shook her head. "I don't believe I have."

He turned to stare at the fire. *Thank gawd.*

FIGHT FOR LOVE

"The closest I came was probably when I first got to London. He was my age and studying art at university. If it was going to be anybody, it might have been him."

He sniffed and frowned at this revelation. "When did it end?"

"Fifteen years ago, give or take."

He inwardly growled. Fifteen years wasn't long enough.

"When ye were like twenty, then?" She nodded. "What happened?"

"I was working full-time and it wasn't getting me anywhere, so that's when I started looking into the possibility of doing a degree alongside work." He nodded he was following. "I was desperate to get things for myself. A nice place. Respect at work. It felt like he was trying to dampen down my ambitions. He said if I went to night school or whatever, I wouldn't have time for him. And he was quite insecure, I think."

"In what way?" *Sounds like a cock.*

"I don't think he liked it that I wanted to do stuff for myself." She tapped her lip with a finger as she thought about it. "He said we'd get a flat together with money his mum and dad would lend us. But I said no. He could do that if he wanted to, but I'd pay my way. He said I wouldn't need to pay my way. You see, he was quite an exceptional artist and thought I was his muse. You might've seen some of his work. He hangs all over the world now. Paul Thornton."

Caelan gulped and wondered if he would have to commit murder, after all. Not him. Not that prick! His most famous piece was a naked woman. Caelan didn't have to think very hard to picture it, not with a photographic memory, and from what he remembered of the headless woman from the neck down, she sure did seem to share some resemblances with Flora.

The bastard.

But she wasn't with him now. Caelan sat up straight at the thought. "So, you refused to let a man to look after ye?"

"I did then," she chuckled. "I still had something to prove. But more than that, he was shit in bed. You'd never know, would you? Not when his paintings make him seem so passionate."

"Ha! Eejit." He hid his smile.

"Well, I guess a lot can happen in fifteen years. Maybe he eventually found someone more forthright and she finally pointed out where the clitoris actually is."

Caelan nearly spat out his precious whisky! "In my experience men who are no good at it, are never good it. And for one reason."

"Oh, yes?"

"They're selfish."

"True. Or, they're married and don't really care. But they also don't make their wives come, either. For them though, the illicit sex is better. Something warped in their brains, I think."

"Hmm." It was blatantly obvious something, somewhere in her past had taken place.

Since he'd been following her around Europe, saving her from gunmen, poisoners, kidnappers and dodgy waiters with cheese wire in their pockets, he'd also noticed her take a lover occasionally. Usually a married man.

"You grew up in a place like this, I can tell," she said, keeping on with the interrogation.

She'd had wine, so...

A muscle in his jaw feathered and he was scared she'd unfurl his entire history. "How can ye tell?"

"I watch people and know things. I can just tell."

"Aye, I joined the army for bigger adventures, I suppose. But Flora, you left home young because you hated your father's enterprise?"

He turned slightly to rest his back against the arm of the sofa, then slung one arm across the sofa cushions, his eyes searing into hers. He needed her away from asking about him.

She swallowed stiffly. "I violently detested what he did. I also hated him, too. I'm not going to lie, beyond the grief, I still remember what he was." She stared into her wine, in pain, he thought. "I hated him for a lot of things. Mostly my mother's death. But I hated what he was doing more than anything else. He didn't think I knew, but oh, I did. I knew. All the men he forced me to call Uncle This, or Uncle That, with their bloodied knuckles and their black eyes, their jackets bulky around the chest, guns holstered. I knew he was addicted to it. Knew he got a kick out of it. I ran as hard and as fast as I could away from all that. I promised myself I would never be like my mother. I'd never be sucked in by a bastard, or relinquish my ambition for some crooked ingrate with nothing but evil in his heart."

He touched her knee gently.

"It's okay," he whispered, as she stared into her drink.

"There's something I never told anyone, not even him."

"Ye need not say it. If it's your secret to keep." He dreaded hearing the words—he already knew he would commit murder to protect her.

She moved to the fireplace, perhaps to give him her back so he wouldn't see the pain in her eyes. "When I was fifteen, one of his guys tried to rape me, Caelan."

"Perhaps it's your secret to keep," he persisted, because he really didn't want to have to kill another man.

Ever.

"When I wasn't a wee bairn anymore," she chuckled, "the whole sordid truth gradually revealed itself to me, the more curious I got. So before that day I'd seen things, definitely wasn't innocent anymore, if you know what I mean. He'd had women over... sex parties in the summerhouse. There was also the underground pool, too. And with so many so-called uncles hanging around all the time, it was hard not to see a cock every day, you know? And that was the least of it. Some of the things I saw... the way women were treated..." Caelan rubbed his forehead, angry at the thought. "I can tell you right now, without the shadow of a doubt, I would've had unspeakable things done to me that day... and I might have even lost my life... if I hadn't fought back. I had no choice but to defend myself. So I killed him... and never told anyone."

Up until that moment, Caelan had refused to believe Sherry's notion that Flora was the killer. It had seemed like a ludicrous, crazy claim—designed to get her what she wanted. Caelan had been determined to close in on the truth, but it couldn't be this easy, could it?

Jimmy wouldn't... would he?

This was someone else. It had to be.

A sick joke.

Sherry had twisted this to suit her own ends. She'd known about the rapist and had twisted it...

Yes, it had to be that!

A young girl couldn't have overpowered his uncle.

Could she?

And...

No, he refused to believe it.

"I don't ever think about it, but it's there, all the time," she said.

He had known she must have been hurt at some point, but this? Knives of anxiety surged through him, like he might die unless he went and found that bastard who'd hurt her, right now, and end the fucker.

"You've killed in your line of work, yes?" she persisted, but he still didn't know what she was really angling for.

What did she want him to say?

He merely nodded his head that he had.

"We're not so different, you and I." He was utterly horrified by the thought this beautiful lady had been forced to protect herself and he hadn't been there. "Both you and me, we're abused people. That's why we're loath to love." But those words, right then, were worse than anything else he'd had to hear that night.

He'd been abused, once. Yes.

She could see him like he was transparent, and what's more, he'd barely told her anything about his life. It scared the fucking worms out of him.

He bit down hard on his bottom lip and stared at his lap, then rubbed the back of his neck, which had turned crimson. He was in a state of shock.

Maybe denial.

He was still taking in her words, dazed and afraid, when she rose to her feet and put her hand on his cheek, stroking his beard. The look in her eye told him one thing and one alone:

She wanted him, but, he needed to know and understand the gravity of things before they took that next step. The desire and fervour in her eyes nearly took his breath away, but…

She needed assurances, and until he could give them to her…

"Thank you for dinner, handsome."

She left his side and headed to bed.

The next day, after a sleepless night (on his part), they made love on the rug downstairs.

There was no stopping it.

She was beautiful. Abused.

And needed him.

He was hers.

She was his.

That's all that mattered.

He said fuck it to everything else.

Even though he knew, one day, for sure, Eric would come for Flora.

Eric, the man who'd bathed in Caelan's misery following Dani's death.

Rather than tell his friend to get help and get sorted.
Nae, instead, he'd watched Caelan implode.
And deep down, Caelan had always wondered...
Was there a moment, when his back was turned, where Dani had been vulnerable and Eric had swept in...
He couldn't think about that now.
His urge to be with Flora obliterated all else.
They'd deal with it all as it came.
Whatever.

Chapter Forty-One

Caelan

HE WOULD NEVER TELL her that he had been unable to reconcile it then, and was still having trouble now. He knew it was the truth—she had actually killed Jimmy—but he hadn't wanted to believe it on first hearing, and it had been even harder when she'd gone into more detail. Of course, he believed his wife, but it wasn't pretty. He couldn't stand to think of the violence she'd had to use to save herself, the way Jimmy must have looked, the whole... sordidness of it. It was so difficult to comprehend. So, a lot of the time, he tried not to. He would tell himself that it didn't really matter about the past...

Yet he spent the next morning telling her about all the times he'd scuppered her would-be killers. Similar situations to the first one. Except, he didn't always have Hamish as backup. Sometimes his buddy would be on operations; other times the logistics were too complex, given Hamish had a family, too.

Caelan was there whenever a bird whispered in his ear that another assassin had been put on Flora's case. Drake had been the only one who'd met a violent end, the rest were easily persuaded not to bother, having heard what'd happened to him.

All that time he was watching her, he never for one moment believed she had actually killed his uncle. At first, he'd looked upon her as an heiress, an unsuspecting victim of Sherry's and an innocent. Of course, part of it was lust, desire... then love that kept him following Flora around. Perhaps curiosity, too.

Maybe a pull that was unexplainable.

Inexplicable.

After he'd told her about the final attempt on her life right before Blake died (a goon had broken into that house in Frinton-on-Sea, but Caelan had been there and scuppered them), Flora said to him, "Tell me why you really couldn't let me die. Why you had to let me live."

He stared into her eyes and said honestly, "I already knew that one day, you'd be ma wife."

She looked relieved and happy. "And so why did you leave me in the arms of a potential monster?" It was spoken so slickly, designed to trip him up. Like she had spoken in the beginning; needling him into confessions.

He'd asked for that, though. Then... and now.

"Sometimes even I dinna ken how this mind works." He pointed at his own head. "Maybe I thought... if ye could make me into a civilised creature... ye could him, too."

"That's really what you thought?" He shrugged. "I need to know more, about Eric."

"Aye, tonight's bedtime story," he said.

"Okay," she agreed. "Today we could go swimming? Spend a day at the beach."

"If you feel up for it."

"I do," she said.

He was glad she was recovering quickly, but it also meant the questions were coming thicker and faster.

She'd been close then to discovering the real reason why Caelan had let it go on between her and Eric. That morning when he first saw them in bed together, yeah, it had seemed like his world was about to end.

Then she'd given herself away—still in love with him—but just a bit in love with Eric, too.

More interesting than that was the fact that Eric seemed to have fallen for Flora.

It was obvious. The way the man looked at his wife.

How his eyes glazed over whenever she was around; the sweaty palms he'd try to dry on his jeans; the slight colour in his cheeks whenever she spoke.

In those moments, Caelan had figured out exactly how he was going to break Eric, once and for all.

Chapter Forty-Two

Caelan – Past

ERIC WAS ONE OF THE cleverest new recruits he'd ever come across. Clever, but deceitful.

He'd asked Eric to relay an instruction to one of the others during a training exercise near Ben Nevis—the message was never relayed, but Eric had claimed it was and the recipient sloppy.

Eric didn't know Caelan had known the message would never be relayed. Eric had already been trying to make his colleagues look bad. Caelan only wanted a chance to show Eric up.

Not explaining what he knew, Caelan told Eric to get down and perform 200 push-ups.

Eric didn't argue. He barely broke a sweat performing the task.

Caelan had occasion to wonder how Eric even got in. Aside from high academic scores and great physical discipline, he was a loose cannon, for sure. He ran rings around his teammates and Caelan was in despair. At this point in time, Caelan was an instructor having suffered PTSD following a stint in Iraq—and Eric was sure making it look attractive, the prospect of getting back out into the field again.

The worst instance of Eric's refusal to break was during an exercise down at Loch Lomond. They had to work in pairs to get across a narrow channel of water that was raging, freezing and treacherous.

Eric got himself and his teammate, Will across by sheer force of will. Eric had practically dragged Will by the scruff of his neck alongside himself, so roughly, he hadn't noticed Will taking in water.

Caelan arrived just as Eric finished performing CPR on Will—who was alive, but barely.

"You've done enough!" Caelan screamed, tossing Eric off Will and nearly ripping Eric's clothes right off his back in the process. Prior to that day, Caelan had never displayed his physical strength, but Eric looked deeply shocked.

Caelan didn't have time to think on how he'd nearly broken Eric's neck on a rock as he checked over Will and made sure he was okay. Raging, Caelan growled, "The task was to get both people across safe! If you'd have looked a bit harder, you'd have seen a much safer crossing just a little further up!"

Safety was never Eric's priority, though. Winning was.

His aim was also, as Caelan had started to discover, to grab attention.

Caelan's attention.

While Caelan shouldered Will to warmth and recovery in one of the tents close by, Eric grumbled, "We were still the first across."

Caelan bit his tongue, nearly slicing it in two. He gave Eric no credence.

WILL WAS SENT TO THE nearest army barracks to rest and recover. Meanwhile the rest of them stayed behind, shivering around the campfire that night. No change of clothes. No deviation from real-world scenarios where you could end up freezing, wet through... and need to make it through the night. Eric scowled from the other side of the campfire, not shivering at all. He'd stripped himself naked earlier, warmed his clothes by the fire, and had put them back on once they were dry. Hadn't cared at all that people would see him naked. Well, who was laughing now? His clothes were dry and he was warm despite earlier suffering the chill.

Caelan hated to say it, but the wee fucker reminded him of himself.

An unusual tolerance for pain. Cleverer than was necessary. Rebellious. Physically stronger than many others without even needing to try. And as deceitful and as cunning as they came.

"You, with me, now," said Caelan, rising abruptly from the log he'd been sitting on, his eyes piercing even across the fire between them.

Eric followed behind Caelan through frost-crunchy ground, leaving behind the frozen soldiers to potentially realise they ought to dry out their clothes properly, too.

Behind the tents, Caelan stood at his full height. In his boots, that was nearly always a foot taller than most other men and women. Eric was wider than him but much shorter, and smarmy, so smarmy.

"My mentor, Logan took us out into the mountains and that's where he broke me," said Caelan panting, because he was annoyed he hadn't yet managed to evoke the same fear and respect from Eric that he had from the others. "You and me, after this. One week. I'll break ye, all right."

Eric only looked delighted and that made Caelan even more determined to break the man.

CROSSING FROZEN RIVERS, scaling ice-slick mountains, surviving off snow and rations—or whatever they could catch—Caelan knew it'd be the starvation that got to Eric first.

Most southern softies had never known proper starvation, not usually.

Again, another instance where Eric surprised Caelan, resorting to eating grass and any other bits from the ground they found which were mildly palatable. Caelan had emergency food in his bag, but he wasn't going to tell Eric that.

If it wasn't starvation that'd get him, then it'd certainly be the sleep deprivation as they slept beneath the stars with no tent, no protection except a sleeping bag and their own wits.

Stags, randy cattle, all sorts of creatures might stumble upon them in the night and find their hoof or paw pressing into a soft, human body.

Eric took it all. Blinked open his eyes every morning like it was a summer's day. Ate grass. Drank the snow. Gritted his teeth and powered through the pain as they prowled the land and were battered by the wind, snow and hail.

On the sixth night before the last day, Eric finally spoke. "What made ya think ya could break me?" The little cockney git spoke like a right scrote.

"Huvna I broken ye yet then, lad?" Caelan smirked, working with his knife on a long, straight tree branch to create a javelin.

He'd catch breakfast for them tomorrow. A treat since they'd made it this far, the two of them, without killing one another.

"I ain't feeling too broken," said Eric, in his rough South London accent.

"You need to be educated. You need to speak properly," said Caelan, adopting his fake English tongue. "You need to be able to play whatever character, whenever, wherever. Do you understand?"

"This mean I'm gonna be your protégé for when you kick the bucket and they need another mug, eh? Cos ain't that what happened to you?"

Caelan ignored the little scrote's disrespect. "Utter one more word about my mentor and I'll gut ye."

"Well, you ain't broke me, but he broke you, right? So I'd say that I'm better than you. After all." Eric waited for Caelan to retaliate, respond, anything—but Caelan said nothing for a long time.

Until his anger had passed.

"I ken ye think yer clever, sonny. And maybe ye are cleverer than me. But what ye'll never be is as strong." Caelan scowled at his protégé. "And yer reckless. And carrying a big chip on that shoulder."

"There's no way you're stronger than me," said Eric, baiting him.

Caelan sniffed. He didn't need to prove himself, but if required...

"Show me, then."

They rose from the frozen, rock-hard ground of a sheep field that was empty of creatures at that time of year. They'd been huddled against one of the boundary walls, the jagged and ancient stones it was made from digging into their backs.

Caelan's legs were thicker and more muscular than Eric's yet even Caelan's legs wobbled as they stood up. It was exertion, lack of food, exhaustion.

Eric tried to throw a punch but Caelan caught it in his fist and squeezed until Eric landed on his knees in the hard ground, bones crunching.

Eric's dirty tactic was to try headbutting Caelan in the groin in response. Caelan kept Eric's strongest hand hostage inside his, then used his other hand to rip out half of Eric's girly ponytail before he could ever headbutt him.

Eric rolled around on the ground clutching his head, some blood on his hand as he rubbed at the wound. Furious, he got up and came at Caelan again.

This time, Caelan wasn't playing games.

He split open Eric's cheek, then his jaw, sending him flying back into the frozen, uncompromising earth.

Eric kept getting up. Kept wanting more.

Caelan gave him more and more, never accepting one blow to his own body.

FIGHT FOR LOVE

Eventually, Eric crawled back to his sleeping bag and huffed a broken laugh, shaking as he recovered, the wind having been knocked out of him by several punches to the gut.

"Who the fuck taught you to fight like that?" Eric could barely speak.

"Yer tank is empty, with all yer showing off and such," said Caelan. "Ye always have to save something for later."

Eric gasped, finally showing weakness. "How could a man save anything after walking fifty miles across this endless, frozen wasteland?"

"That's the difference between you and I. To me this isna a wasteland. It's a playground. I ken these places like I ken my own fist and what it can do." Caelan sank onto his own sleeping bag, sighing. "Are you broken now?"

"No, only injured."

Caelan grunted and settled down to rest. "If ye dinna break, I'll have ye tossed out. I canna have a reckless, thoughtless sociopath on ma team."

"But you could do with someone who's almost as tough as you, right?"

Smarmy little tyke.

Chapter Forty-Three

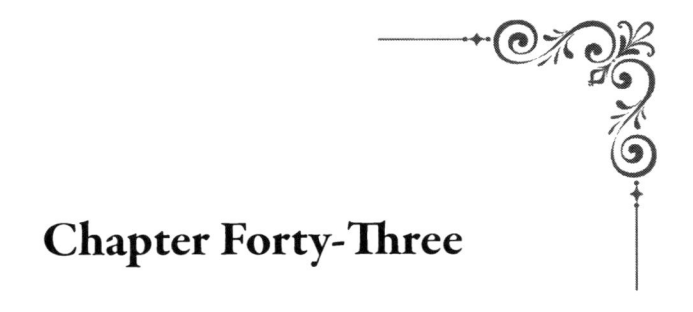

Flora

"HOW DID YOU EVENTUALLY break him?" I asked, after he'd given me that little insight into his first encounters with Eric.

"I ne'er broke, once," said Caelan, who was sitting with me by the pool beneath the stars. We'd just eaten a crab salad, Harold and Morag had gone into town, and the baby was sleeping upstairs, the bodyguard still playing computer games. "And it broke him. That he couldna find weakness, no way to get beneath ma skin. And gradually, I kent he felt more than just a brotherly bond. It was easily ignored most of the time. He did screw women."

"I see." So, that part was true. "He told me he's not gay."

"Aye, he's something... beyond rules. Beyond... well... y'ken?"

"I think so."

"He was jealous of Dani. No doubt about it."

"I can imagine." I took a deep breath, asking the question I wasn't sure I wanted an answer to. "You never, ever did anything, then? Never encouraged him, let him just... nothing?"

Caelan shook his head. "Ma only sin is that I recognised his attachment and did nothing to cut him off. I shoulda done something. Left the military earlier, not gone with them back into the field. But..."

"You felt an affinity with him, didn't you?" It was obvious that's why he'd never been able to force Eric out of his life, not forever.

"It's when you're pretty much the same person, have endured the same shit in life, but it's too much. Too like, close. And yet, nobody else understands." He took my hand across the table. "Until you, o' course. Which is why, I suspect, we ended up here."

"In this triangle," I admitted.

"Aye." Caelan's eyes darkened. "Flora, if it turns out he's a traitor and murdered ma team, I'll have nobody to blame but myself. And I'll have to kill him."

"You wanted to help him, give him purpose, that was all," I tried to soothe, brushing my thumb over the back of his hand.

"Naw, I kent all the way back then, there was something wrong with him, something deep, deep down wrong. I shoulda acted on my fears but I ignored them."

I took a deep breath, still with that hollow feeling inside of me threatening to pull me into myself and away from him—but I wouldn't let it. "We can't go back."

"Nae, and I ken it."

LATER THAT NIGHT, WE were both struggling to sleep. Perhaps it was the heat. Perhaps we were both wired. Maybe we were just so relaxed being on holiday, we weren't tired enough yet. Anyway, I was staring at him as he looked up at the ceiling.

"I want to talk about Jimmy," I said.

His face became lined as he grimaced. "What about him?"

"Do you believe what I told you?"

He turned his head, shooting me a sad but certain look. "Yes."

"Then how do you feel about it? What do you think? I sometimes wonder..." I blew out a big breath, my heart kicking a little.

He lay on his back looking up at the ceiling again. "I tell myself it was the sin in the Anderson family. It corrupted him. It just makes it easier for me to deal with. I just... I like to think of him how I knew him."

I shook my head several times. "I want to say things you won't like."

His hands covered his eyes. "I was afraid o' that."

"I was there, Caelan. It's stamped on my memory." I trembled at the mere thought. Caelan noticed and turned over to reach out, rubbing his hand up and down my arm. "I saw that look in his eye. I remember it clear as day. And I know he knew who I was. I was convinced I'd snuck out of the house unseen, and I thought much later, he'd come after me on purpose. To hurt Blake."

"He'd been waiting? Watching?" He bit his lip.

"I don't think he would've let me live. He'd have let my father go mad trying to figure out who'd done it. And Dad would've killed them all, like they were guilty by association. Maybe that's why Jimmy did it. So he could watch my father undo himself."

"You were Blake's one vulnerability." It was a statement, and, it was oh so true.

"The one thing he had left of her. And so, he buried it; the truth about who'd really killed Jimmy. He must've always known. Seen the change in me." My lip trembled, my chest nearly caved in, and I shuddered. "Dad does love me, but... it's so..." Tears sprang from my eyes. "*That. Thing.* That I can't explain, Caelan. His weird, toxic, but real love for me. He didn't try to fix me, he just allowed me to be angry and to do whatever I needed to in order to survive."

Caelan breathed heavily. "He should've protected you."

I covered my face with my hands. "Yes. But maybe... I dunno."

"What?" he said, sighing.

"Nobody ever protected my dad, so he didn't know how to protect anything. Not even himself."

FIGHT FOR LOVE

Caelan got up and knelt on the bed beside me, stroking a hand through my damp hair. I felt the heat of his gaze even though I was dazed.

"I love you, Flora, so much... but I fell in love with you before we ever spoke. Nobody protected you but you know how to protect."

I sat up too and he made space for me between his legs so I could curl my body into his, snug under his chin, his arms clasped all around me.

"I'd see ye strutting about, looking so fucking beautiful... and then some lonely old soul would stop ye in the street to chat or beg or ask the time. Ne'er would ye bat them off, ye'd always speak wi' em. And the way ye'd smile when people weren't looking, when ye'd see an old couple still in love, or a mum cooing over her bairn. Or ye'd see, I dunno, a piece o' art or a woman with a dress ye liked, and ye'd stop, and tell 'em so."

I pulled myself out of his chest. "That's because she's in me still, Callie. In here."

"I ken it," he said smiling. "But that protectiveness, that ability to live, it's in-built too, in here," he said, pointing to my chest. "Some people learn it, some are born wi' it. You're the latter."

He moved in and swept me up with a daring, passionate kiss that rocked my soul to its foundations. I moved into him, chest to chest, and straddled his thighs. He grasped my butt and my bare breast under my shirt, his tongue rampant in my mouth, then on my throat.

I pulled away, my clit singing with lust, but...

It wasn't time.

He was shaking as we shared breath, our noses pushed together. My eyes closed, I caught my breath and just let myself feel the thwacking of his heart against mine.

"My mother loved me," I whispered, "but she was a victim. She allowed herself to be. I would never allow it."

"I kent it the moment I first saw ye, lass."

I opened my eyes and stared at his body, at all those abs and side abs. His nice big pecs and those lethal arms, not bricks like Eric's, but corded with fierce, determined muscle. No big show-off, nothing wasted, everything in proportion. My towering, violent, rapscallion of a husband. With those utterly delicious lines, dips in his hips, that slope down to his cock. Nobody else had such a nice set of hips and I was reminded how beautiful...

...and why I fell in love with him!

"I would take Logan if it was for the best," I muttered. "Away from it all. I'd do it."

"I ken it," he repeated, "and I'd no blame ye."

"I loved her, and I still love him, but staying a good person? Staying strong? Being, fuck, so alone... for so long, Caelan... it took so much guts. People do not understand." I sucked my bottom lip into my mouth, afraid to say the rest. "I've had to be—"

"So strong, aye," he said, hurt in his eyes. "Then the big twat that I am, I forgot that beneath it, ye've just wanted to be looked after." Tears rained down my face. "Ye'd just had a bairn no long ago. Then I left and ye were afraid, and I shoulda stayed... ye were vulnerable. Ye were broken. By the things Sherry spake, the loss of your da... so many things. And then ye decided..."

"To break it before it broke me!" I cried, shaking so violently, I lost all control and he had to hold me upright. After I'd finished heaving and sobbing, I said, "I was crying every day you were away." My teeth chattered. "I could hardly breathe. I should've told you not to go. Morag spoke as if you might have died out there and I should face the possibility."

"Here, come rest," he said, and we moved so we were lying down again. I was wrapped on all sides by his arms and legs and his breath, his body, his love. "She's just a bit... pragmatic sometimes."

We couldn't help a little chuckle between us.

FIGHT FOR LOVE

"I admit, Eric came along and made me question things. Made me doubt you. But now I've had time, I realise looking back, I was trying to break it before it broke me. Because happiness is still so foreign to me, Caelan. So, so foreign."

"I feel the exact same way," he said, with grit in his voice. "I had whores throwing themselves at me in Ukraine and wasna tempted while sober, but... the drink tempted me while I was out there."

"The drink?" This was new.

"Aye, when I've had a few, I just... tell myself nothing matters... and do things. In the past, that's what happened. I'd have to be filthy drunk to... you know. I think ye were the first woman I made love to... ever... and the first woman I'd been with since Dani without me being drunk."

"God."

"Aye."

"You didn't drink, though?" I held my breath. "Out in Ukraine."

"Nae, there was too much pain there, Flora. Too many broken souls. It would've felt like a betrayal of them. I wrecked myself nearly trying to help everyone from the fisherman to the candlestick maker... I'll no darken your door with the truth about the terrors."

I wrapped myself around him tighter. "I love you so much."

"More than him?" he nearly growled.

"Much more... but I have some sense of what you were saying. Before, I mean." He wriggled a little beneath me. "How you could never do *it* unless you were drunk. I could never do it unless it meant nothing. So long as they didn't know me, not really, and the less they did, the better."

"The stains and all?" he said.

I pushed my nose into his chest. "Exactly."

Then lifting my face close to his, we shared salty kisses that time, his face damp with anguish, probably a few tears, and also some sweaty desire, too.

His tongue raged inside my mouth, needing to taste, to dominate, but also, to lose himself. I let him grab my rear, my back, his fierce hands everywhere.

It was still us. He still wanted me badly. He knew every single secret, but loved me anyway, still saw me for the broken woman I was—but desired me this much nonetheless.

"I'm still bleeding," I murmured against his mouth.

"I dinna care. Just kiss me."

We kissed for a long time, like teenagers again, except this time he wasn't so pent-up he came in his pants. Rock solid though he was, we were kissing to get close again, to relearn one another and be husband and wife, lovers, best friends... all of it... once more.

When we lay there, finally ready to go to sleep, he whispered in my ear, "How'd ye ken ye love me more?"

"Because I'm glad he's gone. The anxiety, adrenalin... the never feeling quite relaxed... might be exciting for a bit. But he was pain; you're my peace. And he didn't keep to the shadows to make sure I was safe, ignorant, and could continue living my life as normal. Like you did. No, he bulldozed his way in... forced himself into my life. Exposed me to danger. And I don't trust him. I might never trust a man like him. He reminds me way too much of—"

"Blake," said my husband, "aye."

"Yep."

"Eric will never figure it out. Doing so would probably kill him. Too much pain beneath the bravado." He clucked his tongue. "Same as Blake."

"And what about your pain?" I asked, sneaking a look at him.

He was utterly resolved. "I was built for pain, to fight, to win, to lead... to love. I've seen a lot of this world, Flora. A lot of people. My pain compared to theirs is so small. Aye, I killed a bad man so he couldna hurt ma mother anymore. Some kids have no choice, no freedom, no control. No education. No guardian like Harold to show them the way. I got lucky. Very lucky."

"Do you know?" I chuckled. "I'd say Harold would argue it was him who got lucky. Without you as a babe magnet, he'd have definitely never pulled Morag."

Caelan grunted and nipped my shoulder. "I'm ready for sleep now, cock's gone right doun."

We both occasionally tittered as we drifted off together.

Chapter Forty-Four

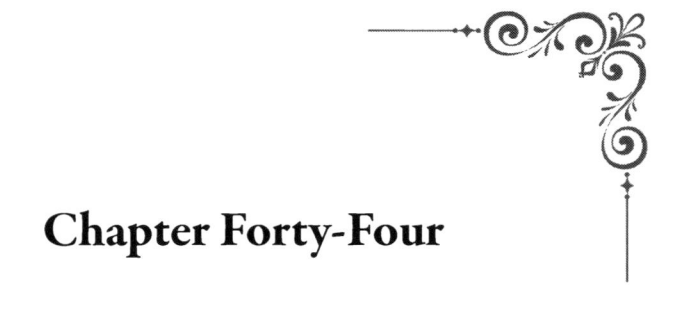

WE SPENT THE FOLLOWING couple of weeks chatting, swimming and walking along the beach beneath glorious sunshine. In short, we fell in love again, cuddling, kissing, talking everything out. He told me little bits about Ukraine but not everything.

We ate gyros, and falafel, and whatever else was available... walking the pram at night until we found somewhere new. Morag and Harold had gone home by this point, having got tired of the relentless heat (it had crept up recently, and it was going to get hotter yet).

Meaning Caelan and I snatched more time together whenever we could, leaving the bodyguard to figure it out when we went to bed early. Often while he shut down the kitchen, clattering around down there with loud music on, we'd use that time to engage in some loud foreplay.

The night I decided I was ready to go all the way, he was already naked and rock solid, lounging across the bed as I kissed his stomach. God, the sight of him was obscene. Here was an Adonis. A man. Vulnerable and breakable, but refusing to ever give up.

I'd stripped down to my knickers and was gazing at him lustfully.

"Would you show me some of your fantasies? Play them out with me tonight." My voice came out huskier than I'd intended. Maybe I was more turned on than I'd realised. "Let me be your toy, or your whatever... show me."

"You sure?" he asked, his eyes blazing with lust.

FIGHT FOR LOVE

"I wanna know what goes in your head. I wanna feel the full force of Caelan Cameron on me, in me, around me, whichever way... whatever... whenever... however the hell you want me, Caelan. I'm ready."

He blinked twice, then licked his lips. "I ask again... are you sure?"

I nodded slowly. "I've thought a lot about it."

"Did you put your cap in earlier?"

I nodded my head. "I did, honey."

"Why don't you call me sir?" he asked, donning a posh English accent. Incredibly husky, with that tinge of wild man. It thrilled me. "Sir Cameron of the Castle."

We held straight faces for about five seconds before we both laughed, a little tipsy from the ouzo we'd had at dinner to wash down our anchovy pizzas.

"I'll have you know," he said, in that accent again. "I've been offered a knighthood, actually."

I shook my head. "Are you joking?"

"Nae, his Highness offered me it. I said no thanks, sonny. I dinna think the choice is mine, however." He raised one sharp eyebrow, grinning.

I raised one back. "How's about you call me Lady Cameron of the Hill. Notting Hill. Sounds good, right?"

He snickered; we were nervous and trying to lighten the mood.

"Love you," he said, then prowled to me, pinning me to the bed. "All mine, tonight?"

"Yes," I said, coquettishly, "but I might let you do really bad things if you speak in that English accent occasionally."

He pursed his lips. "Lady Cameron of the Hill, won't you lie back and think of England?"

"God, yes," I acquiesced, raising my own arms above my head, eyes closed, waiting for whatever he'd decide. "Don't hold back, Sir Cameron."

He began by slapping my boobs playfully. "These gorgeous titties have got tight and high again now you're no feeding."

"You prefer them droopy and big?"

"Aye, but a man canna have all he wants. For instance..." He moved off me and threw me over onto my belly so roughly, I was nearly winded. He began a thorough massage of my bare backside (I was in a thong) and growled, "I'd take just a good arse. But you've also got these legs... this long, supple back."

He leaned down and blew air against my back, making me shiver and bite my lip, giggling. Then he reached into the bedside drawer and pulled out oil, straddling my thighs before he slicked my buttocks, then began a deep massage.

Caelan had massaged me before and was really good at it, having trained as a PT and learnt how to help people with cramp, muscle discomfort etcetera. Plus, it didn't stretch the imagination to believe he knew a few things about the human body. Any killer worth his salt would.

"Is that good?" he said.

"Yes, Sir Castle," I spluttered.

He grunted and I could tell he was struggling not to laugh.

"Why, Lady of the Hill. You're a naughty one, I can tell. Need a good bonking?" He was using his Oxford accent again. "Or is it a good rogering?"

"A good fucking if you please, Sir Castle."

"Filthy language, coming from a lady." He slapped me hard across the rear and it shocked me. My fists grasped the edge of the pillow I was resting upon. "Say something naughty again."

I caught my breath. "I'd like some cock, if you please, sir."

Another thrash.

This time, it really hurt. I had to breathe through it.

The scary thing was, he wasn't even really trying to hurt me. That's how strong he was.

"Not yet," he said, his voice so deep, I thought it was someone else.

He commenced a painful massage of my reddened bum cheeks and it stung so much, I frequently had to bite the pillow beneath my face. Spreading my cheeks apart with his ministrations, I felt the thong getting thinner and thinner, my cleft becoming more exposed the more he worked. All I heard were grunts.

On and on he went, those big hands squeezing, kneading and pulling my buttocks apart. The pulsing inside me had begun and my clit zinged as he kept up with that ruthless massage.

"You're wetting your tiny drawers," he said, clucking. "Quite a lot. And I can smell your filthy arousal."

"I can smell yours too, sir. Don't pretend you don't want to come on me. In me."

With those words, I had my thong snapped in half and tossed away. Then I was really naked. He tucked my knees underneath me slightly and lifted my bottom up, blowing air across my exposed places.

"Speak foully again and let's see what it earns you," he warned.

"I think sir is hungry for cunt."

He growled and slapped me right there, against my soft, wet flesh. I was clenching and he chuckled as he watched, making sounds like he was also licking his hand from having gathered my wetness on it.

"I am hungry for it," he said, "and ye ken I am."

He went for it, sloshing his tongue around, then dipping it inside me. I came on the third or fourth lash of his tongue against my clit, and my walls were gripping the finger he had in my pussy so hard, I thought it might disappear inside me.

Caelan rolled me onto my back and hovered beside me panting. That ravenous hunger of his soon found its way to my breasts, grabbing and then biting, sucking fiercely and hoovering them up between his generous, rampant mouth. I was raw before he'd done, and all the while, he was rummaging between my legs with his fingers, making me suck in breath fast—desperate for something to happen as I remained constantly with my clit humming, never quite making it over the edge.

"When you come, I want you to squirt," he said, "like a fountain."

I lay back fiercely aroused, hurting in places I couldn't really feel anymore—all I knew was that I ached for him in a different way to before—and then even as he was fucking me with two relentless fingers, it was the sharp pinch of my clit between his teeth that made me yell his name.

I wanted him off me but as he took me violently, those incisors finding their intended spot, it was the way he jammed his hand into me that made me spurt all over as I lost control of all my faculties and my pelvic floor, so much so, my anus was clenching too.

Before I knew it, I was on all fours and he was guiding his cock in my mouth.

I could barely fit his head in let alone the rest of him, but he knew just what angle to work with in order to maximise the experience. It was obvious this was all he'd done with women for a number of years, never finding it in himself to really love anyone again... until me.

Grunting because he was trying to fit too much of himself in me, that's when he reached right over me and popped a finger in my arse—so that suddenly it was no longer what was in my mouth that was the intrusion, considering the other space was so tight.

It felt like he was enormous because his middle finger was long and thick... and I was tight.

He kept on probing, going deeper, while swishing his cock in my mouth so I was dribbling everywhere and breathing loudly through my nose.

FIGHT FOR LOVE

"We're gonna come together, and after that, I'm gonna mount ye and make ye scream, all right?"

I nodded my head. *Yes sir, three bags fucking full, sir.*

He really drilled my arse and shunted his cock in my mouth. It all happened so fast, I did stop breathing for a bit. He was coming first, spurting at the back of my throat, his cries so unashamedly loud it made me bounce my bum against his hand. As he kept coming, I felt the thick vein in his cock throb and wondered how in the hell he was still concentrating on touching me, too... but at the same time, his finger was working like a piston... until the deepest, most soul churning orgasm overcame me... waves of burning desire fanning out from the pit of my belly, all my muscles in my pelvis going tense, then throbbing, molten, becoming slack. The sensation travelled along my spine and my knees nearly buckled.

I had to remove my mouth off his cock and moan, then howl, then slump against the bed.

The next thing I knew, he was in the en-suite bathroom and the water was running. I was nearly dead, or so I thought, but he came back.

He yanked down the blankets beneath me to the end of the bed, then lifted me easily into the pillows again. He mounted me as he'd promised, easily slipping into the mess between my legs, his tongue diving for my mouth, tasting himself at the back of my throat.

I clung to his neck and groaned, arching against him, my breasts pushing towards his chest as he sucked my earlobe and groaned, "Do you like me, Flora?"

"Which part of you?" I chuckled, biting his shoulder.

"All of me?"

"Yesssssss."

He pinned my hands above my head and thrust into me deeply, my head hitting the thankfully soft headboard. He was as hard as if he'd never come at all.

I circled my hips and he watched as I lazily swished him around inside me, his hardness eaten up by my desire for him, no matter that he was enormous.

"I was designed for you," he said. "Nobody else."

I gulped and saw the look in his eye. I thought he understood, so I said, "What if I'm designed for more than one? To love more than one? To be yours first and foremost, but also... to be a bridge, the healing power... between three lovers?"

He trembled a little and lowered towards me, kissing my lips softly. "Perhaps."

"Caelan," I murmured. "It's okay."

He wrapped his arms around me and kissed my throat, levering so that his cock rubbed my clit too and I came a little, laughing and gasping his name.

It was then he bit his lip, reached into me for the cap and gently removed it.

Perhaps to re-stake his claim? Anyway, I didn't stop him. I wanted it. Badly.

When he pushed into me that time, I shook all over and bit his bottom lip. Feeling him buried so deep and there being no barrier, it was heaven, and I saw it was for him too, his eyes hooded with desire, all that animal hunger gone, a need for intimacy reigning.

"Yes," I said. "Just yes."

A WHILE LATER, MY BODY beyond exhausted, aching and yearning for rest but still so wired, he lay between my breasts and our legs were tangled, my hands in his hair. He was still catching his breath having pumped into me fuck knows how many times.

"I dinna ken if ye meant it during sex, but I canna share ye again, Flora. Once was okay, to give ye the experience, but I canna do it again."

I swallowed hard and thought he heard that because he lifted off me, grabbed my hand to kiss it, then looked down into my eyes.

"You still love him?" He frowned, nearly angry.

"It's not like that." I didn't know how to explain it. "I think there are things between you two. I think you must've felt something to come so hard in his mouth that time."

Caelan blew out a breath. "It was to give him something to remember me by. I swear."

"What if I did want threesomes and to explore more?"

"Fine," he shrugged. "We'll find strangers. No problem."

I rolled my eyes. "But he's... familiar."

Caelan shook his head and lay on the pillow next to mine, one hand resting on my hip.

"Ye gonna have to explain it," he demanded.

I nibbled my thumbnail before I admitted, "I like it that he loves you, sees you for what you are, and I don't feel so alone in trying to figure you out anymore."

Caelan seemed surprised and my beast of a man even softened. "Okay."

He dragged me across the bed so he could spoon me, but I could still feel him thinking as he rubbed my belly in circles, making those little happy goblins inside me do an even happier dance.

"I mean it. I dinna like sharing." His deep voice was harsh.

"What if we share you?"

He grunted and huffed.

"Caelan, I can live without him. I can't live without you, but... he makes me understand you just that bit more."

"Hmm."

"And you did like it when you both shaved me and you could see how another man liked me too?"

"Sort of," he grumbled.

"It was kinda hot."

"Maybe."

"I got really wet and came... loads."

"I do remember it, lass."

"So, you don't try to keep it buried? Deep down?"

"I kenned you were a whore from the beginning, with even more of a sexual appetite than us men put together."

"Now you're getting it." I reached behind me for his butt and squeezed it. "How lucky have I been? To know two such beautiful men."

He made a growly grunting noise under his breath. "Hmm. There is still that matter."

"I know, I know. He might be a devious killer and all that."

"He probably is," he said sullenly.

"Hmm."

When he suddenly sank into me from behind, I threw my head back laughing and he growled, "Whore."

"Beast."

I tipped my lips up to his and we made lazy, lovely love.

Chapter Forty-Five

WE ATE BREAKFAST BESIDE the pool the next morning, the parasol above our heads beating off the worst of the sharp early-morning sun which threatened to sizzle, even through the thin white cotton dressing robe I wore.

"Was it everything you wanted last night?" I asked, peering at him from beneath sunglasses.

He bounced Logan in his arms as he fed them both bits of banana. "My fantasy is us, Scotland... the dog. That's it."

I held my chin up on my fist. "You want to renovate the castle back to glory and leave London."

He shrugged. "That's what I want."

"Maybe I could get used to it."

He stuck his lip out. "I wouldna want you miserable up there."

"I guess we won't know until we try." He looked infinitely relieved. Perhaps I was desperate to repair things. Whatever the cost. "I think it'd be a marvellous thing to see it restored. I think you could give a lot of people up there something to feel proud of. A new challenge for you, too. Employment for some, even."

"I dinna care about any o' that." He passed me the baby when Logan started to become antsy. It was too hot for him already. I lay him in his buggy and rocked it a little, letting the breeze hit his face for a while before I pushed him indoors into darker shade than the hood of his buggy was capable of.

When I returned to the table, he said, "All I want, Flora... is for you to be happy."

"I'd have to live with Morag and Harold or use the annexe. More workmen will drive me insane." I rolled my eyes. "Or... I could work a few days a week up at Balmoral. They've always got something on the go and would find space for us. I'd like to learn more about tartan weaving. I think we should take up the tradition again. You know? The old-fashioned way."

His face was a picture of happiness. "And maybe, have more bairns?"

I nodded fast. "If you get the castle repaired enough to accommodate us, perhaps."

He cracked his knuckles. "See if I dinna."

I smiled at him. "If we've got the money, I'd like to keep the London house."

He nodded his head. "We have."

"Good, it's got our stamp on it. Would be a shame. Plus, when Logan is bigger, he'll have to go to school somewhere. We might need a house there, just in case."

Caelan's eyes dimmed. He could tell I wasn't one hundred per cent certain on any of it.

"Plenty of good schools in Aberdeenshire. Y'ken? A short drive away."

I inhaled deeply, ignoring his sarcasm. "What? Trekking through snow in deepest winter? With other little wee bairns."

"I hadna thought o' that."

"Yes."

An awkward silence passed.

"We'll review things as we go along," he assured me.

"I agree, we've still got to enjoy our time here first."

"Two more weeks. Whatever shall we do?" He was grinning from ear to ear.

FIGHT FOR LOVE

"I have no idea, whatsoever."

IT WAS LATER THAT DAY, we were wandering around Paphos, trying to stay cool in floaty, light clothing, seeking some dim tavern to have a cold drink inside and a delicious salad or burger, when we saw something in passing. One of the sports bars had a big screen and a news bulletin came on.

Words flashed across the screen that were quickly read by my eyes, but weren't immediately processed, not properly. The scrolling headline was:

Gangster's Moll Escapes Prison, Prison Guards Brainwashed

I kept telling myself it wasn't what I thought it was, but... it was. Her mugshot flashed up, her name... Sherry Rathbone. At least they didn't know yet that she was really Rebecca Horrocks.

"Christ," he cursed beside me.

"You didn't listen to me."

"I thought..."

I looked into the pram and for a second, I was relieved our baby was safe, breathing, and with us. Not in the care of a nanny or his godparents, who were too aged to protect him against someone like that bitch. The nanny, too kind and sweet to know the real dangers of the world.

Caelan had believed her over his best friend. Eric had been right! Caelan's judgement was impaired when it came to that woman.

Our bodyguard had been keeping to the shadows behind us but suddenly sidled up next to Caelan and muttered something to him I couldn't hear. Caelan nodded and looked at me with pensive eyes. "We ought to return to the villa."

I'd never been more in agreement, but I also knew, nowhere would really be safe for us now.

Chapter Forty-Six

BY NIGHTFALL, WE HAD three bodyguards in total. So I supposed we were quite safe, for now, so long as her filthy fingers didn't reach so far.

We ate dinner in front of the TV while the baby slept upstairs. Meanwhile the bodyguards shared hushed conversation in the kitchen, deciding upon a strategy, perhaps.

No more eating outdoors in the dark for us for a while, then.

"You told the prince about her, did you?" It was an educated guess, given the haste with which two more bodyguards had made it here.

I could tell the men we were being guarded by were ex-military turned Royal protection officers. They had that look about them.

"The prince and I huv been drinking buddies for a while. I had to tell him eventually about the things that'd happened to you while I was in Ukraine." The vein in his temple pulsed; I was still getting over him and this bloke who was an actual fucking prince going for pints together. "After I interrogated the Russian asset and it seemed Eric might be innocent after all, I was forced to lay out the alternative. That a woman I ken to be my mother but who is criminally minded and changed her identity, might be the one trying to send a message from prison. And also, yep, about yer father. Together we pulled some strings and let's just say, lass... this could go very wrong for a lot of people if it doesna go right."

FIGHT FOR LOVE

"Nice to have friends though, I suppose?"

He tilted his head. "It sometimes only adds complications. My clearance is higher than his."

I sucked in breath. "We need Eric here, too."

Caelan looked up at the ceiling, his chest expanding with a big, deep breath. "I messaged him earlier."

That gave me such relief. "Thank you."

"We dinna ken what we face. How far she's got already. Who she has helping her. We dinna ken shit and it's nae good."

I tipped my head back and snorted. "Well now we know where you got the cleverness from. It probably wasn't your father."

"Aye, canna disagree."

Neither one of us was really hungry for the cold pasta salad in our bowls. We both kept staring longingly at our glasses of wine, more than at the food—and neither of us had particularly eaten since breakfast.

"Caelan?"

"What is it, honey?"

"Tell me it's going to be all right."

"Sure it is," he said, and kissed my head. "Ye ken I'll make sure o' it."

IN THE MIDDLE OF THE night, I was woken by a body climbing into bed with me.

I knew that smell, and it wasn't Caelan's.

Caelan had been too antsy earlier to come to bed—and had vowed to sleep on the couch downstairs to be on guard.

The windows upstairs were all shut and locked, the aircon in full operation.

"I'm here," he said softly, and I curled around him, burying my face in his shoulder.

"Thank you for coming."

"You knew I would." He kissed my hair and held me close. "It's all going to be all right. I promise."

"You promise?"

"Absolutely, baby."

I didn't hesitate and fell right back to sleep, because there had never been a shoulder more comfortable to snuggle into than his.

WHEN I WOKE THE NEXT day, I knew it was early because the baby wasn't cooing yet, the room was still bathed in shadows and it was cool enough that Eric was the only warm thing near me. Because of the aircon, this was the time of night when I'd usually have to bundle myself up in sheets and blankets.

"Are you awake?" I whispered.

"I am now." Eric was an awfully light sleeper.

He rubbed the sleep from his eyes and I looked down into his face, seeing shadows. He'd been busy, then.

"What do you know?" I asked.

"We were right," he said unhappily.

"You were right," I corrected.

"You knew it, too."

I closed my eyes. "He may not survive this."

"He will."

I slipped my fingers through his. "Did you and he speak last night?"

"Briefly. He's still angry with me." Eric rolled his eyes. "But he's not going to let anything happen to you. Nobody knows you're here."

"Yet," I said.

Eric rubbed his hands up and down my arms as the chill made my hairs stand on end. He looked concerned and said, "He mentioned the miscarriage."

"Yeah." I felt sad again, the reminder painful. "I hope he didn't tell you in a nasty way?"

"No, he just said it'd happened and I shouldn't let it happen again." His sorry gaze was genuinely repentant.

"It's... it was an accident. It could still have been a bad period. It could've been blood left over from the birth. I don't know... these quack doctors here..."

He stopped me, a hand on my cheek, a serious look in his eye. "Listen. To. Me. I'm sorry, angel. Okay?"

"Me too," I squeaked, before crawling into his arms again.

I fell back to sleep easier than I thought I would.

Chapter Forty-Seven

WHEN WE CAME DOWN FOR breakfast, the kitchen was busy with people on laptops. Caelan barely looked up from his except to give a brief nod. I knew I was expected to look after myself and the baby while they got on with everything.

Logan and I sat in the indoor dining room alone and he was grouchy, throwing himself about in his highchair, his eyes darting as he searched for his father. He ate some food and I held him as he thrashed in my arms, eventually getting him back off to sleep for a midmorning nap.

Caelan entered the room behind me, put his hands on my shoulders and rubbed them.

"I needed some space last night. Sorry if it irked you that I sent him to keep you company."

"No, I understand." I looked up into his eyes. "We didn't do anything. I don't think we will, either."

"It's your body, Flora. But I would prefer if ye didna." His sharp stare told me he'd have to bite his tongue hard if Eric and I were ever to... again.

"It was just a cuddle, nothing more," I assured him, and he believed me.

He took the seat next to me. "Everyone is on it. There's been no sign of her. Maybe she's gone into hiding."

"She wants to kill my father and reclaim her daughters."

"Do ye think?" Caelan asked, sounding serious, but also surprised I would assume she needed to see her girls again.

Maybe it wasn't that at all.

"I'm not sure, Caelan. I wouldn't like to put myself in her head."

"In ma heid, she kens how rich we are and would like to kidnap you or the baby and have me cough up what she believes she is rightfully owed."

I shrugged. "She could do that to anyone. I mean, look! She brainwashed a whole prison guard, allegedly."

Caelan was inclined to agree. "She might verra well be on her way to Florida already to visit with yer father if she managed to find him somehow."

"Hadn't thought of that." I chewed the tip of my thumb. "Has he been warned?"

"I should think he keeps abreast of UK news."

"Can I call him?"

He shook his head slowly. "Right now, I wouldna. It's hot right now, lass."

"You're right."

He took my hands between his. "Listen. Our Cypriot friends are working with us, too. We're well covered."

I handed him the baby to hold and Logan mercifully did not wake as he felt his father's strength, heat and scent cradling him.

"There are guys much cleverer than us searching for her, Flora. Let's sit tight."

I wished I could believe we were going to get through this—whatever *it* was.

Covering my face with my hands, I sighed, "I wish I knew what it was she wants."

"It has to be Blake," he spoke coolly. "The timing. She starts up when she kens I'm preoccupied in Ukraine. And by the way, she more than likely has contacts there who transported drugs through the country for them."

"I see."

"She was gonna use you to get to him. While I was gone, she thought…"

"But Eric hindered her… you came back… how could she ever hope to get to me now?"

His eyes darkened… a lot. "Flora, I wish I had ne'er listened to her."

I opened my hands. "But then we'd have never met."

"Aye." He reached for my hand and squeezed it, then leaned down to kiss my knuckles. "This is the price we're paying for daring to love… because we broke their evil mould."

One of the bodyguards Mickey entered the room. I knew it was him without having to look over my shoulder because he was a big fan of Lynx deodorant. Caelan and I turned at the same time to see him say, "Last night, a private plane which departed a small airfield in Norfolk disappeared somewhere off the coast of North Africa a few hours later. Manifest tampered with. Some other paperwork looks dodgy now they've started to comb through."

We looked at one another. Did it mean anything?

"Nothing more?" said Caelan.

"Not yet."

Mickey left the room.

"Is this something people like her do?"

"If this was her, she could've gone anywhere by now. West, east, south! Anywhere."

"But she's not supposed to have any money!" I exclaimed.

"Nae, but if she's got something someone wants, then… she can bargain."

"Like I said, I wish I knew."

"Ak ken, lass. Holy fuck, do I wish I had a magic wand. Christ, I do!" He didn't sound himself and the strain in his body was obvious.

"Caelan, with those stunts she pulled in Brighton, at the cabin and afterwards, she obviously wants to use me to send a message to my father. He has something she wants. Perhaps information."

"Or she's vengeful," he said.

"Or that. Yes."

Eric entered the room and sat beside me, his bulk making the chair beneath him creak. Stabbing his finger into the table, he said, "May I present my take?"

"Tell us," I urged, while Caelan shifted uncomfortably.

"She wants Blake's attention but also, his." He pointed at Caelan. "Because he betrayed her, married the enemy, took her birthright, is a hero, escaped the curse of their family. She despises him because he represents everything she hates. There's no escape for her and she can't handle it. She's got nothing left to lose. Nothing. All she wants is revenge on the people she can't control anymore. And you're the key, Flora. Through you she can get to Blake and him."

I rubbed the back of my neck. "Part of me wants to head back to London, just to see what she does."

"No," said Caelan, without a second's thought.

"I agree," said Eric harshly. "Scum everywhere."

"Then what do we do?" I asked, throwing my hands around.

"This is what we're built for, Flora," said Eric calmly. "So we wait."

Caelan dipped his head in agreement.

"We're the woman's worst nightmare," said Caelan darkly. "Together, we're impenetrable."

"Okay," I said softly. "Okay."

Chapter Forty-Eight

TIME TICKED BY SO SLOWLY. They'd take it in turns sleeping upstairs with me but while Eric and I would only cuddle, Caelan would want me more and more fiercely every night. Concerned we might be overheard, we didn't do any of the freaky stuff, just good old-fashioned foreplay, oral and then missionary. Caelan was becoming obsessed with us getting pregnant again, and I got it, I did. He was holding my legs up as he finished, but truthfully, I was starting to enjoy it less because it was becoming about one thing: him impregnating me again so that I wouldn't leave him.

The nights when I'd lie in Eric's arms, waiting for him to make a move, I'd yearn for that escape I'd once had with him. I would feel him trembling with longing, too. We'd stare at one another, stroke each other's faces, smile. I was glad he was safe and alive.

When my normal period arrived again, I'd never been so glad—but while Caelan scowled as he walked in on me sticking a sanitary towel in my knickers, Eric only hugged me harder that first night I was on. I admit, I let myself get carried away and we kissed and cuddled, me with just knickers on, him naked. I stroked him to orgasm and it was amazing how hard he came for me.

"Still love you, Flora," he said.

I really didn't know what to say in return, I was so confused. I think we all were. My husband was downstairs half the time allowing me to spend the other half of my time with his best mate who

I'd slept with before and who I'd admitted to being in love with, too. Caelan had warned me he wouldn't share again... but...

What the hell was happening?

"It's okay," Eric soothed, stroking my face.

"Nothing is okay."

"He won't relax until it's done with."

"Until she's back in prison?" I snickered. "Look how that turned out."

"He can't kill his mother," he said, "he already killed his father."

"I know," I sighed.

"I'll handle it," said Eric. "Let me handle it."

"That's if she even finds us. It feels like we're the ones in prison right now." Taking food deliveries at the gate which had to be checked, never leaving the villa, only using the pool and gardens during the daytime. Extra guards having to be posted at the perimeter. Never being able to go for a proper walk with the buggy.

I yearned for home! So badly.

"What if this is a trauma he will never move on from?" I said to Eric, rubbing my chest as I became anxious. "It's clear the woman is capable of anything. She did some Jedi mind trick on Caelan to make him kill his father. Yet he won't... can't end her."

Eric rubbed his hands up and down my back and kissed me lightly on the lips. "Neither one of us will ever know what it's like to be him carrying that. That sickness. That hatred for her and for himself because she made him do it. Conned him into it. Coerced. Whatever you want to call it. She's killed who knows how many. She's a murderer. He isn't. He's weak against her. It'll have to be me."

I sighed and bundled myself deeper into him. "I wish we could fuck right now. You feel safe, Eric. He's not always safe."

He kissed my forehead repeatedly. "Isn't that why we love him?"

"I guess," I giggled.

THE MEN LEFT ONE DAY to go running. Cabin fever, allegedly. Not the bodyguards, just Caelan and Eric. I wondered if there might be some ulterior motive, or perhaps they were trying to protect me by saying they were going running and then they'd end up doing something else, like tracking and killing someone. You know, as SAS men do.

However, Caelan arrived back at the villa covered in sweat. Shirtless. I was in the bedroom playing with Logan and a teddy bear, when he turned up in the doorway... like that.

"What happened?" I asked.

"Nothing at all," he said, and proceeded to drench himself in nearly a full bottle of water, quite a lot of it splashing on the tiled flooring beneath his feet. Sure, it'd evaporate off, but this was caveman behaviour.

"Where's Eric?"

"Och, he couldna keep up. Never could. Not built for it."

It was obvious Caelan had intended to ditch Eric and get back here first, a display of dominance, arrogance and sheer alpha maleness. I took a deep breath when he stripped off his shorts and strode towards the bathroom entirely naked... with a semi-on.

Ripped as hell, sweaty, nearly hard, tanned from the sun, a sheen on his body from the exertion... not to mention how severely his calves bulged in the aftermath. I walked across the room, locked the bedroom door and put Logan in his crib with the teddy who he started talking to. Or squawking, rather.

I stroked Logan's belly a few times and he snuggled into the teddy instead, his eyes starting to droop since it was after lunch, we'd done a bit of play and the belly stroking thing always worked—it worked on his dad, too.

I pushed my way into the bathroom and saw him beneath the cool spray of the shower, his cock a little softer but still hanging generously between his legs. Shedding my clothes, I got into the shower

FIGHT FOR LOVE

with him and slipped my arms around his waist, my nails digging in his butt.

Caelan tasted of salt and sweat as we kissed, his hands cupping my cheeks, an erection beginning to form between us.

"Are ye no still...?" He gestured down below.

"A bit. Does it matter?"

"Hell naw."

He chucked me up in his arms, pushed me against the corner of the tiled open space where the shower ran, and slipped straight inside me.

"Caelan," I gasped, grunting—my hands wrapping around his long, elegant throat.

"My one," he moaned, then snapped his teeth around my nipple, his hands greedily clutching my rear.

When he began to swing me along his length, I tossed my head back, utterly weightless as this monster of a man took me, in the most intimate of ways. I'd never let him before. He kissed my skin, every bit he could, bit my shoulders and along my arms, sucked my throat and my nipples until I was nearly crying with pain.

I was so totally gone, shrieking and begging as he pumped through my tremors; one of those terrible, ferocious orgasms that came from spontaneous sex threatening to take me down. He held me still.

When I let go, it was like that ping-pong ball skittering endlessly, bouncing nonstop along an infinite corridor, its velocity undiminished even though it wasn't downhill. Just no end to it, weightless, an invisible force pulsing through me, taking him with me.

Caelan huffed and puffed, his chest pushing hard against mine, his forehead resting on my shoulder as he tried to breathe. He didn't pull out and when he'd caught his breath, he kissed me deliciously. I ran my fingers through his wet hair and licked inside his mouth, his answering smile making me smile.

He let me go and we stood facing one another, embraced tightly. "D'ye love me?"

"More than ever," I said.

"I'm yours," he said, "all yours."

"I know." I bussed my nose to his. "I know."

THEIR RUN HAD HAD ITS desired effect. Caelan had outrun Eric by an hour. A fifteen-mile circuit that he'd completed in sweltering weather in less than two hours. That's why Caelan was the overall beast. He was strong as well as fit; possessing the stamina of a horse plus the dominance of a lion.

When Eric got back and found us locked upstairs together, enjoying an afternoon siesta in bed alongside our babe, I heard him curse in the hallway. We both did. Caelan couldn't hide the way his eyes narrowed and some base thing inside of him seemed to smile. I wasn't going to apologise for having been turned on by my fit-as-fuck husband swinging his dick around—literally—then plunging into me like a wild man even as my period hadn't quite finished. If anything, the bloom in my belly had been more intense, the way he'd been able to push inside too easy.

By evening, as we came down for dinner, Eric had worked himself up into a stewing mess, it was obvious. He didn't say much and stared off into the distance for most of dinner, ignoring us as we got touchy feely and kissed unashamedly.

Yes, it's quite a thing to see your macho as heck husband naked, covered in sweat, radiant and semi-hard.

I'd been reminded why, nearly two years ago, I'd been persuaded to leave single life behind and break all my own self-imposed rules. It was lust, pure lust. Caelan was my sexual fantasy, end of. He wasn't easy to live with and he wasn't always a sweetheart, but he was the man I'd married and chosen as my one. Caelan. Not Eric. Caelan.

That was not easily forgotten.

It'd been Caelan who broke me in, and no man—ever—was likely to match up to him.

No man could protect me in the same way he could.

Eric snarled and went off to bed that night in the spare suite.

Meanwhile Caelan and I spent time on the lawn playing with Logan, and after a drink of ouzo, we went to bed wrapped in each other's arms, no two people ever more content than we were that day.

Chapter Forty-Nine

BREAKFAST THE NEXT day couldn't have been more awkward. Caelan was grinning having enjoyed a complimentary BJ and having not been quiet about it, either.

Logan was starting to make a lot more noise and this also seemed to grate on Eric, who obviously preferred the days when Logan mostly slept, drank milk and only cried, not shrieked with laughter when his father threw him up and down like a yoyo, nearly scaring me half to death, Daddy somehow always catching him.

I drank down orange juice to rid myself of the salty taste in my mouth and Eric's sub-zero gaze made me feel uncomfortable as he watched me swallow eagerly.

"My one," said Caelan, like nothing was wrong with the world, "how about we send one of the guys out to fetch some swim pants for the bairn? He needs to start getting used to the water."

"Great idea."

"And ye can wear that skimpy bikini I packed for ye. Ye ken? The red one." Caelan's eyes danced unapologetically.

"If you like, darling."

"Aye, we'll have a lovely family day today by the pool."

Caelan never once looked over at Eric as he spoke. He didn't need to. His silence and the way he seethed was palpable. Eric ran upstairs, came back down two minutes later and traipsed through the house towards the front door. He was back in running clothes.

FIGHT FOR LOVE

"Good luck to the lad," said Caelan, "maybe if he were a foot taller, he'd match me for my stride and pace."

My husband had reverted back to this arrogant, superior mode of his—the one that might piss off even the most mild-mannered, patient of people. Him in Dickhead Mode could irritate even a mouse to attack and bite back—in spite of the large, monstrous opponent they faced.

Caelan egging you on to fight was like a red rag to a bull, making the person on the receiving end of it so blind with rage, it wouldn't matter that you knew you would get killed—it was better to just rid yourself of the growing anguish bubbling deep down.

"What's going on?" I asked, grinning with what I hoped was nonchalance.

"A bit o' fun to pass the time," he said, mirroring me for indifference.

Hmm, but if I didn't know him better...

ERIC RETURNED JUST before lunch to find us all beneath the awning, sheltering from the sun.

He didn't come near us, preferring to stay by the pool in full sun, soaked with sweat from his run. We'd had a grand old time in the pool and Logan was exhausted, sleeping naked aside from his nappy in his bouncy chair. He was fully in the shade and we wouldn't keep him out much longer. He sighed every now and again with utter contentment, the towel beneath him having absorbed all the dampness from his swim.

Since we'd been outside, all the bodyguards had stationed themselves beneath the other awning on the opposite side of the pool. I'd decided it had something to do with the red bikini.

"I'm gonna take the bairn indoors before we push our luck," said Caelan.

"You're right. He'll be wanting lunch soon, too. Better start chopping some fruit and veg."

"Aye, I can do that."

When I was alone, that's when Eric came over and lay on the lounger next to mine. He looked wiped out from his run, even paler than usual, which was odd considering the heat.

"All those blokes are staring at your arse in that thong," he complained.

"And?" I looked over my shoulder to where the guys were stationed, all of them pretending that they weren't watching from behind their shades. Clearly, they were, as I lay there on my side.

"Doesn't it bother you?"

"Should it? I have a good arse. So what?"

He said nothing more.

After a while, I added, "My husband's not bothered, why should you be?"

He didn't reply and I didn't look across at him to find out if he was reacting.

"What if I wanted one of them next? Caelan says he'd be up for sharing in future so long as it's not someone we're going to have complications with."

Eric made that noise men make when their teeth are clenched and they grunt from the back of their throat. He was quickly learning that in his absence, Caelan and I had got a lot of things straight. And also, that possession wasn't keeping someone wrapped up in layers of clothing for only one person to see. Possession was an invisible thing between two people that only came about through trust, love and a shared life.

"I know what he's doing and so do you."

"Big deal, you'd swing your dick around too if it were as big—"

Eric didn't stick around, launching off his lounger and heading indoors.

FIGHT FOR LOVE

I vaguely heard some cross words spoken indoors, but Caelan was soon laughing as heavy footsteps stomped up the stairs.

After sunning myself for a little while longer on both sides, I went indoors to see what Caelan had cooked up for lunch. He'd made club sandwiches and some skin-on fries. We ate indoors around the kitchen island while Logan slept in the downstairs crib with the aircon on and his net fully protecting him. After he'd fed me, he made the guys their lunches and yelled, "Scran, ye set o' vultures!"

They all came running. Caelan was generous with the cheese and sauces and he made the most deliciously salted fries and deep-fried whole gherkins. Even Eric couldn't resist, grabbing his food before storming back upstairs like a moody teenager.

After they were all fed, the guys outside went back to surveying the land, wandering like dark sentinels in stark contrast with the white house and blazing, white-hot sun they stood beneath.

Caelan and I went to bed for another round of afternoon delight, this time a towel beneath us as he made lazy, disturbingly adept love to me all through the afternoon, his murmurs of, "Those feckers wanted your arse," or, "They'd have all had boners had yer top come off," making me come even harder. I didn't keep my mouth very tightly closed as I yelled his name and begged him for more.

After we got clean and got back into bed for a little snooze, his cuddles were the best thing about the whole event. It felt like Caelan was getting back to himself and didn't need me to reassure him anymore.

It was little things like he knew what my favourite foods were. He knew how I took my tea. He knew I hated him to linger in the shower with me while I washed my hair. Washing my hair was my own personal treat, my feminine time. He knew that I liked a thick pillow so always gave me the thick one if we had odd pillows. He'd take a thin shitty one with no complaint. He knew I liked him to get Logan in the morning because it was important to me they bond. My bond with the baby was forged in the womb, but I'd encouraged Caelan to build his.

Caelan had accepted that I needed cuddles in the morning before he left the bed, even though he was the type to want to be up and at 'em well before me. He was never bothered if I went to the toilet in front of him, but he never did his in front of me.

The thing I liked him to do most for me was bring me the occasional care package. It'd have a bottle of wine, some chocolate, a fashion magazine or a dirty book, a face mask, a candle, some flowers and a few scratch cards for fun. I loved it that I wouldn't have had to say a word about how I was feeling—he would just know.

No wonder I'd gone mad while he was in Ukraine. Losing the reassuring presence I'd come to rely on every day had been much more difficult than I could've ever imagined.

That evening Eric went out, telling us he was going to find his own dinner, and we didn't see him again until the next day.

Chapter Fifty

IT WAS CAELAN WHO KNEW something was wrong before I did. There was a funny smell in the room as we woke up. Like iron, but... rotting.

"Shite," my husband cursed, and was off the bed before I'd even rolled over.

I turned my head and saw the blood spatter on Eric, then the gun in his hand.

There was no more Nice Eric, then. Only the real one. His clothes, hair, face... but it was more than that. Shadows lingered in his features. He was not feral, or animal, no. He was a demon, but vacant. Empty. His soul somewhere else. Just this husk left behind. Dead eyes. No light. No mask anymore.

Eric sat in a chair by the window, not far from our sleeping son whose breathing could be heard. Logan was still tucked up and hadn't made a peep yet. Caelan stood there in his boxer shorts, impotent. Unarmed. He could do nothing.

I swallowed hard and sat up, my breasts tumbling free of the bed linen. Even that didn't so much as move Eric whose eyes were empty, devoid. He would only look at Caelan.

I moved slowly, reaching for a t-shirt, and pulled it on.

"So there's nae more acting, is that right?" asked Caelan, who was obviously not surprised.

Not at the fact Eric was corrupt, anyway. He'd obviously known about that.

No. This had been an elaborate illusion, from both sides.

Caelan had pulled strings to put out the fake story about Sherry.

Eric had come running once Caelan clicked his fingers. Falling right into Caelan's trap.

Yet, Caelan had never, ever expected Eric to slaughter his way into our bedroom like this.

The men downstairs were no doubt all dead—a show of violence, aggression, superiority.

The true Eric Holmes.

Caelan had played his part just as well as Eric had.

The intent had been to show Eric that no matter what, I'd still choose Caelan. No matter if he did have a warped mother and no matter what we had to deal with together, we'd deal with it. We'd proved that, spending all this time locked up here and still liking one another.

Loving one another.

"Why, Eric?" I said, because that was my only question.

He stared at me with those empty eyes and that look inside them nearly made me tremble. It certainly made me want to cry.

"You said to me, Flora that you understand how difficult it is to be a good person when all you've ever known is bad."

I nodded slowly. "I said that, yes."

"Not everyone is as strong as you."

I gulped hard. "Where did you get the money from?"

A laugh caught in his throat. "Breaking apart Sherry's operation didn't mean it all had to be destroyed now. Some of it I kept for myself."

Caelan cursed under his breath and came back towards me, sitting on the edge of the bed so that he was somewhat blocking me from Eric's line of fire.

FIGHT FOR LOVE

"Those in Brighton, at the lodge, even the night you and Caelan hunted them..."

Eric gave a lopsided, sadistic smile. "Her network presented me with options, yes. And a cover."

"So all those people still thought she was pulling the strings."

Eric shrugged. "I guess so."

"What is it ye want?" said Caelan coldly.

"Simple. Her." He pointed at me. "We go, then you two can have your little father-son thing. But we go."

My heart started racing. "Caelan, it's—it's—all right. I'll go with him."

"Nae," he murmured.

"I'd have had to choose one of you at some point. This way, at least our son is safe." I was praying my husband could tell I was faking and he had a plan.

"Nae, I wanna hear first if he's gonna look after ye. I wanna hear that he does care for ye and isn't planning to kill you, too."

Eric laughed darkly. "Why would I kill the only thing that has ever loved me? The one thing that's ever made me feel marginally better."

What did he know of love? Nothing, I thought. If I was thinking that, I was fairly sure Caelan was too. Interesting that he would call me a thing. Twice.

I peered around Caelan to look at Eric. "Why did you set up that thing in Brighton? What were you going to do?"

Instead of being riled, Eric looked unmoved and cold. I didn't know which mode was worse, but probably the one he'd slipped into now. Like he could do anything and it wouldn't register. He could kill ten men and it'd be water off a duck's back. He could murder our son and it'd be justice, in his eyes.

Or maybe there was no reasoning with a thug, a cold-blooded murderer.

When Eric didn't answer, Caelan said, "Ye didna always manifest these traits. Ye were straight all those years. It wouldna huv been possible... they'd have found you out had you always been rotten."

Eric smiled, but still, those eyes were empty.

I swallowed hard.

"I had something to keep me going," he said, and shivered as he stared at Caelan.

That's what this was all about. A love he hadn't found to be reciprocated—and he never would.

Caelan was too clever and not gay, for a start; he'd seen the corruption, the bitterness, the rage and the lack of empathy in Eric all those years ago. Caelan could never love a soul as damaged as his. He saw through him.

"Because I got married and found happiness?" Caelan angrily punched the air with both hands. "I always knew ye were a piece o' work, but this—"

Again, Eric smiled that devoid smile.

Like a psycho.

"The thought was so delicious," Eric began, smirking, "a chance to fuck over my father out there. Yeah, I had Ogarkov convinced I was working *for* my father and Hamish cottoned on. So when I got the call on the radio to warn us of incoming missiles, I may have... made sure they bought it. To uphold the lie with Ogarkov, convince him I was on their side." I could feel Caelan's fists trembling either side of him as he pushed them into the mattress. "Then I thought, if I drag this out, pretend I'm not the get-things-done guy people know me to be, then maybe Caelan will think there's something really wrong and come running."

I swallowed hard that time, but my throat was constricting to the point I was barely breathing. Rage began to swell inside of me. For my Caelan, my family, myself.

FIGHT FOR LOVE

That solid team Eric had shattered. Caelan's friends. His blades. Dead, because of Eric.

How did I not see it?

"And he did come running and saved the day in the way he always does," said Eric, delight shining in those eyes. "To save his poor best mate, or so I thought. No." His eyes dimmed again. "He turned up for glory, of course. Glory and answers. Kicked me out of Ukraine, sent me back to the interrogation room for a week of being ripped apart. So yeah. You bet that the first thing I did was run to you, Flora. And I thought about it, I admit." He licked his lips. "Just taking out a knife and slitting your throat. So I might see his pain. Bathe in it and witness just some smidgen of how I feel every day." He held his hand up and gestured with his thumb and forefinger a small amount. "Just a fraction even of the agony I endure day in, day out, knowing the man I love can never be mine. Will never want me. Will never, ever love me."

"You don't love me." The words came out of my mouth softly. "You never did?"

"Your only attribute is that you are beautiful," he said, while still staring at Caelan, his lip pulled back from his teeth, "and I felt a bit sorry for you, with Blake Rathbone for a father."

"So why do you even want me to go with you, then?" My palms were sweaty and my heart was racing trying to figure out how we were going to play this. I knew I needed to stay calm if possible but this was another level. "I've seen what you really are now. I won't love you anymore!"

He snapped his teeth and looked at me like I was dirt. "It's the only way to hurt him. Make him feel as I do. This pain. Of living without him."

Caelan moved a hand behind him and signalled for me to be quiet now. Let him handle it. I covered my mouth and tried to take a deep breath, but my chest was about to explode with the anxiety creeping through my limbs. The tension. Rage. Fear.

"How many bodies will be enough before you give up?" said Caelan.

"I don't know." Eric stared into space. "I don't know if it'll ever stop."

"You'll take ma wife back to the UK, and what? Take up with the drugs business, get yer rocks off that way, eh?"

Eric laughed a desperate, despotic laugh. "Yeah! Like we'd ever be able to go home now!"

Eric was right; it wouldn't ever be safe for him to go back to the UK. Not with all these bodies littering the place, Eric's fingerprints all over them.

"She winna make ye happy, Eric. She's a wild woman who cannot be tamed. She belongs on home soil and will rebel at every turn because she's no victim. Not ma wife."

Just the fact Caelan really knew me and still loved me made tears well in my eyes. Eric caught that and snarled, teeth gnashing.

"She'll soon learn her place."

"Then ye'll have to kill me before I let you take her." Caelan sat up straighter. "Kill me and be done wi' it. Do it. Finish it now. I should ne'er huv trained ye, I admit it. I shouldna have given you a chance. I tried to kick it out of ye, I saw the pain you couldna hide from me. I wanted to fix you. Help you."

"You admit it, then?" Eric spat. "We're the same?"

"Aye, I admit it. But I was strong enough to go the right way. You only stayed on the path while you had me."

Eric grimaced. "You don't know that. I'm trained, like you are. I know how to cover my tracks."

Caelan's swallow could be heard even by me and this seemed to delight Eric.

FIGHT FOR LOVE

"Ye've been killing before recently?" My husband sounded disturbed.

"Had to get it out somehow."

This was about more than Eric's alleged love for Caelan. This was a warped, twisted person who'd earnt himself a tiny amount of self-esteem by being Caelan's student—while deep down, beneath, he was still that boy. Unloved, unwanted, lost... afraid.

I sat on my knees and Caelan saw my shadow move. His hand gestures urged me not to speak again, but I couldn't keep it in. Not now.

"In the back of your mind, you're still that boy." Eric's fury showed as I spoke. "What did he do? Try to beat the gayness out of you? What did he do?"

"He never beat me," he growled. "But he never loved me. Neither did she. She accused me of being the one to break them apart, but it was her, it was always her... she was always drunk or high. When he got the call, he was off, and he didn't look back." Eric trembled finally and looked down at his lap. "I wasn't the son they wanted."

"What about the marks, on your arms?" I wanted to know if any of it had been real. Even a small amount... I thought we'd...

Eric turned over one arm. "I'd hurt myself to vacate, because, this was a pain I could control."

"You kilt ma oldest friend," said Caelan, in a meeker voice than I'd ever heard him speak with. "A father of three. A good, solid man. A man whose wife you looked in the face after the fact and apologised to. Only a monster does that."

"Yes, I am a monster," Eric admitted, eyes gleaming with a mixture of tears and rage. "Like you, Caelan. And like her. We've all killed. When she killed those men at the cabin, I knew then, what a monster really looks like. Someone like her." He grinned from behind that existential sadness. "Someone who delights in the killing, spilling guts everywhere."

I didn't say it, but it was because one of them had threatened my son, like he was now.

I'd tear apart anyone who threatened my family. I'd gladly rip them limb from limb to keep my loved ones safe.

It wasn't a good idea to remind him of my specific motivations, not in that moment.

"She was so wet after she made those kills. She came so damn hard it was insane. She made me do her up the bum even though she hadn't completed yet that morning. She wanted it rough, Caelan. Really rough. She wanted me to do things to her she can't do with you because you're too big and too much. She came so hard, so many times with me. Do you know why?"

We both remained silent. This was a pointless conversation.

"So, she gets off on hurting people," said Caelan gleefully. "She told me about all the times she kicked people's heads in at class. How many instructors she put in the hospital. So yeah, I'd say, she was probably getting off on the thought of hurting me because I'd left her. It probably had nothing to do with you. But see, I ken you, Eric also. From the very start of all of this, it was obvious your intention was to hurt me. To punish me by trying to shack up with ma wife. Fair do's, she had every right to punish me because I'm her husband and I left her, but you? You have no rights to me!"

"See?" Eric tapped the gun against his knee, reminding us he had one. He was smiling. "No, she didn't come hard because she was trying to hurt one of us, or even herself. That wasn't it. She came hard because I remind her of Blake. Isn't that right, sweetheart? The classic. Daddy issues."

Before I could say anything again, Caelan was on his feet and stalking around the room. Perhaps he'd decided Eric wasn't going to do anything, therefore, he wasn't afraid for my safety anymore—and didn't need to be my human shield.

FIGHT FOR LOVE

"So we've all got Daddy issues. We're all monsters," said Caelan darkly, "but ye've only been playing at being a killer. Guns are nice and clean, are they no? Easy though, if ye ask me. See, you've no idea what it takes to save yourself from an abuser. You've no idea of the strength she and I share. And I would remind you again, ye'll have to go through me to get to her." He walked to Eric and held the barrel of the gun against his chest. "Go on, do it! Because there's no way we're all walking out of here alive today. So end me and be done wi' it. Leave this house and let ma wife and bairn be. Go off and take over Sherry's drugs cartel. Do as you fucking please, but dinna think I will ever allow you to take her from me."

Right on cue, the baby began to stir and my panic set in. If the baby started to cry, it would set Eric off, demanding that a decision be made and this thing finished with.

Caelan ignored the baby's little mewls and turned his attention to Eric again.

"You are no a new thing for her, y'ken? When I was trailing Flora to protect her from Sherry's thugs, I saw her go into hotel rooms and public bathrooms with filthy married men." Eric's dark smile appeared and unnerved me. "I believe what happened with ma uncle scarred her, made her feel dirty. True. But more than any of that? She had to watch as her father nearly crumbled under the weight of grief, cried himself to sleep for decades because of the loss of her mother." The recollection sent tears streaming from my eyes. "She used to tell herself that a love like that was designed only to destroy. That it should be avoided at all costs or face the potential fallout if it was lost." I saw Caelan gathering himself to go on, when Eric looked at me differently, with a more sinister glare, frightening me. Thankfully Caelan chose that moment to sit in front of me once more. "All ye are pal, to her, is another one of them. Another blank face to get her rocks off with. Freedom from all the hurt of the past. Because sex can be just sex. Remember? We examined her like she was a piece of meat that night and she loved it. Women want that sometimes, but no all the time. Most of the time, they want a man who listens, holds them, is there to pick up the slack... no very often, they're most of the time stronger than us... but she found a friend in me before she found anything else. That's why you canna break us."

Eric glared. "I can't break you, but, I can separate you." He raised his gun. "You'll let her come with me and I'll show her a good time, buy her things, let her ride other men if she wants... though she'll need to wear a rubber with them. I had a vasectomy years ago to prevent more of me being visited upon the world."

I slapped two hands over my face. It'd been easier to imagine...

Oh, god.

Not *our* baby. Not *ours*.

We'd lost mine and Caelan's.

Caelan grunted at that. "You fucker."

Eric laughed sadistically. "As if I'd want to impregnate her. Me crossed with her? It'd be an absolute horror show. Nah, that one time I was off work, it was for the vasectomy. I'd had to pay for it myself with not being married etcetera."

"You hateful prick," Caelan spat.

"Never said I wasn't."

Caelan gestured behind him for something under his pillow, jabbing his finger in that direction.

The baby let out a yell and I moved as if wanting to go to him, but shifted my hand under the pillow instead when Eric warned me to halt. I tucked the knife I'd found up against my arm and moved up behind Caelan, handing him the weapon carefully. Eric's attention had been momentarily focused on the baby.

"Please, let me sort him out. Then I'll come with you. I promise." I stepped around Caelan and held out my arms in Logan's direction. "Let me soothe him and change him, feed him, one last time. Then I'll come with you. I swear. If you let them live, I'll do anything."

FIGHT FOR LOVE

Eric cackled as I stared at the crib; at my yearning to go to the crying baby and cuddle him.

"Who said anything about letting anyone live? Now that you've both admitted you despise me and that I mean nothing, there's absolutely no reason for any of us to live. Right?"

He was about to raise his gun, when I thought I heard Caelan begin to move, and everything that happened next took place in slow motion...

The gun was coming for me first, seeing as though I stood in front of Caelan, desperate to go to my boy. He'd probably pop Caelan next, then maybe himself—leaving the baby to be raised by an ancient set of godparents, or by my friend Sophie in her chaotic household.

The level of hate in Eric's eyes made me breathless as he aimed for me, the one obstacle standing in the way of him and Caelan continuing as they had done all those years.

Eric as the big man's wingman. That empty, soulless existence—but, at least he would have had Caelan in his life if they'd stayed that way.

They were mates, best mates. Or so he thought.

The truth was, Caelan had never been close to anyone, had never revealed his true self or capacity for love to anyone—not before me.

My heart stopped for a beat as I imagined Logan being raised by Eric.

That would be the ultimate revenge: kill us, then raise Logan to be a monster, just like him.

Before I could do anything, a shock to my side sent me flying across the room like I was being cleaved from myself. I crashed into the floor and went sliding towards the wall.

A unmistakable noise, then. A shift in the air. Even above the crying baby.

That brutal cut.

Then a gasp.

All I heard in that moment was my baby's crying and I scrambled across the room, knees scraping across the cold, hard floor. I nearly tipped the crib over grasping for him, and the moment I had him in my arms, wailing against me—I held him safely.

"It's okay, Logan. Mummy's here."

When I looked behind me, Caelan sat there on the edge of the bed, lip wobbling. Arms dangling at his sides. Tears leaked from the corners of his eyes.

"This will... get you that knighthood now for sure..."

I took to my feet and held out the baby to his father, the babe gratefully accepted.

Caelan consoled himself in the son who'd never know anything about this.

I walked to Eric, took his gun, flicked on the safety and tossed it into the vacant crib.

The kitchen knife Caelan was very fond of sharpening was embedded in Eric's heart.

"I loved the person you were pretending to be," I told him. "But deep down, that wasn't you. You knew Caelan would be suspicious if you behaved differently when he was around."

Eric was taking his last breaths, stuck to the spot. Caelan's aim had hit the mark. Eric's arms were numb, his fingers twitching.

"You didn't love Caelan, and I know that, because I love him," I whispered. "And I know he's a big dumb softie underneath it all. If you'd ever loved Caelan, properly, you'd have seen that. You weren't looking for him, but for some self-worth, which he gave you. Caelan only ever tried to help you but you couldn't find a way to let go."

"Stop—" he begged.

"Real love is when you take the fall for them."

FIGHT FOR LOVE

I whipped the knife out of his chest and Eric's breathing became much shallower. His entire body seemed to crumple and he had to look up from beneath his sunk form.

"Now you'll die at my hand," I said proudly, "because you brought a gun into a room where my baby was sleeping... and only a truly, truly brutal monster would do such a thing."

"Sorry—"

"Ever wonder why he didn't kill you sooner, Eric?"

His face had completely drained and he was barely breathing at all. "He's better... than me... always was... hated him for it... hate you... hate myself... hate the world..."

"No," I said, "because in his way, he loved you too."

Eric took his last breath and was gone.

He would never have stopped.

That level of hate only had the power to destroy.

Not even Caelan had been able to save him from himself.

I went to my husband and son and we wept together.

Chapter Fifty-One

A COUPLE OF DAYS LATER, the first person I called once we were cleared to go home was my father. At the airport, while we waited for our flight, I walked off to a deserted corner of the departures lounge and video called him.

"Jesus, Flora," he said, before taking a hit of oxygen from the portable machine at his side. "I've been worried sick waiting for your call."

Somehow, it'd got out about the son of a Russian military advisor trying to murder one of the UK's greatest military heroes—in retaliation for his covert op having been scuppered. Something about him being a mole inside the British military all these long decades. He hadn't, but, it explained away all the dead bodies including Ogarkov's, not to mention those of our protection officers whose families were now no doubt devastated. The actual truth would never be revealed. It'd been personal, of course. Just as Caelan had recently explained that Sherry's actions of two years ago were down to her personal vendetta against Jimmy's killer.

It looked like Dad was in a big house with glass everywhere, a sumptuous sectional group propping up his tired body. He'd got to the point of only wearing pyjamas, I saw.

"I'm safe, we're shot of him," I said, shutting my eyes and breathing. "It's over."

"What about my ten mil?" said Dad, but with a wry smile.

FIGHT FOR LOVE

I shook my head and snorted. "Oh, Dad."

"I know." He inhaled some more oxygen. "Tell me everything."

So, I did. I told him how the news story was faked. Sherry had even been moved temporarily to a medical wing and segregated to bolster the narrative, so that even her fellow inmates would believe it. Caelan didn't even tell me it was a sting because he knew Eric would scent the lie if I had to pretend with him.

Caelan had wanted Eric to wonder if he'd actually got away with it—then start questioning everything once he realised Caelan no longer feared his influence over me. Nor cared for his company anymore. Eric had been consigned to the sidelines once more, forced to bear witness as we fell even more deeply in love; he'd had to realise slowly, painfully, he hadn't got away with anything. He'd only made us closer. He'd become surplus to requirement.

The mind games made him crazy enough to do what he did. Not to say Caelan had expected it to get as bloody as it had done, but it'd been obvious Eric was desperate for the fiction to end and was ready to confess. And confess he had.

My husband had taken a big risk and gambled with our lives, I knew that. However, I also knew Eric would've kept getting away with murder otherwise. They'd have never been able to pin anything on him, not concrete. Personally, I felt relieved to know none of it had ever been real and I could now go home with my husband and child and start again, with a fresh start and a clean slate. No more torment, my heart no longer divided in two.

Once I'd reported everything that'd happened, Dad wheezed a bit, caught his breath, and then told me, "I've got days, Flora. But I don't want you here. Do you understand?"

I didn't let myself cry. This had been the second chance most people never got. We were lucky to have had that when far worthier people never even got chance to say goodbye once, let alone, twice.

"I understand," I said, "this is easier."

"Thank you," he breathed, taking another hit of oxygen.

"But I want to say something," I said, cupping my mouth while I gathered myself. Shaking my tired limbs out, I gazed into the camera. "Thank you."

"What for?" he asked, puzzled as to what I could possibly have to thank him for.

"For the strength inside me to overthrow a tyrant."

Dad sucked in deep breaths, then smiled. "Don't tell Caelan, but I actually like him."

I laughed. "You never like anybody!"

He shrugged, eyes popping. "I know!"

Dad looked tired and ready to depart, so I sighed and waved goodbye. "Dad, say hello to her for me."

He shut his eyes and smiled from ear to ear. There was such peace in his expression then. "I will."

"Go with peace."

"Promise me something, Flora?"

"Anything," I said.

"Don't let that man involve you in any more SAS shit, all right?"

I huffed a laugh. "I won't. It's all castle renovations from now on, more babies, more royal garments to fix and display, and such like. All the way. Nothing but."

"All the way," he murmured.

"I promise."

Chapter Fifty-Two

Caelan

A WEEK SINCE THE DRAMATIC events in Cyprus had unfolded, he strode into the prince's private members' club like an utter nobody. To most people here, he was nothing. He preferred that. The anonymity. Being treated like a normal nobody was perfect. Here, it wasn't the done thing to draw attention to anyone—no matter who they were or how many front pages they'd just been splashed across. All were afforded utmost privacy. A coveted thing in some circles. He saw why the prince liked it.

Rather than it being so businesslike as it usually was, the prince was waiting with open arms to embrace him. Caelan allowed a quick manly hug, the prince clapping him on the back.

"So happy to see you well," said his friend.

"Me too," said Caelan, chuckling.

They sat opposite one another, then Caelan said with an air of reluctance, "So, about that knighthood..."

"Ah. Yes. I've already had a word with some people." The prince tapped his nose with an index finger. "You'd already been suggested by someone else, anyhow."

Caelan felt incredulous. "Who?"

"The last outgoing prime minister apparently added you to their honours list. Something about you talking to his son at one of your training camps." Caelan didn't remember such a lad. "He'd used a false name, of course. Apparently, your words saved the young man's life. Something about it being okay to talk. Lots of other young men also mentioned your training camps were invaluable. It's all online but I expect you don't have a lot of time to go trawling for casual testimonials."

Caelan was speechless. He'd often run free camps in the past for under-25s, since he didn't need the money and had spare free time, but he'd never done it for any kind of special recognition. He'd done it because he knew how giving men space to be able to talk and be themselves meant the difference between loving life and beginning to despise it.

"I can see you're taken aback," said the prince.

"Aye, more than a little."

The prince tapped his fingers on the arm of his wingback chair. "How are you, really?"

Caelan sipped from his glass of whisky and took a deep breath. "Dreadful."

The prince nodded his head. "She still doesn't realise?"

"He pretended to hate her, at the end."

The prince and he sighed at the same time. Caelan's eyes gave it all away, the prince mirroring his expression. Neither one of them would ever speak of this again, not outside these walls anyway.

"Self-preservation," said the prince.

"Maybe, or..."

The prince caught his meaning. "He knew you'd never give her up, so he welcomed death because it was better than having to watch her live her life with you."

Caelan had double checked Eric's medical records. Nothing about any vasectomy. He'd really gone to town severing the ties—allowing her to let go.

FIGHT FOR LOVE

It was possible Eric had realised that if you love them, that's what you do. You let them go.

Especially if you're past the point of no return. Such as, if you met the love of your life after you'd already given up your soul to the Devil. Not even a woman like Flora might save a man from the amount of sin he'd stacked up.

The prince and he merely sat drinking in companionable silence for a bit after that. No cigars today. It wasn't that kind of meeting. They both watched as traffic passed by outside the windows, as the world kept turning, oblivious.

"I wasn't going to tell you this, Caelan... lest it skew your judgement."

Now he was awake again, peering at the prince. "Eh?"

"My friend Johnny Feathers who was killed in Ukraine?"

Caelan nodded that he remembered the man.

"He'd suspected Eric to be a spy. Something about him demanding it be their team that went out to collect Ogarkov. Eric had petitioned hard for it."

Caelan knew now why the prince had been so passionate about getting to the bottom of this affair.

"And then," the prince continued, "something about other missions across Europe having coincided with Russian state visits." The prince waited for the penny to drop, his expression one of suspicion and certainty. "Plus, British envoys repeatedly requested Eric's team as guard when it came to meetings with Russia. Coincidence?"

"I dinna ken," he said, not wanting to be drawn on theories that were unprovable now. "Maybe it was Eric's linguistics skills. He spoke Russian as the Russians do. It would've been useful, I reckon."

"Oh, come on, Caelan. Was he their spy? In your professional opinion?"

The Scotsman worried his lip. "I dinna think we'll ever ken for sure."

"Hmm. It'd be conjecture only, I suppose. There's no evidence."

"Aye, there's no evidence at all." Caelan pinched his mouth between thumb and forefinger as he looked out on the world.

The heir to the throne took to his feet and gave a crooked smile. "I hope we don't have occasion to see one another again for a while."

"Me too," said Caelan.

"What about an MBE?"

Caelan tried not to grimace. "Aye, less suspicious. A nice MBE. That'll do. For now."

"For now?" laughed the prince.

"Aye, the knighthood might come in handy when I'm trying to push through permissions for the castle."

"Ohhhh," said the prince, pleased as punch. "All the very best with that. Please let me know when we can visit."

The prince, not one for royal tradition, bowed his head and grinned as he left Caelan where he was, still seated.

Caelan's complicated emotions when it came to Eric and what had become of him caused him pain on a daily basis. For a moment, sat in that room alone, he allowed himself to feel the agony of Eric's loss. All that talent, knowledge and life... wasted.

It was tragic.

Caelan couldn't help but think he'd given Eric a nasty, wicked end.

Maybe everything Eric had been doing was just a way for him to get back to his da. A lost boy wanting to be back with his father, that was all.

Caelan knew if it had been Jimmy out there in the world and he'd known there might be some way to reconnect with him, Caelan would've been sorely tempted to do whatever was required. In spite of what Jimmy had done in the past, he'd have jumped at the chance. Just to have five more minutes with him. Whatever slim odds they were, and even if it would only mean getting his uncle back for a

FIGHT FOR LOVE

split second in time, he would've taken that chance, just to speak to him one last time. Perhaps say goodbye. Exchange confessions. Understand.

There were however some things Caelan would never do to get five more minutes with Jimmy, so he supposed, in his heart of hearts, Eric had got what he deserved.

There were lots of things still unanswered. Like Dani's death. Plus, how much had Hamish really known about Eric? Is that why he had to die? Had Eric ever loved anyone before Flora came along? He somehow didn't think so and he somehow knew Eric hadn't expected it, at all.

Love and hate. Such a fine line between them. Caelan was sure it'd never been love Eric had felt for him. It'd been frustration that he couldn't break Caelan, whose mental strength was beyond most people's understanding. Even Eric's. Which had fascinated Eric, of course. A sociopath couldn't understand how someone could appear to be so cold on the surface, while beneath, possessing such humanity and goodwill. Eric had no doubt gone to the grave still angry he hadn't been able to figure out what made Caelan tick.

Well, if your only motivation in life is to see other people suffer, then for sure, Caelan could see how that kind of a man wouldn't understand that his only motivation in life was to be better, do better and help others find better ways of living.

Sometimes though, Caelan still missed Jimmy. He couldn't help it. His uncle had been kind to him, never warm, but just... not awful. Eric's father had been a tyrant to him, which made the thing even more perplexing to think of.

Caelan expected Eric hadn't ever planned on falling in love. Pity. It can be the deadliest weapon in the world, love.

He'd have to carry the burden of that forever, knowing he'd risked his wife to take out a murderer. He'd have to pray she never figured it out. Never left him because of it.

Something had told him, however: if you need a difficult person dealt with, you send in an even more difficult person. One whose true strength and power isn't always visible to the naked eye.

Nae, her true power lay hidden beneath all that beauty, glamour and intelligence.

That inner psycho she wielded which few people ever got to see.

Sometimes, with some people... it's there. Lurking.

It might just require a little coaxing.

One thing was for sure, Caelan would never forget those few whispered words from Ogarkov after he finally broke in the interrogation room, it dawning on him that he would not be allowed to live:

"Tell my son he did his best, but again, it just wasn't good enough."

Chapter Fifty-Three

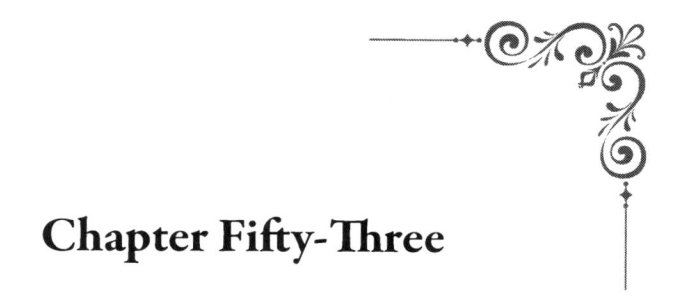

Sometime Later

THE SUMMER HOLIDAYS are my favourite time of year. We come up to the castle, let the air into our lungs and the sun into our bones. We swim in the loch on very hot days, and on cooler days, paddle around in canoes.

The castle looks remarkable. It's obviously not the same as the original incarnation, because most if not all of it had to be rebuilt, but it's really a jewel of the area with thousands flocking to it every year now.

After the terrible events in Cyprus, Caelan needed some time to recover and this project was the healing he needed. A way for him to say fuck it to the people who let the place go to rack and ruin; and also, a way for him to make good on all the bad this place ever saw. He made it new again.

Meanwhile I kept my career in London and was very glad I did. Once he accepted the knighthood for (undisclosed) services to King and country, doors started opening for me.

I'd be asked to advise on this or that, and suddenly, my expertise on fabrics, furnishings and preservation were highly sought after. So once I'd trained up a team at the Royal Collection to continue my work there, I left and set up my own business restoring, procuring and also selling on antique and high-end fashions and fabrics. It was a no brainer and finding things to furnish the castle was made even easier by the connections I was beginning to build.

Logan and Caelan Jr come running up to me from the vegetable garden having been digging for worms. Showing me what they've found, I survey them with a haughty eye.

"I hope you haven't dislodged my herbs again, lads."

"No, Mummy!" says Logan, with those shining hazel eyes and all that wild blond hair. Seven years old and already a terrible heartbreaker.

"Mummy, mine's bigger!" yells Caelan Jr who's darker with blue eyes, like me.

"I'm sure it is," I snigger, as they both wiggle their dirty worms in front of me.

They run back off while I watch from the kitchen window as they lob bits of dirt at one another and make a mad scramble to see who can find the longest worms. Gross! Bringing up boys has been an education to say the least since I never knew many boys growing up, going to girls' schools and all. The male species wasn't very well represented during my youth, not with Dad's cronies constantly hanging around. Needless to say, Caelan is a great father to them both and should write the guidebook on bringing up boys. Hence why they're always doing gross things, because apparently, that's all boys want to do and we should let them. So long as they let me hose them down at the end of every day, fine.

My phone rings and it's Soph. I smirk and answer, "Yessss, this is your ladyship speaking."

"I'm sure it's your turn to have them. I'm absolutely sure!"

I go to my calendar on the fridge. "Nope, it's yours. Valentine's day when you were seeing that chiropodist. Remember? It was half term and I let the kids have a big snowball fight."

"Ugh, god. Can't I owe you one?"

FIGHT FOR LOVE

"Another one?" I splutter with laughter. "How's about you take them tonight and I take them any other night. Name it."

She thinks it through. "Why can't you be here all year?"

"Cos I'm a super fandango fabricky person and all that." Plus I need concerts, shows, the cinema, Oxford Street and Harrods; the boys need private school; and Caelan needs his work for the Royals as their Head of Security. (Something about his regular guys' night with the prince has often screamed that they're in league on super-secret projects together, but whatever...)

"Oh yeah, and you roped me into running the castle while you keep your dual citizenship." It's a joke we share. "Remind me how I got sucked in again? Cos sometimes, in the dead of winter... I mean, it looks pretty right now, but..."

I laugh loudly into the receiver. "You were a wreck. Remember? He'd had you sign a prenup you never even knew about. So you had no money and he was already on his second wife the moment you two got divorced. Right so far?" She sighs loudly. "You needed a home. And well, we let you stay in our annexe while you helped project manage the reno's since project management is kind of your forte and all." She sniggers; he paid her quite well for that. But it was a weight off his mind while he split his time between here and London. "So then you found yourself a cottage in the nearby town having fallen in love with the area. And when Caelan asked you to run the castle during spring and autumn, you jumped at it. We allow you to take a lot of holiday days and your kids can play with mine when we're up here for the holidays, too. Sound about right?"

"Hmm," she says dreamily, "and it had nothing whatsoever to do with all these tall Viking men that live around here and swan about in their kilts, trekking across hills in all weathers... sometimes needing a warm bed."

I double over laughing. "Just wait. One day one of them will get you pinned down again."

"Yeah, which is why I'm calling. Might have found a special one this time..."

"Ugh, well, take them tonight, then name your night."

"You got yourself a deal!"

After we hang up, I text Caelan right away: *Just got us a child-free night!*

His response comes quickly: *Hell, does that mean I can finally sleep?*

Absolutely not!

Hahahaha...

CAELAN'S BEEN DOWN at the stud farm all day. That's another of his little hobbies, so when I text him: *Kids are now with Soph. Where the hell ru?* I see him receive the message, then start replying: *Have a surprise here for you. Come down!*

I just went past there on the way back here from Soph's. I grumble and get in the Land Rover, setting off at speed to hopefully find a naked body waiting for me when I get there.

Instead of Caelan laid out in the hay like a human sacrifice awaiting my plunder, I find him and one of his new stable hands still busy at work. The boy is scrubbing down one of the few mares we have here with a ball of hay in his hand. Caelan grins like a loon, wearing his kilt, boots and a surprisingly bright white shirt.

"Why are you looking so shifty?" I ask, walking to him and kissing his mouth.

He tastes like the horses and sweat. It's a bit high in here tonight.

"I want you to meet Timothy. He just joined us."

Timothy swings around to look at me and blushes furiously. He must be eighteen at the most. I eye up my husband and wonder...

Has he found me another treat?

FIGHT FOR LOVE

"Timothy caught sight of ye in the village last week and remarked upon how much of a bonnie lass ye are."

"Oh, thanks Timothy," I gush.

"Aye, I'd be most pleased to serve you, Lady." He tosses away his bit of hay and bows deeply, nearly making me blush.

I survey Caelan carefully. How does he always know which ones are submissive? This is the first stable boy he's found me, but all the other boys or men he's found for me have always been equally eager to submit.

"He needs a lady who might show him the ropes," says Caelan, winking.

"Let's have a look at you, then."

Timothy draws closer and I grin at how pretty he is. Big blue eyes with dark brown hair falling into them, tanned skin and muscled forearms poking out from beneath the rolled-up sleeves of his check shirt. He's going to be a real heartthrob when he's older. Not that he isn't already on his way...

"Do you like Caelan as well?" I ask gently.

He gives a lopsided grin. "Aye."

"I like to watch men suck him. He's very big, you see."

"Ah ken. He doesna wear no knickers." Timothy snickers and I throw my head back laughing. "Ma'am."

Caelan folds his arms and shrugs.

"Well, why don't you close the stable door and then show me what loveliness you're hiding under those clothes."

Eager to please, he hurries to shut us inside, then begins stripping out of his clothes. I was feeling hot and aroused already but then he reveals his tight muscles from all that bale tossing, horse riding and no doubt, horny fucking with girls and boys around the place.

"You always choose so well, Sir."

"I aim to please, my Lady," says Caelan, smirking.

The lad's lovely young cock is already hard but certainly not too big.

"Let's tie him to a stool or chair," I suggest, asking Timothy with my eyes if he consents.

"Yes, Lady."

"Got just the thing," says Caelan, heading for a corner of the place to grab a simple wooden chair. Probably for sitting on while inspecting hooves or the underside of a big horse.

Timothy acquiesces all too-easily and it thrills me. Little young sub for me to play with. Caelan ties him to the chair and fetches me a riding crop, a well-used one that's become a bit more lethal than a fresher, softer one which hasn't been moulded to the act of thrashing yet.

I keep checking for signs he's not up for this, but Timothy is only too eager, licking his lips as he watches me. Starting with a bit of play, I stroke the flat edge along the length of his shaft. Timothy shivers and chuckles when I stroke in circles around his ball sac.

"Good?" I ask.

"Some pain, please."

"Have you done this before?"

He shakes his head.

"Then how do you know how much pain you can take?"

He grins. "I don't. But I know I'll like it anyway."

"How do you know that?" I say, gazing at him lustfully.

"A feeling."

I tap the crop against his chest gently. His cock bounces in response. So, he really does like it.

"He told me you're a real-life domme," says the boy. "I think I nearly came in my pants knowing *you*... with the way you look... enjoy hurting people."

I give him a lopsided smile. "Oh my dear, you have no idea..."

Another tap, and he starts leaking fluid.

FIGHT FOR LOVE

Caelan and I share a look. It's obvious this one is going to go all the way.

Him sucking off Caelan while I suck him. Double penetration (perhaps a first for him).

Both men licking me simultaneously.

Welts all over Timmy's body.

And everyone will be happy.

How it could and should have been.

Have you enjoyed this book?

Please consider leaving a short review.

It takes just a few seconds and can help other readers decide whether this series is for them.

Thank you!

Books by the Author

THE ANGEL AVENUE SERIES:
Angel Avenue
Beyond Angel Avenue
Hetty
Guilt
THE THISTLEWICK DUET:
The Thistlewick Curse
Goodbye Thistlewick Cottage
THE LOVE DUET:
Loath to Love
Fight for Love
THE CRIMSON DUET:
Surviving Him
Becoming Me
THE CHAMBERMAID SERIES:
A Fine Profession
A Fine Pursuit
The Chambermaid's Tales
THE NIGHTLONG TRILOGY:
The Contract
The Fix
The Risk
THE SUB ROSA SERIES:
Unbind

Unfurl
Unleash
Dom Diaries
Worth It
His Deadly Rose
Epilogue
THE LEGACY TRILOGY:
Kismet
Karma
Killer
THE BAD SERIES:
Bad Friends
Bad Actor
Bad Wife
Bad Girl
Bad Guy
Bad Lover
Bad Exes
Bad Night
Bad Endings
STANDALONES:
Tainted Lovers
Christmas Lovers
Fantasy Man
PARANORMAL ROMANCE:
Fabien & Leticia
POETRY COLLECTIONS:
Punctures
Naked Observations
THRILLERS/SCI-FI BY S. M. LYNCH:
Chimera
Panacea

Exodus
Ruthless
Careless
Endless
The Radical
The Informant
The Sentient
The Awoken
The Rising

Printed in Great Britain
by Amazon

7dbaf1d7-d334-4ff8-a2dd-ee679050f781R01